LIFE LIKE STARS

BY

C. R. KELCHNER

To my college friends

AUTHOR'S NOTE

This story is a fictional quest
on which I embarked to answer
one question: what is sin?
If you are not interested in such a quest —
or in encountering potentially contentious
opinions — then please
do not flip any further.

1

OH SO PRETTY

NASTIA SOBIESKI TURNED her eyes away from the setting sun and back to the small table inside the Dallas Airport, where she sat alone. Two thick red drops of smoothie oozed down her straw, causing a mess on the lid. She elegantly wiped it clean with her paper napkin, just like problems.

She tossed a newspaper article to the side and placed her drink back on the table. Her eyes were simply hazel; yet, once you looked closer, they became mysterious jewels lost in some exotic country. But her skin — white as the rare desert snows — was the most precious part of this twenty-one-year-old woman — soft, lightly freckled, and naturally radiant. Her selfless mother gave her that skin, but she was not to be thought of.

A tanned beauty glared out of an advertisement across the room, mouth slightly open, a tropical paradise in the background. What's that you're trying to say, dear? Nastia thought to herself. Do you need something? Or are you unable to breathe through your nose? Yes, you look perfect — but you aren't anything more than glorified plastic for the disgruntled boys to long for. And no, princess, you won't be sweet as strawberries.

Nastia flashed her smile — one that was different from all others — a white flame that had singed the hearts of many a young man. Even while she sat alone and oblivious at her table, a male onlooker wished he could have her.

After a bite of her mozzarella, pesto, and red tomato sandwich that tasted of airport memories, Nastia returned to the article she was reading entitled "Why God Does Not Exist." The supposedly distinguished author rambled about this thing and that, making it sound nice and stuffy as he mentioned "galaxies," "stars," and "the cosmos."

"I'll show you the cosmos," Nastia muttered right before another careful bite. Who did this man think he was, criticizing God like a science project? If the writer ever needed anything, it was pity. And boy, would he need pity once his days ended.

The clock digits informed her it was time to leave. Nastia pulled the latch out of her suitcase and started walking toward her gate, leaving a trail of clicks in her wake. People bustled around her, and many noticed her slim-fitting dress, but she didn't think the tiniest thought about them. People were not her favorite subject at the moment. They had hated her in college for being openly Christian. Her professors hated her so much they made her fail. She was an unacceptable "disturbance," especially considering her striking beauty. They could permit ugly Christians on their campus, but not beautiful ones. That was too much.

Nastia felt a sting from the rejection memories. The pain pulsed through her whenever she thought of the past three years. But that pulse was like a pop beat that you play over and over again. She was beginning to know what it meant to be persecuted because of righteousness. She had battled for her faith, regardless of what others said. This was the confidence in her stride.

The gaunt travelers stood anxiously in line. A man babbled into his phone; two elderly women chatted intimately. But then instructions resounded over the intercom, and the line began to move.

Once Nastia found her seat inside the jet, she peered out the small window. Like a snake, a baggage car tugged its trailers over the windy tarmac. Nastia felt like the wind — free and boundless; there was nothing she couldn't do. A new life waited for her in

Washington D.C. with a good Christian friend Nastia had known almost all her life — a black American woman named Lauren Henson. She had invited Nastia to live with her, and even found her a job. How good it would be to live with a sister in Christ.

A stray lock of red hair slipped over her right eye — hair that was oh so pretty. That's what Nastia's friends would say to her: "Nastia! Your hair is so pretty!" Even her ex-boyfriend mentioned her hair when he broke up with her once upon a time. "I'm sorry but it just isn't working out, but oh, such pretty hair." She had quickly jerked away from his sly fingers and put the scene to right. "Don't touch me, and please get out of my face." She didn't miss him. *Yeah, sure, he had been faithful — about as faithful as a leech wants to be to your throat. Good thing I kept myself and stayed pure all through the college temptations.* Like the red sandstone of Arizona, Nastia Sobieski's hair was oh so pretty.

———◆———

ANTON SHEPHERD, A tall young man with the stature of a football player, searched for his seat number, 18, 20, 22…

He saw a young woman with perfectly straight red hair sitting alone by a window. She reminded him of a dream he loved. The sight of her head, the smell of the plane, and the numb rumble of the engine felt so — right.

He discovered that the seat beside her was his. "Excuse me —" He saw her face. *Wow, this is going to be a very enjoyable flight.*

2

ANTON

HMM, HE'S CUTE, was the first thought that entered Nastia's mind as the young man slid his belongings under a seat. It didn't necessarily mean anything though; Nastia had thought the same about many guys before.

Over spring break in her sophomore year, Nastia had visited Paris with some friends. While she examined a mystifying statue in the Louvre Museum, a young man strolled up beside her. *Hmm, he's cute* was her first thought.

Later during that same trip, as she nibbled a savory crêpe near a tumbling fountain, her friend said, "Oh my goodness, that guy is cute!" Nastia had looked up to find the same man from before; something about him made her stop and wonder.

A similar curious feeling tickled her now, but Nastia resented it. What did she care about this stranger beside her? He was just another guy among millions of others.

But the curious feeling persisted, and Nastia decided to pray. That's what she usually did when unsettling emotions swept through her. She prayed quickly, *Lord, please bless this man, heal his hurt, redeem him, and save him. Amen.*

An outline of the Skylink railway appeared outside the window upon the sunless blue sky with black lampposts, now illuminated, as the plane moved. Nastia felt better after the prayer, as if God were saying, "You did right, Tia." God was there. The presence of God was clear to her at that moment. She could feel Him around her when she gazed out the window and when she closed her eyes; God was there. His presence was as certain as the hissing air nozzles inside the plane.

Nastia could imagine people saying, "How do you know there is a God? You can't see Him or prove his existence." Ha! Could they see air? Could they prove its existence absolutely and completely? No, but they could feel it, and they could see how a gust of wind moved things. God existed just like the air around her.

Nastia laughed inside at the silly doubts of humans, especially at the author of "Why God Does Not Exist." Of course God exists! All who denied that were extremely silly. This man — this scientist who had spent his life studying and accumulating walls full of plaques — was nothing but a lost child when it came down to it. But Nastia was not! She had eternal life. She not only recognized the existence of God but also the need for his atoning sacrifice. God had conquered death and sin forever at the crucifixion and resurrection — including her death and sin.

Suddenly, out of nowhere, an image overcame her mind: she was lying in a white bed with this young man, bright morning sunlight flooding over them. He was still and smiling with his eyes closed while Nastia readjusted the position of her arms and head on his bare shoulder, a smile on her face too — one that meant complete happiness.

Nastia shook the thought out of her head. *Where in the world did that come from?* Ashamed of herself for thinking it, she prayed, *Lord, please forgive me. And please help me to tell Satan off!* She imagined the evil one and said in her mind, *Get out of my face, Satan. You can go to hell. Oh wait, you're already there. My bad.*

A giddy smile slid onto Nastia's face, and she laughed blissfully. *Uh-oh.* She opened her eyes. The cute guy was looking at her with a questioning expression. *Oh crap, now I have to talk to him.*

"Sorry, that must have been awkward. I was just thinking."

"Don't worry about it." He had a vibrant good nature in his countenance, a strong neck, and tanned skin. "My name is Anton, by the way."

"Nice to meet you. I'm Nastia. Why are you traveling to D.C.?"

"I just graduated from grad school and got a job there."

"Really? What was your major?"

"Political Science," he said.

"We always need good people in politics."

"Yes, for sure. What's bringing you to the capital?"

"Not politics." Nastia smiled and breathed deeply. "I was going to college in California, but they kicked me out because I refused to compromise my Christian faith."

"That's not right." His broad torso turned as a golden tinge glimmered in his brown hair. "What exactly happened?"

"They gave me a lot of trouble for my unwavering convictions," she explained. "When I got into this one class required for graduation, the professor threatened to fail me if I wrote my paper from a Christian perspective. I did anyway." Leisurely, Nastia turned and gazed out the window, the city lights gleaming far down in the black.

Who is this girl? Anton thought. She pulled her shoulders up to her neck, like a stretch for comfort, and lightly glided her fingers down the shoulder closest to Anton. Glittery lime-green nail polish sparkled before his eyes.

"What a jerk," he said.

"Yes." Nastia crinkled the newspaper beside her.

"I was reading that article, too," Anton said. "What do you think of it?"

"Oh this? The author is," she paused and smirked, "a complete scumbag."

"Wow, that's quite an insult." He laughed, showing his clean white teeth framed by rounded dimples. "Actually, he is one of my icons. You may be a Christian, but I am a devout atheist."

"Are you? Well, I'm sorry I called him a name in front of you."

"But you're not taking it back?"

"No. My loyalty lies with God, not social subjectivity."

"You are entitled to your own opinions. We all have them." Anton might have said the same thing on regular occasions, but this time he had a motive — he wanted to get to know her.

The flight attendant's opinion leaned in favor of beverage choices. She held a plastic cup in one hand and an ice scoop in the other — eyeliner stretched and chin forward.

"Cran-apple juice, please," said Anton.

"Thank you, sir. And you, miss?"

"Nothing for me, thanks." Nastia thirsted for something else — something that would satisfy her spiritually.

"Would you mind if I asked you a question about your faith?" Anton inquired once the flight attendant had moved on.

Nastia's face brightened. "Not at all." She wanted to listen to him. His voice was enchanting, like a sports broadcaster who draws you in with crisp, resounding tones.

"When I look at the world around me, I see a product of natural processes — of evolution that progressed over the vast expanse of time. I see as much evidence for a God as I see evidence for fairy tales and myths. How have you come to the conclusion that there truly is a God? What is it about the world around you, and everything you have seen in your life, that convinces you to believe in such an idealistic being?"

"Oh gosh, I could spend days answering that question." Nastia was not at all offended by Anton's bluntness but rather delighted by the challenge. She thought for a moment. "I like to go back to the start of things. We could reason for hours and hours about proof and evidence, but it comes down to one question. Where did all this come from?" She gestured around her, pointing at the window, the air valves, and Anton in one sweep.

"Biological development sparked by the Big Bang."

"Where did the Big Bang come from?"

Anton was enjoying himself. "Molecules that collided over time."

13

"Where did *they* come from?"

"No one can know. I could ask you the same kind of question. Where did God come from?"

"God has *always* existed," she replied. "There was never absolute nothingness. He is the foundation that has always been."

"How do you know?"

"Because God created time and is above and beyond it — and all things. Molecules don't just appear out of nowhere. You can't say the molecules that miraculously started the entire universe could have always existed. There has to be a beginning. God doesn't need a beginning because He is beyond all beginnings and ends. But as far as the earth goes, there *has* to be someone who started it." She glanced at Anton's juice-filled cup and napkin. "Do you mind if I use this to demonstrate?"

"No, go right ahead." Anton decided it was better to just listen for now. Even though he wanted to refute her arguments, he enjoyed hearing her voice.

Nastia petted her cup with her sparkling fingers. Anton wished those hands could do that to his shoulder or his arm — or anywhere on him really. Nastia poured some of the red liquid into her hand and sprinkled it onto the napkin.

"There," she said. "Even this pointless splatter needed someone to start it. How much more does our extremely complex universe need someone — an intelligent designer — to create or even just start the universe?"

"Here, wipe your hand with this." Anton gave her the stained napkin. "I can see how you could believe in God. I still think it's idealistic, though. If there is a God — which is very unlikely in my mind — then he certainly isn't active in the world he created."

Nastia looked him straight in the eyes, noticing that their rustic beige centers were surrounded by rings of deep blue like the evening outline of a northern mountain. "Then let me ask you this, where does care come from? Where does *love* come from?"

3

SINGED

ANTON STARED AT his cup of juice but saw memories instead — memories of love and its many types. He knew which type of love Nastia was referring to — the desire for the good, wellbeing, and success of someone else.

His eyes drifted to the tray latch on the chair in front of Nastia and then over to the young woman herself, who waited for his answer.

"Love is a product of biological development," he said confidently. "Scientists have found the functions in the body and the brain that produce feelings and emotions, such as care and love. Over many, many years love has evolved from the growing productivity of the surviving organisms. In humans, it happens to have progressed the farthest. Pain also exists, but that is because evolution is not perfect. Absolute perfection — as our minds see it — is impossible to attain because chance does not allow it. Chance, and the great decree of evolution, can only permit so much, and that is our existing world."

Nastia smiled. He didn't get it; he didn't understand. She had to keep trying. "So, you think love and care just came out of nowhere like everything else?"

"Not out of nowhere. It evolved."

"Okay. You think it evolved. Then why do people want to be loved? What makes love so different from everything else that you say 'evolved?' If the world is ruled by chancy evolution, why is there a desire to be cared for, and a desire to care for others? You think it's from a highly evolved 'biological function?' "

"Yes," he confirmed, "from the need to preserve your species."

"Then who cares about love? If all of us just accidentally wobbled into existence, what meaning do we have beyond ourselves? Simply to preserve our species? There can be no meaning if God did not create us. There can be no true purpose, no goodness, no standard for happiness and enjoyment. God *does* exist. There has to be a source for love, or else love would be nothing."

"There doesn't have to be a source."

"Yes, there *does*," Nastia asserted. "Everything has a source. How did this plane get here? Did it just plop out of the sky ready to take us up? No, it was constructed by intelligent beings — people like us — using different sources and materials. Think of all the time and resources that went into building this plane. The parts had to be purchased and manufactured; the metal ore had to be dug out of the earth. A lot of intelligence went into the process of constructing this aircraft. Have you ever seen a plane evolve without being built by the intelligence of humans?"

He contracted his eyes slightly. "No, I have not."

"Then how could even more complex things — like living organisms, people, and the human mind — just evolve over time without any direction? There are so many things that are too complex to evolve. An existing world without a designer is not possible. It goes beyond the bounds of logic and reason! There must be a source. Without a source, nothing could exist. Without a source, there wouldn't be anything at all."

Anton grinned. He didn't want to argue with her anymore, even though he thought of a response. He wanted to get off the topic and allow her to believe as she wished. "You have constructed your thoughts very well."

Nastia relaxed a bit and smiled. "Thank you. I get so impassioned with conversations like this."

"Yeah, you do. It's not a bad thing."

"I have been very angry with people in the past. There were times when it was a bad thing."

The steady rumble of the engine soothed Nastia as Anton watched her with a curiosity he thought had been resolved. Usually, he could get a satisfactory grasp of a person just by seeing their face and hearing them talk for ten seconds. Anton never struggled to figure people out. But now, as he looked at the enigmatic face of this red-haired girl, Anton found the exception to the rule. He didn't understand her at all.

Anton was not a lady's man, but he possessed an exceptional ability to empathize with all kinds of people — including the opposite sex. Some girls wanted idealistic romance with a guy more than anything else; others just enjoyed friendliness because the desire for romance was satisfied or pacified somehow. Almost all girls loved to talk with Anton.

He couldn't decide which type was Nastia. He couldn't simply pass her off as one of those delusional, needy girls who became Christian out of desperation. She was much deeper. She was a mystery that he wanted to solve.

"We all have times when we're not at our best," he said. "But honestly, you are a very good debater."

"So are you," she replied. "It *is* nice to meet you, Anton."

"It's very nice to meet you too, Nastia."

They both smiled and looked away from each other. Nastia turned toward the window to gaze at the light-speckled vista below, reminding herself that she was talking to an acquaintance. Hopefully her words had helped him.

Anton reached for his black bag and removed his iPhone. Nastia seemed to be done talking for now. As he adjusted the ear buds, he found a good country song and let it play.

A few minutes passed, and curiosity got the best of Anton. Nastia was still gazing out the window. What in the world was going on in her head? Why was he so interested? He noticed one of Nastia's sparkly light-green earrings, dangling in reticent curves.

"What kind of music do you like?" he asked, thinking it best to make conversation while they could. She would be gone once the plane landed.

"All kinds. I like a lot of contemporary pop artists but not everything they make. I enjoy some soundtracks. What about you?"

"A lot of the same. Some rock, pop, country and, on occasion, I listen to soundtracks. I'm listening to my twenty-five most played list." He motioned. "Would you like to listen with me?"

Nastia adjusted the black ear bud in her own ear and turned to look out the window again.

God is such a mystery — a magnificent mystery, Nastia thought. What was it I wanted to meditate on? Oh yes, I am not of this world. What a beautiful assurance; such a fulfilling idea, knowing that the present world with its tears, suffering, and endless agonies will soon fade away but I will not. I will be in the eternal kingdom.

The song changed, and Nastia turned toward Anton. "Do you know how far I believe the power of God can reach?"

Anton smiled. "How far?"

"Farther than our minds can grasp."

He chuckled. "How do you understand that?"

"I don't have to. All I need is complete faith in Christ. I don't mean blind faith of course. Blind faith is stupid. I play with ideas that support my belief. Like your iPhone."

"How does my iPhone help you?" he asked.

"I use the idea of it because it is available to me now. Think of how complex technology is. God can change whatever he wishes with technology. He can control anything. He could make your iPhone switch to whatever song he wanted. He could shut down the entire world of electronics in less than a second. God's control permeates through the whole world and society, through all of everything."

"Would you say that God is good?" he inquired softly.

"Yes! Yes. Without a doubt, yes!"

"How did you come to that conclusion? How do you explain all the pain and hardships that people suffer? If there is a God and if he is good and has absolute control over all things, then how can he make us suffer? Why is there pain?"

"The fall." Her voice was remote but sweet as strawberries.

Before Anton could ask his next question, a voice sounded on the speakers, announcing the plane's descent.

"Are we there already?" Anton remarked, slightly disappointed.

Nastia handed the ear bud back to him. "Yes, I suppose so. Thank you for the conversation, and good luck with your new job."

"Thank you. I hope you have an awesome stay in D.C."

After the plane landed, Anton let Nastia go ahead of him. The passengers filed out, each receiving a thank you from that one flight attendant. Anton ducked his head and hurried up the jet bridge until he reached Nastia. She smiled casually, and together they made their way through the airport. They didn't talk much as they passed rushing businessmen, magazine stands, and coffee corners. It was enough to head toward the same destination, each pulling a suitcase and keeping in step with the other.

They arrived on the street, cars zooming by. Nastia gazed at the dark above as she stopped near the curb. "Do you see the stars? Those few precious stars?"

Anton looked up at the scattered lights. "Yes."

"That's what it's like to be a Christian."

"What do you mean?"

"Those stars have been up there for ages and ages," she said. "They are basically immortal. That's what it is to be a Christian. I know that when I die and leave here, I will keep on living forever, like a star."

"What about the stars that go out?"

Nastia's face became somber; she glanced at a discolored pebble. "My ideas aren't perfect. I find symbolism in lots of things, but that doesn't mean they are just like the ideas I compare them to."

"So, you haven't related a symbolic meaning to dying stars?"

"I didn't say that." Her face was serious. "Oh look, my ride is here!" She smiled again, worry free. "Thank you for walking me out. You really didn't have to." She loaded her suitcase into the silver SUV that pulled up.

"Wait, what did you say your last name was?"

"I didn't. It's Sobieski."

"Nastia Sobieski?"

"Yes. Thank you again!" she waved a farewell.

The SUV drove away as lights flashed like white flame. Red disappeared too — red that was oh, so pretty.

She's gone? What the heck! Anton felt lonely and disappointed. Her face became the most prominent image in his mind, like the one pop of color in an otherwise black-and-white photograph. As he stood alone at the curb, he almost wished he had never met Nastia Sobieski because he couldn't think of anything else.

4

JUST A GOOD MAN

THE SILVER DRAGON was a grand restaurant. Leaders from around the world visited when they came to the United States capital, making reservations months in advance. You couldn't go to D.C. without a night at The Silver Dragon. And of course, everyone had to ask about the legend. The interior design didn't let you forget the other characters in the story, especially the blue tiger and the red canary.

Guests dined under faint spotlights in the mostly black interior of the restaurant. The place was full of art. Silver carvings of Chinese-style dragons were everywhere — engraved on the stone walls, slithering up the lamps, aligning the great wine cooler, and especially in the lobby as the floor-to-ceiling sculpture behind the hostess stand.

Two elderly women scrutinized the legend on the backs of their menus, eyebrows rising. "It says here that each of those enormous watercolor paintings has the dragon, the scarlet canary, and the blue tiger in them."

"Really?" The other examined the closest painting. "I see it in that one! There is the tiger and the canary beside the cherry tree and the dragon in the shadow of the boat."

"Oh yes. *Marvelous!*"

Simply being in The Silver Dragon was a treasured experience.

◆

NASTIA RESTED SILENTLY in a cozy booth with her friend Lauren Henson and the calmly joyful overseer for her future job at the church, Stephanie Rivers.

Beaming with happiness, twenty-two-year-old Lauren talked through stories with wide grins and billows of laughter. She was black American with puffy cheeks, endearing eyes, and the largest grin in the restaurant. Her many jiggles of wonderful laughter could lighten the heart of the most troubled person because it was pure comfort. Everyone struggled to keep a straight face when Lauren Henson laughed. She was also perceptive and kind. She even understood Nastia Sobieski. No one else in the world knew her like Lauren Henson.

Lauren was encouraging Ms. Rivers to explain more about Nastia's job at the church, when a flag shot up in her mind — something unusual was bothering Nastia.

"You've been pretty quiet tonight, Tia," Lauren said, addressing Nastia by the nickname she had used ever since high school.

Nastia traced the silver dragon design on the edge of her plate, like the stroke of an Asian brush. "Have I?"

"Yes." Lauren's smile glowed in the night. She tried to lighten the air and imitated Nastia's relaxed manner. "Girl, you're lounging like a world traveler. It's as if you're saying, 'I've seen the temples of Bali,' " Lauren's quick hands moved like the flow of water as her tone spoke hilarity, " 'walked upon the stones of the Great Wall of China, climbed the steps of the Eiffel tower, galloped past the pyramids of Giza, and pinched the sand of the Colosseum. Coming here is, well, ho-hum.' " She patted her lips and faked a yawn, which was quickly replaced by her beaming smile and a pure laugh, like the assurance of a strong bridge. Nastia laughed as well, and Stephanie timidly brushed her hair behind an ear.

"I've only been to Paris, you know that. I'm just happy," said Nastia. "It's great to be here."

"It's not like you to be quiet. You usually have an abundant harvest of stories to share after a flight," Lauren responded, certain that Nastia wasn't "just happy."

"Maybe she's tired," Stephanie chimed in. "Traveling can wear you out."

Nastia tapped her ceramic teacup, gaining the slightest ding. "Yeah, maybe I am, Lauren darling." She flashed her white-flame smile with dominantly sweet eyes.

Lauren could tell that something was going on, but Nastia obviously didn't want to share yet, so she decided to wait until after dinner.

———————◆———————

"GOODNIGHT, STEPHANIE." BLUE light shone in the quiet car as Lauren and Nastia waved farewell to Stephanie and drove off. "She is such a dear. I think you'll like working with her, Tia."

"She's nice."

"Oh, I was going to tell you!" Lauren changed the subject. "I quoted you the other day."

"Did you? How's that?"

"A woman asked me why my day wasn't ruined when everything was going wrong with a mentally ill patient at the hospital. I told her that I don't find my satisfaction in life, I find it in God."

"Good answer."

"Remember when you said something like that in a Facebook message to me once when I was down in the dumps?"

"Yes," Nastia replied. "Vaguely."

"It certainly cheered me up; what you said is true indeed." Lauren gave a warm glance. "It's so good to see you, Tia. You will be the best roomie ever."

Lauren drove down the smooth roads, past shadowy buildings and peach-colored lights. Nastia remained quiet, and Lauren had to ask, "What's on your mind?"

"Nothing," she chuckled. "I am just happy, Lauren."

"Yeah? What makes you happy?"

"Today. All of today," said Nastia. "Life was different in a way it hasn't been in years. I have a new beginning — and I can feel it! Something wonderful is happening. Wow, just looking over this day. I stepped out of my dorm for the last time in California this morning, then I flew to Dallas, and I had a great conversation on the plane with a nice atheist guy. Now I am here, riding in the car with my best friend after a delicious dinner at a high-class restaurant. I am just happy. After all of that, how could I be anything else?"

"OOOOHH! You met a *guy* on the plane? That explains it."

They both laughed.

"Oh gosh, Lauren. After all the guys who have gone after me for three years at college, do you really think one conversation with a stranger would be so special? You're silly."

"Did you think he was cute?" Lauren prompted.

Nastia rolled her eyes. "Yes, actually he was very handsome. So what? He was a likable person. We debated about God and the existence of the world."

"My goodness. You get right to the issues, don't you? I'm glad."

"Yeah, it was great. He presented his side very well, and I was able to articulate my thoughts effectively. He said I was a good debater."

"I think he liked you."

"Come on, Lauren. He was just a travel acquaintance."

"Was he?"

"Yes. I mean — I think so. Of course he was." Nastia pondered for just a second. "I don't know. God bless the man, and I hope he becomes a Christian. No, of course I didn't like him in *that way*. Maybe God just wants me to pray for him."

"Maybe. Why do you say that? Have you been thinking about this guy ever since the flight?"

Nastia was surprised by the question. "Yes. I guess I have. But that doesn't mean anything. I think about all kinds of people."

"It is definitely okay to think about people. God very well might want you to pray for him. I'm sorry," Lauren reached over and rubbed Nastia's shoulder. "I know how it is to be confused. But I sensed something about you today. Something is off balance inside you — and that bothers me."

"Off balance? Oh Lauren. Today was pure blessing. There's no reason to worry."

Lauren decided not to say anymore on the subject, and they switched the conversation to other topics.

LAUREN AND NASTIA had been best friends for years, ever since high school in Arizona. They were the best of friends in the immature days of chatting about the football players Nastia pursued every now and then. They were the best of friends when Lauren almost moved, and Nastia joined the cheerleaders because she was depressed at the thought of losing Lauren. They were the best of friends when the Sobieski family was going through a fire of hard times, and Nastia visited Lauren's church more than the church led by her own father.

The Henson family members were always welcoming and joyful people. Mrs. Henson was a tall, keen-eyed woman who could tell whether you needed prayer by the slightest glance. Nastia remembered when she had wandered over to the Henson home after school, perplexed by life's growing hardship. As always, all four Henson children raced through the rooms of the house to greet Nastia with their beaming smiles.

Lauren was the youngest and only girl. Her brothers were tall and broad football players. Mrs. Henson would come out of the kitchen with the happiest smile you have ever seen spread across her face, ready to give Nastia a firm hug. "Come right into the kitchen. I just made a batch of chocolate and peanut butter bars, and you need to have one before my famished boys scarf them all down."

Knowing what had been going on with the Sobieskis, the Hensons invited Nastia to their church. She was immediately considered part of the family as they sang at the top of their lungs in that blessed Baptist church with Mama Henson's hand upon Nastia's shoulder.

Mr. Henson, who liked to be referred to as Daddy James, was a towering man with broad shoulders and a deep ebony face. Daddy James was a serious-minded Christian man, but he had a thread of humor in him that seemed to bubble over at just the right times. He always seemed to be completely content, unlike Nastia's father.

Those times with the Henson family were the greatest blessings of Nastia's high school years.

Lauren and Nastia first met sitting next to each other in class during their freshman year at a private Christian high school. Nastia opened up with a complaint about how long it was taking the "stupid" teacher to write on the board, but she quickly changed to a sweet smile and said, "I'm Nastia by the way. What's your name?"

"Lauren."

"Nice to meet you. I haven't seen you before. Did you just move here?"

"Yes."

"You'll like it in Sedona. It's small but, you know, it works. We should totally be friends."

"Yeah, we should," Lauren replied.

Looking back, Nastia thought she had been a selfish and bossy teenage girl. Nastia would unload her many grievances onto Lauren, who usually listened with interest. When other people were around, Lauren would interject a humorous remark, which was quickly followed by a scolding stare from Nastia. Lauren would shrink away momentarily and return the glare with shy, *wishing-to-be-innocent* eyes like arched lamps in a cool night.

Tension sometimes challenged Nastia and Lauren's friendship, but they were best friends regardless.

There was this one recurring inside joke between them that had stuck through the years. One day, while they thumbed through swimsuits in the mall, Nastia found a black suit with white polka dots. "This is like you and me. You're the black that complements me, the white dots."

Lauren didn't exactly like the unapproved arrangement and found a white bathing suit with black polka dots. "No, no, Tia. You are the white that complements me, the black dots."

Nastia grinned and slowly started to put the white suit back on the rack. "No, Lauren. You are *such* an amazing friend. You are loyal, kind, and *very* supportive. You are the polka to my dotta."

"Haha! Actually, *you* are the polka to *my* dotta, Tia." The two exchanged artificial death stares and burst into fits of laughter. They laughed so hard the other shoppers peered over the racks at them, wondering what in the world could be so funny.

Yes, Lauren and Nastia went way back.

———————◆———————

"YOU ARE THE polka to my dotta, Lauren." Nastia grinned and turned to her friend at the wheel.

Lauren was quite pleased that her previously distant friend had remembered the joke from the past. "No, no, Tia. *You* are the polka to *my* dotta."

The two laughed together as best friends do, just like old times.

———————◆———————

"SO, THIS IS your apartment?" said Nastia. "I like how you've decorated the place — very rustic French with a modern twist." She pointed to the floor. "Hey, your blue and cream carpet matches your fleur-de-lis throw pillows. Clever."

"Thank you, Tia. But it's *our* apartment now."

"I guess so, huh? I like it." Nastia approached the window and looked into the dark sky. "You know what I've been thinking lately?"

"What?"

"That I don't need pleasure or luxury or any of the opulence of life to be happy. All I need is God."

"That's fantastic. I know what you mean." Lauren listened eagerly and realized just how much she had missed her best friend. Nastia could be insensitive occasionally, but Lauren loved her anyway; she even appreciated her bluntness most of the time. Right now, she didn't care if Nastia was as blunt as a rusty knife. Seeing her in person was too wonderful.

"As I've gone through college and lived in tiny dorm rooms with sometimes no food," said Nastia, "I have come to the point where I don't really care about my surroundings. I could live in the slums and be just as content because — like you said in the car — I find my satisfaction in God. My soul is clothed in His divine protection. What more could I want?"

"Being a Christian is the only way to live, isn't it?" Lauren grinned proudly.

"Yes, it certainly is. But what do we mean when we say that?"

"What?"

"When we say 'only way,' what do we mean?"

Lauren thought for a moment. "We mean that Jesus is the best way, the happiest, and the most fulfilling way. What makes you ask?"

"Oh, it's just that I seem to hear the phrase 'only way' a lot. I wonder if it scares non-Christians."

"We say 'only way' because we care about people, because we want them to live in complete satisfaction with God in eternity."

Nastia nodded slowly. "Yes, you're right."

Lauren sat on her couch as Nastia turned to explore the apartment. "Aw…what a cute kitchen. Your dishes are adorable, Lauren." Nastia held up a dinner plate, displaying the pale blue fleur-de-lis icon in the middle. "Am I noticing a theme here, perhaps?"

Lauren clutched a fleur-de-lis pillow. "You got me."

After Nastia unpacked, the two women sat around the unstained kitchen table, talking away.

"Okay, I've figured it out. The reason I couldn't stop thinking about that guy on the flight is…. Don't say it, Lauren, don't say it!"

"What? Me say something? What are you talking about?"

They laughed.

"No, listen. The reason I couldn't stop thinking about the guy is because he was the nicest atheist I have ever met. He respected my opinions and didn't seem offended when I talked about God. He seemed like a good man. I don't meet good men every day. He was so different from my dad. Ich! the last thing I ever want is to end up like my dad. But this guy — he was special. I got the impression that he is a very loyal person."

"How refreshing," Lauren chortled, sipping her strawberry lemonade.

Nastia raised her cup of lemonade and said in a purposefully silly, witchlike tone, "Drink this, my child. Drink, yes, yes, and you will be more than refreshed. I will give you treasures beyond your imagination."

"Treasures!" Lauren played along. "Oh please, wicked witch of the strawberry lemonade, what treasures will I gain?"

Nastia lowered her voice and whispered, as if uttering the secret of the world, "You shall receive a great forest of *strawberries*."

Nastia couldn't hold her act any longer and the two burst into tearful laughter.

As Lauren left to wash the dishes, Nastia returned to her thoughts. She remembered Anton and how he looked at her with steady care. She found herself wishing to sit next to him again. Whenever she closed her eyes she saw his face and his strong shoulders beneath a blue button-up.

Nastia prayed, God, please bless Anton.

5

A BEAUTIFUL MAN AND
A LEGEND

"OH, MY GRACE! Why hasn't he replied yet?" Nastia whispered as she sat at her desk beside the window, glancing around to be sure no one heard.

Two days after she landed in D.C., on Monday, she began her new job at the church. The official title of her position was Administrative Assistant of the Head Pastor's Secretary, which really meant that she was the schedule girl. Over the past three days, she had begun training, been assigned to a desk, and answered countless calls from people with either the wrong number, a need for a counselor, or something to schedule. But it was good work, mostly because it gave her a chance to talk about God and the gospel with whomever called. Stephanie Rivers had been understanding and kind, yet professional. Nastia thought she would enjoy the job, even though she occasionally got bored.

Recently, however, boredom was the farthest from her mind, and lack of ability to focus on work was the closest. On Tuesday, that guy she had met on the plane sent her a Facebook friend request. *So that's why he asked for my last name*, Nastia thought initially. Of course, she couldn't help but smile, click confirm, and scan through Anton Shepherd's photos. Last night, while she was online messaging a friend from college, Anton began a chat:

Anton's message: "Hey. How are you settling into DC?"

Nastia's message: "Hello there, Anton. I like it here so far. How are you settling in? What is your job anyway?"

And so, the conversation began. As the night progressed, Nastia said she needed to get to bed and Anton sent her his number.

Anton: "Text me if you want, and we'll finish our conversation."

Nastia: "Ok."

Thus, on this Thursday, she was texting Anton Shepherd.

But was he still texting her? The last thing she had sent could have been taken the wrong way, "Did you ever consider yourself a Christian before?" Nastia had felt the menace of offended non-Christians whenever she asked if they believed in Christ. Was that happening now? She earnestly hoped not. She really wanted to get to know Anton. Why? Why was she so eager to find out more about him? He seemed to respect her and think well of her. Did this question change that? *Please, please no, God. Help him to respond!*

Has he replied? She checked her phone again. *No. Darn it! Of course he hasn't.* There was no way she could have missed the distinct vibrating buzz of her phone in the quiet church office. *Okay, this probably means that he was offended and doesn't care to talk to me anymore. He has probably disregarded me, deciding I'm not worth his time. I can deal with it, right? We are just two strangers continuing the conversation we started on the plane. If he never wants to talk to me again, that's fine. I'm fine with it. What the heck, whatever.*

After feeling like she was almost peaceful about the situation, Nastia finished the report she had been typing all day. And then she checked her phone. Oh goodness, she hated that blank screen! She wanted to throw her phone out the window and shout, "Jerk!"

What is wrong with me? Why am I waiting so desperately for a response that will probably never come? I have to forget him now.

The first step to forgetting someone was to think of something else. One technique Nastia liked to use was what she called *memory replacement.* Since all hurt and struggle to forget people was rooted in some memory of them, the best way was to supplant that memory with a different one and then transition to a new focused thought, if necessary. She closed her eyes.

———————◆———————

NASTIA ENTERED HER memory library in the middle of a forest — a library that resembled an abandoned glass greenhouse with no roof. Gray leaves floated down from the overcast sky. Everything was black and white, except for the memories in the books.

After pondering for a second, Nastia removed a clean brown book from the shelves and shuffled through the "Kindness" section. The memories were like moving photographs. There was the wonderful Mrs. Henson and her boys welcoming her into the house. There was the understanding face of Lauren, and then Nastia's beautiful sweet mother. Six entire pages were filled with pasted memory-photos of Nastia's mom. *Oh, Mom, oh my dear mom.*

In one special photo, Mrs. Sobieski sat in front of a large canvas, gracefully painting. As the women left the picture to get something, a young girl entered, gazed up at the painting in wonder, clutched a dish of paint, and splashed it on the bottom piece of the canvas. Mrs. Sobieski had seen it, and the girl ran to her in shame. "I'm sorry, Mommy! I ruined your painting!" She wept and buried her head in her mother's skirt.

Mrs. Sobieski knelt. "Nastia, my sweet Nastia Jane. I forgive you, just as Jesus has forgiven me. Don't cry anymore. Come, and I'll show you how to sign your name." Mrs. Sobieski had a smile like a warm white flame and such kind hands. The photo memory ended with the mother helping the little girl sign the canvas.

A cold wind began to blow the wonderful memory away. Along with dark, crumpled leaves, it swept in the memory of her father onto the pages. *No! I will not remember him!*

Nastia closed the book and the wind calmed. Why did painful memories always have to follow the ones of her mother? Always! That's why she tried not to think of her mom. The leaves rested on the rustic brick floor, mingling with old, blurry photos.

A new, freshly sliced picture floated onto the coffee table, vivid and bright like an image of solace. Anton turned toward the onlooker, removed an ear bud, and asked in his soothing voice, "What kind of music do you like?" Nastia stared at the photo, sighed, and watched his caring eyes blink.

For the love of wisdom, that guy was gorgeous — totally gorgeous! My word, what a beautiful man. He didn't look that completely attractive at first. But now, goodness!

———————————◆———————————

BUZZ!

Nastia nearly leapt out of her desk chair and reached for her phone faster than she had in her life.

Anton: "Yeah. My parents took me to church every once in a while, until I got to high school."

Thank the almighty God of heaven, Anton does not hate me.

Nastia: "Really? Do you mind if I ask these types of questions?"

His reply came much faster this time.

Anton: "No, not at all. Sorry, I had to work something out with my boss. But I'm good now."

Nastia moved her shoulders up and straightened in her chair, displaying her beaming white-flame smile. *Yes! Victory!*

Nastia: "I understand of course. I'm at work, too."

Anton: "Do you have any more questions? Feel free to ask."

Did Anton know what he had just invited? No way.

Nastia: "Okay. Let's see. Why did you stop going to church?"

Anton: "I didn't believe in God. He seemed like an imaginary friend that some deceptive politicians created to make people follow them."

Boy, no one created God! She shook her head.

Anton: "Does that offend you?"

Nastia: "No, I understand. I'm sad for you, though."

Anton: "Thank you, but I'm happy."

Nastia: "Are you? Have you made any friends at your lovely workplace yet?"

Anton: "Not really. No one I can foresee being a real companion. I consider you a friend."

Nastia: "But you just met me."

Anton: "I met you before I met my coworkers."

Nastia: "You got me there."

Anton: "Do you consider me a friend?"

Nastia: "Yeah, I guess."

Anton: "DC is a big city full of people striving for things."

Nastia: "What are you striving for?"

Anton: "Um...I'm not really sure. I thought it was an advanced career, but work is only a part of life. I guess I'm searching for the other part."

He was soul searching! Nastia knew a ministry opportunity when she saw one, but she wouldn't push. She would be careful.

Nastia: "I've searched for that other part before. How are you going to go about your journey?"

Anton: "I don't know. Any suggestions?"

Nastia: "Hey, I'm a Christian. I'm gonna say find out more about God."

By this time, Nastia had finished her work and began packing up her things to drive home. As she pulled out her keys in the parking lot, her purse buzzed.

Anton: "I would need someone to tell me about Him then."

Was that an invitation?

Nastia: "I would love to tell you more about God."

She didn't read the next text until she walked through the door of her and Lauren's apartment.

Anton: "Really? Then would you like to meet for dinner tomorrow? There's this quiet place I just visited by the river. It's nice."

As Nastia entered the apartment living room, Lauren greeted her with a joyous, "Hey, Tia! What is it?"

"You know that guy I was telling you about, the one I met on the plane?"

"Yeah. Did he contact you?"

Nastia shrugged. "We were texting, and he just invited me out to dinner tomorrow."

"Really? I told you he liked you."

"You were right."

"Are you going to say yes?"

Nastia licked the edge of her pretty teeth. "Maybe. We'll see."

———————◆———————

A CAR DROVE across the bridge beneath a dim streetlight as Nastia watched from an illuminated window, her finger delicately gliding in swirls on the wall beside her. Anton Shepherd was out there. Where was he? Who exactly was he?

"Did you read the legend on the back of the menu the other night?"

"What?"

Lauren was sitting at her computer. "The Legend of the Silver Dragon? I have it up right now on the restaurant's website. Let me read it to you. It's really neat."

Nastia sat on her bed as she took a sip from her cup of chamomile tea. "All right."

Lauren cleared her throat and began:

Long ago, in the Everlasting Kingdom, there was the Great Emperor and his court. The members of the court were animals of all kinds. Being immortal, they glowed as they displayed their splendor of colors and variety for the Emperor. One of the members of the court, the dragon, was especially beautiful; he had many colors and intricate designs all over his body. The other animals admired his appearance and gave him compliments. Even the Emperor himself was pleased and granted the dragon a high position in the court.

During the festival of worship, when all the animals prepared something to give to the emperor, the little crab made some very special dumplings. He spent hours and hours preparing the dumplings. The other animals talked about it among themselves. "Did you hear that Crab has been working with all of his strength to cook dumplings for the Emperor?"

"Yes, I did hear. Isn't it marvelous? Watching him worship is always enjoyable."

The dragon overheard this talk concerning the crab, but he was not happy about it. Usually, everyone talked about the dragon and gave him all the compliments, but now they were complimenting the crab, the least and most humble of the court animals. Envy started to grow in the dragon's mind.

Once the dumplings were finished and the crab had gone to rest, the dragon rushed in from behind a pillar and approached the delicacy. He glanced around and took a bite. Immediately, his paws drained of color, and so did his entire body. While he gasped in disbelief, his body was coated in a reflective sheen.

Overcome with fury about the resulting consequence, the dragon stole the remaining dumplings and raced away to his chamber. Once alone, he writhed and slithered in violent convulsions, destroying everything in sight, including all the gifts and treasures from the Emperor. Such violence had never before occurred in the Everlasting Kingdom.

Suddenly, the Emperor appeared in the doorway. The dragon froze and bowed, not out of respect, but from the sheer power of the Emperor's presence. "You have stolen the worship created for me and have destroyed the generous treasures I had given you," said the Emperor. "Never before has sin and rebellion occurred. You are cursed from now and for all time. You will suffer endlessly. You shall be separated from me and cast out into a colorless kingdom. You are my enemy. One day, you will receive the judgment you deserve."

And so, the dragon became the silver dragon and went to his gray kingdom, departing forever from the emperor and his light.

"Aw…that's cute," said Nastia. "It would make a great children's book."

Lauren swiveled around. "Do you see the symbolism?"

"Yes, the fall of Satan. Fascinating." Nastia went over to the computer. "Is that it?"

"No. There's more. Would you like me to read the rest?"

"No thanks. I think I'm good."

Lauren decided to stop beating around the bush. "Have you made up your mind about dinner tomorrow?"

"Yes. I just sent him a text."

"Are you going?"

"Mmhmm," Nastia replied ever so calmly as she sipped more tea.

6

TALL, STRONG, AND CUTER

ANTON: "I HAVE a table for us."

Nastia slid her phone away and smiled as her car confirmed with a beep that it had locked. The name of the restaurant was Shalom Shy — a modest American cuisine establishment.

As she entered, Nastia noticed the grayish-white décor with vivid blue and magenta touches. Anton waved, the sinking sun glimmering through the window behind him.

"Hi," he said, standing as she walked up.

"Hello, Anton. Thank you." She took the seat that he pulled out for her.

"Thank you for coming," he said. "I don't really have any friends right now, except you. It's great to meet with a friend."

"Aw. No, I wanted to come. Really, I should be thanking you for inviting me."

She observed how his grin revealed adorable, toned dimples and bright teeth. Nastia wondered why he had occupied her thoughts every day almost constantly. Yes, he was cute. So what?

"The first thing I'd like to say is please be honest," Nastia continued. "Don't stop yourself from saying something because we are supposed to talk about God. I want our conversation to be real. I know some people are afraid that we Christians will judge everything about them, but please don't feel that way. I might not agree with you on some subjects, but I won't judge you."

"Thank you. I will be honest if you will also," Anton said in a light-hearted tone. "It sounds like you don't remember how rude I was with my imposing atheism."

"You weren't rude."

"I wasn't? That's nice to hear. But tell me more about yourself. We've texted, but we haven't really asked the basic questions like, 'Where did you grow up?' and 'What did you do in high school and college?' "

The magenta beads in the table centerpiece cast tiny shimmers below Nastia's face. "All right. Where did you grow up?"

"Denver, Colorado. I miss the mountains. Where did you grow up?"

"Sedona, Arizona. I miss the sunsets."

"Nothing like a western vista is there?"

"Nope, but I think I like it here anyway. I don't particularly want to go back to Arizona."

"Why not?"

"I've moved on. Going back might cause me to forget what I've learned about myself," Nastia replied.

"I don't know about that. If anything, you would solidify what you've learned about yourself by taking a look at the past."

"I still look at the past and remember, but I'm glad to be here in D.C., where God has put me."

"Has he put you in this restaurant?" Anton prompted.

"Yes. God is sovereign. But I didn't ask you the second question. Tell me a story from, say, your freshman year of college. Did you play any sports?"

"All right, back to that," he said, accommodating the topic switch "Yes, I did play a sport. Actually, I got a football scholarship and played all through my senior year — but I had to drop it when I went to grad school."

"Did school and football consume your life?"

"No, I definitely have a few wild stories to tell about my social life."

"Tell me one," Nastia urged.

The waiter came by; Nastia and Anton both ordered water.

"Let's see. What's a good story?" Anton thought for a moment. "I hope you don't mind if it's a bit raunchy?"

"Don't worry about it. I probably have similar stories."

"Well," he began, "in the first few weeks of freshman year, I went to a party with my teammates. Two of the guys had been following me around like insecure kids — acting like they had to impress me to survive the day — but I didn't really care. Anyways, we were standing in a corner, drinking punch out of plastic cups when one of the guys said, 'I so want to have sex with that Latin chick right now.'

"Me and the other guy shook our heads and were like 'Dude, we've barely walked in the door.'

"He was like, 'What do you think freshman year is for?' and went over to talk to the girl. The other guy and I laughed as we watched him. This other dude seemed all excited to talk to me alone and began pouring questions on me and going on about how he wanted to shoot his slob of a roommate.

"Then he said in a kind of desperate tone, 'We should be roommates.'

"I started sensing that he had some form of insecure gay crush on me, and I didn't want to deal with his obsessive talking. So, I went to talk to some girls who had been staring at me. They were all smiling and giggling, and I was being the guy saying stuff like, 'The dude who is throwing this party is such a creeper.'

"The girls were like 'Yeah, I know!'

"Anyway, once a band began playing music, I started making out with one of the girls. We kissed for about five minutes, with everybody watching. To this day, I have no idea why I did it."

"That wasn't so raunchy."

Anton raised his eyebrows. "You don't think so?"

"No. I went to college too. I told you, you don't have to worry about me judging you," said Nastia.

"Yeah. I guess I don't."

Anton blushed, and Nastia thought, *Poor guy. Must be the change of moving to a new city and having to live alone. Aw...* "Once at a Christmas party, a guy kissed me, and I didn't really care until I thought about it ten seconds into the kiss."

"For real? I didn't think you the type," he said.

"Yeah, it happened, but I regret it. I was in a very careless spiritual phase at the time."

"So, you think kissing someone you aren't dating is a sin?"

"It could be. Sin is an action or thought that goes against God's law. He never said 'thou shall not kiss random people,' but he did promote faithfulness. In our modern culture, a kiss isn't just a greeting; it's a way of saying 'I want you' or 'I love you.' Romance and kissing are almost the same to us."

"I agree," Anton said. "Hey, I never asked you. What was your major?"

"Art history," she responded. "I liked your story, though. I can definitely relate about people obsessing over you. In college, people either hated me, gossiped about me, or were starry-eyed over me."

"People gossiped about you?"

"Oh, definitely," Nastia continued. "I guess I was one of those people you could call *outspoken*. At least that's what a lot of people called me because I always talked about my faith and God in class. People like to slander those who hold to their morals."

Anton's eyes glistened with faint admiration.

"Have you decided what you want?" The waiter asked, approaching with a click of his pen.

"Oh, um. I'll have the special, thanks," said Anton.

"All right. How about you?"

"Crab cakes with a side of the dumplings, please." Nastia elegantly handed the menu to the waiter.

"Perfect choice. That's exactly what I would order. Your meals will be right out." He grasped the menus with shuffling hands and left.

"Did you see the way he looked at me?" Nastia smoothed the vivid blue napkin on her knee.

"Yeah, I did. He likes you."

"He is a perfect example of what I've had to deal with throughout college. The first semester of my freshman year was crazy. In high school, I was never such a popular person. Yeah, a few people liked me, and we hung out sometimes, but I didn't stand out very much. College was completely different. I don't know if it was just northern California or the new environment, but everybody wanted to get to know me. Everybody!"

"That doesn't sound so bad," Anton remarked.

"It wasn't at first. I didn't know how to handle it except to say 'hi,' be myself, and treat people like I would anyone else. Maybe it was the way I carried myself in that first semester. I have always been able to make great first impressions, but when people get to know me, they think they have figured me out and pass judgment because they want to get rid of the mystery of me — or something like that. I honestly don't know. Many guys tried hitting on me and asking me out on dates. A lot of the insecure, lesser-known guys wanted to hang out with me, maybe because I wasn't insecure at all. I tried to be nice and accepting toward them. And at every meal, I usually had a few girlfriends hanging around me. That brought more jocks over."

Anton's shoulders slackened, as if deflated. "Wow. What changed?"

"I was myself, and people didn't like the way I talked about God all the time and gave my opinions freely. Some of the guys who I refused to go on dates with became jealous and talked about me behind my back. In class, several guys would chuckle when I spoke. I think they were trying to strip away my security. I shrugged it off and didn't care. But many of the professors didn't like me because I had a tendency to talk about God when we had serious class discussions. Some of the girls who hung out with me thought I was judging them because I had said a few times that premarital sex is wrong. They would take every little thing I did as a way of judging them when I wasn't. I knew they didn't agree with me; I didn't tell them what to do or look down on them. But no one cared about the truth. They got mad at me for no reason at all and refused to talk to me.

"I tried to work things out and be nice, but by the second semester, a lot of people scowled at me as if I had personally offended them. Many people said it was because I would never hang out with them or I didn't enough. I couldn't hang out with *that* many people! It simply wasn't possible. And the girls or guy friends who I did hang out with got mad at me because I wouldn't text them or I didn't open the depths of my soul to them. I don't know. But guys never stopped asking me out every now and then."

"Yeah, the first year is always crazy," said Anton. "People tend to hold unrealistic expectations about friends and what they want."

"Yes. Exactly."

"Did you ever say yes to the guys who wanted to go out?" He grinned.

"Yes," Nastia laughed, "to a few. Most people I couldn't really consider at all, but there were a few persistent guys. On nights when I didn't have anything else to do, I would say, 'Sure. Why not?' Usually they were just harmless, free meals — for me at least."

Anton laughed now. "Usually? When was it not?"

"Well, you know." Nastia sensed that he might think she was categorizing him as one of those guys. "Sometimes they would take me to college events like football games or basketball. Ah, here's our food."

The waiter and his server friend set the plates. "Enjoy."

Anton watched Nastia pray. When she was done, they picked up their silverware and began eating.

"Did you ever have any serious stalkers?" Anton asked, right before he took a bite of his grilled halibut.

Nastia gulped. "*Stalker*. I never liked that word. In my experience, people use it to belittle others. In high school, I liked a guy on the football team. Once he told me, 'You're such a stalker.' That hurt — very much. I try not to use the term. But, yes, I have had a few stalkers."

Anton's forehead rumpled at the word *football*. "Can you tell me a specific incident? You never really told your story from college."

They both laughed.

"All right." Nastia scooted her two crab cakes apart. "One night, in the fall semester of sophomore year, I went out with a group of girls to a rock concert. The place was packed. Everyone was going crazy over the slightest movement of the singers and the changes in the lights and the LED screens. Somehow, near the end, I lost my friends. While I searched for them in the dark forest of people, this guy — who had been interested in me for over a year — offered to drive me back to campus. I really wanted to get out of the concert, so I said yes. But he had more in mind than just driving home. On the way back, he randomly pulled over to the side of the road. I was like 'What are you doing?' He didn't answer, and I became suspicious.

" 'Ever since I met you I haven't been able to get you off my mind,' he said in a yearning voice. I could see his wide eyes despite the darkness of the car. He touched my hair and said, 'Please, I just want a kiss. Just one kiss…' He was far too desperate, and I backed away.

" 'No,' I said. 'I don't just kiss people.'

" 'Please make an exception for me — just this once. You don't know how much pain I've suffered over you. *Please.*'

"He kept saying please, and I kept saying 'No!' But he didn't listen and came closer to me and grabbed my arm. I didn't like it at all and managed to open the door, pull away, and start walking on the side of the road.

" 'Don't do that!' he shouted at me. 'How are you going to get back? There's no way you can walk all the way to campus.'

" 'I don't know,' I shouted, 'but I *will* get back. I'm not going with you!'

" 'Please just give me what I need, and I'll drive you home.'

"I didn't care what he said at that point. I started running down the street. The next morning, I shot him a satisfied smile as I entered the library."

"How did you get back?" Anton inquired.

"That's another story."

"I'm interested."

"I was very upset," Nastia went on. "While I ran along the side of the road in the chilly night, I prayed, 'Lord God, please provide a way back to campus. Please help me.' I kept muttering the same prayer over and over. Eventually, a car pulled up next to me. At first, I thought it was the dude who wanted to kiss me, but the car was different.

"I stopped running, the window rolled down, and an elderly woman squinted at me. 'What do ya think you're doin', running 'round out here at a time like this? Someone could pick you up, chil'!'

" 'I know, I know,' I replied, nodding my head. 'It's hard to explain.'

" 'Get in,' she said, 'and I'll drive you to wherever you're goin'.'

"I did, and she drove me back to campus."

"Wow. How lucky," Anton commented, starting on his sautéed asparagus.

"Luck? Is that all you think it was?"

"Yes. A fortunate coincidence."

"Just like the evolution of mankind, right?" Nastia grinned, shaking her head.

"What do *you* think it was?" Anton responded.

"God answering my prayer."

"I can see how you would believe that."

"But you don't?"

"No."

"I hope you change your mind one of these days," she said.

"You can hope if you want. As far as my thinking goes, there are a lot of things in this world that don't make sense — a lot of good things and a lot of bad. Your story is an example of one of those good things."

"You certainly phrase it nicely." Disappointed, Nastia took a sip of water.

"*You* make sense to me," Anton said out of the blue.

Nastia stopped drinking, put her hand over her mouth, and laughed after she swallowed. "Do I? Huh. You might be the only one who thinks so." He was grinning — those razor-edged eyes grinning. "What?"

"Oh. Nothing."

She displayed her prettiest smile without even thinking about it.

The sun had set by now. A boat slowly made its way up the river. A plane crossed the darkening sky.

"Do you know what it's like to be a Christian?" she said.

"Like stars?"

"You remembered! Yes, but I was going to say something different. Being a Christian is like my crab cakes."

"What?" He chuckled. "They must have used very devout crabs for your dinner."

"You silly. I guess it is funny. I mean, being a Christian is like crab cakes in how they make them. Everyone knows that the best crab cakes are made almost completely of crabmeat."

"I didn't know that."

"Well, you know it now, precious." They both laughed, and Nastia continued. "But the seasoning and ingredients are like art, personality, and creativity. Say the crabmeat is like Jesus, the colorful bell pepper pieces are like art, and the seasoning is personality. True Christians have Christ living in them, ruling over their desires and thoughts — while their personalities, talents, and artistic abilities are the flavor and dazzle. The cakes would taste horrid without the crab."

"Huh. That's a different way to look at it."

"Are you making fun of me?" said Nastia, although she wasn't offended in the least.

"No, I'm not. Really. I've just never heard of anything deep compared to crab cakes before."

———————◆———————

AFTER THEY FINISHED dinner, while Nastia washed her hands in the ladies' room, she saw bead necklaces of bright blue and magenta pink in a basket beside the sink. She took one of each color.

Fresh air and the sound of distant cars greeted Nastia and Anton as they stepped onto the parking lot.

"Would you like to walk along the river?" Anton suggested. "It's nice."

"Sure."

Emotions rushed inside Nastia as they strolled by the dark river. Everything was so perfect now, with Anton and the cool city air. Why could she never find a good man for herself? Nastia wanted someone just like Anton. He was so strong, natural, and experienced. His personality was comfortable and exciting. She would feel perfectly safe with a guy like him, especially in a vicious city full of millions of people galloping through the mad circus of life.

They didn't say much as they walked until Nastia spoke, "I found this. You should put it on." She handed him the bright blue necklace.

"Huh?" He laughed as she placed it around his neck. She laughed too and put the pink one on her own neck.

"How tall are you, Anton?"

"Six three."

They walked on.

"I should probably leave soon," said Nastia, thinking realistically.

"Yeah. I should too, I guess."

He stopped by a bush of flowers, leaned over, and smelled one. *Guys are so hot when they smell flowers,* Nastia thought, attempting to restrain a giggle. Anton noticed and flashed a playful smile. *Oh gosh, could he get any cuter?*

"I was meaning to ask you something." Anton rubbed the back of his neck.

"What?"

"There is this big gala that my company is putting on. I was asked to bring a date. Would you like to come with me — tomorrow?"

The chilly nighttime emotions leapt inside Nastia, like the intro of a pop song that makes you want to dance. "Yes, I will go with you."

"*Yes!* Thank you. I was afraid you would say no."

"You feared for nothing then," she grinned.

"I guess so." Anton picked a flower and took the privilege of placing it in Nastia's hair. She let him. He removed his necklace.

"What are you doing?"

"Pretty glittery beads look much better on you." Anton laid it over her neck.

Nastia removed the pink one. "If you're going to give me yours then you must have mine. I insist." She draped hers around his neck, brushing his hair as she removed her hands.

"Is pink my color?"

"It's magenta, Star Boy."

He laughed. "Star Boy? What does that mean?"

"It means you're adorable."

"Then call me Star Boy as much as you like, Nastia."

"I was planning on it."

They returned to Nastia's car, holding hands.

"I guess I'll see you tomorrow then," he said as she opened the car door.

"Yes. Where do I need to go?"

"I can pick you up. My hotel is over there." He pointed at a towering building.

"All right. Call me." Nastia hesitated to leave and hugged him tenderly. At the last second, she kissed the side of his face. And oh, his smile afterwards! *Wow, he could get cuter.*

Parting strained the night's emotions and raised hopes. They waved to each other, and Nastia drove off.

Anton closed his eyes and exhaled, feeling exceptionally satisfied with the first date.

7

YOU KISSED ME TONIGHT

NASTIA SILENTLY CRAWLED into her twin bed, trying not to wake Lauren. Her friend had been happy for Nastia when she had entered the room like a dreamer.

"Do you have tomorrow off?" she had asked Lauren excitedly.

"Yes. Would you like to do something?"

"Oh yeah! Tomorrow we are going shopping for my dress!"

Lauren was supportive as always, but she had been uneasy. "Tia?"

"Yes?"

"I know you are excited and all, but you might want to be cautious tomorrow."

"Why? What's wrong?"

"He's not a Christian, right?"

"No. It's just a party date with a guy who has no one else to take," Nastia replied dismissively. "Don't be so worried!"

"No, I *need* to be concerned and so do you. Celebrations can turn into defeats if you don't watch yourself."

"You're mistaking a ray of light for a staining splotch, Lauren. Come on, it's all fun. You are worried over nothing."

"You could have a staining splotch on your heart if you aren't careful. I was reading second Corinthians six today — "

"Who said anything about marriage? I am barely on the tropical islands of dating. Marriage is a far away nation in the mountains, Lauren."

"What do you think romance is for, Tia?"

Nastia had suppressed the conversation and gone to take a shower. Despite how much she resisted Lauren's cautioning, Nastia thought about her words. *What is romance for?* She didn't want to answer the question. *This is simple, innocent fun. Isn't it?* The mention of second Corinthians six did not comfort her.

The memory of Lauren's words prevented Nastia from finding sleep. Her phone buzzed. Who would text her now? She hadn't received a late-night text in a long while.

Anton: "You kissed me tonight."

Nastia: "Yes, I did."

Anton: "During our discussion about kissing, you said it should only be used for romance and dating."

Nastia: "That's right."

Anton: "I hope you don't think me bold to talk about this."

Nastia: "No. Not at all. It is a little late, though."

Anton: "Yeah, it is. Sorry about that. Were you saying you want me for romance, or was it just a kiss despite what you said before?"

Nastia: "I don't know. I'm not sure what I'm feeling now."

Anton: "I really enjoyed our dinner together. Thank you."

Nastia: "It was my pleasure all the way. What are you feeling?"

Anton: "Something, I think. I don't really know. That's why I texted you. It was probably crazy to receive a text that said, 'You kissed me tonight.' "

Nastia: "Not too crazy. You have a good reason to wonder."

Nastia put her phone back on the nightstand, ready to sleep this time. She decided not to pray about the conversation, telling herself she was too tired. Feelings were so confusing, like neon lights blinking in a dark night.

———————————◆———————————

IN HER DREAM, Nastia was hiking with Anton on a snowy mountain beneath a swirling green sky. He said he wanted to get back to the stone house of death. "What? You don't live with death!" she said.

"Yeah, I do. It's no big deal. Just fun." They arrived at the stone hut, and two hideous goblins hobbled out.

"These are Emotion and Desire." Anton introduced the goblins like old friends. "They keep the fires burning up here."

"But they are so horrible, Anton! Get them away! Push them over the edge!"

He just laughed as if she was joking.

———————————◆———————————

THE DISTURBING MOOD of last night's dream lingered as Nastia thumbed through racks of dresses with Lauren, testing and deciding with the slightest touch of her eager fingers. Fortunately, Lauren seemed to have forgotten last night's conversation.

"How about this one?" Nastia asked, holding up a periwinkle gown.

"That's nice, but I'm not sure it fits your occasion."

"Hmm…I agree. Back to the rack, you inane piece of cloth!" Nastia enjoyed shopping with Lauren. What a pleasure to go out with her best friend again. Just like old times.

Nastia kept thinking about Anton, but her nightmare hindered the pleasing association. She knew that dreams didn't mean anything most of the time, but there were a few occasions in the Bible when dreams were quite significant —Joseph's and Daniel's for example.

Nastia didn't want to believe this dream meant anything. Anton did not live with death! Goodness, the guy was a sweetheart. Yeah, he was not a Christian. But he could become a Christian, right? Maybe God wanted to use her to bring Anton to Christ. Of course — that must be why God allowed him to be attracted to her. Nastia settled with the thought in her mind; it was much easier than thinking in constant circles. God was using her to point Anton to Christ.

"Oh! Tia, I think I might have found it." Lauren held out a sleek garment.

"Gold?" Nastia hadn't thought of that.

"Yes. Gold. It would go perfectly with your hair and the gold eye shadow you've wanted to use for months."

The possibility dawned on Nastia as she held the dress up to the mirror. "Yes! You have a wonderful eye for fashion, Lauren. I *have* to try it on."

After purchasing the dress — and gasping with raised eyebrows at the sight of the malicious price —the two friends made their way out of the mall. "This will be a dress you'll keep for life," Lauren reassured Nastia as they rode up an escalator. She nodded and glanced to the side. A blue tiger sauntered through an aisle, swaying its tail back and forth.

"What in the world?" she exclaimed.

"What?"

"Over there, look it's a —" Nastia dropped her sentence and reeled back. A lady pushed a blue cart with two kids in it. Both wore tiger hats.

"A mother pushing her kids?" Lauren finished the sentence.

"Yeah. Never mind."

What is wrong with me? Nastia thought. Earlier, when they first entered the mall, Nastia thought she saw a moving blue tiger image on a displayed T-shirt. But when she looked back, there was no tiger at all, just some senseless graphic T. Also, while they passed the food court, Nastia thought she saw a red bird flying toward the large skylight, but when she looked closer, it turned out to be a dove.

Nastia hadn't thought about it until now, as she and Lauren entered the sunny parking lot.

And then it hit her.

When Nastia was five years old, her mother painted a picture of a blue tiger and a red bird because Nastia had just lost her favorite stuffed animals of those kinds, and she was sad. She remembered jumping up and down and hugging her mother after the painting was finished. It still hung in her old room back in Sedona. *I can't believe I forgot. It was the most precious gift Mom ever gave me!*

But that still didn't explain why she was seeing things.

Nastia didn't want to dwell on these memories. Recalling her mother's love made her want to cry. Today she was thinking about Anton Shepherd, not the past.

———◆———

"HE'S HERE!" ANTON heard a voice say after he knocked on the door. *So this is where Nastia lives.* She was still a mystery to him, but a shade of understanding added to his conception of her. The clean walls and modern-style interior of the apartment building suited Nastia Sobieski.

"Hi. Well, what do you think?" Nastia opened the door and smiled like a princess waiting for executive approval.

Anton's heart leapt. *You are the most beautiful person I have ever seen.* But speaking was different. "Wow! You are — stunning." He observed her satisfied expression and the light glittering on her single-strap gold dress that fit snugly around her body. "Are you ready to go?"

8

IF YOU WANT

DID THE DRESS or emotion cause Nastia excitement and tension as she followed Anton through the grand resort lobby and onto a dinner boat? Inside the boat, quiet caterers wore white gloves as well-dressed people chatted. They socialized lightly, standing in the buffet table line as business allowed for the business of eating. The boat began to cruise down the river.

"There is my boss," Anton motioned and introduced Nastia formally. The man was very pleased to meet her. Nastia felt nervous behind her beauty.

"What's wrong?" Anton asked after his boss moved on.

"I don't know."

"Don't worry. It's just a party, people, and a boat."

She looked up at his eyes. "Everything is new these days."

"It's only been a week hasn't it, since we first met and flew in?"

"Yeah. Only a week," she responded passively.

"And now dating."

"This week seemed longer, as if each day were two. Last night was fun."

"Yeah." His eyes softened. "Yeah, it was." They found glass plates as the servers offered food. "Hey, here is something familiar." He looked to her, grinning.

"Crab cakes?"

"Yep. Being a Christian is like crab cakes, remember?"

"Haha. Yes. What is being an atheist like?"

58

Anton glanced around and saw a guy slicing tuna rolls. "I know. Being an atheist is like sushi. You are cooked to perfection, and I am raw." They both laughed as they helped themselves to a few pieces of sushi.

They took their food up to the top deck with no roof and found a table by the railing. The wind fluttered Nastia's hair.

"Are we talking about Christians and atheists or you and me?" she asked.

"You and me. More who we are, I guess."

"This better be fresh sushi, then."

Her white-flame grin thrilled Anton. "And the cakes better be ninety-percent crab."

"Do you think I am really such a good Christian? Dependent upon God?" she inquired, reflectively.

"You would have to ask another Christian. Why, do you doubt yourself?"

"Oh, I guess that's what it is to have faith in Christ. You don't trust in your own strength but God's instead. I wonder about goodness. I'm not so sure what and where it is exactly sometimes."

"What happened to make you say that?"

She hesitated but decided to be honest. "You happened."

His wide grin spread across his face. "So you think I'm a good guy? Awesome." His eyes became extra sweet. "Oh, I forgot the drinks. What would you like?"

"You can decide. Just nothing alcoholic, please."

"Okay. I'll be right back."

Nastia felt doubtful as she stood alone in the cool wind. She gazed at the water and thought she saw black stripes on something blue. *I must be imagining things.*

They were being very sweet on each other, like a couple. "And now dating," he had said. *Maybe he was right,* she thought. *After a kiss, things just happen.*

Anton returned with two glasses. "Here we are."

"Cran-apple juice?"

"Yes. This is our drink. Remember?" he said proudly.

"Hopefully this time, I won't dip my hand in it."

"You can dip your hand in my beverage whenever you want." He smiled.

"Anton?"

"Yeah?"

"Are we really dating?"

"Yes, I think so. I would love to date you. Do you —"

"Did you see that?" Nastia exclaimed as she stared out at the water.

"What?"

"I was sure I saw a blue shark down in the water!"

"I highly doubt it. Maybe it's just the light."

"What is light doing swimming around?"

He laughed. "No idea."

"Maybe I'm going crazy. My feelings are so confusing."

"Back to feelings. I've been thinking about it, and I'm sorry for being so blunt with my texting last night," said Anton in a humble tone.

"Don't worry about it."

"I'm pretty sure now, though. I do have feelings for you,"

"Really? Huh." She took the news casually, as if she knew his feelings would disappear soon, as if all romance was hopeless.

"Here, I'll show you what I mean." He opened out his white napkin. "Do you mind dipping your hand in the juice again?"

She smiled. "Sure." Gently, he took her outreached hand, poured a splash, and pressed it onto the napkin.

"Okay, say this white napkin is my heart, and your handprint is my feelings for you," he said.

"This isn't right."

"What?" He didn't understand until Nastia grabbed his hand, poured on some of her drink, and pressed it onto her napkin.

"This is more like it. The napkin is *my* heart, and your bigger handprint is my feelings for you."

"So, you like me too?"

"Yes." She smiled. "I think I'll take this home with me as a souvenir."

"Take me instead." He meant it half as a joke, half as a hint.

She giggled. "That would be nice. I'll tell my roommate, 'Oh this? Just a souvenir. Don't mind the muscles.' "

He laughed. "How can you tell I have muscles under this stuffy suit?"

"A girl can tell when a guy is strong. You can count on it. Besides, you told me before that you used to play football."

"Yeah."

Nastia touched his fingers lightly.

"We're back at the hotel. There is dancing inside. Do you want to go?" Anton asked

Nastia brightened. "I hope it's wild dancing."

———————◆———————

BLUE FLASHED, TWIRLING across the room; magenta shone, leaping from table to table as the music pulsed in the mostly black room. In the corner by the bar, Nastia and Anton entered the hotel ballroom. A young guy looked up from his seat and immediately had to talk with his coworker.

"Hey, Anton. How's it going? Who is this you brought? You are amazing, man, to find a date so quickly."

Nastia could tell immediately that he liked her. Anton could tell, too. "Hey, man. Yeah. We sat together on the plane from Dallas."

"Really? Cool, cool." He turned to Nastia. "What's your name?"

"Nastia." She wanted to leave the acquaintance and dance. "We would love to chat more but the music is calling. See ya!"

"All right. Bye…"

Nastia pulled Anton by the hand, leading him through the crowd and to the dance floor. No one else was there, yet. Anton watched as

Nastia went over to the DJ and made a request. The song changed and a thicker, catchier beat started to play.

Anton was mesmerized as the music played loudly, and he danced with Nastia. He wasn't the type of person to give into his feelings easily, but now they were so strong! Nastia was phenomenal. She made him forget everyone else in the world. She was the most attractive human being he had ever met.

Nastia thought she glimpsed a silver creature slithering in the shadows. *What is that?*

The song ended, people clapped for them, and Nastia smiled. "Anton, could you buy me a drink? I'm thirsty."

"Oh yeah. Definitely. Let's get something." They went over to the bar and made the orders.

Anton's boss approached. "Hey, Anton. Looked like you had fun on the dance floor. Allow me to introduce you to a gentleman visiting from Hawaii."

"I'll be right back." Anton told Nastia as he went with his boss. What the heck was happening to him? He felt great, but his urges were strong and his feelings wild. All he wanted to do was be close to Nastia — very close.

Nastia wasn't alone for long. As she sipped her virgin mojito, the guy who introduced himself earlier came over again. "Hey. You dance very well — so natural."

"Thank you," she managed to say, but she was actually thinking, *Oh gosh, not this guy again.*

"Do you want to go out there again — with me?"

"Oh, um, no thanks. I'll wait for Anton."

"He'll be talking for ages. I know my boss. But you don't have to be bored for a minute. I can show you some moves. You'll like them. I promise you."

Oh, my grace, is he asking what I think he is asking?

Anton saw Nastia's look — a look that said, "Please save me from this guy." He politely ended the conversation with his boss and went to rescue her. "Excuse us," he told his coworker as he led

Nastia out of the ballroom and into the illuminated hallway. "What's wrong?"

"That guy was totally hitting on me. He was pushy and weird and…yeah. You know what I mean."

"Okay. What do you want to do?"

"I don't know. Let's just walk around this hotel a bit."

"All right." They began making their way down the long halls and through the decorated rooms.

Nastia started to express herself to Anton. "Why does this always happen to me at parties? Everywhere I go, there *always* seems to be a guy who tries to be around me every minute. What is this? Do I have a problem or something? I don't know, I don't know. And why do the guys have to act so *weird?* It's like they don't care about me; they just care about getting me. You know? I don't like it. I'm waiting for the right guy to come along, you know? I can't act like a slut or anything. That's not okay. I don't want to do stuff with crazy people. Weird guys are stupid. Oh! Anton. Where do you live, by the way?"

"Here, in this hotel."

"Really? You're kidding? You live in a resort?"

"Yeah, my room is on the tenth floor. It's like an apartment. Do you want to see?"

"Sure." They got into the elevator and Nastia started acting unstable and giddy, laughing every now and then. "Oh, what a cool elevator! This is a really nice elevator. It's like gold or something. Don't you think this is a nice elevator?"

"Sure." He smiled at her funny mood.

She giggled. "Hey, do you have a shower in your room?"

"Yes, I do actually —"

"Oh! The door's opening. I like the *ding*. Isn't it a pretty *ding*, Anton?"

He didn't know how to answer. She ran in front and pointed down the halls like a street sign, ready to giggle again.

Nastia didn't know why she was acting like this. She wasn't drunk because she didn't have any alcohol. Maybe it was some strange combination of her emotions and the late night. She didn't know, and she didn't care. It was just nice to get away from all the people and enjoy Anton's comfortable company.

"Which way? This ways or that ways?" Nastia giggled again.

"This ways." They laughed like college students, for they both knew that Nastia was being a funny strange. Once they got to the room, Anton opened the door and let her in. She turned on the lights immediately.

She gasped. "Wow! This is gorgeous! A combination of modern and Colonial décor. How much do they pay you? I love your coffee table and the TV, and you have a separate bedroom, and it's so roomy. I love the slate blue couch."

"Yes. It's a suite," he chuckled. He wondered why she was in such a silly mood.

"Oh, and a balcony!" She ran over, opened the door, and inhaled the fresh air, dim city sounds entering. "Ah...I like it." She turned and sheepishly started to ask a question. "Um, Anton?"

"Yes?"

"I feel really icky right now. Would you mind if I took a shower?"

"Not at all. Go right ahead. I'll order you a bathrobe."

"Yay! I get to go to Lystra!"

"What is Lystra?" he laughed.

"Just some city in the book of Acts. I liked how it sounded so now I call the shower Lystra."

Anton didn't think this made any sense but he decided to play along. "Hopefully my Lystra is clean."

Nastia thought she saw a small red bird fly outside the door. She expressed her pleasure without thinking about it, "Oh, pretty!"

"What?"

She recovered herself. "Oh, um. Nothing. Sorry. Thank you. I'll go take my shower now. See you in a bit!"

"All right." He headed for the door. "Take your time. I'm going down to the party for a little longer. Your robe should be up soon."

"Awesomeness! I shall see you soon, Anton Shepherd."

NASTIA FELT REVIVED after her shower, although she didn't understand what she was revived from. How cozy the creamy bathrobe felt! She wanted to hug it and lay down in its warmth. Feeling spontaneous, she opened the door, raced over to the couch, and curled up on the silk cushions, shutting her eyes. She heard the sound of the opening door.

"Did you have a nice visit to Lystra?" said Anton's soothing voice.

"Lystra was wonderful, quite refreshing. Just what I needed. Thank you for the robe. It's cozy."

"No problem." Anton paused, and there was a silence but only for a moment. "Do you mind if I lock the door?"

Nastia opened her eyes. She saw a blue tiger and a red bird poised in the hallway behind Anton's silhouette. "If you want."

9

RED, BLUE, AND SIN

NASTIA SAT QUIETLY in her office on Wednesday afternoon. Stephanie had asked her a question when she first came in on Monday: "I didn't see you at church on Sunday? Where were you?"

Nastia regretted her reply. "Oh, I was invited to a high-class D.C. social event, and with all the stress of moving and starting a new job, I simply wasn't able to make it. But I wish I could have. How was the service?"

At least her words prevented Stephanie from asking any more questions. Ever since Nastia returned to Lauren's apartment on Sunday afternoon, an uncomfortable aching feeling had settled inside her stomach. The memory of Sunday morning replayed in her mind once again.

———◆———

ANTON'S FINGERS TWIRLED Nastia's oh-so-pretty hair as she played with her sparkly cross necklace, tapping it on the side and letting it spin and spin. She prayed softly, "Thank you, Lord." And displayed a giddy grin.

"What was that?" Anton asked, lying beside her in the bed, his eyes still closed.

"Oh, nothing. Good morning, handsome." They kissed.

"Thank you for doing this with me. I wasn't sure if you ever would."

"I wanted to."

He sat up. "What was your pet name for the shower again?"

"Lystra."

"That's right. I'm going to Lystra now, would you like to come?"

Nastia jumped out of the bed and raced over to the bathroom, Anton laughing lightly. "You'd better hurry, Star Boy."

"If I'm Star Boy, then what should I call you?"

"Hmm...what do you want to call me?"

"Let's see." He pondered for a moment, rubbing his lower lip with his thumb. "How about my Galaxy Girl?"

"My Star Boy has divine ideas."

———————◆———————

NASTIA SIGHED. HOW could she have sinned so thoroughly, without even the slightest bit of regret? She didn't even consider it a sin until she returned to the apartment and started to talk with Lauren.

———————◆———————

"WAIT, NO KISS goodbye?" Anton prompted after pulling up in front of the building.

"Oh, sorry." Nastia giggled and kissed him. "Bye, Star Boy."

"I'll text you, my Galaxy Girl. Bye."

After she walked up the stairs and entered the apartment, guilt crept inside her heart. Once she entered the room and saw Lauren, her mood changed completely. "I'm no longer a virgin," she said simply, smiling to try to soften the severity as she began to cry. Lauren immediately came over and gave her a hug.

When Nastia finished crying Lauren spoke, "I'm here for you, Tia."

"Thank you." Nastia dried her eyes.

"But I have to ask you a question. I've known you for a long time."

"What's the question?"

"Are you crying because you sinned against God or because you aren't a virgin anymore? Which part makes you sad?"

Nastia was nailed by the question. She felt sorry for herself because she didn't have glorious virginity to make her feel like a good girl any longer. "I'm sad about both," she answered.

"Okay, now, here's another question," Lauren continued very gently. "Know that I ask both of these things because I love you. I was praying for you very much last night."

"Okay."

"Do you regret it? Do you truly and honestly regret it?"

"Yes. I mean I —" She sighed. "I don't know. Remind me again, how is it a sin against God?"

"Tia, you know the answer to that! Don't let your feelings get in the way of your beliefs. Please think. The most obvious example I can think of is the eighth commandment. Do not commit adultery. You aren't married to anyone, but why do you think it would be adultery? Also, I told you about 2nd Corinthians 6, do not be yoked with unbelievers. Even if he were a Christian it wouldn't be right. Sexual immorality — in this case fornication — is a sin against your own body." Lauren exhaled. "We can't serve two masters. We have to choose between God or ourselves."

"Okay, okay — I mean, yes, you're right. It was obviously wrong. Very wrong."

"He didn't force you, did he? That would be entirely different."

"No, no. He was actually very honorable about it."

"Honorable?"

————————— ♦ —————————

AND SO THE conversation went. Now, three days later, Nastia felt the reality of what she had done. She had prayed for forgiveness a number of times — Sunday evening with Lauren, Sunday night before she got into bed, and more than a few times on Monday. She prayed nearly every time she thought about it.

Nastia kept shaking her head, reviewing the events of Saturday night over and over in her head. *What got into me to just do it so willingly and thoughtlessly? I threw my convictions and love for God out the window without a second thought. How did it go so wrong so easily? Darn feelings!*

Yet, at the same time, she kept trying to find any possible idea to reason herself out of the responsibility, even doubting whether it was wrong or not despite everything Lauren had said. Nastia remembered how difficult it was at times to keep her virginity in college. It took work, especially when most of her friends didn't have the same moral framework or determination.

One girl named Bonnie, who had grown up in a Christian home and continued to go to church regularly in college, gave into the temptations. Bonnie was one of those unstable and dependent girls who would get upset when Nastia didn't respond to her texts, phone calls, or Facebook messages. "Why didn't you respond to my text?" Bonnie would ask with such a hurt expression on her face. Nastia always tried to abide, but sometimes she was busy with other things. Bonnie used to come to Nastia for advice and encouragement.

But after she lost her virginity, Bonnie tried to free herself from the guilt by saying, "I know it was wrong, but the guy was so nice to me, and I really enjoyed his company. Sometimes closeness can be so wonderful. I yearn for closeness more than anything. In modern times, I don't know if it's really practical to keep yourself, unless you're willing to be alone. I didn't want to be alone. It was the easiest way to feel close."

At the time, Nastia couldn't believe Bonnie had gone back on her convictions. Now Nastia was faced with the very same doubt. *Is sex outside of marriage really so wrong?*

Nastia caught herself doubting again and shook her head. How could she regress to human reasoning when she knew the truth — the superior truth of God? Sometimes moral lines appear as smudged brushstrokes that seem to curve and turn in uncertain places. Is this or that really so wrong? What is wrong anyway? Is it a societal disturbance or the accepted result of an imperfect world? What is morality? Is it just a personal set of rules? Morality felt like a foggy day where light bounces everywhere, and the shadows seem to be gone altogether. Nastia was utterly confused.

Maybe Nastia's mistake was just another result of an imperfect world. Maybe the ideal conception of morality simply isn't possible or "practical," as Bonnie put it. Nastia was still uncertain, but in the presence of her uncertainty and mingling guilt was a dirty feeling. She felt dirty, as if she were entering a high-class ball wearing running shorts and a sweatshirt after a long workout. She wanted to give her soul a shower. *Why didn't begging for forgiveness from God suffice as a cleansing spiritual shower? What else can I do? Is it my persistent doubts that give me this dirty feeling? Is it my human reasoning?* Nastia didn't understand what was happening inside her, but she did know that it would be wrong to go back to Anton.

The thought of Anton rushed into her mind. Nastia had to admit that she missed him. He was a wonderful guy — a handsome, kind, honorable, and caring man. She missed him.

He had texted her on Monday: "Good morning, my Galaxy Girl."

But Nastia didn't respond. At the time, Nastia was thinking she could never talk to him again. She erased his contact from her phone to help her resist the desire to respond.

A text from an unknown number appeared later on her screen: "Are you all right? Do you want to talk?"

Monday night had been horrible as a result. Of course she wanted to talk! But she couldn't talk to him! She had to put him in the past and move forward. "I can never talk to Anton Shepherd again," she told herself on Tuesday when that "unknown" number called her once, then again. As for Facebook, she dared not even log in. Facebook was how he found her. If she logged in now, she would probably give into the urge to look on his page and scan through his photos, staring at his gorgeous masculine face that was a dream come true.

Good gosh! Forgetting him is very difficult.

◆

HER KEYS JINGLED in the apartment door and Nastia entered, turning on the living room light with a quick tap. She was alone for the evening. Lauren attended a woman's ministry group on Wednesday nights, but Nastia didn't care to get involved quite yet. "I'm tired. I need to go to bed early and get some extra rest tonight," she had told Lauren after receiving an invitation to the group. Nastia didn't want to see other people today. Not now, not when she would only feel uncomfortable with the discussions. Did anyone understand her struggle? She was tired and weary. The past few nights had been restless. The last thing Nastia wanted to do was see other people. She was glad to have the apartment to herself.

One calm light illuminated the kitchen table as Nastia poured a cup of juice. She turned.

A small bright red bird rested on the clean table. Nastia gasped, but remembered how she had seen a bird like it on Saturday night.

"Go away, bird. I'm done imagining things that aren't real."

"I'm not a product of your imagination, Nastia," said the bird with a voice like a woman.

Nastia raised her eyebrows in disbelief. "What? Did — did you just say something?"

"Yes. Hello, my name is Aini. I am an angel. But I do not come alone." The little bird pointed to a dark corner of the kitchen. "Please meet my companion, Jianyu."

Nastia winced, trying to distinguish something in the shadows. A blue tiger, as tall as the kitchen counter, emerged from the darkness. "Hello, Nastia Sobieski." The tiger's voice was deep and strong.

"Wait!" Nastia addressed the tiger. "I saw you in the mall when I went to buy my gold dress. I thought I was seeing things."

"Yes. I was there." The tiger sat casually, flinging his tail over the tile floor.

"Who are you? What is this?" She turned to the red canary, calmly perched on the table. "What do you mean you're an angel?"

"Please sit down, Tia. We have a lot to explain," the bird replied. Nastia scooted out a chair and hesitantly sat, fearfully watching the blue tiger.

"Is he going to eat me?" she whispered to the bird.

"We have been sent to help you," the tiger responded. "We will never harm you."

Nastia didn't know what to think. "Uh, are you an angel too?"

The bird spoke again. "We are both angels. As Jianyu said, we have been sent to help you. God knows you are having a difficult time. We are here to help you through your current struggles."

"You are angels? I thought angels were awe-inspiring giant people with wings like eagles."

The bird answered again. "We took on these forms because it works best for you. Humans have been known to worship angels instead of God. Our purpose is to help you grow closer to God and come to know Him more. We are merely his servants."

Nastia was still suspicious. "What do you mean by the word God?"

The tiger answered this time, his voice rumbling. "Yahweh, the triune God, the creator of the universe and all that is. And Jesus Christ, the one who sacrificed his life for the sins of humanity, the one who will come again in complete glory."

The shadows whimpered, and the red bird spoke in a sweet tone, "Very good, Tia! The holy word of our Lord says to test the spirits in order to be sure they are from God."

"You know my nick name. What all do you know about me?"

"We know everything we need to know to help you," purred the tiger.

Nastia was still confused and suspicious. *Honestly, a red canary and a blue tiger? Who ever heard of such a crazy scene? Angels don't appear like this. Do they?* "Okay, why exactly are you here? If God has sent you to help me, then why now? I have gone through many trials in the past. What makes this time so special that God would send two angels to help me?"

"I was hoping you would ask." The bird fluffed her scarlet feathers. "For one thing, we aren't here randomly. We have followed you on the path of your life for many years. In high school, you were interested in cute boys and talked about them quite a lot. In college, boys were interested in you almost constantly, and you liked it, but you kept yourself and didn't give into the temptations. But now, after going through a difficult rejection from many people at your college and moving to a new city, you yearn for a higher level of companionship. We know what happened between you and Anton Shepherd on Saturday evening and Sunday morning. If you remember, we were in the hallway outside his hotel room before he closed the door."

"Yes. I do remember."

The tiger picked up where the bird left off. "You *willingly* submitted to the temptations and promptings of the evil one. You aren't sure what you believe anymore. This is *very* dangerous. We also know that you want to move in with him."

Nastia felt exposed. "Really?"

"Yes," the red bird continued. "As Jianyu said, this is very dangerous. It is not right for a Christian to take part in a physical relationship without being married. Nor is it right for a Christian to become romantic with an unbeliever. But do you agree with us,

Nastia? Do you believe that it would be wrong for you to live with Anton?" The two angels waited for Nastia to reply.

Oh Anton, Anton! That name sounded like the dream she thought up years ago — the dream she had craved as a girl, swinging alone in the backyard. It was the dream she tried to find in her tumultuous high school years when she became a cheerleader because she liked a guy on the football team, the guy who broke her heart. It was the dream she gave up in college and thought would never come true, when she read her Bible for joy and made sure to keep herself while all the other girls ran after guys and often came back wasted. Anton was the dream of a truly amazing man who loved her. And she loved him.

"Well," Nastia answered, "I don't know. I'm not sure. Things aren't as clear as before."

The angels lowered their heads in a solemn motion, and the red bird spoke, "We were hoping you wouldn't say that." Aini looked into Nastia's eyes. "Do you see now why we are here?"

"Maybe. I think so."

"For your knowledge, I represent kindness and Jianyu represents authority. Things will change for you from now on."

"What things?"

"For one, we will always be somewhere close by, but only you can see us. Secondly, you will encounter another spirit whom no one else will see as you do — a demon called Lunosh. He will appear to you in the form of a Chinese silver dragon or a silver snake. This will help you distinguish between good — in what we tell you — and evil — in what Lunosh tells you."

"Do you mean he will talk to me too?" Nastia inquired, amazed.

"Yes," said the red bird. "Also, your physical perception of yourself will be different. You will not see your true physical appearance but that of your soul as if your body was your soul."

"What? I don't understand." Nastia was growing frustrated with their talk. Did she even believe it? She didn't want to.

"We will show you. Please come with me." The red bird flew out of the kitchen and toward the bathroom. The blue tiger followed as Nastia decided to do the same. Aini flicked on the light, landed on a bottle of lotion, and spoke again. "Look."

Nastia faced the mirror and saw her gorgeous reflection as usual, along with the red bird and the blue tiger. "I don't see anything different about myself."

"This will be the last time for a long while that you will see your reflection like this. Consider your appearance the same as your soul from now on."

Nastia looked at her image, turning her head and opening her eyes in different ways in the mirror. "How will my appearance change?"

Jianyu exposed his white fangs as he growled, "Since you are considering living in sin with Anton Shepherd — rebelling in your heart against the one true Lord Jesus — then you, Nastia Sobieski, are guilty of the sin of pride."

A small rusty bullet ball appeared on the hand towel and rolled off. *Ding… ding…* it sounded as it bounced on the counter tiles and onto the floor. After the second bounce, the ball unraveled into silver wire and slithered toward Nastia's left leg like a snake.

"What's it doing?" she gasped, her breath growing faster and faster. The angels didn't answer.

The wire leapt into Nastia's ankle and spiraled up her leg, underneath the skin. She screamed.

10

CAN I SEE YOU TODAY?

NASTIA TOUCHED THE skin above the wire on her leg, ruminating over what it meant as she sat in her office. It hurt like cavity-infested teeth, and she stopped thinking about it, trying to ignore the fact that the wire was her sin. Was it really her pride? It hurt again, and she decided to stop touching and get back to work. Aini and Jianyu were there too. The bird preened her scarlet feathers atop a stack of books as the enormous tiger lay beside Nastia's feet, sweeping his blue tail over the floor.

Nastia addressed the bird. "I don't like this. I don't like it at all."

Aini fluffed herself one more time and turned her black bead eyes toward Nastia. "You don't like your sin or the whole situation?"

"Of course I don't like sin. But yes, the whole situation! Honestly, do I have to constantly be reminded of the fact that I struggle a bit with pride? Ow!" The muscle beneath the wire in her leg pulsed like a swollen sore.

"The pain is there to prompt you to bring your sin before God and ask for forgiveness," said Aini.

"I *have* asked for forgiveness — again and again!"

"But you have not dismissed the possibility of living with Anton. That's the problem. You pray but only because you hate the guilt, not the sin. You haven't truly repented yet."

"Whatever. I have stuff to finish." She turned back to the computer screen, annoyed and frustrated as Aini hopped onto the desk and waddled over to the keyboard.

"Oh, Tia. Don't you see how all this is because Jesus loves you?"

"No. I don't see that at all."

"You have been granted a phenomenal gift that many wise people in history have wished for. God gave you a tangible physical glimpse of the reality of sin."

"Why would anyone wish for this pestering pain?"

"It isn't so much pain. It could be a lot worse. Wise people would wish for the tangible reminder you have because it would help prepare them for eternity. You see, this life on earth will only last for a short time. Even though a lifetime might seem like forever to you, it is really only a grain of sand on the beach of eternity. God loves you more than the whole of this world will ever love you. The love of Christ is eternal.

"Say your dear friend Lauren gives you a mug for Christmas. You are grateful for the mug not because of it but because of the pure love Lauren has for you. That is like a speck of love-sand, and the love of Christ is like the golden beach that the sand came from, shining in the light of pure fulfillment and endless satisfaction."

Nastia paused and tilted her head in thought. "Wow. I don't know how to respond except *wow*. God loves us a lot."

"Yes, he does," said Aini. "The unpleasant pain of this life is only temporary but closeness with God is everlasting."

Nastia breathed more calmly and considered the glimpse of eternity. "Okay. I won't consider Anton anymore. He is in the past."

"You don't need to run from the memory of your experience with Anton. God would have you face it and then move on. What you need to recognize is that living with Anton would be wrong because you love God more."

Jianyu lifted his striped head from his paw, hoping.

Nastia responded, "Okay. I recognize that living with Anton would be wrong. I turn away from that."

Aini sounded a sweet birdcall and flew into the air. "Wonderful! Hurray! You are repenting!"

Nastia smiled as Jianyu stood and released a kind, soothing roar. "Scoot out your chair, Nastia Sobieski. The wire is about to fall off!"

Nastia pushed her chair back and glanced at her cell phone. It was shimmering silver. What happened to her magenta case? She heard a sound like a long exhale. Aini landed on the back of the chair as Jianyu stood still and gazed up attentively. The silver material slid off the cell phone, rising up like smoke, revealing the magenta case. The smoke turned into the shape of a small Chinese dragon and slowly floated toward Nastia.

" 'You kissed me tonight,' " the dragon said, quoting Anton's text message in a deep, tranquil voice. "If you turn around now, there will be no more love from him, no more words of endearment, no more *My Galaxy Girls*. It will be very hard to forget him — very hard. And don't forget his touch." He brushed Nastia's cheek and swirled around her arm, tickling her skin. "Remember how he glided his fingers through your hair, kissed your lips and neck in that special way, and more. Remember how he —"

Jianyu roared powerfully, and Aini leapt into the air, flapping her wings around the smoke. The dragon diminished and blew away.

"Was that Lunosh?" Nastia asked softly, chills of teasing desire for Anton racing up and down her skin. Her life's dream was in sight! She could have the most wonderful romantic closeness she had always wanted with the most wonderful man she had ever met. Did she really have to say no to that?

"Yes, it was." Aini landed on the desk. "I hate smoke. It has an awful smell that sticks to my feathers."

"He did have a point," Nastia admitted. "It will be very hard for me to forget Anton."

Jianyu sighed, his deep voice rumbling. "It will be hard to get past Anton, but God is more powerful than any struggle. With Him you can face this challenge."

"I can't see that," said Nastia. "Honestly, I don't know if I have the will power to fight it right now. All I want to do is be in Anton's arms, nothing extravagant. What is so wrong with that? All I want is to spend time with him and talk. What I would give to talk to him right now!"

"You're right," Aini responded. "Talking to him isn't so wrong. But right now, you yearn to be with him romantically. That would not be right. God cares about your heart. He doesn't want you to suffer unnecessarily. If you go to Anton, your pain will only increase."

"Pain? More pain? I'm too tired for pain! I just want to rest with him and chat. Come on. I'm tired of arguing with you. I can't think about this anymore."

"Okay. I understand your need for rest." The red bird turned away. "Remember God cares for you more than anyone —"

Buzz. Nastia grabbed her cell. "It's him. Please give me a break. We're just going to chat."

———◆———

ISOLATED IN HIS office cubicle, Anton rubbed his forehead, stressed from his endless thoughts of Nastia Sobieski. Ever since he dropped her off at her apartment on Sunday, an aching need for her pulsed through him. It made him sad not to receive replies to his texts. *Would she ever respond?* He had tried calling and Facebook messaging as well as texting, but she continued to ignore him. Today, he sent a simple *Please respond* in a text. He had to keep trying. That night with her was different than the other times in his past. She was different from other women. The mere memory of her breathtaking face and her mystifying smile made him yearn for Nastia Sobieski more than anything. He was infected with desire.

How could she give herself to him so thoroughly and just pull away? Should he stop trying to contact her and focus on work and his new life? Work felt like prison; it didn't have the answer. Anton could appreciate his job, but when he compared it with the deep intimacy he had found with Nastia, paper piles and digital files were nothing. The memory of her personality felt like poison in his veins, flowing through every part of him

He checked his phone and leaned back in his chair triumphantly as a pleased grin stretched across his face. He felt like hugging his bros, lifting his hands, and shouting as if a teammate had just made a game-winning touchdown. She had responded! He read the text:

Nastia: "You are like a curse to me, Anton. You haunt me like the reminiscence of a horror movie."

Whoa. He wasn't expecting that. Was she serious? What exactly did she mean?

Anton: "No, it's the other way around. You haunt me. I can't stop thinking about you."

Nastia: "I have to tell you something."

Anton: "Okay?"

Nastia: "That night was my first time."

He put his head back and pressed his hands against his face. *Crap!* He never intended to do that. The way she acted made him think she had done it before. *Darn it!*

Anton: "I'm sorry, Nastia. I didn't mean to take advantage of you. I really don't want to cause you any hurt."

Nastia: "You didn't take advantage of me. I went with it as much as you. I'm not supposed to do that though. My faith says it's only right in marriage."

Anton: "I was wondering about that, but I decided not to say anything. I'm sorry. I didn't mean to lead you away from your faith."

Nastia: "Do you think it was wrong?"

Anton: "I didn't at first, but now I'm not so sure. Since you're hurting, maybe it was wrong. I don't know."

Nastia: "I miss you, Anton. I really miss you."

Anton: "I miss you too. I've been so mad at myself. I thought I ruined what we had."

Nastia: "Don't blame yourself. It was my fault."

Anton: "Can I see you today?"

Nastia: "I'm almost done with work. Could we meet somewhere?"

Anton: "Anywhere."

Nastia: "Okay. I'll meet you at your hotel. It's not far from here."

Anton: "Perfect. Text me when you leave."

Yes! They were meeting! Now all he had to do was take care of work.

THE DARKENING SKY was gray. Nastia imagined glowing red letters in the clouds saying, "Perfect."

Nastia shut the door to her car and began to drive. As she turned a corner, she noticed the blue tiger and red bird in the passenger's seat. "Good gosh, you startled me! What are you doing here?"

"Tia," said Aini. "We know where you intend to go."

"Yeah, to Anton's hotel. We are just going to talk. It's no big deal. What's wrong with you? You can't stay here or people will notice."

"There is no need to shout and panic," the bird replied. "When you talk with us, no one can see your mouth moving or your head turning. You will appear as if just thinking."

"Terrific."

"Please don't give into this attitude. We want to save you from pain."

"Okay. Great. Then tell me why God let me fall in love with Anton? Why would God put the one thing I have always wanted into my life if he is just going to take it away?"

"We don't know the absolute will of God. We are only angels. You can ask him yourself. Pray like you used to."

"So, you can't tell me? Then how the heck are you helping me at all?"

Jianyu responded in his deep growl, "Anton was created in the image of God both in body and spirit. He is valuable, but he is not part of God's kingdom because he has not placed his faith in Christ, the only redeemer of souls. I cannot say why God allowed you to meet Anton, but you can trust that God will never allow you to be tempted more than you can bear. However, you recently gave into temptation when the right choice was clear. You are doing the same now."

"How am I giving into temptation? We are just going to talk. Stupid car! I'm turning here!"

After the turn, Aini replied, "It's your intentions, Tia. God can see your heart. Everything you want and feel is open to his eyes, and he understands you completely. He loves you and wants you to experience love from others. But love is not only physical closeness. That can be *very* harmful. We know you intend to spend the night with Anton."

"You guys don't know anything about me! What you don't understand is how much Anton means to me right now. He is the man of my dreams, Aini!"

"Is this about you or him?"

"Him! He is hurting too."

"But you know that sleeping with him is wrong," growled the blue tiger. "If he does mean something to you, then don't do evil with him. True love can only be within the realms of God's law. Stop blinding yourself and look to the light of true love."

"I can't do this anymore, Jianyu. Both of you are really stressing me out! You don't understand. I am weary, tired, and about ready to cry." She drove into the hotel parking garage, found a spot, and parked. "I'm here now, and there is no way I'm turning back. I love him. There is no way I'm passing up this opportunity."

Jianyu's cat eyes glared at Nastia.

"That's it! I can't take this anymore! Please, get out of the car."

The angels' faces filled with sorrow. The blue tiger opened the car door with his paw and jumped out. The red bird flew away.

"Thank you," Nastia pulled the door shut and exhaled. "Thank God they finally stopped pestering me!"

As she sat in the welcome silence of the car, she lifted up her left hand and noticed a rusty bullet on the tip of her index finger. She shook her hand, but it didn't fall off. "What the crap?"

She tried pulling it, but it hurt. Once she removed her fingers, the bullet unraveled into silver wire and slithered around her hand like a snake. Slowly, it slid beneath her fingernail and up her arm. Nastia tried to muffle her scream and hit the dashboard with her other hand. "Darn it! Darn it! This isn't fair! This isn't fair!"

Soon, the pain subsided, and she breathed slower, trying to reason herself out of it. "I'm okay. This isn't happening. It's just an illusion. It isn't there."

She lifted her arm and observed the dark outline of the wire curving just past her wrist, rusty orange staining her skin. Feeling half guilty for yelling at the angels and half angry at the new wire of pride, Nastia quickly got out of the car.

"Aini? Jianyu?"

The hollow air of the forlorn parking garage resounded with each step. Nastia thought she saw a blue tail move behind another car.

"Jianyu? Please tell me, what did I do?"

There was no answer.

Nastia searched for the angels as she approached the elevator. She unconsciously touched a wide cylinder pillar and another rusty bullet rolled up her arm along the spiraling wire. The ball unraveled into six metal ants that crawled up her arm. Nastia tried to brush them off but she couldn't. One ant went down to her side and imbedded under her skin, another on her neck, two on her back, and one on her wrist. "What is this? What's happening?"

Loneliness and shame swept over Nastia as she stood alone on the cold concrete. White lights flickered as a disturbing exhale sounded. Darkness dripped from the ceiling and transformed into the floating silver dragon. "They have abandoned you, haven't they?"

"I'm not listening to you, Lunosh."

"No? I can help you more than they can. I want you to know the pleasures they keep trying to hide from you. Awfully cruel of them, isn't it, to try to take away the best comfort you've ever had?"

"Just because I'm mad at them doesn't mean I don't believe them."

"Trying to listen to angels is like trying to live in Cinderella's castle. They are never there when you need them." Nastia watched as the light-avoiding dragon swirled around her. "How *horrible* of them to harm your body like this when you only want to talk to a beautiful boy. The wires were ugly enough, but metal ants! That's going too far. They obviously don't care about your attractive charms. And you *are* very attractive."

"All I want is for things to be the way they were. I just want to be a normal person again. I hate all this weirdness!"

"I know, isn't it horrible? I've heard of a way to cover it up, but I know you believe the angels so I'll leave you alone." He started drifting up in peculiar curves.

"What way?"

A vile screech resounded through the parking garage — an ear-piercing sound like scraping metal. The dragon turned back down and gazed at Nastia with pale eyes like raw fish meat.

"What was that?" she asked.

"What?"

"That sound. Didn't you hear it?"

"Oh, that. I don't know. Maybe it was a car a few levels up. Wish I could help. So, you want to learn the technique?"

"Yes. Is it hard?"

"No, no, it's actually very easy. Simply press your palms together, slowly pull your fingers down, pinch, and you'll have pretty injustice-covering ribbons. Wrap them around your arm and leg or put pieces on the ants and you will not see them anymore." The dragon quickly swirled up and disappeared.

Nastia played with the strips of odd cloth that came out of her hand. They were cold like ice when she wrapped them around her arm.

A familiar SUV drove by and parked near Nastia. Anton climbed out with a big smile on his face. "Hey."

Nastia ran to him. "Oh Anton! I'm glad you're here."

They had a sweet moment as Anton stared down and Nastia gazed up — her eyes needing him. They kissed, and he put his hands on her neck, his fingers entwining with her hair.

Anton removed his briefcase from his SUV and loosened his top collar button, keeping his face full of cheer and calm. "Do you have everything?" he asked.

"Yeah. It's just me and my purse. Nothing much." She loved how he was so relaxed as if nothing ever fazed him, as if he had his life fully under control. "Should I have brought more?"

"I don't know. It's up to you." He winked boyishly. "What would you like to do? Do you want to go eat somewhere?"

"Actually, um, is there any way we could eat up in your room? A quiet meal sounds so nice right now."

"Yeah. We can do that. I haven't ordered from the room service menu yet. Someone told me the food is really good here. Hey, maybe they have crab cakes and cran-apple juice."

She smiled, soothed by the simple joke. "Who knows? Maybe we can try something new and go on a different food-tasting adventure."

He chuckled. "A new adventure. I like that."

They walked to the elevator — his arm around her and her head caressing his shoulder. How good it felt to be in a nice hotel rather than a lonely, maddening parking garage! Nastia felt like she was in a completely different world as she walked down the high-class halls with Anton, laughing and commenting here and there. Nastia loved the stylish furniture, the pristine carpet, and the simple subdued lamps on the wall. She was still recovering from the pain under her fingernail, but it seemed to diminish altogether once Anton stood by the dark wood door and turned the stainless-steel handle. Nastia adored the smell of a clean, newly furnished hotel room.

"Make yourself at home," said Anton. Nastia wondered if that was a hint. She hoped it was.

"I love your suite. It's so elegant and vogue."

"Yeah, it's nice." Anton wondered if her comment was some kind of signal. He hoped it was, but he didn't want to take a chance. He was too happy to ruin this evening. He liked being sweet on her.

As Anton changed into something more comfortable in the bedroom, Nastia found a menu resting on the coffee table. She perused the choices: *Sirloin Steak, Braised Duck...*

"Found anything you want?" Anton asked as he emerged from the bedroom and sat on the couch beside her. "Don't be afraid of the prices. I've got it."

"How generous of you. I'm not sure what I want. What are you getting?"

"Hmm, let's see. I think I'll get the sirloin," he said.

"You like steak?"

"Oh yeah. A football player has to love his steak."

"I'll have that too," Nastia decided impulsively.

"You sure?"

"Yeah. I want to eat what you eat."

"All right."

Anton ordered the food over the phone while Nastia found his iPod. They played his music, listening, dancing freely, and discovering how many songs they both liked. Once the meal arrived, and Nastia removed the outrageous centerpiece from the glass table, they started eating. Anton intentionally exaggerated the pleasure of tasting "steak like victory" as he called it, and Nastia laughed at him.

"Do you like that cow or something, Anton, you carnivore?"

"Yeah, it's delicious." He gave Nastia flirty eyes, causing her to giggle.

SOMEHOW, AMIDST LAUGHTER and the fun of spontaneity, Nastia convinced Anton to help her move the two-person couch onto the balcony. He didn't care. Whatever was fun for Nastia was fun for him tonight. As they sat together, watching the city lights cast a glow on the low-lying clouds, Anton put his arm around her and decided to get personal. "I'm sorry for taking what wasn't mine."

She looked up at him. "What do you mean?"

"Saturday night. I'm sorry for taking your, um, virginity."

"Who says it wasn't yours to take? I gave it to you," said Nastia.

"Wow. That's quite a gift. Thank you."

"Can I ask you something deep?"

"Anything."

"When was your first time?"

"Sophomore year of high school," he answered. "I had a girlfriend, there was trouble between my parents at home, and I wanted to."

"Do you regret it at all?" In the back of her mind, Nastia wished Saturday night had been his first time also.

"Not really. I was careful, even then."

She sighed and looked back at the glow on the clouds. "What kind of trouble between your parents?"

"My parents divorced when I was sixteen. They argued a lot."

"My dad cheated on my mom when I was fourteen," said Nastia.

"That's hard."

"He was the pastor of a small church," she explained. "A lot of my best friends growing up went to his church. After everyone found out about my dad, most of them left and stopped talking to me."

"People can be jerks."

"Yes, it was hard."

"Was that the most difficult thing you have ever experienced?" he asked.

"Yes. Definitely."

He held her closer, and her heart leapt.

"What was the most difficult thing you have ever gone through?" she asked.

The wind brushed their necks as Anton thought for a moment. "Probably my parents' divorce. I tried to stay out of the house and get involved in high school stuff like football, but it was difficult. It was harder on my younger brother, though."

"How old was your brother?"

"Thirteen."

She grimaced. "I can empathize with both of you."

"I got so angry with my dad when he and my mom argued and argued. I would get up and yell at him sometimes."

"I argued with my dad a lot during high school. I shouted at him too." She giggled. "Anton angry? I can't imagine."

"Yeah, I got angry. One of the things I love most about sports is they allow me to take out my anger."

"You seem like you don't get angry much."

"No. Not for the past few years," he replied.

Nastia decided to pose another deep question. "What is your worst fear?"

"My worst fear? I don't know. That's a hard one. I'm not afraid of much."

"Everyone's afraid of something," she prompted.

"Maybe. I guess my worst fear is losing my grasp of reality. I want to always be able to discern truth from lies, even if it's hard."

Nastia didn't reply.

"What about you? What do you fear the most?"

Nastia was afraid to open this part of herself. Her fear was directly related to him. How would he react? Would he pull away because of the pressure? She decided to stop worrying and answer even if it did ruin everything. "Okay, I'll be honest."

"Okay."

"My worst fear is that the guy I fall in love with will treat me like my dad treated my mom. I couldn't stand that. Never, never."

Anton touched the side of her face lightly and put his head close to hers. "I will never cheat on you, Nastia. I like you a lot."

"I like you too, Anton."

"Would you like to live with me? You could move in tomorrow and we would be together every night." He eagerly waited for her answer.

"I would love to live with you, Anton. Actually, there's nothing I want more in the whole world."

Their kiss sparkled more than the city lights.

———————————◆———————————

THE WHITE RESORT sheets felt warm and soft, like Nastia's favorite dream, especially because of the person who was already between them. She snuggled up beside Anton. In the glass covering the painting above the TV, Nastia saw a silver dragon writhing in wild contractions.

"Lunosh?"

"Do what?" Anton stared at her.

The dragon's fish-meat eyes glowed ravenously as Nastia watched. "Oh, nothing. Never mind."

11

THE ROACH

THE DIM LIGHT of the foggy glass window was like the presence of God. Nastia awoke in the dark bedroom; Anton was somewhere else.

Strangely enough, God seemed close. He was watching. He knew everything that had happened. Nastia felt a twinge of guilt, as if she had betrayed her favorite person. She wondered how long it had been since she really talked to God. She wanted to speak with him again.

"Hello, God," Nastia prayed in a whisper. "I live with Anton now. Please forgive me and save his soul. I love him. Please heal us both."

Some warmth left the sheets. Why do I feel cold? Where is Anton?

After throwing on a robe, Nastia wandered out into the main room and turned on the kitchen light, her arms wrapped tightly in front of her.

She saw a white piece of paper on the granite counter:

Good morning, my Galaxy Girl. I put a plate of breakfast in the fridge for you. Can't wait to see you tonight. I love you.

Your Star Boy

A smile overwhelmed her face as she lifted the room key card, hidden beneath the paper. "He loves me," she said with proud pleasure. "I am loved by the man I love." She giggled blissfully.

Nastia adjusted the blanket and lounged on the couch, eating her cold breakfast with cold orange juice — the plate cold, the cup cold, the leather couch cold. "Good gosh! I need some light in this dreary place." She approached a lamp by the wall and flicked on the light. Around the neck of the lamp was a red metal bird. *That's odd.* She hadn't noticed it before. *Wait! Is it Aini?*

Immediately the red metal turned into soft feathers as the bird fluttered off the lamp and onto the couch. "Good morning, Nastia."

"Aini? What the heck! Where have you been? Lunosh talked to me yesterday. I got another wire and some crazy metal ants, and you and Jianyu were nowhere to be seen!"

"You did yell at us and tell us to get out of the car." The bird looked hurt, and Nastia felt a pang of guilt. She remembered her skin and raced to the mirror on the wall.

"Oh, my grace!" Nastia noticed the wire curling under the skin of her right forearm surrounded by a growing greenish bruise. Down on her left calf was the first wire and bruises. Her face was different too, sickly as if she hadn't eaten in days. "What has happened to me?"

In a grieved voice, Aini replied, "You are living in sin, Nastia. Until you turn away from this life and back to God, your soul will grow uglier every day."

Nastia breathed faster. "But Anton has already invited me to live with him! He wants me, Aini. He really wants me. Look, he even gave me a key to this hotel room."

The enormous blue tiger leapt off the glass table behind Nastia without disturbing anything except her nerves.

"Good gosh! I nearly jumped out of my robe!" She stared down at Jianyu's piercing cat-eyes. "Do you have something to say?"

"You *don't* have to do this, Nastia Sobieski," the tiger purred. "God has given you the strength to resist the temptations crawling around you."

"Yes, exactly!" Aini chirped. "God is strong. Ask him for strength. He will always be faithful."

Nastia glanced between the two, pushing her lower lip to the side. "I can't. God is faithful, but life is confusing. When Anton invited me to live with him last night, and with this key, my deepest dreams started to come true. I feel like a convertible sports car just starting to race down a clear night highway with no one to block me. Finally, no one to block me! And you are telling me to slow down? I can't do that! I must race with the speed of my realized dreams, blaring music of this new life with Anton. Please, just let me do this."

The two angels let their eyes fall to the ground, disappointed.

"Why won't you say anything?" Nastia wanted them to support her decision. "Do you understand me now?"

"Yes, your choice is definitely understandable." Aini's gaze drifted toward the window opposite Nastia.

"But we can't stop *it* now," said Jianyu.

"Stop what?" Nastia felt a jolt of fear. "What's going to happen?"

Ding… ding…

Nastia turned around to see the silver dragon floating above the sink and a rusty bullet ball bouncing on the countertop and onto the carpet. Wind escaped Lunosh's feverish grin, and Anton's note flipped up, drifting down to the bullet.

As Nastia leaned over to retrieve the paper, the bullet uncurled into a vile metal cockroach. Immediately, it raced toward her right leg, darted up the wire, and entered her skin at the knee. She screamed and jumped for the couch as the roach scuttled beneath her skin as if nibbling a tunnel. Nastia kicked and hit the leather-covered cushions. "No! No! Gross! Detestable! Not again!"

The roach stopped at her waist.

Soon, the pain softened, and Nastia breathed slower. Tears came. "What is this?" She looked at the bug beneath the skin of her waist. "Why?"

"That is a roach of lust," Jianyu growled. "And the metal ants from yesterday are ants of idolatry."

"Lust, idolatry, pride? They are all so disgusting and horrible! I hate this! I hate this!"

"Yes, they are disgusting," said Aini. "Sin *is* horrible."

"Then what do I do?" Nastia lay on the couch, her face cringing. "How do I deal with it?"

Aini flew closer and landed on the edge of the coffee table. "Go back to Lauren's apartment, ask God for forgiveness, and explain to Anton why you can't live with him."

Nastia shut her eyes, squirming, and pulled her chin. "But I love him too much! So very much!" She sighed. "I can't."

"Yes, you can, dearest child of God," said the bird. "Show Anton the love of Christ — love that comes with soul-saving morality. There is no love more beautiful than the love of God — none more glorious or satisfying. If you truly love Anton, then show him God's love and gently explain how you made a mistake and why you can't live with him. This would be a testimony of how much greater God is and how phenomenal is His forgiveness. You can point Anton to Jesus. Don't you want him to be saved?"

"Of course I want him to be saved! Good gosh, of course I do." She shook her head in confusion. "But I don't know. I don't know, I don't know! I can't think."

"All right." The red bird's voice was kind. "Will you let us help you deal with your sin?"

"Yes, *please.*"

"Then just lie there, and Jianyu and I will help you."

Nastia lay still and watched as Jianyu swayed over with a ruby bowl in his massive paw. He brought it close to her. The bowl had a lid with gold lettering. "What's that?"

"This is protection lotion," Aini said as she flew over, lifted the lid, and dipped one wing into the pure cream. "Otherwise known as Calvary Balm. Stretch out your arm."

Nastia let her right arm fall out as Aini gently spread the lotion on the wire and bruises. "It's warm."

"This is God's patience and comfort," Aini explained. "If God allowed sin to take its full effect, you would be dead. But ever since Adam and Eve first sinned, God wanted to give his masterpiece of humanity a chance to know him, to be free from the slavery of sin. God's love is infinite. He is the most patient being in all existence. His comfort will give you the strength to face each moment. This lotion helps to soften the effects of sin. God does not want you to suffer."

Aini rubbed her lotion-covered wing onto the roach in Nastia's waist, on the wire of pride on her calf, and on the ants around her neck.

"The silver dragon taught me a way to cover up the wounds," Nastia confessed. "I pull strips of cold cloth out of my palms."

Jianyu spoke this time as Aini applied the lotion onto Nastia's wrist. "Those are soul strips otherwise known as shreds of Babylon. They are human reasoning. When you try to reason yourself out of the responsibility of sin, shreds of Babylon will appear on your soul wounds. However, they will be difficult for you to keep, since you are a Christian and you know the truth."

Nastia glanced around uncomfortably. She saw the time on the kitchen stove. "Oh crap! I'll be late for work!" She leapt off the couch and headed to the bathroom. As she brushed her hair, she noticed a strange, icy slime — like mechanical grease — on the lock of hair beside her temple. "What happened to my hair? Aini! Aini!"

The red bird flew into the bathroom and landed on the counter, her eyes sad. "Yes?"

"What happened to my hair?"

"All I will say is blessed are the meek."

95

"What kind of answer is that? This is disgusting!" Nastia tried to wash the icy grease out but nothing worked. "I don't have time for this! Will anyone else see it?"

"No," Aini answered. "Just you."

"That's all I need to know." Nastia raced into the bedroom, dressed, grabbed her keys and purse, and left. The angels accompanied her down the hall. "Can't you at least tell me about this grease in my hair?"

Jianyu replied, "The more you depend on your own strength rather than God's, the more grease will stick in your hair."

Nastia shook her head, upset at the situation, and refused to discuss anymore. After driving to the church, she entered the office and apologized for being late.

Stephanie was understanding. "That's okay. But are you all right? You seem a little stressed."

"I'm fine," Nastia responded almost too quickly. "Don't worry about me." Stephanie shrugged and went on with her work.

After she took care of a few things, Nastia checked her phone and, to her surprise, found only one message in her inbox from Lauren saying simply, "Okay." The night before, Nastia had texted Lauren, telling her that she was spending the night with Anton. She then hid her phone away for the rest of the evening. Nastia expected to receive at least two messages from her friend trying to convince her not to sin again. But oddly enough Lauren said "Okay." Nastia wondered if Lauren was hurting today.

Buzz. After lunch Nastia received a text.

Anton: "Good morning, Nastia. Are we still on? Are you going to move in with me tonight?"

Nastia: "Definitely!"

From her resting place on the pen and pencil cup, the red bird stared at Nastia after she sent the text. "Don't look at me like that,"

Nastia shot back, and the bird turned away. The blue tiger lying by Nastia's feet groaned. She received another text:

Anton: "Wonderful! I'm going to work a bit late, but you can go ahead and order dinner for yourself at the hotel and charge it to my room whenever you get off."

Nastia: "Thank you. Where do you get all this money? I'm going to get my stuff from my friend's apartment after work. I hope she takes it all right."

Anton: "Yeah, I hope so too. Text me when you leave there."

Nastia: "Okay."

Once work ended and Nastia was in her car driving to Lauren's apartment, she thought of Anton's face. There were plenty of handsome guys in the world, but Anton was different. His face had a youthful glow to it; his tan-prone skin held a subtle masculine attraction. She liked his golden-brown bangs that slanted as if brushed by a high-altitude wind. And of course, his admiring bluish-hazel eyes dazzled her every time, for they cared deeply for her and seemed to catch things that other eyes couldn't. But the feature Nastia liked most about Anton was his smile. Anton had perfectly-aligned, white teeth that gleamed whenever she looked at him. When he smiled, he didn't seem to worry about anything; he only wanted Nastia with him and that was enough. Every time he smiled, Nastia couldn't help but notice his rugged dimples, as if God had left thumb-prints in his cheeks. Anton Shepherd had a classic profile that explained why he had been popular in college, but his kind character explained why so many people liked him. Nastia hoped he really did love her.

Nastia was glad to find the apartment empty. Lauren wasn't home from work yet. Maybe Nastia could pack up her things and leave without ever having to face her friend. Even though it made her feel a bit guilty for sneaking out, she wanted to escape the sight of Lauren's sad face.

Nastia clicked open her bags and began folding and stuffing hastily. The door opened, and Lauren Henson entered.

"Hi," Nastia said with a smile, trying to brighten the atmosphere as best she could.

"Hi. What are you doing?" Lauren asked, her strong lips pushed together in dread.

"I'm," Nastia sighed, "moving in with Anton."

The white of Lauren's eyes flashed. "What? No, Nastia, please don't. You don't know what you're doing."

Nastia steeled herself. "Please, Lauren, let's not do this scene. Things are hard enough as it is."

"But, Nastia, this isn't okay! This is very bad! How can you move in with this guy? Don't live in immorality, my dear friend, please. Don't turn away from God. There is nothing worse for a Christian than to turn her back on God. I don't want you to get hurt, but you *will* if you go ahead with this. Don't blind yourself to the truth you know. *Please*. Drifting away from God will be —"

"I'm in love with him!" Nastia blurted out, her eyes growing moist. Lauren went silent. Nastia bit her lower lip, glanced at the ceiling, and shrugged. "I'm in love with him, and he loves me. You don't know how it has felt getting to know Anton. Ever since I met him two weeks ago on the plane, I haven't been able to think of anything else but him. This week when I was trying to get over him and forget, I just couldn't. It was too hard."

"But you *can* move on," Lauren pleaded. "I'm here to help you. I will be your friend as I have always been. Let's pray together. There can be nothing wrong with that."

"No. I'm not going to just sit here with my eyes closed as you ask God to stop me. I would be putting on a false face if I did. But you don't understand, Lauren! Anton is the best man I have ever met. I can't believe God wants to just take him away from me. You know better than anyone how much I have needed a good man in my life. You met my father. You know what hell my family went through because of him. And they are still going through hell! I have never had a truly good man care for me like Anton does. Anton is different from the other guys I've met — he actually loves me."

Lauren recalled the high school days in Sedona and all the turmoil the Sobieski family went through because Nastia's father committed adultery. The Henson family was a part of Mr. Sobieski's small church until he refused to listen, and the elders had to dig deeper. Mr. Sobieski started to blame the people who cared for him and his family, shouting maliciously at them.

Lauren remembered peering out the backdoor window as her father and another elder talked to a guy she had seen only a few times, maybe at a potluck or two. Her mother, Mrs. Henson, cooked with a heavy frown on her face that day, muttering to herself, "He manipulated her. Her even! Lord, bless her sweet soul. She must be the kindest woman I've ever met. Heal her, Lord. And bless the Sobieski family. Oh Lord, heal that family. The children, Lord!"

Lauren had heard all this from the kitchen entryway. Mrs. Henson had turned around and stared at her daughter for a long while, her sigh pressing against her flour-dusted apron.

"What's going on, Mom?' Lauren had asked.

"Go call your friend, Nastia, and invite her over." Mrs. Henson ordered. "Go!"

Those were hard times. Lauren knew how much Nastia had dreamt of a man to love her. Nastia would complain about her father with great dislike as they hung out in Lauren's upstairs bedroom.

"I hate my dad!"

"No, you can't hate your dad."

"Oh yes I can, and I do!" Nastia would walk over to the window and gaze out saying, "Someday, I'm going to find a guy who actually cares for me. He will love me and I will love him. Just watch, Lauren. It's going to happen. You'll see. Everyone will see!"

Now Nastia was standing before Lauren, talking about a guy who actually loved her.

"Yes, I remember the hard things you went through. I do understand, Tia. I do." Lauren reached for a tissue and started dabbing her eyes.

A tear slid down Nastia's cheek, carrying a bit of mascara with it. "Then please stop making it hard for me." She swallowed the choking in her throat. "I'm going." She stuffed the last of her things into the large suitcase and headed for the door. "I'll see you at church on Sunday."

"I will always be here for you, Tia," Lauren said as Nastia stood in the hall, clutching the doorknob. "I'm just a text away. Remember that."

"Thanks. Will do. Bye!" The door shut.

Lauren got on her knees and began praying, "Father God, please heal Nastia's heart. Show her what she is doing and draw her back to you. But most of all take care of her. There's no telling what she will do in this frame of mind."

———————◆———————

THE CAR WAS cold as Nastia crawled in, slammed the door, and started texting Anton. It was odd how her car could get cold when the late summer sun shone directly on it; very odd. But she didn't care.

Nastia: "I'm in the car. It was hard."

Anton's reply came almost immediately.

Anton: "Ok. I'm sorry it was hard but soon it won't be. How bout we go down to the Jacuzzi tonight after dinner?"

Nastia: "I would love to. I love you, Anton!"

Anton: "I love you too, my Galaxy Girl."

Nastia: "You'd better get back to work, Star Boy. I'll be there soon."

Anton: "I can't wait."

———————◆———————

NASTIA TURNED THE wheel as she leaned with the curving on-ramp. The sun left the sky as the silver dragon slithered around the passenger's seat, whispering, "This is the best thing you could do."

Sometimes, thinking just goes numb when you drive through a big city, cars racing past and the radio singing.

12

WOULD YOU LIKE TO COME OVER HERE?

CLAD IN HER black bikini, Nastia stepped into the Jacuzzi tub with muscular Anton holding her hand as he stood in the water. The aquatics room was lit by the glow from the Jacuzzi, the pool, and the window of the workout room one floor up. Nastia glimpsed a young man jogging shirtless on a treadmill. The large windows on the opposite wall provided a spectacular view of the glittering city lights of Washington D.C.

The two lovers were alone, except for the sight of the young man on the treadmill. But soon, he abandoned the pursuit of fitness and left. The red bird and the blue tiger lay at the far end of the pool, watching calmly — but they didn't count as company

"You don't know how glad I am that you're moving in with me," said Anton, the watery glow illuminating his bright smile.

"You don't know how glad I am that you invited me." Nastia thought he looked superbly masculine with his arms stretched along the edge of the tub, his head back, and his eyes shining.

"Would you like to come over here?" He motioned to his shoulder. The bubbles hissed as she slid over and rested her head on his shoulder. "There we go. Much better."

They kissed.

Nastia looked up at the ceiling and saw the outline of a large dragon moving among the shadows. Two alluring white eyes appeared and flickered like fire. The dragon slithered around the LED lights of the exercise room, dancing in wild jerks.

"Go away," Nastia said aloud.

"Do what?" Anton asked, lifting his head and opening his eyes.

"Nothing." She touched the bubbles. Apparently, others could hear when she talked to Lunosh but not when she talked to Aini and Jianyu. *Huh.*

Anton wondered about her. "Was it hard, leaving your friend today?"

"Yes. Her name is Lauren. Didn't I tell you about her?"

"I don't think so."

"She has been my best friend for nearly ten years," said Nastia.

"Wow. Must be a good friend." He blinked. "What did she have against us living together?"

"She believes it's immoral. She thinks living together is only okay for married couples."

"She's allowed her opinion. But why does she have to impose her beliefs on you? It's your choice."

"She's not imposing exactly." Nastia tilted her head. "Lauren wants the best for me. She thinks not living with you would be better. I disagree."

"You must be pretty dang-good friends for her to tell you what you should and should not do." He shook his head. "I believe this is very good. What's so wrong with a girl and a guy living together when they love each other like we do?"

Nastia hated the silver dragon's grin. "Yeah, I know. It's confusing sometimes. But she and I will still be friends. I'll see her at church on Sunday."

"Oh. So, you're still holding on to that?"

"Holding onto what?"

"Christianity."

"Of course I am! I will always be a Christian, Anton. Always."

He shrugged. "Okay. And I will always love you."

They kissed again, and she pressed her head close to his naked shoulder. "Don't you think it's kind of crazy how quickly we fell in love?"

"Yeah, but it's working out. It *is* crazy, though. We haven't even known each other for two weeks. But you're different from any other girl I've met. I don't know how to explain it."

"You're different from any other guy I've met."

"That's easier to believe." He grinned.

"What do you mean?"

"Please don't take this wrong, Nastia." He chuckled. "But from what I've seen of the Christian church, most of the guys are sissies."

"I don't think that's a fair assessment. Maybe a few guys are but…" Her voice trailed off as she thought about the Christian guys she knew.

Anton smiled. "See what I mean? When my mom made us go to church, I felt like the people there were trying to take the man out of me. Ever since, all I have seen is more evidence supporting that suspicion."

"You think Christians want to remove manliness from guys?"

"Yes, exactly. Being myself — a strong, actual man — is very important to me. I avoid anything or anyone who tries to remove masculinity from me. Losing masculinity is like losing myself. I'm never going to let that happen. Church is a clean-carpet prison."

Nastia could sense how much this meant to her lover. She felt vulnerable in his arms. "I understand. You don't want to lose yourself."

13

FADING LIGHTS

PEOPLE SAUNTERED IN line, waiting to order, with hands in pockets or holding phones. A bell jingled as others entered the sub shop. Nastia carried her small turkey sandwich dinner to a metallic table that wobbled. The blue tiger swayed past the line, thoroughly unnoticed by the other customers, as the red bird flew overhead.

"Hello, Nastia Sobieski," said Jianyu.

"Hello." Nastia was not in the mood to talk. The angels understood.

Why is it so hard to eat? Nastia had looked forward to dinner, but once she held the sandwich, her appetite abandoned her. She forced herself to eat but didn't enjoy it. The same had happened at lunch and last night's dinner. Eating seemed to be a chore now. Nastia found herself thinking that the only way she could enjoy food again would be if Anton ate with her. She tried to imagine him in front of her, saying with love, "You need to keep up your strength, my Galaxy Girl. A sad city it would be without markets full of food." She imagined his prize-winning smile. She missed him even though she had seen him last night. *Why do I miss him? I must be very much in love to want him every moment.*

Earlier, Anton had sent her a text saying, "I have to work late again tonight. Go ahead and order whatever you want at the hotel restaurants and charge it to the room." Nastia felt bad living off of Anton's generosity and decided to eat something cheaper tonight, on her own dime.

Nastia addressed Aini, who was preening on the napkin dispenser. "I was meaning to ask you, how come I can talk to you two without anyone noticing, but when I talk to the silver dragon others hear?" She recalled how Anton heard her last night in the hot tub when she asked the silver dragon to go away.

Aini directed her black bead eyes toward Nastia. "Lunosh controls that. Sometimes no one will hear what you tell him, and other times, he will want to make a fool of you and allow others to hear."

"I hate Lunosh," she said, rubbing her less-than-cold shoulder. She was warmer when the angels were near.

Jianyu lifted his head from his spot on the floor. Nastia marveled at the way people walked right through him as if he were a ghost. "Then love God," he said, "and tell Anton about your faith."

"Yes, point Anton to God," Aini agreed. "We picked out a story that you could tell Anton tonight."

"What story?"

"You created it during your sophomore year. 'The Lighthouse Church.' "

Nastia recalled the tale. "Oh yeah. Why that one?"

"It brings the church, people, and God into a better perspective," Aini answered. "You need to realize this so that Anton can see the truth of Christ."

"The end of Second Corinthians, chapter five conveys what we mean best," said Jianyu. " 'We implore you on Christ's behalf: Be reconciled to God. God made him who had no sin to be sin for us, so that in him we might become the righteousness of God.' "

"Now you're quoting scripture at me." Nastia winced immediately after the words left her tongue. "I do like that verse, though."

Jianyu continued, "Christ took on the burden of your sins so that you might become the righteousness of God. But if you live willingly denying Christ and his authority in your life, pressing on with sin, then how can you be the righteousness of God? Take this first step

106

and tell the story to Anton tonight. Without regular reminders of God's presence, life is but a ticking of worldly time. Remember God's presence tonight."

Nastia swallowed, an aching feeling overcoming her. "All right. I will tell him the story when we are together tonight."

———◆———

THE TWO ANGELS found still places to rest in the main room of the suite as Nastia waited for Anton. *How late is he going to work tonight? Hopefully not past nine.*

She crawled into the cold bed as the clock changed to nine. *When would he come back?* She started to worry. *Couldn't he open the door already!* She hated the quiet, lonely suite without Anton. The serene lamp didn't comfort; it only cast shadows and a motionless glow. Nastia wondered if this was God's way of punishing her for her sin. She had turned her back on God. But he understood, right? An itchy fear tingled on the bruise surrounding the metal ant imbedded on her neck. She pulled out the Bible from the bedside drawer and began reading a psalm. Maybe if she read the Bible, God would bring Anton back.

As Nastia glided her gaze over the words of a psalm, a terrible idea swept through her mind like an icy wind. *What if Anton never returned?* She shook her head and pulled the blanket closer. "Of course he will return!" she told herself. She didn't like the absence of her angels. "Jianyu! Aini! Can you come in here, please?"

"No, Tia," the blue tiger's steady voice replied. "We cannot enter that bedroom."

"Why not?" Nastia hated being alone. She closed the Bible, flung aside the bedspread, and hurried out into the main room. She turned on a light. Aini flew out of a picture on the wall as Jianyu emerged from a dark corner. "Why can't you come in there with me?" Nastia demanded.

"Because that is where you have sinned," Aini answered in her kind voice. "We love you dearly, but we love God much more. Hopefully, you can realize how right that is."

"Then where do you expect me to sleep?" Her voice was laced with fearful anger. "On the couch? Where do you expect me to tell him the story?"

Aini responded as calm as ever. "Where do you think we want you to sleep?"

"Don't reply with a question!" She grimaced again. "Wait — I'm sorry. I'm just so upset right now. Why isn't Anton home yet?" The angels didn't answer. "Good gosh, if there was any time I needed a man it's now. Now! I want Anton! I want him to hold me again. Is that so wrong?"

She heard the beep of the unlocking door and instantly sighed with relief. Anton entered with his head low and a black briefcase strap across his chest. She tried to calm herself.

"Hi, Nastia," he said in a tired voice, smiling vividly.

"Anton!" Nastia raced over to him. They kissed. "How was work?"

"I'm glad it's over," he said, allowing his briefcase to slump to the floor while he stretched his arms. "Oh man! I'm glad it's the weekend. I would take you out and do something tonight, but I'm just so tired."

"That's okay. I don't really feel like going anywhere tonight either."

"How would you like to go sightseeing tomorrow?" He faced Nastia. "I haven't had a chance to see any of the famous D.C. places yet."

"Yes, I would like that."

As Anton showered, Nastia muttered a "Thank you, God!" and crawled back into bed.

Anton groaned wearily as he cuddled up with his girlfriend. "How 'bout we sleep in tomorrow?"

"That would be lovely." Nastia stroked his forehead and brushed his hair, her boyfriend closing his eyes and exhaling deeply. "But I have a bedtime story to tell you first."

He chuckled. "Yes, please, teacher. What is the story about? Is it okay if I'm in love with my teacher?"

Nastia smiled back at the flirty man-grin resting on her lap. "Yes, you may, Star Boy. Simply close your eyes, rest your head on my thigh, and I will tell you."

Anton curled up, pressing his head against her soft white skin. "I'm ready."

"Remember how you called church a clean-carpet prison last night in the hot tub?" she asked.

"Yeah."

"This story is my response to that statement."

"Okay. Tell away."

"Imagine a lighthouse overlooking a cold ocean with cloudy skies above."

"Where is this lighthouse?" he asked.

"I don't know. Maine maybe? It's fiction." Nastia continued stroking his head as she began.

ONCE THERE WAS an old man who lived alone. He was the caretaker of a lighthouse. One day, he felt that God wanted him to build a church. Very excited, the old man decided to place the church right beside his lighthouse tower. He found a man to be the pastor and soon people from all around came to the church. The old man remained a simple Christian regularly attending the church and quietly living his life.

After two years, more and more people moved into the houses that were being built near the lighthouse. Some of the neighbors found the rotating white light annoying and asked the pastor to turn off "the pestering light." Wanting to keep peace with the neighbors, the pastor finally gave in and ordered the lighthouse lamp turned off. The congregation was outraged at first, but eventually they stopped complaining and went on with their daily business.

One of the people attending the lighthouse church was a nine-year-old girl named Faith. She joyfully looked forward to church every week with her kind and loving parents. During one of the services, while she sat in the handcrafted wooden pews listening to the pastor give his sermon, she saw a woman in front of her trying to adjust her husband's uplifted collar. Faith thought for a second that she saw right through the man's neck as if the lower part of his neck were invisible. The man instantly grabbed his wife's reaching hand and pulled the collar back up. Faith told herself that she must have been seeing things.

Now, Faith's parents had told her about this thing called invisibility slime of doubt. They said that everyone doubts God, and it's important to talk about it when you do, but when you don't talk about it and allow the doubt to stay, the invisibility slime appears somewhere on your body. Faith thought everyone knew this.

The following Sunday, right after Sunday school, she saw a twelve-year-old boy tying his shoe with his pant leg lifted up. His leg was completely invisible.

"What happened to your leg?" she cried out. The boy immediately pulled down his pant leg and stared back in fear.

"Who do you think you are, coming in here like that?" he said. "You'd better not tell anyone!"

"I won't," Faith responded innocently, wondering why her friend was so defensive. "You should talk to someone about that. Doubt is dangerous when you don't clean it up."

The boy shrugged and replied as he walked out the door, "Who would listen?"

As the day continued, Faith felt more and more burdened with the knowledge that people in her beloved church were struggling with doubt and not addressing it. With concern written on her face, she listened to the pastor's sermon attentively. She looked to her left across the aisle and saw a middle-aged woman trying to hide her invisible hand with a glove that was falling off. Their eyes met, and Faith saw the desperate fear in the woman's eyes. With a shaking hand, the woman put her finger to her mouth as if begging Faith not to tell anyone. Faith shook her head as if to say, "Don't worry, I won't." She looked away, sadder than before.

After the service, once everyone else had left, Faith walked up to the pastor and said, "Pastor, can I talk to you about something?"

"Of course, dear," the pastor answered with a rehearsed smile. "What is on your heart?"

"I was listening to your sermon, and I think you're missing something," she said.

"Really?" he replied. "And what is that?"

"You never talk about doubt or the things that normal people struggle with." The pastor knitted his brow as if asking the girl to go on.

———————◆———————

"WOW. WHAT AN intelligent nine-year-old," said Anton, interrupting the story.

"Yes. She is a marvelous girl." Nastia stopped petting her boyfriend's head. "Anton?"

"Yes?"

"Hush."

Anton sensed that Nastia wanted very much to finish the story and decided to let her.

———————◆———————

FAITH CONTINUED TO tell the pastor about the burden on her heart, "You talk about David being honorable toward Saul, how the Israelites disobeyed God over and over, and what the food was like in Jesus' time, but you don't talk about the things that normal people deal with every day."

"I'm not sure about that," the pastor started to say.

"Some of my friends here are seriously struggling with doubt, but they don't talk to anyone about it," said Faith.

"Can you tell me who these people are?" asked the pastor.

"No, I can't. That would be unfair to my friends."

The rehearsed smile suddenly reappeared on the pastor's face. "I think you are too young to understand these things. I suggest you leave the leading of a church to the pastor. Okay?" Faith could tell that the pastor wasn't going to listen anymore and left to walk home.

That night, Faith felt too sad to sleep and decided to walk over to the church to pray. As she approached the concrete tower in the darkness, she saw someone placing a bag into a rowboat down by the water at the bottom of the lighthouse. Curious, she walked down the warped steps and onto the dock.

"Who is that?" the person's voice demanded as he lit a hand lamp.

"Just me, Faith," the girl answered somewhat fearful of the dark form. The man raised the lamp to his face and squinted. Faith could see that it was the good old man who owned the lighthouse.

"What are you doing out so late?" he asked.

"I was just going to the church to pray," she replied.

"What would a little girl like you be praying about at this hour? Go back home. Your parents will worry." He began to walk her back up the slippery steps.

"But I can't sleep. I'm too sad," she exclaimed, and the old man stopped.

"What are you sad about, Faith?"

"I found out that at least three of my friends have invisibility slime of doubt on them, and no one is helping them clean it off! I talked to the pastor today, but he wouldn't listen and told me to leave the leading of a church to him. I wasn't trying to stop him from leading, I just want to help my friends, but I don't know how. I was praying because I'm concerned. What will happen to them if they leave their doubt alone and not talk about it?"

The old man sighed deeply. "You are one of the few people who have noticed this problem. I can show you something that will help you understand. But it might make you even sadder, so go back now if you don't want to be sad."

"I can't go back. I have to know, or I will never be able to sleep."

"All right then, get into the boat. Carefully now. It's slippery."

Faith and the old man climbed into the boat as the old man began rowing. The lamplight had blown out. To keep warm, Faith pulled the edges of the big frayed coat that the old man had given to her. She tried to distinguish the shapeless waves and the dark horizon. She prayed that the Lord would help the old man to see through the darkness. Eventually, they arrived at a small cliff island.

The boat hit the sand, and the old man picked up the girl and put her on his back as he stepped out into the shallow water and dragged the boat onto the beach. He carried her, along with his bag, up the ancient stone steps and onto the top of the cliff. The wind blew powerfully as Faith stood in the enormous coat, watching the old man work. He knelt around a stone fire pit dug into the ground. "Please open the bag, Faith," he said.

She opened the brown nylon bag and looked inside. "It's all wooden crosses!"

"Please hand me the matches," he requested. She saw a small plastic bag with matches inside and handed it to the old man. "Now hand me the crosses one by one." As Faith passed the crosses one after another, the old man explained, "Each cross represents a lost soul who died this week in our country."

Faith gasped. "But there are so many!"

"Yes, that is the sad part. Christians need to address their doubts before they can practice the great commission. When they don't,

113

more and more crosses appear. When the pastor ordered me to turn off my lighthouse flame, I asked God to give me some way to grieve those who have not come to believe in him, those who are lost to the world. He gave me these wooden crosses."

"Where do you find them?" Faith asked.

"In the basement of my lighthouse," he replied. "I place the empty nylon bag on the floor every Monday morning. And every following Sunday night, I find it filled with small wooden crosses."

A tear rolled down Faith's cheek as the old man struck a match and lit the crosses. They watched the whipping flames consume the wooden shapes. The wind stole the ashes, and there was nothing left.

"Each cross represents the sacrifice given by Jesus," said the old man, lifting Faith into his arms. "Nothing is more horrible than a soul who does not accept the freely-given, truly-saving grace of Jesus Christ."

NASTIA PAUSED, INDICATING the end of her story. When Anton did not comment immediately, she asked, "So? What did you think?"

Anton moved up and placed his head on the pillow beside her. "I don't know. I'm really tired, Nastia. Tomorrow we'll talk when we go sightseeing. Let me sleep on it, okay?"

"All right." Nastia clicked off the lamp. "Good night, Star Boy."

"Good night."

NASTIA WALKED ON sapphire water in her dream, causing single ripple rings with every step, the only movement on the perfectly still, endless ocean. She stepped onto one spot of surfacing black stones and reached down to clench one. She rubbed it with her thumb and threw it into the ocean. Ripples came and went.

Suddenly, she couldn't walk on the water any longer and had to swim. If only she knew what was in the water beneath. A snake swam over in writhing turns and said, "All alone are you? Why can't you walk upon water?"

"I'm trying to find God, Lunosh! Get away! Get away!" A waterspout glided somewhere in the distance only to disappear.

Lunosh spoke again. "God doesn't love you. Why would he? You turn your back on him every moment of every day."

"No! You're wrong! Shut up!"

The blue changed to black as the snake clutched Nastia's legs with his tail and pulled her down, down, down into the dead fathoms.

————————◆————————

NASTIA WOKE WITH a start, a bead of sweat trickling across her eye. She heard Anton's steady breathing beside her. Careful not to rouse him, she slid off her side of the bed and quietly walked out of the bedroom, closing the glassy door.

In the darkness of the main room, she felt a tingle of fear like a rushing chill all over her skin. She wanted to talk to her friends from heaven. "Where are my angels?" she whispered. In the dim city glow on the balcony, she saw the silhouettes of a tiger's head and a small bird on the railing. She snuck out to the balcony, leaving the door cracked open. "I just had a nightmare. Do you know what happened or do I have to explain it?"

"We know what happened," Aini replied calmly. "But tell us, what is bothering you the most about the dream?"

"He said that God doesn't love me!"

"Lunosh said that," Jianyu responded. "Lies are his specialty."

"Yes, it is a horrid lie!" said Aini as Nastia dropped onto the leather couch that she and Anton had moved onto the balcony. "God loves you more than anyone has or ever will!"

"Then does anyone love me?" Nastia felt confused and weary.

"Yes, Tia, yes! Many people dearly love you. But God loves you more than all of them combined. He wants you, but do you want him?"

"I do want him, but God is always there and always will be. Anton won't always be here, and sometimes, I won't connect with him as well as I want. I have to get to know Anton as best I can because I might only have him for a little while."

"Let me ask you this, Nastia Sobieski," said Jianyu, "If God is always with you, don't you think a relationship with him matters more than anything else? Don't you think God matters more than relationships that will fade away — relationships that don't always connect, even while they last?"

"I don't always connect well with God," said Nastia. "In fact, it seems like ages since I've connected with him. When was the last time? The plane ride the day Anton and I met?"

The dark shape of the blue tiger sauntered over to the glass door and pushed it open. Aini flew in after him.

"Wait! Where are you going?"

Aini hovered in the doorway for a moment. "It's time for you to talk to God again. Pray, Tia. Pray because you need God."

Nastia stared into the black night and instantly felt guilty. She began praying, "Okay, God. I told Anton the story like the angels asked. I'm talking about you to him. Can't you make it all okay? Could you please save Anton's soul now? Then I can marry him and we will be a good Christian couple." She didn't feel any better. "No man has ever loved me like Anton does! You know how horrible my dad is. You know the broken relationships I've been through. God, can't you just let me live with him? I'm in love with him. Can't you understand? Why do I still feel guilty? I can't leave him! It's too hard!"

CHAPTER 13

Nastia ended the prayer, mad at God for calling it wrong to live with Anton.

14

TO FEEL WORTHLESS

ANTON CONTINUED SLEEPING steadily as Nastia woke beside him on that Saturday morning. She carefully displaced the covers and raced over to the bathroom, closed the door, and turned on the light. Maybe it was only cold because of the early hour. She stared into the mirror and gagged. "No!" she wanted to shout, but it came out only as a hand-muffled whisper. The mirror revealed an increased sickly appearance on her face with more icy grease in her red hair. The wire beneath the skin of her right forearm had climbed past her elbow, now with a darkening bruise; the wire in her left calf had reached her knee and felt as if it were beginning to pierce the bone.

"I'm hideous," she murmured, removing her hand from her mouth. Hesitantly, she lifted the lower part of her nightshirt to reveal the roach underneath the skin of her waist. Immediately, she released the cloth, closed her eyes, and shook her head again and again, squeezing out a groan.

Nastia forced herself to breathe calmly, suppressing the urge to scream as she thought of some way to see what her actual physical appearance looked like rather than the disgusting image of her soul. A weak possibility came to her. She snuck out of the bathroom, retrieved her laptop computer, and snuck back in, hoping not to see the red bird or blue tiger. To her great pleasure, the computer's camera app revealed her actual physical appearance. She muttered a quick but sincere "Thank you, God!" Now she could apply makeup, brush her hair, and feel like a confident woman again as she observed her own beauty in the screen. *Anton will like me even more today.* She giggled.

After showering with an extra dose of shampoo and applying most of her makeup, Nastia crept out of the bathroom and placed her laptop in its previous spot in the main room. She reentered the bedroom and found Anton out of bed, stretching his head back with a hovering yawn.

"Did I wake you?" she asked.

"No," he smiled at her with his wide, winning set of teeth, his pressed dimples appearing. "I slept great. I do remember hearing some water rushing in my dream, though. I think it was your shower."

"What were you dreaming about?" She watched him rumble a drawer open and retrieve his clothes.

"Let's see, I know there was a forest, lots of leaves, and you." He happily said the last word with a glance her way. Her bosom expanded with pride as she smiled back. "Are you ready to go see the amazing sights of Washington D.C. today?" he asked.

NASTIA'S RED HAIR fluttered lightly as she stood on the concrete of the subway, waiting for the racing train cars, her right hand wrapped in her boyfriend's strong, loving hand. Anton smiled every time Nastia spoke.

Nastia spotted a blue tiger resting on the other side of the tracks with a red bird flapping overhead. As windows raced by, the metal wailing, Nastia felt the gaze of the two angels. She thought she saw the silver dragon as well, writhing around the dark tracks.

NASTIA AND ANTON walked the tourist paths as the sun shone brightly in the sky, scattering warmth. People from countless races and worldviews strolled past while the two calmly observed the sights and memorials of the Mall. The Washington monument towered above, shining so brightly it could have been made of the stones of hope. The World War II memorial caught Anton's eye, and he turned the corner, still holding his girlfriend's soft hand. Nastia spotted sadness in his eyes.

"What's wrong?" she asked.

"A lot of people died during World War II. It's horrible. Even though we were on the winning side, that war is a deep scar on world history."

"Have you studied World War II?"

"Yes. Many times." He sighed and turned to smile at her again. "I wanted to go into the military for a long time. It was all I thought about as a kid."

"Do you mind if I sit for a minute? I'd like to rest." The fountain splashed behind her.

"Sure. I'm going to look around a bit." Their hands slid apart as Anton walked off.

Nastia watched the water glisten in the sunlight. The red bird flew through the mist and landed on the white stone beside her. "Hello, Tia. How are you?"

"I don't know. I'm pretty tired today." She gazed at the small red bird for a moment. "My wounds are hurting, Aini."

"You mean your sins?"

"Whatever. There is more grease in my hair, my face is *horrifying*, and the wires have grown with the bruises. Not to mention the detestable ants and the thoroughly disgusting roach. Ugh!"

The red bird fluffed up her feathers, as if to shrug. "How is your boyfriend?"

"Why do you ask me questions when you already know the answers?" She cringed. "He seems great. He smiles at me all the time."

The blue tiger sauntered toward the rushing fountain and stopped beside a fully oblivious young girl, who reached out to catch droplets.

"You love him, don't you?" Aini asked.

Nastia was surprised by the question. "Of course!"

"Are you angry?"

"I don't know. I'm not angry exactly; I just hate what is happening to my soul. Why does everything that happened to me before I met Anton seem like nothing in comparison to now?"

"Because you feel as if your deepest desires are being satisfied by living with him. Romance is a wonderful creation of God."

"I think you forgot something there, Aini. Weren't you going to say, 'But only in a marriage between a Christian man and woman who waited to have sex till their wedding night?' " said Nastia.

"What you just described is the ideal situation. It is God's desire for all who take part in romance. That's why it has the greatest blessings." Aini winked, and then flew off as Anton approached.

"Are you ready to go on?" he asked.

The presence of God was more certain than the bold sun, clearer than the shimmering lake, and more fearless than the tall American flag moving with the wind as Nastia and Anton walked down the path. Nastia gazed up and viewed her surroundings. God was there and watching — without a doubt. He knew everything she had done and every desire in her heart. Nastia missed God. She wanted to talk to him.

Nastia prayed silently, expressing her weary heart, The truth is, God, I feel filthy and worthless, but I don't know how to change. I don't know if changing is really possible for me. Repentance is like a lofty dream I can never reach. As she prayed, she felt that changing was possible. She remembered that anything is possible with Christ — even leaving Anton. Maybe she could start repenting by going to church tomorrow. Yes, she told herself, knowing God was listening. I will go to church tomorrow.

Once the couple arrived at the Vietnam memorial, Anton searched up and down the endless list of names. Nastia did the same, quietly. She saw her reflection in the polished black marble. *Oh, my grace, I'm so ugly.* The carved names blew as if they were feathers, forming a glossy dragon. Nastia bit back the urge to yell, because she didn't want Lunosh to make a fool out of her again.

The silver dragon spoke smoothly, "Remember when everyone in your dad's church found out about his affair — the way they looked down at you with such pity?"

Nastia remembered all too clearly. She hated that kind of patronizing pity. She had always wanted to tell them, "Don't look at me like that. You act as if my father is the worst person alive. But he's not! We all make mistakes. Please, never talk to me again." But what she never wanted those people to know was how she hated her father. Why was she remembering this now?

The couple walked on and climbed the steps of the Lincoln memorial. The silver dragon curled around a pillar, leaned out, and whispered to Nastia, "The truth is you *are* worthless; you're filthy as rags. If people could actually see your soul, they would run from you because you are so completely disgusting. Do you want to know why?"

"Why?"

Anton turned around, grinned, and said, "Do what?"

Nastia hated how she couldn't talk to Lunosh without others hearing. "Oh-uh, I was just saying. It's really cool, isn't it?"

"Yeah, it is." He looked up at the statue and the words behind with admiring eyes. Nastia saw a group of three young women in the corner. One pointed at Anton, and they all covered their mouths, giggling.

Nastia could read their lips, "He's so cute!" She wished she could tell them he was hers. Thankfully, Anton was oblivious.

She whispered, "Why?" again and listened for Lunosh's answer.

"You are so worthless," the silver dragon began, "because you know what sin is, but you do it anyway. You know how wrong your actions are, yet you continue. God doesn't want you because you have turned your back on Him. God will never want you again."

Nastia felt her soul sink, believing the words of the dragon. Anton put his arm around her and said, "Are you okay?"

If only he could understand the despair of a Christian's sin. Or was it better if he didn't? Would he think she was weird and delusional if she told him about Aini and Jianyu and Lunosh? Of course he would. She told herself that she could never tell him, or he wouldn't love her anymore. Losing his love would be absolutely unbearable.

He touched her face softly.

"I don't know. I'm feeling weird today," she replied.

"Would you like to go sit by the lake together for a while?"

"That would be nice."

Nastia glanced around as they descended the stairs. Two women walking up saw her and then Anton. They made an effort to stare at Anton, as they grew farther apart even craning their necks back, tripping and nearly falling on the top step. Nastia didn't like those women.

They found a bench in the middle of the long reflecting pool, the bright sun warming their skin. People strolled hither and thither as Anton put his arm around her, and she rested her head on his comforting muscular shoulder.

Is that a silver snake swimming in the lake? The snake slithered onto the side walk, facing Nastia. "That was why the people who left your dad's church looked down at you. They could see the evil in your eyes. Anyone could tell that you are worthless except for men blinded by love. But their love always fades away, doesn't it? Every boy who has liked you eventually hates you. Everyone hates you, Nastia. You hurt everyone who once loved you."

The snake saw the blue tiger approaching and slithered away. Nastia sniffled as a tear dropped.

123

"What's wrong?" Anton asked, compassion in his blue eyes with the beige rings that loved and discovered.

"Oh, nothing," she lied.

Aini flew in front of her and hovered in the air, saying sweetly, "It's okay, Tia. You can be honest with him. Even if he doesn't completely understand, he will somewhat. Try it."

Nastia decided to be honest. "Anton, I need to talk to you about something."

"Okay. Shoot."

"You know that I'm a Christian."

"Yeah," his tone changed to serious. Nastia wondered if she could do it. Aini smiled kindly.

"I'm not supposed to live with you. It goes against my beliefs and convictions. I have turned my back on God by living with you."

"Yeah, I was wondering about that," Anton said calmly. Nastia wondered if he had a solution behind his eyes.

"I really do enjoy your company, and I think you are the best boyfriend I have ever had. But…" her voice trailed off.

"But?" he prompted. "It's okay. You can tell me."

"But I love God also, and he says that I should stop living with you."

"Do you know that for sure?"

Nastia thought about it. Aini, Jianyu, and Lauren told me not to live with Anton, but God hasn't told me that exactly. It's not like I've actually heard his voice saying, "Don't live with Anton." The Bible frowns upon sexual immorality, but what exactly was sexual immorality? There wasn't a verse that said, "Thou shalt not live with thy boyfriend." But Nastia did feel guilty. Amidst her confusion, she heard a smooth voice hissing in her left ear, "Maybe this guilt is just something other people have created. You aren't really living in sin. These convictions belong to someone else. They aren't yours."

Nastia turned to her left to see the close-up face of the silver snake. She remembered herself and addressed Anton, "Yes. I know for sure."

Anton sighed. Nastia hated the downcast sound. "I was hoping you wouldn't say that." His tone was serious. "I don't want to hurt you at all, but I do really want you to continue living with me. I've grown attached to you, Nastia. I keep thinking about it. We have only known each other for two weeks, but I love you. I really love you."

Nastia's heart melted. She felt bad for being honest, but at the same time, she didn't because she could talk to Anton on a much deeper level now. "I love you, too. I was just thinking today how everything that happened to me before I met you seems to fade as if it doesn't mean anything when compared to my time with you."

Anton's winning grin stretched across his face. They kissed and gazed back at the water, their arms around each other. "This would be the perfect spot," he said in a lighter, happier tone.

"Perfect for what?"

"For the Nastia Sobieski memorial." They both laughed.

"What exactly would this memorial look like," she asked coyly.

"How about a glass bridge from here to the other end of the lake with gold and brass. Do you like that?"

"Yes. Very much."

His eyes sharpened as he pieced together the remaining vision. "And on the four corners there will be four glass statues with golden eyes and brass touches here and there."

"Wow, how glorious. But are you sure you want to dedicate it to me? You deserve it more."

"Yeah I'm sure!" he laughed. "You are the best girlfriend I have ever met. Actually, I think you are the best woman I have ever met. No one else is quite like you. Just watching you do your normal thing is a sight to behold."

She laughed. "Maybe I'll secretly make a memorial for you. I think you are the best guy ever. I'm not the only one who thinks so."

"Who else does?" A suspicious smile crawled onto his lips.

"Easy. I'll show you." She placed her hands on his head and pulled him back to look at the people walking by. "See those girls approaching?"

"Yeah?"

"They are giggling and watching you."

"It seems like it," he admitted, hesitantly.

"The blonde one on the left. I can see what she's saying, 'Oh my gosh! He is so cute!' "

He laughed it off. "I don't know. It's just an impression."

"They are thinking exactly what I think every time I look at you. 'Oh my gosh, he is so cute!' " Even while she looked into his eyes, she saw the blue tiger staring at her. Jianyu made her shiver sometimes. "People have been looking at you all day."

"No, well, maybe. That's happened before. It's no big deal."

"Oh sure, right," Nastia teased. "People stare at you all the time. You have grown bored of it by now." They both laughed.

"Hey, people have been looking at *you* more than me."

Nastia blinked. "What do you mean?"

"Ever since we got out of the hotel, almost every guy we pass has checked you out. You are really beautiful, Nastia — unusually beautiful. People just like to stare at you. And remember the party I took you to last Saturday?"

"Yeah."

"All the guys there were checking you out, and that one guy was drooling over you. We went upstairs to my room because you were so uncomfortable with it. Then, you know, things happened between us."

"Yeah, I know," she laughed, wishing to keep the atmosphere light.

"Don't tell me you don't notice it." Anton grinned triumphantly, knowing he was right.

"I might notice, in the back of my mind. But ever since my freshman year of college, people have been staring at me. I guess I've just gotten used to it."

"Oh yeah. You're just used to it," Anton teased back. "People think you're amazingly beautiful. No big deal." His big smile appeared again, placing sharper edges on his eyes.

The sun began to sink as they comfortably embraced each other.

"Are you hungry?" Anton asked.

"I could eat. Is it already time for dinner?"

"Yeah. But don't worry, there's a whole night ahead of us." He couldn't help but laugh. Nastia joined in. They laughed not because anything was funny but because they enjoyed each other's company.

The D.C. atmosphere was peaceful as they made their way toward the shops and restaurants. They saw one restaurant named Beyond This.

"Let's try that one," she said.

"Okay," her boyfriend replied.

———————◆———————

LIGHTS WERE DIM in the restaurant; only soft murmurs filled the air. Some unusual abstract paintings hung beneath kind lights — colorful and expressive. Was that a tiger outlined in the blue pigments? As Anton scanned through his menu, Nastia looked up from hers to see a red canary shape in the painting right beside them. The bird flew from one branch-like brush stroke to another. Nastia marveled at the aesthetic movement.

"Cool painting, huh?" said Anton.

"Oh, uh, yes." Nastia was thinking about Aini, but she might as well agree. "Do you like art?"

"I love it. Do you?"

"Definitely!"

"Oh, that's right. You majored in art history," he said.

"Yes. We should go to the Smithsonian art museum sometime."

"Would you like to go tomorrow?"

"Sure." She glanced at the tiger shape in the painting across the room. "I want to go to church tomorrow, though."

"Oh. All right."

They continued chatting about inconsequential subjects. Once their food arrived, Anton asked a deeper question, "I was thinking today. Who is the person you resent the most?"

"My dad." Nastia didn't need any time to think.

"Why is that?"

"Like I told you, he committed adultery. But maybe it was more his character and how he treated our whole family. He would always pull away from us and go work or play around with his hobbies instead of spending time with his children. But what I hate the most is how he treated my mother."

"Did he abuse her?"

Nastia shook her head. "Maybe he did a few times, but he didn't physically abuse her exactly; he manipulated her. That continues to infuriate me. I hate how my dad manipulated my mom. She would always defend him, even after he cheated on her. I remember talking to her one night while people were leaving my dad's church. I asked her if she hated Dad like everyone else. She said, 'No, your father is really a good man. We all make mistakes. You don't know how sorry he is.' " Nastia shook her head again as if she completely disagreed.

"You don't think he was sorry?"

"Absolutely not! He did it again with a different woman two years after everyone left our church. I went to my friend's church by then, so it wasn't as hard on me as it was on my siblings. Anyway, I left for college soon after. My dad didn't care for his family enough to control himself. It makes me so angry when I think of how he lied to us."

"Wow. That would be tough." Anton took another bite.

"What prompted the question?" Nastia asked.

"Oh, I was just thinking about my mom today, for some reason. She was completely different from your mom."

"Do you not like your mom?"

"No, not really." He squinted.

"Aw…why not?"

"She never respected my dad," said Anton. "My mom is probably the person I resent most in the world. She always talked behind my dad's back and looked ashamed of me when I defended him. Remember how I told you that my parents got divorced?"

"Yeah." Nastia glanced at her water curiously.

"My dad honestly tried to stay with my mom, but she was very disrespectful. My mom caused the divorce, not my dad. My dad liked to watch football every now and then (I would join him when he did), but my mom would nag him all day, saying ridiculous stuff like, 'You don't care a thing about your family' or 'You love that stupid pig sack more than your wife.' I hated it. I tried to stay out of the house as much as possible during high school. That's the main reason I played sports. My mom would sit around watching her TV shows, and I would ask why she was such a hypocrite, pestering Dad about football when he was the one who worked. That was just on my mind for some reason."

Nastia had a horrible feeling that she might remind Anton of his mother. "Would you like to go to church with me tomorrow?"

"No thanks, babe. I sleep in on Sundays. But you go, if you want. Enjoy it for me."

Anton smiled as Nastia watched the silver dragon slither up the leg of a passing waitress.

15

PRETENDING

ARMED WITH A leather-bound sword of truth, Nastia bravely approached the humble church door. What would Lauren say when she saw her? Nastia dreaded the possible future image of Lauren's grieving eyes above her motionless cheeks. But even if her best friend remained sad throughout the whole service, Nastia felt confident because she was actually here. Coming to church had been a battle.

Anton had mumbled while turning in the bed, "You off to church?" in a tone calling her to retreat as Nastia dressed and prepared herself. Why did the silver dragon have to point out how attractive and warm Anton looked amidst the sheets, making her want to abandon the church endeavor and curl up by his side? Relaxed talks in bed were one of Nastia's favorite parts about her relationship with Anton. But she wanted to prove to herself that she was still a Christian by going to church. She had to!

And here she was.

Nastia opened the door to see various people casually greeting one another. Why did this modest setting feel so intimidating? The confident faces of the red bird and blue tiger answered the question without words — because God was there.

"Please take your seats," a man on the stage requested politely, bending his head toward the microphone. She spotted Lauren talking cheerfully with a few women among the clean chairs. Nastia walked up and said nervously, "May I sit with you?"

Lauren whirled around. Her lamp-like eyes burst into a bright array of surprised pleasure. "Tia!" She hugged her immediately. "You're here! And what kind of a question is that? If you didn't sit by me I would drown in embarrassment." Lauren released her full, resounding laugh that never failed to comfort Nastia.

As the congregation hushed, Lauren leaned over and whispered in a humorous but sincere tone, "Will you accompany me to lunch after the service, Ms. Sobieski? I would be most delighted."

Nastia grinned, "Thank you, Ms. Henson. I believe I can fit that into my schedule." The two giggled softly but hushed each other at the same time as someone made an announcement.

After a few moments, Lauren couldn't hold in her comment any longer and whispered to Nastia, "I've missed you."

"But I've only been gone for three days," Nastia whispered back. "How could you miss me already?"

"Because I have missed you."

Nastia knew what she meant and proceeded to listen to the sermon quietly.

———————◆———————

FOLLOWING THE SERVICE, Nastia accompanied Lauren to a small Sunday school room, where a women's Bible study group prepared to discuss the sermon. Why did the topic have to be spiritual cleansing? Nastia thought the pastor must have said, "We must turn from *all* our sins" a dozen times. Now the leader of the study group said it again. Nastia was uncomfortable and used a great deal of her reserved strength to appear normal, innocent, and humbly attentive. At least five times she hastily offered a silent prayer, *Lord, please help them not to call on me.*

By the end of the discussion, no one had asked Nastia to talk, but the leader of the group came up to her while the other women chatted loudly. "I'm glad to see you back."

131

"Thank you."

"You were very quiet, though. Are you all right? Do you want me to pray for you?"

Oh, good grace! Nastia thought. Of course she didn't want this woman to mention her name in her woven prayers. Good gosh! This middle-aged woman was a stranger and, frankly, Nastia didn't like her at all. But if she said no, this woman would tell her friends to pray. Nastia could imagine her asking her family at their dinner table in a high-pitched voice, "Could you please pray for this red-haired girl at church? She was such a burden on my heart today, and when I asked if I could pray for her she said no." Oh dear! What shall the American church do? Someone said no!

Nastia didn't like this woman who looked like a nosy squirrel, but she responded with a forced smile, "Oh, thank you. I would greatly appreciate it. It's just been a stressful week, relocating you know?"

The wire squirmed in her leg.

"Yes. I definitely know what you mean. Have a blessed day."

The woman moved away as Nastia told herself, Lauren is a much better Christian. I may not be, but Lauren certainly is.

———————— ♦ ————————

LAUREN AND NASTIA'S Jewish lunches quickly arrived at Judah's Café.

Lauren prayed before the meal with an emphasis on thanksgiving. Nastia bowed her head and closed her eyes, smashing her lips together in discomfort. She didn't feel uncomfortable because of Lauren (never Lauren), but because of her own guilt and the resounding voice of her conscience saying, *Turn away! Turn away! Leave all sin and love God.*

"How have you been?" Lauren asked.

"Good, very good. We're happy together," Nastia said as if she had lived with Anton for years.

Lauren tilted her head, noticing something deeper. "Truly, Tia? How are you behind this new lifestyle?"

Nastia dearly wanted to tell Lauren about her suffering, the temptations, the spiritual pain, the confusion, and whatever else might come out. She decided to try a little, "I don't know how I'm doing. Okay, I'm not doing well at all. I love Anton and living with him. You don't even know! It's phenomenal, but I am constantly going back and forth in my mind, round and round in countless circles, wondering what I truly believe." She was proud of herself for opening up.

Lauren's eyes filled with empathy. "It must be very hard."

"But it's only the first week. Things should get better soon." Nastia tried to be optimistic with a light smile.

"So you plan to continue living with him?"

"Yes, as far as I can see now."

"But you just said you aren't feeling well at all," Lauren reminded.

"Yeah," she shrugged. "But it's not like I can go back to life without him."

"Don't tell yourself that. You *can* stop this."

"Lauren! Don't be so serious." Nastia was surprised at her friend's grieving passion. "We're fine. It's not that bad. Really. Sleeping with him hasn't been so different. Sex is just another part of life. We're still human; life still has problems and daily trials. I've just moved to a different, better phase that is really making me happy —
"

"Tia, no!" Lauren shook her head. "Don't you hear what you're saying?"

"Yes. It's perfectly fine. He's sweet, and it's all good —"

"Stop!" said Lauren unexpectedly.

Nastia fell silent and glanced at the couple looking her way from the next booth. She wanted to tell Lauren to tone it down, but her friend was too agonized.

"Tia," Lauren looked straight into her eyes, "you are living in sin, and you are a Christian. You are living like you're dead and lost when you are saved and free. Come back and live with me in my apartment like we had planned for months. We talked about it through all of your last semester. You said that you were eager to work with a ministry and see what God has in store for you."

"That's just it, Lauren. Anton is what God has for me. Why else would God have him sit right next to me on the plane? Why else would God allow me to meet my dream man, even before you picked me up from the airport? Anton is right for me."

"No, it doesn't work that way. God doesn't put knives in your path so you can stab yourself with them. Yes, you met him, but he's not a Christian and you're not married. Please come back. Stop this sin."

"No, Lauren, you stop!" Frustration rose in Nastia's face. "I can't stand it when you push and push! It doesn't help me. You have no idea how it is. You have no idea how much I'm missing him even now. I love him, and that's it. This is the way it is. Accept it!"

Lauren fell silent this time. She picked at her matzo ball soup. Nastia sat tall and faultless in her Sunday attire, like a dominant queen silencing a rebellion.

After a few long moments, Lauren spoke, "You know how God said in 2nd Corinthians 12:9, 'My grace is sufficient for you, for my power is made perfect in weakness.' "

"Yes."

"Even though you might feel incapable of leaving Anton, you are not, because you have God. Ask God to help you leave him."

"I'll consider it," Nastia responded as if she were dealing with a business associate. Silence visited again.

"I need some time to think," said Nastia. "I'll take care of the bill. You can leave now."

Lauren felt as if she was visiting a business woman and her appointment had ended. Tia was acting like a stranger. But Lauren wanted to be respectful. "All right. I'll leave." She stood. "Remember, you can call or text me anytime."

"Thank you," said Nastia in a final tone.

"Well, goodbye."

Lauren walked out, leaving Nastia to stare into space.

16

THAT LOOK IN HIS EYES

NASTIA'S THOUGHTS REMAINED entrapped in morose confusion as she entered the hotel suite, placed her keys and purse on the counter, and looked around for Anton.

"Hey, beautiful." He sat behind a computer.

Nastia saw pornography playing on the screen.

"What are you *watching*?" She marched up behind him, aghast.

Anton paused it and turned around with a calm grin as if he watched it every day. "Just looking at some porn videos. How was church?"

It was true! "Can you please turn that off?"

Anton sensed her serious mood and exited the internet. "What's wrong?"

"What do you mean 'what's wrong'? You were looking at pornography!"

"Yeah," he replied casually. "I look at it every now and then. I'm a guy who has sex often. I was researching different moves."

Nastia's jaw dropped. She turned and headed for the bedroom. He's cheating on me! He's cheating on me! She kept thinking and switched to prayer. God, what the heck? Who is this guy? What am I doing? I've been such a fool! Get me out! Please get me out! I'm leaving. Now, whatever! Just get me out, please! What have I done?

Anton stood in the doorway, sweet but sad compassion in his handsome features. "Nastia?"

"It's all wrong! It's all wrong!"

"What is?" His voice was soothing and tender. "Pornography?"

"The porn and all of this. I could almost thank you rather than kill you for watching it because you have handed me glasses. I can see clearly now." She hurried into the bathroom and started to detach her earrings. What a horrifying face! She looked like a dying hag. She tried to ignore the orange lines growing around the metal ant beneath the skin of her neck. She loathed the arm-clutching wire.

"I love you, Nastia." Anton was by her side. "You're the only woman for me."

"Ha! You think you love me? Then why are you looking at that trash and at those other women? Don't you dare talk to me about love!"

"I'll stop if you want. I won't look at it again. I'll do anything for you."

He was touching her slowly. Father in heaven save me! She prayed. No! No! He's touching me more! Get me out, Lord. Please get me out!

———◆———

WRAPPED IN SHEETS and Anton's arms, Nastia petted her glittering cross necklace, the one her mother gave her, the one she wore to church just a little while ago. Why was the room so dark? Wasn't it daytime? Nothing made sense. She searched for meaning in the golden shape. She felt helpless and unable to do anything but what Anton wanted her to do. It wasn't just another part of life.

She could feel six more ants beneath the skin around her neck.

A silver snake toppled off the bed, glancing back with a hideous grin. "Go away, Lunosh!" Nastia said aloud.

Anton heard and was somewhat concerned. "Who are you talking to?"

Nastia realized she had spoken outside her spirit. "Oh, um, life and things."

"Okay."

"Anton?"

"Yes?"

"Would you like to take me to the National Gallery of Art now?"

"Whatever you want."

Nastia scowled back at the snake's face, as if it helped.

NASTIA DIDN'T SAY much as she wandered through the museum and neither did her tall boyfriend. Compared to all the people around, Nastia could see his impressive six-foot-three form tower above almost everyone, but it was only a form. When she looked at him regardless of the others, she was disappointed. She didn't want to talk with him. Did she even want to be with him at all? Dates can be such silly things.

They entered a big, echoing room with a dome and sky lights. Anton's phone rang.

"I have to take this, Nastia. Can you wait here?"

"Yes."

"Okay, I'll be right back."

"Don't hurry," Nastia said in a clearly sarcastic tone. Anton walked out, ignoring the comment.

"What the crap am I doing? This day feels like forever," Nastia said to the air as she sat on a cold marble bench. "I miss God." Her face was sad.

She gazed up at the ceiling windows, light descending, and warmth finding her. Hope followed with freedom, peace, meaning, and purpose. Purpose! The light was like purpose in a world that didn't make much sense. *God, come to us, and we will shout your name among the unbelievers! Christ, I need you. Oh, I need you more than anything! I've been a fool, an idiot. I want you, Lord God. Please, forgive me. I want you!*

Her eyes were moist.

The faithful blue tiger sauntered into the large room, past oblivious people, and stood before Nastia. The selfless red canary flew in with the light and landed on the marble bench.

"I hate sin, and I want God," Nastia said with deep yearning in her eyes. "Can you please help me?"

Aini sang a wonderful song of victory as Jianyu pressed his paw on Nastia's leg. The wire disappeared without any pain. He touched her forearm and that wire disappeared too, then her waist and the roach vanished. Jianyu sprang onto the bench. He placed his heavy paw on the back of Nastia's neck, nearly pushing her off the bench. Suddenly, all of the ants were gone.

She was free.

"Thank you, Lord!" she prayed and turned to the angels. "What do I do now?"

"Explain to Anton why you can no longer live with him and that what you did was wrong. Then return to Lauren's apartment," said Aini with encouraging joy.

"Why do I still have the bruises?"

"Because you haven't finished the steps yet," Jianyu answered. "Once you pray in Lauren's apartment, they will disappear."

Nastia couldn't wait to return to her best friend and live like a Christian again. If she lived simply that would be fine. She wanted closeness with God.

The angels headed down the hall, leaving Nastia on the bench as Anton reentered from the opposite direction, a victorious grin framed by his dimples.

"What is it?" Nastia asked.

"I just got off the phone with my boss. He wants me to go to Hawaii this weekend and represent the company. I asked if I could take you with me."

"And?"

"He said yes."

17

HOW CAN I DO THIS?

NASTIA FRANTICALLY PONDERED the news as she and Anton traveled back to the hotel through the subway system. She didn't know how to take it. What did this mean? *I will repent anyway, regardless of the temptation to go to paradise with Anton. Honestly, Hawaii! What could be more tempting than that?*

As they entered the door of their grand resort hotel, Nastia felt like a millionaire's wife (or mistress).

"Anton, we need to talk."

"Okay. You want to go up to those seats by the window?"

"Sure."

The light entered differently now. Nastia put on her sunglasses. "How should I start?"

"Is this about the videos I was watching today?" he asked.

"Not exactly. It's kind of hard to say this with you sitting right here but," she took a deep breath, "I can't live with you anymore."

Anton thought she would have been happier to hear the news about Hawaii. It must be something deeper. "Why not?"

"Honestly, I don't even know how I slept with you at all. I really wasn't supposed to. We Christians call it sinning. We're not supposed to do it."

"But you did anyway."

"Yeah, I did. I thought I was in love with you, and I let that distract me from God's law, but I can't do it anymore."

"So, you're *not* in love with me?" Anton asked.

"Well, that's another thing confusing me." Nastia glanced out the window.

Anton could barely see Nastia's eyes behind her dark glasses. "You're saying you want to leave because you believe it's wrong for us to live together?"

She nodded.

"I'm still in love with you."

This caught her attention.

"I'm sorry about the porn thing this afternoon. I really don't want to lose you. I love you and I want to live with you. I believe *you* are worth it. Please don't go, Nastia. I only make it through my work hours because I get to see you every night when I come home. Yes, texting helps but it's not the same as now, face-to-face with you."

"Thank you, Anton, but I don't love you." She knew it was a lie even before it left her mouth. The sadness in Anton's eyes didn't help at all. "I thought I did, but I can't do this. Please, if you ever cared anything for me, stay down here while I pack my stuff and leave. It will be easier for both of us."

She got up and began to walk away. She could feel his stare behind her and imagined his face, his handsome face. He was more than a hot guy. He really seemed to love and care for her. Even though he had looked at porn, Anton was a good man. Nastia knew she would miss him as she rode the escalator to the second floor and headed for the elevators.

Something wrenched her heart as if the world was ending. She felt like she would die once she pushed the elevator button. The slow hum of the machine was like the crushing of Anton's heart. Tears filled her eyes. *How can I do this to him? He will be miserable and alone when I could have made his life happy and full of relationship. What will happen to me? Can I really live without him?*

Nastia couldn't do it, or at least, that's what she thought as she approached Anton Shepherd standing between two plush lobby chairs. Oh, that look in his eyes! Nastia felt like she had just discovered love.

18

HATE OR LOYALTY

HAWAII!

Nastia beamed with excitement as she sat in her office Tuesday afternoon, thinking about the upcoming trip with Anton. The red bird and blue tiger rested calmly beside her desk, ready to talk when she needed. As for now, the only thing Nastia would think about was Hawaii. Oh, the glorious paradise! She couldn't wait until they arrived in warm, tropical Honolulu. She could almost feel the cleansing Oahu sun enliven her skin in showers of light.

Anton had conveyed to her their plans: they would travel all morning Friday, arrive in the islands at around 3:00 p.m., spend three nights in a luxurious resort right on the shore of Waikiki beach, and leave to fly back over the expansive United States on Monday afternoon. Was it really happening? Nastia dearly hoped so; she had sacrificed much for this trip with Anton.

Last Sunday night, Anton had told her, "Thank you for staying with me. From the bottom of my soul, thank you. I won't look at porn anymore."

"Yeah, I'll stay with you as life is now."

Ever since, Anton proceeded to treat her as if he were deeply in debt. Frankly, Nastia agreed. She had rejected God by making the choice to continue to live with Anton, so of course he was in debt to her. Jianyu had phrased it as rejecting God, and Nastia had to concur, but she tried desperately not to think of it that way. Even though she knew the truth, Nastia ignored the fact that she turned her back on God every minute she lived with Anton. She tried to remove the unfavorable guilt by muttering little eloquent prayers every now and then. Little aesthetic prayers made Nastia feel better about herself, as if she were a good person.

Hawaii! Nastia remembered when she would sit in the sand of the California beach, dreaming of visiting the popular paradise as she watched the proud sun sink into the watery horizon. She was exhilarated! Honestly, Hawaii!

Her phone buzzed, and she read the text from her lover. They had been discussing sexuality, and Anton was talking about some secretive gay guys who had confessed love to him in college. "What did you tell them?" Nastia asked in her last text to him.

Anton's reply was the text she read now: "I would say 'No way! I'm not gay at all!' "

"Yeah, I hate homosexuality," she typed and sent quickly. What she loved most about their relationship was how open they were with each other. Nastia felt free to express her opinion to Anton whenever she wished, and he would listen attentively. She loved how he respected and tolerated her opinions so well.

The phone buzzed again. Nastia read the text casually: "My brother is gay, and he's fine that way."

What? Oh no! Maybe they weren't as similar as she thought. Anton's brother was gay? She could imagine her lover sitting with a hurt expression on his face, wondering how he was living with such a cruel woman. This was terrible, a thoroughly unwanted barrier in their relationship. How could she get past it? She had offended Anton. Suddenly, Nastia didn't feel like Anton was in debt to her anymore, but that she was in debt to him. Would he reconsider taking her to Hawaii with him? Was he reconsidering their relationship altogether? This couldn't be happening! She had to fix it even if a lie was necessary.

ANTON LEANED INTO the corner of his swivel chair — upset and troubled. Was Nastia a homophobe? Traditionally, Anton was disgusted by homophobes, considering them too incompetent and insecure to accept the differences in others. He was absolutely not gay, but he did understand it somewhat, or at least he thought he did. Anton could never imagine being attracted sexually to a guy. It simply didn't work that way for him. He was attracted to women. That was his nature.

Anton turned his eyes toward the ceiling. His brother, on the other hand, was different. Anton's only sibling, Julias, was three years younger. As far as his sexuality went, Julias was different; he was gay. Homosexuality was his nature.

Anton remembered how hard the divorce was on his brother. Julias was thirteen when it happened. Sometimes Anton would get angry at his mother and father and try to break up their fighting. Julias simply watched television in a daze, not really caring what was playing just as long as something was on. He would hold the remote loosely as he sat on the couch, allowing it to slip away, as if only the remote would slip out of his hands but not the two-parent family life he cherished so dearly. Anton grew to be concerned for his brother and would act as a counseling friend.

Anton resented most people who disapproved of homosexuality — those who called it wrong and especially those who said, "I hate homosexuals." Enmity would naturally build, and Nastia was no exception. Anton resented hypocrites more than anyone. There had been a few guys on the football team in college who always demeaned and talked down about homos. Anton later found out that those same men had done homo things. He hated two-faced hypocrites.

Was Nastia a hypocrite? She certainly wasn't gay, but she was judgmental. Anton's phone showed him a new text:

146

Nastia: "I don't hate gay people. I think they are treasures. What I hate is how homosexuality seems to harm the treasures."

Hmm... maybe that was an all right response. Anton still had the feeling Nastia was a homophobe. Yes, there were times when Anton disapproved of his brother's actions, but that wasn't necessarily caused by Julias's sexuality. Everyone had character flaws. Anton thought that being gay must be hard, especially when so many people were homophobic.

Anton wanted more clarification from his girlfriend and replied with a text saying:

"So you don't resent gay people at all, but treat them like everyone else?"

The responding text read: "Yes. Exactly."

———————◆———————

NASTIA CRINGED AS she sent the lie. The six metal ants beneath the skin of her collarbone squirmed. "Ow!" she exclaimed, reminded that sin still clung to her soul.

After she had asked for forgiveness from God and all the sin was removed from her body-appearing soul, Nastia intended to repent and leave Anton, but at the last minute, she went back to him and tried to ignore Aini, Jianyu, and especially God. She didn't let the guilt get to her that night but enjoyed Anton's praise, compliments, and tender love. Once Monday arrived, Nastia tried to ignore her conscience and acted happy before her supervisor, Stephanie, who sweetly welcomed her.

But today was different. She felt like she couldn't ignore the angels any longer.

She touched the back of her head and felt the cold, sticky grease in a lock of her hair. She had tried to ignore that, too. Nastia sighed and turned toward the kind black eyes of the red bird. "Aini," she said drearily, "there is so much grease in my hair."

Aini waddled over to the keyboard on her tiny feet. "Tia, how good to speak to you again. I have missed you."

"Oh, good grace! You have seen me every moment of Sunday, yesterday, and today. How could you miss me?"

"I have missed talking with you and pointing you toward your faithful savior. And, yes, there is grease in your hair because you are not drawing your strength from God."

Nastia frowned. "Oh. Then why did ants come back on my soul again?"

"Why do you think?" Aini asked with pure love in her eyes.

"Because I have idolized Anton and our life together," she answered hesitantly.

"Yes. Correct."

Nastia shuffled through some papers, not wishing to talk anymore. She received a new text.

Anton: "My boss asked me to keep working longer. I won't be back in the room until 8 or 9. Go ahead and eat without me."

"Crap," Nastia sighed. She was very disappointed. Just as before, she could not enjoy food when Anton wasn't around. "Good grace, no!" she groaned. Was she losing Anton? She wanted to eat with him and feel close like before, but she had to wait longer now. Did he resent her? She couldn't help but feel an agonizing distance between them. *No, no, no!* Nastia couldn't stand the thought of losing Anton.

Was God taking him away from her?

———————————◆———————————

THE BLUE TIGER moved slowly in line beside Nastia's leg as she made her order at the quiet Mexican restaurant. Once she purchased and received her food, she sat at a stainless-steel table scratched copiously with illegible letters.

"Nastia Sobieski," said Jianyu, poised by the table in noble form.

"Yes?" she was afraid. "What is it?"

Aini stood on the back of an unused chair. "We need to speak with you about your judgmental and superior attitude concerning gay people."

"But I disapprove of homosexuality, just like God does."

Jianyu spoke, "Giving into homosexual temptations isn't good, but that's not the issue. Yes, those who live in the gay lifestyle are living in sin, but so are you. How can you despise homosexuals when you are just like them?"

"Don't say that! I'm not gay at all. How could you accuse me of something so horrible?"

"We aren't accusing you of being gay," said Aini. "We are pointing out that you are being a hypocrite whether you express it outwardly or not. You look down on gay people as if you were better than them."

"Well, yeah. I am better than gay people."

The angels waited for her to explain.

"Honestly, there is something different about homosexuality. It's so wrong! I mean a guy in love with a guy or a girl in love with a girl? Gross! I've met gay people before, and I treated them just as I would treat any other acquaintance, but there is something much more destructive and evil about gay sin. I feel like gay people are more evil than most of them realize. There is something about them that destroys goodness no matter how nice they are."

" 'Why do you look at the speck of sawdust in your brother's eye and pay no attention to the plank in your own eye?' " said Jianyu, quoting Matthew 7:3.

"That's just it, Jianyu. That verse doesn't apply to my situation because I am living with a guy not a girl. God designed one man to live with one woman, which is what I'm doing with Anton. Even though the way we live together isn't exactly how it should be, we are still faithful to each other and are growing slowly closer and closer to becoming husband and wife. That is a very good thing! Homosexuals, on the other hand, live a lifestyle that is completely off track from what is good. The gay lifestyle is clearly wrong. My living with Anton is much closer to the ideal good life than any gay relationship."

Aini and Jianyu glanced at each other. The red bird spoke, "Sin is sin, Tia. A gay sin makes someone just as unworthy of God as a straight sin. Any and every type of sin makes a person worthy of hell. You are a sinner just like Anton's brother, but *you* know the truth and the right way. You don't know if Anton's brother knows God or not. But you do know God, Nastia. You know God and his right path toward life, yet you chose a path to death."

"I am still better than gay people because their sin is worse. I'm going through a confusing time, that's all. Things will be right soon."

"Then let me challenge you with this," Aini began. "What is worse? A sin that is obviously very wrong or a sin that you can convince yourself is not so bad? I would say the latter is more dangerous because you can grow complacent and slowly drift away from God when you tell yourself that your sin isn't so bad. This is very dangerous to your soul! When you think this way, you idolize your own reasoning; you place God and his word to the side. Gradually growing accustomed to sin is the most popular road to hell."

"Don't get off track," said Nastia. "We are talking about the nature of homosexual sin. Just admit it; homosexuality is worse than my sin. Why would God single out homosexuality as detestable in the Old Testament Law of Moses and burn Sodom and Gomorrah because of it if homosexuality is equal to other sins? Do not deny the truth! There is something extremely evil about homosexuality that makes it different than other sexual sin."

Jianyu growled and responded, "Homosexuality is a smothering spiritual condition that clings to the desires of identity. It is an evil sin, but all sin is evil. Jesus the Messiah treated sinners with compassion rather than condemnation. So should you. When you look down on homosexuals and see them as inferior, you are preaching a gospel contrary to the gospel of Christ."

Nastia shook her head and shut her eyes. She faced the dark window and said, "I'm not even going to respond to that."

The angels weren't beside her anymore. The air was still and lonely.

Ding, ding. A rusty bullet ball bounced on the scratched steel table and unraveled into a slithering wire. Nastia cringed in agony as the wire penetrated beneath her fingernail, tunneling up her arm.

"No! No! Not again! I thought I was done with the terrible wires of pride!" Nastia hated the pain and hit the seat three times. Immediately, she remembered herself and glanced around. Two people from a table across the room stared at her.

How was she supposed to know what other people saw, and what they didn't? Where had the angels gone? Frustrated, Nastia chucked her trash into the bin and left the restaurant.

NASTIA STOOD ALONE and separate in the center of the hotel room, wearing a risqué gown as she waited for Anton. She wanted to see his adoring face.

The wooden door opened. "Hey, babe. Will my Galaxy Girl accept my gay brother?" He noticed her breathtaking beauty.

Nastia giggled with her white-flame smile, the smile she knew had made Anton like her the moment he saw it. "Of course!

Whoever my Star Boy loves, I love." She walked close to him and he touched her Arizona sunset red hair. She didn't like his silence.

"Oh Anton! I hate it when anything comes between us. I love gay people. I really do. But I love you more than anyone. Please tell me there is nothing between us." They embraced as Nastia eagerly waited for his reply, holding her breath.

"I've been thinking about that all evening. We're very different from each other, you know. Sometimes I wonder if I'll ever figure you out."

"But that's okay. Every couple has differences."

"You're right. We can work it out. I guess I just realized today how much I don't know you," he said.

She sighed, pressing her head on his chest, feeling his heartbeat. "How can there be such a distance between us when you are holding me so close? It doesn't make any sense."

"There is always going to be a distance between people who don't know each other that well. This really isn't a surprise when you think about it."

"Then how do we remove the distance, Anton?" she asked with an ache in her voice.

"We have to date each other, not just sleep in the same bed. Any couple grows apart when they stop trying to get to know each other. We need to spend more time together."

"That's what I want more than anything! You are the most important person in my life."

"Don't worry, Nastia. We'll have lots of time together very soon. We're going to Hawaii this weekend." He grinned.

"Yes! I can't wait! Oh, my grace, Hawaii with you? That sounds like the most romantic experience in the world."

They kissed.

Some distance diminished between the lovers. They had one thing on their minds — each other. Anton couldn't take his eyes off her as they entered the bathroom. Nastia was afraid of seeing the mirror and pressed her thoughts to think of Anton only.

Anton started the faucet. Water rushed. As Nastia reached for her toothbrush the clear water changed to inky silver — and soon the entire sink filled with silver liquid. Nastia turned off the water.

"Why'd you do that?" Anton asked.

Nastia grinned. "Oh, no reason. The bowl is full enough, and I like the quiet."

He chuckled. "Okay."

Nastia glanced at the bowl, gravely. *Has the silver dragon returned?* She hoped not. She hated the silver dragon.

The still pool gradually separated into clear water and condensed gray. The gray became a twitching silver snake.

Why is Lunosh taking on the form of a snake so much lately?

Nastia diverted her eyes to the mirror and bit her lip. The wire beneath the skin of her arm nearly touched her shoulder. It was so high on her arm! And the bruises clung to the wire's edge. Nastia's face was sickly again as the six metal ants around her collarbone writhed. They had collected orange bruises of their own. *So, this is my sin?* she thought.

Anton dipped his toothbrush into the clear water, and the snake licked the bristles with its tongue. He put toothpaste on and started brushing.

"Don't —" Nastia began but caught herself.

"Do what?" Anton stopped brushing.

"Nothing."

They laughed about talking with toothpaste in their mouths, forcing Anton to spit in the bowl. Nastia liked how the snake bathed in the dirty water. *Take that, Lunosh!* she thought. *My man spit on you!*

"You're amazing," Anton said after his laughter subsided.

"Thank you."

The silver snake glided around the sink rim. Nastia waited for Anton to finish flossing.

"Aren't you going to floss?" he asked.

"I'll wait and use your floss thread after you."

He chuckled. "That's kind of weird. Why?"

"Because it will help me grow closer to my distant star."

"Okay. Whatever."

Nastia held the string of floss before her eyes. "You know, floss is like rules. They help us to clean our teeth, but it's stupid when we let them command us."

"Exactly. Rules and standards are just things created by imperfect people." Anton started laughing and shook his head slightly.

"What?" Nastia smiled as she flossed.

"Oh, I just remembered something that Julias used to say." His eyes brightened as he told the story. "I don't know where he got it, but when Julias would floss, he would intentionally make his face go wildly blank and then he would say in a weird voice, 'Flossy! Flossy!'"

She chuckled but only to please Anton. She didn't want to hear about gay Julias.

The snake slithered up the faucet spout and disappeared from sight as the lovers continued to joke with each other.

⸻ ◆ ⸻

NASTIA WENT TO drink something from a clear glass in the kitchen. *Why are all the beverages laced with inky silver — the water, the orange juice, the tea, everything?* She sipped a little water. Once she turned around, she saw Aini standing on the counter.

"Aini."

"Yes?"

"Why is there silver stuff in all the drinks? What the heck is going on? This didn't happen before."

The red bird blinked, flashing over her tiny eyes. "You have been judgmental today. The silver liquid is your sinful condescension of others — your superior attitude. It is called *hypocrites brew.* As you continue to judge others and consider yourself better, everything you

154

drink will contain hypocrites brew. Everything you drink will taste bitter. Just as the Nile turned red with blood when Pharaoh refused to free the Israelites, all the liquid you wish to drink will gradually fill with the bitterness of your hypocrisy."

"What! Now you're taking away the taste of beverages from me? What about the sweet Coke I like to drink at lunch every now and then? Will the taste of purified water always be bitter now?"

"Yes."

She threw her hands to the side. "Then how the heck do I stop it?"

"Repent," Aini replied simply.

Nastia sighed, scolding herself for asking the question.

"Nastia," Anton called from the bedroom.

"I'm coming." She turned to the bird. "I'd love to stay and chat, but I'm in love with my man. Bye." The red bird followed as she approached the bedroom. She stopped at the doorway. Anton lounged on the bed, gazing up into Nastia's eyes with obvious intentions.

"Don't lust," the blue tiger said, standing nobly behind her.

Nastia was a little intimidated by Jianyu, but she stared back at Anton. "Me lust after him?" she scoffed. "No, he is the one admiring my body." But she liked it. She wanted him to lust after her body because it made her feel powerful and significant. This was a special kind of love from Anton — the most thrilling.

As he looked at her, in such a way, one of Anton's eyes began to fill with darkness. "What is that?" Nastia asked the angels.

"Just watch," Jianyu replied.

The eye grew to a deformed size, disgusting Nastia. Once he blinked, a cockroach rolled out of his eyelid and landed on his bare chest, tapping its antennae as it slowly crept over his skin. She lusted in her heart and the roach scuttled across the sheets of the bed, over the carpet floor, and up Nastia's leg until it reached her waist, where it burrowed savagely.

Nastia did her very best to ignore the pain as she went to lay with him.

WHY DID SLEEP abandon Nastia when she wanted it the most? Why did darkness tear her heart? Nastia hated this night for she could not join Anton by sleeping. She was weary and tired but thoroughly unable to sleep.

She thought she heard the glass door of the balcony slide open. Was it the angels calling her? She climbed out of the bed, threw on her robe, and strode out to the balcony, wrapping her arms together as a defense against the cold. She slid the door closed and stood in the dim glow of the city lights. Wind swirled.

"I can't sleep," Nastia told the dark outline of a small bird and a large tiger resting on the leather couch. They moved and she could feel their eyes.

"You're not the only one in the world who struggles with insomnia," said Aini.

"But I want to sleep. If I can't sleep, then distance will grow between Anton and me. I can't stand that!"

"Maybe this distance you feel has a purpose," said Jianyu, leaping off the couch to make room for Nastia. "Maybe this distance between you and Anton will make it easier for you to reform your ways and turn back to the satisfying companionship of Jesus the Messiah."

"Easier? It's not easy at all!" She crawled onto the couch and wrapped herself in the blanket as tightly as she could. "Can you make it warmer for me so that I can rest? I'm not lying beside Anton right now."

"Yes. We can," said Aini, touching the blanket with a flutter of her wings. The blanket warmed and the stark cold vanished, allowing Nastia to sleep.

19

DOES GOD TAKE THE PLANE?

"THANK YOU FOR flying with us," the flight attendant said in a genteel voice. Her small dragon pin writhed and stretched, flashing a blink at Nastia. She ignored it and boarded the plane.

Nastia honored a few leather chairs in the aisle by touching them with her graceful fingers. Her pretty periwinkle blouse had two slits in the sleeves, exposing her shoulders. She identified the number of her row and slid into the seat. She turned casually and noticed the man in the opposite aisle, gaping at her. She winked her white-flame grin and turned back to the window. She giggled with calm pleasure inside and then felt sadness pressing on her heart again.

"I have to take this call. Go ahead, and get on the plane. I'll be there in a minute." Nastia remembered what Anton had said just before she boarded. She was glad for the break. It gave her a chance to gain composure over herself and think clearly about the trip. She felt that this trip to Hawaii would be a decisive point in their relationship.

The night before, Thursday night, Nastia had asked, "Anton, did you ever live with another girl before me?"

"Yeah. I had a few girlfriends in college."

"What was the longest you have ever lived with a girl?"

"I slept regularly with one girlfriend for about seven months."

Nastia had gasped when she heard. She was jealous. She wished she had been Anton's first girlfriend. She had been with Anton for only three weeks, and he had lived with another girl for seven months? She hated the idea! Ever since that conversation, Nastia felt that Anton was slipping away from her. She wondered if she even knew him. Yeah, she was living with him, but she didn't know him nearly as well as she wanted to. She realized that they were strongly attached, but they had not constructed a secure relationship yet. She feared if this trip didn't go well, Anton would tell her sensibly, "Nastia, even though I love you, I think it's time for both of us to move on with our separate lives."

No! She dreaded the thought. *I can't let him slip away from me!* She remembered the lesson she learned in high school with the boy she pursued. Because she had been obsessed with him, he wanted nothing to do with her. Nastia was determined not to let that happen now with Anton. Anton was so much better than any other man she had ever met.

Nastia realized she was getting very close to becoming obsessed with him. *Am I obsessed?* she wondered, painful panic growing in her feelings. Maybe she was. She sighed with despair. She knew how obsessions ruined relationships. She knew the horrible hurt that always came with desperate desire for someone.

"Hey, baby," Anton grinned, calming Nastia as he slid into the seat beside her and placed his briefcase on the floor. He looked curiously into her sad eyes. "What's wrong?"

"Nothing," she lied with a smile. "I'm just tired."

He put his arm around her and kissed her. "Thank you for coming with me. This is going to be an amazing trip!"

She smiled, her heart melting.

As the plane ascended into the air and Washington D.C. diminished far below, Nastia thought, *I am obsessed with him.* She felt a form of depression growing in her. She leaned her head back and closed her eyes. She decided that she would fight the obsession, but she had to make sure she didn't go too far and act as if she didn't care at all. *True love is the height reached between the two dark valleys of obsession and apathy,* Nastia thought. She had to find and apply the proper balance.

The red bird flew down the aisle and landed on Nastia's knee. "Good morning, Tia."

Nastia appreciated the company. "Hello, Aini."

"Why are you sad?"

"I think I'm obsessed with Anton, and it's painful."

"Obsessions hurt."

"What am I supposed to do? How do I deal with all this pain? I can't look sad to Anton. He has already noticed, but I can't tell him. But at the same time, I can't stop being sad."

"God loves you," the red bird counseled her. "You are safe in his hands. Return to him, Nastia. Turn back to God and he will comfort you. Remember how he died for you? He bore the weight and pain of *your* sins, Tia! He gave his divine life for *you.* He loves you more than anyone ever has or ever will."

Nastia tried to realize what this meant. She missed God and dearly wanted to talk with him again, but she knew she needed to stop living with Anton in order to get back to God.

"But I can't repent, Aini! I can't! I'm already on the plane. It's literally impossible now. I can't just walk away and leave him. I have to be his lover for this trip to Hawaii because he's paying for my living. Living with him is my only option for this weekend."

"I understand. I know it's difficult, but you can talk to God now. You don't have to wait. He has provided the way to break through the barrier between you and God. He has given you the strength. Break through the barrier and pray."

Nastia wanted to pray.

Anton lifted the armrest between them and slowly pulled her close to him. "Hey, Nastia?" he said cheerfully.

"Yes, Anton?"

"Are you asleep?"

She smiled. "Yes, I'm far away in dreamland."

"I have a pillow for you."

"Where is this pillow?"

"Right here. It's my shoulder. I've been working out to make it especially big for you."

They laughed and Nastia began sleeping. The morning was very early.

◆

THE PLANE SLOWLY rumbled as Nastia opened her eyes and looked at Anton.

"Good morning," he said. "You were asleep for a long time."

"Sorry. I was really tired."

Anton continued working on his laptop as Nastia gazed out of the small window. She felt the presence of God as certain as the light on the bright white clouds. She saw the land far below — mountains and greenery.

Wow, she prayed. Lord Jesus, what an amazing creation you have made. I don't know why, but you feel close right now. I haven't prayed much. Oh, God, I miss you! Please help me with this confusing situation with Anton. I don't know what to think anymore. Am I being a ridiculous fool? Do I even know him at all? Oh, God, please forgive me of my sins and help me to leave them.

She felt peaceful and secure as if God had everything under control and she didn't need to worry at all. God felt real and life felt confusing.

"How is your work going, Anton?" she asked.

"Oh, it's coming." He exhaled and saw something sparkle in her eye. "But I could use a break." He put down the computer. "Is anything on your mind?"

"Yeah, Christian stuff."

"Please, enlighten me."

"Okay." She tilted her head to the side. "I was just thinking about the reality of God compared to this life. God is so much more real than anything else in all the world."

"More real? What do you mean?"

"I mean that God is greater than all of time and every daily thing we experience. Even you, even people who I get to know seem less real compared to the realization of God's presence."

"Huh, I don't know if that makes any sense. I don't think anything can be more or less real. Something is either real or not. There is no in between."

"It was just a thought." She stared at him. "Can I touch your face?"

He chuckled. "Sure."

She pressed her fingers lightly on his cheeks, touched his nose, and poked the masculine dimples that appeared with his smile. She even touched his white teeth.

"What are you doing?" He laughed.

"Checking you out," she said calmly.

"Why? Are you unsure whether I'm real or not?"

"I know you're real, I just don't experience your reality to its fullest. You really do have a nice face, Anton — your manly cheekbones, your mountain blue eyes, and your hair." She brushed his short bangs, and he winced humorously. "You could do a lot more with your golden-brown hair if you grew it out."

"I thought it was dark brown?"

"No. It looks almost blond with the light shining on it."

He smiled.

"And your body." She squeezed his bicep with both hands. "You are six-foot-three with nice, plump muscles but you're still slim and fit." She removed her hands. "You're just — perfect."

She realized her obsession was obvious. *Oh crap! Now I've lost him.* Her heartbeat quickened in panic.

He didn't seem to notice. "Perfect? I wouldn't say that. You saw me looking at porn on Sunday. A perfect guy wouldn't do that, would he?"

She started to feel as if he were in debt to her again. "You're still human."

———————◆———————

AFTER FLYING OVER endless miles of nothing but ocean, Nastia finally saw the Hawaiian Islands below. She felt excited to be so far from the continents. *Please take care of us, Lord*, she prayed.

Inside the Honolulu airport, Nastia and Anton stopped by a shop, where they purchased dark chocolates, roasted macadamia nuts, and shortbread cookies. As they exited through the automatic doors, the blue tiger approached.

"Yes, Jianyu?"

"I have something to tell you."

"What is it?" Nastia prompted impatiently.

"Here in Hawaii, you will see much more of the truth about you and Anton. You will encounter strong temptation and a symbol of your own faith."

The tiger's words lingered in Nastia's mind, but she didn't try to wrap her mind around them yet. She was too distracted by the warm Hawaiian breeze welcoming her to paradise.

20

A PINCH OF PARADISE

SUNLIGHT FLOODED EVERYWHERE, causing Nastia to squint.

"It's bright, huh?" said Anton, adjusting his black sunglasses. Nastia did so as well, covering her eyes with large brown sunglasses. She looked around at the dry beige hill beneath a cloudless sky and then the overwhelming sight of the vast ocean. Suddenly, she felt a pang of vulnerability as she watched the battling white caps.

"Oh, my gosh, Anton! It's gorgeous!" She hopped with giddy excitement and touched his muscular arm.

The good-natured wide grin took over his face as he looked at her. "Yes, it is. The rest of the island is even more beautiful, they tell me."

"I'm just taking it in one piece at a time." The wind tugged at her red bangs, and she brushed them back. "Anton, we are actually here! In Oahu, Hawaii! I didn't let myself believe we would actually come until now."

"You can believe it. We are here together, and it's real."

She giggled, and they kissed.

They found a plush silvery rental car and began driving toward Honolulu.

Suddenly, the red bird appeared on the dashboard in front of Nastia. "Welcome to Hawaii, Tia."

"Thank you," she replied, enjoying the tropical scenery. "Don't you have more to say?"

"Yes, I do. You talked about a beautiful truth on the plane."

"Yes," she smiled. "God felt close again today. It was wonderful!"

"Do you think Anton understood?"

"Maybe. He's a good man."

"Tia, you know you are using God's name in vain every moment you continue living with Anton, right?"

She gasped. "Oh no, I never use God's name in vain!"

"Yes, you do, Tia. When you call yourself a Christian and live a life that does not reflect the righteousness of God, you are using his name in vain."

"You mean I am using his name in vain right now?" Her smile faded.

"Yes. That's why it really doesn't matter if you talk about a beautiful truth like God's superior reality when you live in sin. It would be better for you to communicate guilt than to pretend everything is okay. Every moment you live as a hypocrite, you throw mud at the beauty of Jesus."

Aini fluttered through the glass and out of the car.

"What are you thinking about, babe?" Anton asked cheerfully.

"Oh, uh," Nastia tried not to look at his endearing eyes. "Hawaii is beautiful, isn't it?" She forced a smile.

"Wrong."

"What?"

"That's not what you were thinking. Come on. Tell me. What has been bothering you?"

"Christian stuff."

"You can't tell me what kind of Christian stuff?"

"It's kind of hard to explain. Ask me again after the banquet tonight. Maybe I'll have all my thoughts put together by then."

"Okay. I'll let you go this time," he teased.

"What kind of people will be at this dinner, anyway?"

164

"All kinds. It's a really big deal. A lot of major investors from around the world will be there tonight. I'm here to represent my company."

"Wow. That must be a big responsibility. Your boss really trusts you, doesn't he?"

"Yeah, he does. It's crazy."

"All around the world, huh?"

"Yeah," he grinned. "Hey, they might invest just because you're with me."

She released a soft, enchanting laugh, as if she were humming a magical song. "What makes you say that?"

"Because you're so beautiful! You really are, Nastia. Sometimes I can't believe how gorgeous you are."

"You're sweet." Nastia didn't feel beautiful. She wished she could see her own physical beauty again — the beauty everyone else could see. The screen on her computer wasn't the same.

"The hotel is right on Waikiki beach," said Anton, following the signs through downtown Honolulu. Multiple people, adorned in colorful summer clothes, strode on the sidewalks past glimmering shops beneath billowing palm trees.

"Here we are," Anton pulled in front of a resort made of two tall white towers that stood out among the many other hotels.

"We're staying here?" A thrill swept through Nastia. "Isn't this one of the most famous hotels in Hawaii? I've seen it in so many pictures."

"Yeah, it's pretty famous." He grinned as a young man dressed in sharp white approached their vehicle. "Are you ready to go in? The valet guy will take care of the car."

The chills of a dream coming true pulsed through Nastia's veins. "Yes, I'm ready, Star Boy."

Love overcame Anton's eyes, and Nastia felt truly valued.

They walked up the steps together and into the three-story lobby, marble glistening beneath the huge golden chandelier. As Anton checked in, Nastia observed the enormous photograph of a crashing blue wave covering the entire wall behind the attendant. The unfamiliar vulnerability rippled through her again. She was very glad to stand right beside Anton.

Their room was on the seventh floor. They entered and Anton placed the two suitcases to the side. "Anton, look at the view!" Nastia ran for the white curtains, pulled open the glass door, and gazed out at the endless ocean. "Oh, my grace, the sky is so blue!" She looked down, leaning on the railing. "And Waikiki beach is directly below us." Anton came over and embraced her, softly rubbing her arm.

"There are a lot of people," he observed. "We are looking at one of the most renowned beaches in the world." He glanced at his watch. "It's only four o'clock. Would you like to grab some food and then walk on the beach? The opening luau dinner isn't until seven."

"Yes please. That would be marvelous."

Wearing short pink shorts and a thin white shirt, Nastia wrapped her arm around Anton's, who wore orange-splashed swim trunks and a blue striped tank top, their sunglasses back on. They treaded the sidewalk without a care as the afternoon lengthened the shadows.

"Hey, there's a sushi place. Are you up for raw fish?" he asked with a laugh.

"Sure. Why not?"

"There's a table for two. How about you save it for us while I get the food?"

"Perfect. I'd like to sit under the sun."

Alone for the first time all day, Nastia waited at the small table and looked around. Two stories of restaurants across the patio were already filling up. A group of five young and pretty women sat in a booth laughing while a group of burly guys entered the same restaurant. Many different people came and went, contentedly enjoying paradise.

After they enjoyed a California roll topped with mango and spicy sauce, Anton and Nastia began strolling down the beach, holding hands. The sound of the waves and the beauty of the sunset enchanted Nastia like nothing else she had experienced before, and she was living it with her lover — her good man. *I wish life could always be like this*, she thought, *simply perfect.*

"We should probably go in and get ready for dinner," Anton whispered in her ear as they hugged on the end of the walkway-pier, watching the sailboats.

"Okay," she whispered back, her eyes closed in absolute enjoyment.

After they got back to the hotel room and Nastia was adjusting a necklace, her back toward the large mirror, she thought, Maybe life can always be like this. Maybe I can live with Anton for the rest of my life. Oh, that would be paradise! Not Hawaii, not praying and reading my Bible, but living as lovers with Anton. Yes, yes. This is it. Anton is the one!

She changed to prayer as she looked out the window with enflamed passion in her eyes, O God, living with him like this is all I've ever wanted. Please, please, please make this last forever!

Ignoring the blue tiger sitting on the balcony in noble form, Nastia gazed up at the first twilight star. *He is my everything.*

21

A NIGHT TOO REAL

ABOVE THE BEACH and beneath the stars, Anton and Nastia sat together on the second-floor deck, watching the luau performance. Drums played dramatically as three shirtless men danced wildly around a slender woman in white, who calmly smiled and rotated her hips with elegant skill. Suddenly the three men fell to the ground, bowing to her, and the dance ended with a final beat of the drums.

Applause rose and fell from the many circular tables filled with finely dressed investors from around the world. A tall middle-aged man with graying hair strode onto the cleared stage. His face was handsome, experienced, and peacefully enigmatic. Nastia thought that many women must have fallen for him over the years. He spoke in an admiration-inspiring voice that made you want to listen carefully.

"Thank you for your gracious approval. Performances like these show us what we truly love about the islands and why we love it so much. Please enjoy the rest of the evening. I look forward to seeing all of you in our sessions tomorrow."

The following applause was more eagerly honoring than gracious as the man stepped off the stage and back to his table.

Nastia turned to see Anton in his sharp business mood. She smiled for him, her hair cascading onto her shoulders in sparkling red curls.

"Oh, grieve me, that dance was *thrilling*," said the only other person at their table. She was middle-aged with glossy short hair and a flat chin. "Thank Elysium for Luaus. My name is Enyo Barlas. What are your names?"

"I'm Anton Shepherd, and this is my girlfriend, Nastia Sobieski."

"Nice to meet you," said Nastia politely.

"Very nice to meet both of you." Enyo leaned back into her seat as her face fell into boredom.

The servers set the food before them and poured more pineapple juice.

"This is *delectable*," Enyo blurted out, dropping the fork so she could press her collarbone and close her eyes.

"Yeah, it is delicious," Anton agreed.

"Where are you both from?" Enyo asked.

"Washington D.C.," he answered. "How about yourself?"

"I live on an island mansion off the coast of Athens." She seemed quite proud of the fact.

"Wow, that's awesome. I've never been to Greece. How is it?" Anton asked.

"Perfectly stunning in the right places. But you have to know where to go." She turned to Nastia. "Speaking of stunning, that is a breathtaking dress you have on, darling!"

"Thank you," Nastia replied simply.

"How long have you two been together?" Enyo swiveled her head back and forth between them, waiting for an answer.

"We met three weeks ago," Anton admitted.

Enyo gasped. "Only three weeks? Did you fall in love the moment you saw each other?"

"Pretty much." He looked at Nastia with a grin. She smiled more vividly.

"How adorable. I love hearing the stories of young couples. Are you living together yet? That's a stupid question! Of course you are now, up here, but back in D.C. do you live together?" Her head swiveled again, but Enyo seemed to want Nastia to answer.

169

"I moved in with him twelve days after our first conversation." She didn't feel proud or ashamed of the fact.

Enyo gasped then giggled oddly. "What passionate lovers you are!"

An older man approached the table and said something to Anton.

"I have to go talk business now." He kissed Nastia. "It was nice meeting you, ma'am."

"Oh, so nice to meet you too," Enyo giggled oddly again.

They watched Anton go over to a group of men in Hawaiian shirts, smiling and shaking hands. Nastia grinned, amused because she knew he was acting.

Enyo scooted her chair in, put her elbows on the table, and looked at Nastia with shockingly large, round eyes.

"Yes?" Nastia leaned back, surprised by the sudden intensity of the acquaintance.

"Dear, I have something very important to tell you — something that will save you a world of unhappiness for the rest of your life. And you *must* listen. Will you?"

"All right," she answered sweetly. "Say it."

"Whatever you do, do *not* live for him. Live for yourself. You don't know how these crazy-love relationships can backfire. I know from far too many years of experience how it makes a woman into a slave." She shuddered. "Live for yourself, not for him."

Nastia remained silent for a moment, not knowing what to say. "Thank you. I'll think about it."

"Do more than that, girl. Live it."

———————◆———————

THE COOL WIND blew as Nastia and Anton arrived at the outdoor pool area. Wearing their swimsuits underneath, they draped their outer clothes on a deck chair and stepped into the glowing hot tub.

"Did you enjoy the luau?" Anton casually wrapped his arm around Nastia.

"Yeah. It was all right. I like this better, though."

The infinity pool caught both their eyes at the same time. Distant stars reflected in the water before plunging over the edge. Large and healthy foliage rustled behind the hot tub in a ritual dance, flowers bowing and palm trees making sweeping gestures with their branches.

"So, now that we're both alone, don't you have something to tell me?" He flashed his eyebrows.

Nastia felt sad, guilty, and angry at the same time. She hid her emotions and laughed carelessly, "You mean my Christian stuff?"

"Yeah, the part you refused to tell me in the car."

She shrugged and decided to be honest. "I feel that it's wrong for me to live with you. Christians shouldn't do this."

"Do you really feel that way?"

"Yeah." She didn't sound convincing. "But I have other things on my mind that I want to talk to you about."

"Okay. Shoot."

"I am really jealous of that girl you lived with for seven months. And I'm angry at you for only just telling me."

"When did we talk about this?" Anton looked as if he didn't remember.

"Last night." She shook her head, disappointed at his forgetfulness.

"Oh, right. Sorry. Must be all the time change and traveling." He paused. "Do you think I should have told you sooner?"

"Yes, before we started living together."

"You're right. That probably would have been better. What exactly bothers you about it?"

"What bothers me?" She was annoyed that he didn't already know. "Anton, I have put my entire life on the line for you, and I feel like I don't know you at all. I had never slept with a guy before you, and suddenly you tell me that you had lived with a girl for seven months? How do I know our relationship won't end like that? Why are we even dating at all if we really don't know each other? I feel like I'm your mistress away from home. It makes me feel insecure and exposed, like you are using me as a pleasure toy."

Anton pulled his arm away from Nastia's neck, and she was about to rebuke him for it, but he merely scratched his head, spraying a few droplets and put his arm back with a slow exhale. *Is he going to say something? Or is he going to let me suffer?*

"I didn't know you then. At the time, it seemed fine. And I did learn from the experience. I wouldn't be the man you love now if it weren't for that relationship."

Oh, good grace! What does he expect me to do, bow before his ex-girlfriend and thank her for making Anton into such a marvelous man?

"Shame on you, Anton." Her voice quivered slightly but with strength as she glared out at the ocean, watching Anton turn his head toward her from the corner of her eye. "Even now you are trying to justify your life with her. Every word you just said confirmed that you really don't love me. You're hurting me, Anton. I love you more than any other man alive, and this is how you treat me? Why don't we all just sleep with everybody and forget about faithfulness and the value of each other! I was hurting all day because of that relationship you had. Now, my heart is screaming in pain. You have abandoned me."

She felt his gaze remain on her face, but she refused to look back at him. She straightened her back and made sure her pretty eyes displayed her suffering. She slowly pulled his arm from behind her neck, scooted over, and looked straight at him. His masculine face seemed less handsome than before.

Anton shook his head, groaned, and threw his arms out in exasperation. Nastia felt like she had won and he was about to argue, but her competitive mindset faltered when he thought more and said finally, "It was wrong. I never should have lived with her. Okay, I'll admit it; I feel pretty broken whenever I remember my relationship with Alison. All it did was cause me pain. I honestly wish you were the first girl I ever got intimate with. It would have been much more special, you know. I wish I could have had that. But since I didn't, I feel divided." He pressed his face with his palms and continued. "It takes time, Nastia. We are still getting to know each other. We can't give up especially in tough, questioning times like this. Trust me, baby. I am putting everything I am into my relationship with you."

"How can I know for sure?" She hesitated to trust him again even though she desperately wanted to.

He smiled. "Look at this," he gestured to the resort and the ocean. "Hawaii. I had never planned to take a girl with me on my business trips. But then I met you, and now I don't want to go through another day without you."

They quietly soaked in the warm water for a long moment just looking at each other. An older couple shuffled by, the man roared a remark, and the woman sniggered.

Nastia didn't want to resent her boyfriend anymore. She went back to her spot under his arm and said, "All right. I'll trust you."

"You're wonderful, Nastia. Thank you." He bent down and kissed her.

She noticed a light tattoo on his right bicep. Nastia hadn't thought about it much before, but this time she realized she didn't know what it was. "What is your tattoo supposed to be?"

"You don't know?" His eyes flinched.

"No."

"Huh. I thought we had talked about it before. It's a silver dragon."

Nastia froze. Suddenly she remembered her sins. The metal ants around her neck pressed into her collarbone, the roach painfully pulled the skin around her waist, and the wires of pride clenched her left leg and right forearm. A shiver raced up and down her entire body as if the hot tub had never been warm. "Say that again?"

"A silver dragon."

The shiver raced through Nastia's body again, stabbing at the sins. "Oh. When did you get it?"

"I thought for sure I had told you."

"No, you didn't."

"I got it in college. Some other friends were getting tattoos as well. I thought this design was cool."

"Does a silver dragon have any special meaning to you?" She hoped not.

"Funny you should ask." He grinned. "I was just thinking about it. I see the Asian silver dragon as a symbol of strength, independence, and solid identity."

Nastia slid out of his arm and held it in her soft hands. Yes, she could see it now; it was a dragon. The edges had sharp, straight lines and angles like blades. She could see the outline of the face. Were those eyes? Suddenly the tattoo had glowing white eyes and a vile grin. It stretched out on his skin and flicked its tail, as if in victory, and then went back to its original position. Nastia gasped.

"What's wrong? Do you not like it?" Anton wondered.

"Oh, uh, no — I mean that's not what I meant. Yeah, It's cool." She wanted to change the subject. "You make it awesome, though." She pressed her head onto his shoulder, knowing the tattoo was right below her neck. How could she have not seen it before? Anton had a silver dragon on his arm all this time? It was crazy!

She felt a terrible, overpowering need to get much closer to him, closer than she had ever imagined closeness could be. She wanted to be inside every part of his heart and mind. She wanted to know everything about him, every memorable glance from the other women in his life, every hard disappointment he had suffered, every life-founding childhood memory. Everything. She felt like she would die if she couldn't get closer to him. Oh, she had to have that closeness with him. And she wanted it now.

———————◆———————

"YOU CAN HAVE the covers. I'm hot," said Anton, tossing the sheet over himself after they had finished making love for the night.

"Okay." Nastia pulled the covers up to her neck. She was cold, very cold, and she didn't know how it was possible. Maybe she would warm up soon.

Time passed. How long? She couldn't tell. It was too late to know anything. "Anton?" she whispered. He didn't answer but continued breathing steadily. She felt a sting of agony in her heart and squirmed around wanting to scream. Tears grew in her eyes, and she tapped them away with the covers. One tear stayed on her finger. She reached over and touched Anton's face with it. He didn't move. She placed her hand on his chest for a moment and then quickly removed it. He was cold as ice.

Feeling alone, she pulled her legs up and tried to get warm. Why couldn't she sleep? She was so tired but she couldn't sleep. She felt weak and wondered if she was going crazy.

"You are just like your father," said an overly soothing voice. She watched the silver dragon tattoo rise off Anton's arm and float into the air. The pale eyes glowed with a wicked grin.

"No, I'm not," she whispered, knowing others could hear when she spoke to Lunosh.

"So sure, are you, so very sure? No, you are the female version of him. Both of you are going to hell."

"No!"

Lunosh laughed, making the sound of scraping metal.

Nastia covered her ears, but the scraping continued. Suddenly it stopped, and she was alone.

Her heart beat faster and faster. She couldn't rest at all. She shivered and shivered but couldn't stop. She had to soothe herself and get warm. She quickly changed back into her wet bathing suit, threw on a shirt, and tip-toed out of the hotel room.

As she headed down the hallway, forgetting what Lunosh had said, the two lamps beside her flickered. Suddenly a memory flashed through her mind:

———————◆———————

SEVEN-YEAR-OLD Nastia crept into the kitchen and removed a popsicle from the freezer. Mrs. Sobieski entered, her tired red curls hanging over her forehead. She noticed her daughter. The constantly sweet, plump, and pretty face changed to saddened disappointment, and she said, "I just told you that two was enough. Why did you go ahead and disobey me? You are just like your father — you only believe in your way."

———————◆———————

NASTIA LOOKED AROUND the resort hallway. Mrs. Sobieski had not punished her for that one incident many years ago. Nastia thought she had won over her parent's rules at the time, but after she saw the sad look on her mother's face, she felt guilty and apologized for stealing the ice pop. Mrs. Sobieski responded with her extremely sweet and loving smile and gave little Nastia a tender hug.

The same guilt plagued her heart now, but her mother wasn't there to show forgiveness.

A horrible idea filled her mind: if her mother knew that Nastia was living in sin, would she be as hurt as she was after Mr. Sobieski's adulterous affair? Was Nastia as selfish as her dad?

"Yes, you *are*," the silver dragon whispered, suddenly appearing in a cloud of smoke that clung to the walls. His whiskers curled like vines as he glared straight into her eyes. "You are going to hell. Why would anyone love you? Nastia — the Christian girl who shunned God. He will never love you again. Why would he? You are worthless."

She felt like she was swallowing a handful of thorns. Her throat swelled, and she had trouble breathing. She had to get out! She had to get away from Lunosh!

Nastia started running. *Run! Run!* was all she could think. The silver dragon pursued. Dark smoke filled the lamps on the walls once she reached them, the light disappearing like the hope in her heart. *Am I so bad? Am I saved at all?*

She reached the elevator and gasped for breath. *No, Lunosh, you can't get in here! God, what is happening to me?* She didn't feel God's presence. Where was he? Why couldn't she feel his comfort like she had on the plane? If only she were on the plane again!

Red outlines of the dragon appeared on the screen above the door — his wicked grin vicious, ready to devour Nastia's soul. Finally, the elevator reached the first floor. Nastia leapt into the lobby.

Where was the indoor hot tub? The darkness of the room was eerie and unnaturally void of life. Why wasn't the attendant at the front desk? Why were the doors open? Nastia squinted and thought she saw an enormous silver dragon writhing in the doorway. The darkness was maddening.

The faint hint of scraping metal came in with the wind. *No!* It grew louder and louder. Where could she go? Where was the room! Nastia ran down the hall and turned at a sign that read Coral Spa. The scraping was louder than ever. The voice of Lunosh said, "Come now to hell."

More terrified than she had ever been in her life, Nastia raced down the narrow hallway, jerked open the door, and shut it behind her.

The room was calm, steamy, and dimly lit. Vapors listlessly rose from the tile-lined hot tub, softly bubbling. A small cooling pool rested below the Jacuzzi, motionless and serene.

Nastia exhaled with great relief, tears stinging her eyes. She removed her blouse and stepped into the tub. *You are going to hell* repeated in her mind, but much softer now.

She looked up at the mosaic illuminated by the quiet lights hidden above it. The mosaic was a brilliant depiction of a coral reef that stretched from wall to wall and floor to ceiling, forming a half moon around the tub. Brightly colored fish swam past the pink brain coral and green seaweed in front of the ocean blue background. "Wow, what a hotel." The magnificent beauty dazzled Nastia.

She thought she heard a peaceful wave brush the green seaweed. Did it move? Nastia gasped as the mosaic came to life right before her eyes. The fish wiggled out of sight except for a single red one, who bounced over the coral and smiled. "Hello, Tia."

"Aini? Oh, Aini, please help me! I just had the most horrible experience of my life! And I'm not exaggerating."

"What happened?" The red fish's tiny bead eyes became sorrowful with compassion.

"Lunosh said I'm going to hell." Two tears slid down her cheeks.

The mosaic made a deep sound of rumbling water as a hammerhead shark swam into view, filling a great deal of the large artwork. "Do not listen to him," it said in a deep voice. "Lunosh constantly tells lies. He wants you to think God hates you, but he is wrong. God's love never ends. No matter what you do, you will never be beyond his love. Jesus has paid the price for all sin."

"Oh, Jianyu!" Nastia cried. "I have never doubted my salvation as much as tonight. In high school, I asked the questions every teenage Christian does. But tonight, oh my goodness, tonight was worse than anything! I felt like I was going to hell. I have never felt like that so strongly before. Please, *please* help me."

The red fish leapt out of the mosaic, changed into a red bird, and landed on the flat edge of the tub. Jianyu followed, causing a splash in the tiles as he transformed into a blue tiger — wild and powerful.

"Do not be anxious about anything," Jianyu began in a calm tone, "but in everything, by prayer and petition, with thanksgiving, present your requests to God. And the peace of God, which transcends all understanding, will guard your hearts and your minds in Christ Jesus."

Nastia recognized the passage from Philippians 4:6-7.

"Yes," said Aini as she hopped onto Nastia's shoulder. "Listen and believe these words. They are true. 'Do not be anxious about anything.' Not *anything* Tia, not even the fear of hell. Trust in God. Pray and tell him how you are afraid."

"I already prayed today," she tried to reason, but the strong gaze of the blue tiger changed her mind. "Father God, please help me. Forgive me for my lack of faith and all my sins. May I live in your truth one day. Just help me through tonight, Lord. Have mercy on me." She looked back at the Angels. "Okay, I prayed. I still feel horrible. What am I supposed to do?" She splashed some of the hot tub water onto her face and started to sob. "Oh, God, save me!"

Aini stroked the back of Nastia's neck with her velvety wing. "Believe and love Jesus, Tia. He will never leave you. Do not doubt his ability to forgive, but trust that he will work through your life. Everyone is broken in some way. If you did not realize this then how could you ever depend on Christ? You do realize the brokenness of your life, don't you?"

"Yes, definitely, my life is broken. I feel like I'm going mad. I feel like I'm barely hanging on."

Aini continued gliding her feathers up and down Nastia's neck. "Do you believe in Jesus? Do you love him?"

"Yes. I believe Jesus is the son of God. I believe his death paid for my sins. But I know that I need to love him much, much more."

"Then you *are* saved!"

"It doesn't make sense. Why doesn't my life match up with my faith? How can I be a Christian and have such an overwhelming need to be close to Anton? I know Jesus is the answer; I just don't know how to apply his truth when I'm so confused by my need for Anton. I don't know what to think."

Aini flew off her shoulder.

Nastia felt tired. She got out of the hot tub and removed a white bathrobe from the tile shelves in the wall. "Do you think I can sleep down here?" She saw the lounge chair that didn't look too uncomfortable.

"Yes," said Jianyu. "Sleep will find you here, away from Anton."

"Thank you."

"We will leave you with one more quote from God's holy word, Psalm 130 verse 7."

"Okay."

" 'O Israel, put your hope in the LORD, for with the LORD is unfailing love and with him is full redemption.' "

"Full redemption, Tia." Aini flew over to Jianyu, who lay down by Nastia's feet. "Put your hope in Jesus. Rest in his peace."

Nastia closed her eyes as she breathed the clean, humid air and murmured, "Redemption?"

22

PIÑA COLADA

A CHILL RACED over Nastia, then she was warm again. She turned in her sleep and felt like she had a fever as another chill flooded through her body, and she shivered. Slowly, she opened her eyes and saw the red bird flapping before her.

"What's wrong?" She noticed where she was sleeping and looked around at the barren pool and Jacuzzi room. "What time is it?" she demanded, her voice panicking. The blue tiger gestured to the clock on the wall.

"It's 5:30. Oh my grace, Anton will be waking soon!" She heaved the towels she had been using as blankets to the side, gathered her things, and headed for the resort room.

She ignored the stare from the attendant at the front desk, pleased that no one else saw her. Once the elevator reached their floor, she sped down the hallway to the room door and inserted her key card.

The hotel room was dark and quiet. Nastia had to force herself not to make a sound. She saw Anton sleeping peacefully just as he had when she left. *Good*, she thought to herself, exhaling, *he hasn't noticed*. She felt tired and dizzy, but she didn't want to lie back beside Anton. She decided to take a shower.

Nastia could hear Anton moving around the room as she dried her hair and applied makeup. She had to guess what would look good. She hadn't brought her laptop into the bathroom this time because she thought Anton would get suspicious. The mirror showed the reflection of her soul, which Nastia decided was hideous. She looked like a starving old maid who hadn't bathed in weeks.

"Good morning," Anton said with a smile as Nastia exited the bathroom. He was rushing to fasten his tie. "Are you about ready to go down to breakfast?"

"Yes. What time do you have to leave for all your meetings?" She dreaded the thought of spending the whole day without him.

He shook his wrist and looked down at the shimmering silver watch. "About thirty minutes."

Her heart sank. "Oh. Then we'd better go down now. I think they just opened at 6."

"Good idea." Anton appeared lighthearted and purposeful. Somehow, this made Nastia feel even worse. *Why do I feel so distant from him?*

After they gathered their food at the buffet bar, Anton pointed at a table by the window. As they sat down, Nastia observed the waves crashing on the beach just below.

"Are you okay?" Anton asked with concern in his undecided-blue eyes.

Nastia knew she must look depressed for she certainly felt it. "I wish we could spend the day together."

His masculine face became deeply kind. "Don't worry. Today is the only full day I have to work. Tomorrow I only have one session in the afternoon. Maybe we can go visit Pearl Harbor in the morning. I'll be back for dinner tonight, and we can do something together afterwards. I promise. All right?"

She shrugged. "Okay."

"But you don't have to wait for me to have fun. Go outside and do something you would enjoy. There are some shops not too far from here that you could look through."

"Nothing would be fun alone." She knew she sounded hopeless. *Maybe I should encourage him or something.* She didn't feel like trying.

"This is Hawaii, Nastia — paradise! I know you will meet some people. You're not a shy woman." He grinned, and she smiled weakly in return.

He quickly finished his food, grabbed his briefcase, and stood. "Okay. Time for me to go." Nastia walked with him out of the dining room, into the enormous marble lobby, and down to the rotating doors. They stopped at the top of the stairs where cars pulled up and drove off, escorting ambitious professionals.

Anton placed his hand on her shoulder. "I hate to leave you alone. I really do. But it's just one day. We can do this." He kissed her. "Bye! I'll text you when I'm on my way back."

She waved.

Nastia stood alone at the top of the stairs for a long moment after Anton had disappeared from sight. Various people loaded and unloaded their baggage. A well-dressed elderly couple knitted their brows at her as if she was an odd plant, but she didn't care. "What am I supposed to do, God?" she muttered softly and headed back inside.

More sunlight filled the breakfast dining room. Clean white tablecloths framed small bouquets of pink-and-orange flowers.

Nastia mixed a cup of coffee and sat back down at the same table. She watched the watery horizon, her thoughts dissipating. All she wanted to do was go back to bed and sleep, but she knew she couldn't — not because of the coffee but because she was not peaceful inside. She would only toss and turn.

A lone surfer in red shorts maneuvered his board onto a distant wave. He glided faster and faster, standing to his feet and balancing. But soon he was back on his stomach, paddling with his hands. Nastia thought it would be cool to meet a surfer in Hawaii.

She turned from the window and gasped. The blue tiger stood before her, strong and authoritative, his yellow cat eyes pierced by a controlled gleam. "What is it, Jianyu?" She was intimidated by his presence.

"Watch yourself today, Nastia Sobieski. Be careful of idleness. As it says in Proverbs 1:32, 'The waywardness of the simple will kill them, and the complacency of fools will destroy them.' "

"Okay." She nodded, but the blue tiger didn't move. She felt awkward and glanced around the room to see a red bird flying just beneath the ceiling. "Why did you tell me and not Aini?" she asked, but Jianyu had disappeared. She looked back up at the ceiling only to find a circling fan. "Hmm…" Nastia didn't feel comfortable anymore and decided to try taking a nap after all.

Even though the hotel room was the perfect temperature, the curtains were drawn and the soft pillows were thoroughly cozy, Nastia couldn't sleep. After trying for fifteen minutes, she sighed, bounced herself onto her knees, and clicked on the TV. She scanned channels and watched something about a glamorous celebrity for a little, but quickly got bored. She sauntered over to the window and recalled Anton's words: *Go outside and do something you would enjoy. This is Hawaii, Nastia — paradise!*

"Okay then," she said. "I will!"

———◆———

NASTIA ADJUSTED HER jeweled sunglasses as her lime-green blouse rippled in the Pacific wind. She wore especially short jean shorts as she strode up the sidewalk, carelessly swinging her flip-flops around. Two small children hurried for the sand, passing her. "Slow down!" the mother called from behind, giving a quick smile to Nastia as she stepped quickly to rejoin her children.

Once she got to the sand, Nastia observed the bright colors all around her, and the countless people on Waikiki beach. Just in front of her, a tall man with an impressive long torso chatted with a girl in a bikini as he stood by a display of several stacked surfboards. Nastia was thrilled to see him at first, the edge of her heart turning over, but

184

once she looked closer at his sunglasses, she determined that his face wasn't very good-looking and walked on.

"This is as good as any." She found a spot on the warm beach in front of the green park, positioned her branded hotel towel, and sat on it before it blew away. The waves crashed and lingered. She saw a handful of swimmers far out from the shore.

Nastia took a swig from her water bottle and grimaced, remembering all too clearly what Aini had said the previous weekend: Everything you drink will taste bitter. Just as the Nile turned red with blood when Pharaoh refused to free the Israelites, all the liquid you wish to drink will gradually fill with the bitter darkness of your hypocrisy.

"So, I'm an Egyptian now? Is that it?" She chuckled, and the wind blew her oh-so-pretty hair over her face.

Even though she knew she would be thirsty later, she didn't care to drink anymore of her gray water and poured it onto the sand. The freshly moist sand started to move and transformed into a three-foot long silver dragon. It writhed slowly and began to speak in a smooth, icy voice. "Why are you alone, Nastia? You know that you could never enjoy life by yourself."

"Oh, I know," she replied carelessly. "But Anton is at work and my angels are — uh — busy or something. So, what am I supposed to do?"

"Oh no!" The silver dragon imitated compassion. "Even your beloved angels have abandoned you? You really are alone now. Poor, Nastia."

"They haven't abandoned me exactly." She shrugged. "I never really know when they come or go."

"So, they just left you hanging and yearning?" The dragon hissed.

Nastia frowned as she watched a group playing volleyball to her right. A dark-haired young man dove for the ball, and a bikini-clad girl on his team jumped up and down victoriously.

"I think I'll take a dip in the water. It looks so inviting," Nastia decided. She pulled off her shorts and shirt, revealing her dusk-blue bikini, and headed into the waves. The water was warm, and she quickly went all the way under. She hit her foot on a rock and squealed, looking around to see if anyone had noticed. A young blond-haired man in red shorts stared at her from the closest corner of the volleyball court.

"He's beautiful, isn't he?" the silver dragon whispered. "Do you remember Enyo's advice? 'Whatever you do, do not live for him, live for yourself. You don't know how these crazy love relationships can backfire. I know from far too many years of experience how it makes a woman into a slave. Live for yourself and not for him.' "

"I remember *now*." She tried to laugh, but it didn't come out. The blond guy was still staring at her. She turned away and headed for the warm sand and her towel.

"Just imagine what it would be like to enjoy any guy you wished, any and every sexy man you met. Think of how free you would feel. What liberation…"

Nastia noticed how attractive the blond guy's body appeared. He was leaner than Anton, and his muscles were more sharply defined. "He doesn't have an ounce of fat on him. Must have been a scrawny little kid in high school." She smiled.

"But he isn't in high school, is he? Maybe he has just graduated and has a more interesting personality than Anton. What would you do if you were living with him instead?"

Nastia lusted in her heart. The silver dragon blew away.

Some drops of salt water fell from her hair and onto the towel. The wet spot swelled bigger and bigger. Suddenly, a metal roach crept out from under the towel and scrambled onto Nastia's waist. "Oh, crap!" she cried and leapt to her feet, trying to brush off the insect, but it was already beneath her skin. She clapped her hands over her mouth to muffle the scream, but the sound came out her nose. Soon the roach stopped moving, positioned right beside the other one. Nastia now had two roaches of lust inside her waist.

"Crap, crap, crap!" She lay back on the towel and wormed around, trying to lessen the pulsing pain. "I hate it, I hate it!" she breathed rapidly. "God, *why* does this have to happen to me? Why me? I just want to be normal! Please, please make me normal again!"

She lay still for a moment with her eyes closed, listening to the rumbling ebb and flow. She exhaled the last of her enraged frustration.

"Hi, are you all right?"

Nastia opened her eyes and gasped in surprise. The blond guy she had just lusted after was standing above her. He wore a black necklace that was close around his neck with a polished blue stone hanging from it. His keen eyes were exactly the same color as the stone. "Good grace, you scared me!"

"I'm sorry. I just heard you shouting and wondered if you were all right. What are you doing out here all by yourself?"

Darn! Why did he hear me? "Oh, just soaking in the sun." She grinned, and he smiled back. He didn't say anything, and she searched for something to comment on. "I saw you playing volleyball over there. Were you having fun?"

He shrugged and looked away. "Not really. I'm here on vacation, visiting my grandparents. I just jumped in on the game those people were playing because I have nothing else to do. They're strangers to me."

"You can sit down if you want." Nastia patted a vacant section of the towel. "It feels strange for you to stand over me like that."

"All right. Thanks." He sat on the towel, leaning on his elbows with his legs stretched out.

"What's your name?"

"Erlend."

"Sorry. Say that again?"

"Erlend. Like air that you lend. People get confused with my name a lot. It's weird, I know."

"I don't think it's weird, it's just different. Erlend. I think it's a very cool name. I don't know what's wrong with those other people."

He smiled. "What's your name?"

"Nastia. Nastia Sobieski."

"Good to meet you, Nastia. Your name is cool and different also."

She smiled, her captivating white-flame smile, complementing her dominantly sweet face. "Thank you. Pardon me if I'm wrong, but did you just graduate from college?"

He looked at her suspiciously. "Yes, I did. How did you know? Do I look like it somehow?"

"No, it was just a guess. What did you get your degree in?"

"Business." He didn't seem very excited.

"Good major."

They watched a surfer get buried by a large wave. Finally, Nastia said, "I don't care for a superficial conversation right now, and I'm sorry if I seem weird to you. I know we just met, but if you would like to continue talking to me then please tell me some of your deepest secrets, and I will tell you mine. If not, then it was nice meeting you."

Erlend looked at her searchingly, his dirty-blond hair flapping in the wind. "Okay, I'm willing to try this."

"All right. Be my guest."

"I'm a Christian —"

Nastia laughed. "Is that your secret?"

"No, you didn't let me finish. I'm a Christian, and I think I'm addicted to pornography."

"Oh," she wasn't shocked. "Don't worry, it's not uncommon."

"Unfortunately. Your turn."

"Okay. I'm a Christian also, and I'm living in sin with my atheist boyfriend. He is here for work and decided to take me with him. That is why I came to this sunny Waikiki beach by myself. He is working all day today." She knew she would feel exposed and vulnerable if she blurted it out like that. She winced as she waited for his reply.

"Sounds like we're both messed up."

"So, you think it's wrong for me to live with my boyfriend?"

"Yeah. But you do too, don't you? You just said you were 'living in sin' with him."

"I guess so. I'm not always sure. I really love my boyfriend. His name is Anton, and he loves me. That is good, isn't it? Why would God want to take goodness away from me?"

"I think God has something better planned for you," said Erlend. "Living with this Anton guy might seem amazing, and the only way for you now but," — he paused — "you're missing out on something more beautiful."

Nastia sighed and allowed her expressions to sulk. "I don't know if I agree. I honestly don't know what I believe now. What about you? Are you a virgin?"

"No. I lost it one night but never did again, although pornography is almost as bad. It's the same sin just not physical."

"You sound like you're more resolved, and I guess a better Christian than me, Erlend." She smiled for him.

"I don't know. Just saying that shows your humility."

She laughed, trying to lighten the atmosphere. "Me? Humble? I don't know if I could ever be truly humble. I've always been proud in one way or another."

He looked at her for a while. Nastia wondered what was happening behind his piercing stone-blue eyes.

"Are you hungry?" he said almost indifferently. "Would you like to have lunch with me?"

"Sure. Why not?"

They got up, and she put her shirt and shorts back on. He went to retrieve his shirt then led her to an outdoor grill nearby, where they ordered sandwiches at the bar.

"And two pineapple juices," Erlend added to the order.

"That sounds tasty," Nastia said as she noticed the black letters reading *Staff* on the back of Erlend's red tank top.

"Do you think so? Hawaii isn't the same to me without the taste of pineapple juice. My mom would serve it to us all the time when we lived up here."

While they were eating, Nastia reached for her glass of juice and tasted the bitterness in her mouth along with the pineapple. She wrinkled her nose.

"What's wrong?" Erlend's eyes stayed wide open with a look of blank disbelief.

This stuff must be important to him, Nastia thought. "Oh, nothing. Don't mind me. I do that whenever I drink any liquid these days."

"Why?"

"I can't tell you."

He remained troubled. "Can I taste it?"

"If you want."

He tasted the juice and scowled. "Ugh! You're right that's awful. It tastes like someone spilled cold grease into it."

What? He can taste it, too? Aini never told me that.

"I'll get you a new one."

"All right." She didn't really care.

"Hey, dude." He waved at the waiter.

The red bird flew in from the bright sky and landed on the counter.

"Aini, what have you been doing? Lunosh tempted me, and I lusted, and now I have another roach on my waist!"

"You can't depend on us, Tia. You need to put your hope in God and his unfailing love. We are only angels."

"Hmm...I don't think I know how to put my hope in God's love. But anyway, why did Erlend taste the Hypocrite's Brew? I thought I was the only one who noticed these things."

Aini's black-bead eyes wilted. "Hypocrisy affects everyone. They won't see the darkness like you, but everyone can taste it after you have taken a sip."

"How am I supposed to stay hydrated if it tastes so awful?"

Aini simply looked at her.

"Okay. I understand." Nastia leaned on her elbows despairingly, and Aini flew away. Nastia was glad that Erlend couldn't hear or notice when she talked to the angels.

"So, what are you going to do this afternoon?" he asked.

"I don't know. I have no plans," she replied.

"Would you like to go snorkeling with me? There is a reef nearby that my family used to go to. I went there by myself two days ago, but I would love to share it with someone else."

"That sounds wonderful." Nastia brightened. "How would we get there?"

"My grandparents own a motorboat. The dock is just a short walk away. They even have a bin of gear onboard."

"All right. Lead the way, Erlend."

———————◆———————

THE MOTORBOAT BUZZED away as Erlend brought Nastia out into the ocean. She watched the white surf crash behind them while the Pacific wind swept over her face. Soon Erlend stopped the boat and threw the anchor overboard. He opened the blue plastic bin and pulled out a snorkel with goggles and a pair of fins. "These might be a little big, but you can fasten them so they stay on well enough. Here." He handed her the gear.

"Thank you." She calmly started to put on the fins. He watched her for a moment. Nastia saw something she didn't understand on his face. "Aren't you going to put yours on?"

"Yeah. I will." He glanced around curiously. They were the only boat for at least a mile. "You are very trusting, Nastia. How do you know I wouldn't do something to you?"

She was surprised. "Well, you did say you were a Christian."

"I could have lied."

"But you didn't. Did you?" She smiled.

"No. I am definitely a Christian. But you are a very attractive woman. Some guy might want to put on an act so he could take advantage of you."

"Hopefully I am a better judge of character than that." She giggled lightly, not wanting a heavy atmosphere.

Erlend dropped the topic, and put on his fins and snorkel. "Okay, Nastia. You go first. Just put on your goggles and jump in. I'll follow."

Nastia stared at the waves as the boat rocked. "I have a better idea. You go in first, and show me how to do it, and then I will follow. Someone told me recently that I'm too trusting."

Erlend merely blinked at her joke. "All right." Keeping a straight face, he moved over to the edge and positioned himself. Nastia wished Anton were there. He would have laughed and smiled calmly rather than being serious and grim like Erlend. He jumped in and shook his head as he came back to the surface. "Okay, just do what I did, and be careful," he shouted.

"Don't worry," she said, adjusting her goggles. "It's easy." She jumped in and bobbed up right beside Erlend. "See. I told you." She laughed at his gaping face.

"We'll stay at the surface first. When you're ready to go down, motion to me. But remember, you only have so much air, and you'll need to come back up soon."

"Really? You mean I'm not a mermaid? Oh, darn." *Gosh, he needs to lighten up*, she thought as she placed the end of her breathing tube in her mouth and tested it.

They swam on the surface for about five minutes, but Nastia was eager to see the colorful fish down below. She took a full breath and dove. Erlend followed immediately.

The reef wasn't very far. Nastia glided around the orange, pink, and red corals. A school of small silver fish raced away from her, and she spotted another group of larger fish colored in black, yellow, and blue. Erlend tapped her shoulder and pointed up. They returned to the surface.

"What's wrong?" She was feeling fine.

"I just thought you needed to take a breath."

She grinned. "I think I can decide that for myself, thanks. Do you need more time, or are you ready to go back down?"

"I'm fine," he muttered, adjusted his mouthpiece, and disappeared below the waves. *I hope I didn't offend him. Poor sensitive boy.* Nastia tested her breathing tube again and went under.

Erlend glanced at her but instantly turned away. Nastia ignored him and continued to swim through the reef. A tiny red crab crawled on a rock as two stingrays raced over it. She touched the rock and twirled around, enjoying herself tremendously. She spotted a shell with spiky white branches half buried in the sand.

Suddenly, Erlend tapped her on the back. *What is it now?* She was slightly exasperated. He put his finger over his lips as if motioning her to be calm and pointed. A sleek tiger shark drifted in, looking as if he was strategically avoiding them. Erlend pointed up toward the boat and headed toward it, assuming that Nastia would follow. She hesitated. Even though she was terrified of the shark, she wanted to get the shell also. *I just have to take something with me. I just have to!*

She reached for the spiky shell and pulled. *What? It's broken!* She felt like she was being extremely stupid and headed up, the shell under her arm.

She sighed, relieved when she had made it to the surface and removed her goggles.

"What are you doing?" Erlend shouted. "Get in! Now!"

"Okay, okay!" She swam over, and he helped her get inside the boat. The shark drifted past the boat, as if foiled.

"Are you an idiot?" he screamed, his blond hair treacherously spiked. Nastia pulled away from him, but he grabbed her shoulder, his eyes panicking wildly. "Why didn't you come up immediately with me? You could have been killed!"

"Good grace, calm down! I'm all right. God was protecting us."

He shook his head angrily, rushed to the wheel, and started driving back toward the shore. Nastia wondered what was going on but was afraid to ask him. "I'll give you a tour of some of the coast," he said finally. "The green hills are really spectacular."

"Cool. That should be nice," Nastia tried to sound cheerful, but Erlend didn't look back at her. He still seemed upset.

After cruising slowly for almost thirty minutes, Erlend spoke, "Mind if I make some modest Christian conversation?"

"Yes, please," Nastia nodded rapidly and muttered *thank you, God* under her breath.

"What is your favorite Bible verse?"

"Oh gosh, that's a hard question." She thought for a moment. "I don't think I have one favorite. John 3:16 is always a good one, but I read the Psalms mostly. I really like Philippians 4:6–7: 'Do not be anxious about anything, but in everything, by prayer and petition, with thanksgiving, present your requests to God. And the peace of God, which transcends all understanding, will guard your hearts and your minds in Christ Jesus.' " She was satisfied with her answer.

"Yeah, I know that one," he said without emotion.

"What is your favorite verse?" Erlend was still faced away from her as he drove, and Nastia sat in the back of the boat. She wondered what expressions were on his face.

"My favorite verse used to be John 15:7: 'If you remain in me and my words remain in you, ask whatever you wish, and it will be given you.' But I've found over the years that God hardly ever answers my prayers, especially the ones I want answered the most. So, I changed my favorite. A lot of people don't understand why I like this verse so much, and you probably won't either but I'll tell you anyway. Ecclesiastes 7 verse 3: 'Sorrow is better than laughter, because a sad face is good for the heart.' "

He was right, she didn't understand why that was his favorite verse. "I'm sure it has its place, just like every verse in the Bible."

"It definitely does."

"My favorite passage in Ecclesiastes is the first part of chapter three. You know the one that says, 'There is a time for everything, and a season for every activity under heaven.' I wish I had the rest memorized."

"Yeah. That one is very applicable to life." He went silent again, and they cruised for a while longer.

After looking and commenting on the different shapes in the jagged emerald green hills and the mountain behind (without much response from Erlend), Nastia had enough. She scooted down the bench until she was right behind him, and put her hand on his shoulder. "Erlend, we began our friendship today with abrupt honesty. Can we please continue that now? Can you tell me what is wrong? You've been moping ever since we left the reef. Besides, we should probably head back to the dock."

Erlend began turning the boat around and picking up speed.

"Are you going to tell me?" Nastia prompted.

"Yeah, I'll tell you if you'll come to my grandparents' place, and let me make you a drink. I'm thirsty again."

"Sure. Let's do it."

———————◆———————

BY THE TIME Erlend drove Nastia in his car away from downtown Honolulu to his grandparents' house and they stood on the front porch, Nastia was extremely curious. "Are they home?"

"No, they both work on Saturdays. That's why I went to the beach. I don't like being in this house alone."

The house looked well-furnished and good to Nastia. Erlend unlocked the door and they entered.

"What's so special about this drink that you have to bring me all the way here to make it?" she inquired as they walked into the kitchen lit by the afternoon sun.

"Because I'm going to make you a homemade piña colada. The restaurants don't make it as well."

"Oh, so you're the master chef?" She took her seat in one of the tall counter chairs and rested her arms on the polished black granite. "I'll watch you."

He pulled out the blender and started gathering ingredients.

"Can you talk while you cook?" she hinted.

"Sorry for making you wait," he said in a much calmer voice than before. "Do you still want to hear why I was a little upset?"

"Yes, please."

"Okay. Here it goes. How should I start? I was born and raised here on Oahu. We moved when I was thirteen but before that I had a best friend here who I would do everything with. We were best friends ever since first grade."

"What was his name?" she asked.

"Derek, but my little sister and I would call him Eky. He would call me his air-lender. Whenever he would come to our house, he would make a melodramatic display, acting as if he were suffocating as he slowly made his way to me. Once he reached me, he would gasp, as if he was only then able to breathe, and would say 'Thanks, man. I really needed that air.' I would chuckle and roll my eyes.

"When I was twelve, Derek and I went surfing. We surfed a lot together. But one time we were really far out, and he was saying that we should probably go back, but I saw another wave starting to form farther out that I thought would be really good and said, 'Okay, but I have to catch this last one.' He said okay and waited while I surfed it.

"But when we started paddling back to shore, a shark rose toward us and bit him in the head. He was screaming and bleeding like crazy, and I was panicking, frantically pulling him to the beach."

"Did he live?"

"Yes. My dad drove him to the hospital. They were able to fix him up and save him. He was in a coma for a few days."

"Wow," said Nastia. "What a miracle! I can understand why you were upset about the shark. It must have been horrible to watch…" Her voice trailed away. Erlend had stopped chopping pineapple and was looking at her. He shook his head.

"That's not the whole story," Erlend continued. "After he woke up, he was a completely different person in a bad way. He didn't recognize me at all. He had lost his memory. His personality changed, and he has been mentally handicapped ever since. It was really hard on me and my sister. She had a crush on him before the accident and would tag along with Derek and me all through childhood. My dad saw how badly it was affecting us. He found a job in Oregon, and we moved.

"But the worst part about it is I would pray and pray and pray for God to heal Derek and make him remember me, but it never happened. I so wanted my best friend back, but no matter how much I believed Derek would come back and trusted that Jesus would heal him, no matter how many nights I spent drying my eyes on the carpet as I prayed, God never healed Derek. In college, I lost my belief in prayer. I don't pray much anymore. I read my Bible and maybe even talk to God every now and then, but I don't ask him for things because I don't believe he'll answer."

Nastia didn't know what to say.

"I saw Derek yesterday," he continued. "This is really what makes me upset. I went to his house just to visit him. He was sitting on their front porch completely bald and didn't recognize me at all. He was worse than the last time I saw him, which was four years ago when we came up to visit my grandparents. He didn't understand a word I said and just sat there, scowling at me. I went inside and talked to his mom. She told me the doctors diagnosed him with brain cancer somehow induced by his accident, but they were unable to treat it. They expect Derek to die within the next three months."

Nastia searched for something to say to comfort Erlend. "That's terrible. I can't imagine how hard it has been for you."

197

"Do you agree with me that God really doesn't answer prayers?"

"No, I don't," she said firmly. "You can't fall into unbelief like that, Erlend. I know this is crazy, coming from a girl who is living with her boyfriend, but," she exhaled, "we live in a fallen world. It's as if our world and all of humanity has a sort of cancer. Sometimes the infection sprouts up and stabs us right in the center of our hearts, forcing rivers of pain. I know exactly how it is to pray and pray but get no answer at all. My dad committed adultery when he was the pastor of a small church back in Arizona about eight years ago. All of my friends' families left, and almost all of them stopped associating with us. I would pray and pray that my dad would be sincerely sorry and everyone would come back, but it never happened." She paused. "Do you think this has anything to do with your addiction to pornography?"

"You mean Derek's condition or my lack of faith in prayer?"

"Both."

Erlend glanced to the side. His hair was less spiky. "Maybe. I sometimes watch it just for the numbing effect."

"Does it make things worse or better?"

"It definitely makes my life worse. I know it's bad."

"I think I know of a Proverb that could help you." She got off the tall chair and looked around the kitchen. "Do your grandparents have a Bible?"

"Yes, they do." He walked over to a short bookshelf and pulled out a soft Bible. Nastia thought it was amazing and crazy how she could have this conversation with a stranger. Was Erlend still a stranger? She felt connected to him in a way she didn't feel with many other people. He was another Christian who was living in sin.

Erlend handed Nastia the Bible.

Nastia flipped through the pages for a bit. "Here it is, chapter 1 verse 32, 'For the waywardness of the simple will kill them, and the complacency of fools will destroy them.' I know it's pretty harsh, but the point is: don't become complacent or idle or you will sin, and sin destroys." She returned the book to him when she noticed he was staring at her. "What is it?"

"Oh, nothing." He quickly put the Bible away and began pouring the white smoothie-like beverage into two glasses. "Would you like to go to the backyard and drink this?"

She glanced at the digital clock on the microwave. "Actually, it's getting late. Can you please drive me back? We can drink on the way."

The eagerness in his eyes disappeared. "Sure. Let's go."

They listened to music on the drive back as Nastia was saying how much she loved one song and dancing a little to it while Erlend laughed.

Once they arrived in front of the two white towers of the resort, Nastia said in a light-hearted tone, "Well, here we are. Thank you for the snorkeling and the piña colada. Just to let you know, I could tell it was virgin."

He smiled more than he had all day. "Well, we've got to start somewhere, right?"

Nastia laughed, thinking he must be referring to their sins. "Yes, we do." She was about to open the car door, but he kept staring at her. "Is there anything else you wanted to tell me?"

He hesitated, but then it all came out, "Nastia, you are unlike any other person I have ever met. You are gorgeous, but it's more than that. You have a certain quality about you that I have never seen before." He leaned closer to Nastia as he said slowly, "I don't know how I will live without you."

With a sudden push forward, he kissed her passionately, and Nastia let him until she remembered — *Wait! I'm dating Anton!* She pushed him away.

"Um, Erlend. I'm with someone else. Do you understand?"

He nodded, looking at her as if he couldn't breathe without her.

She sat silently in the car for a few moments longer, watching the clouds in the east turn pink.

"I think it's time for me to go. Thank you for an amazing day. I won't forget you, Erlend."

He barely shook her hand. "There's no way I will forget you, Nastia."

She smiled, nodded, and finally opened the door. After a few steps, she turned around.

"Yes?" he said too hopefully from his opened window.

"I was just going to ask, where did you get that stone from — the one on your necklace?"

He held up the stone pendant, rubbing it between his fingers. "Derek found it when we were playing hide-and-seek with my sister."

Nastia's face went sad, and she walked into the resort.

23

THE NIGHT BEACH

THE LIGHTING IN the restaurant was too dim. Nastia wondered how the servers, attired in black Hawaiian shirts with blue flowers, were able to see anything. The candle in the center didn't help. Yes, it was a nice place, residing in the top floor of their hotel with wide-open walls, allowing the warm wind to enter, but Nastia had to remind herself again and again. Somehow, she didn't care how nice the restaurant was.

The sky was almost completely dark; Nastia could tell from her table right beside the edge of the walls. A distant boat displayed clear lights as did the large city of Honolulu.

"Here is your pineapple juice, ma'am."

"Thank you," she replied in a sarcastic tone. She took a sip but wasn't thirsty anymore after the initial taste. The glass was blue with etchings of white on it — fish, seaweed, and a hammerhead shark. "A shark? Hmm…Jianyu?" The etchings came to life, and the fish raced away as the shark looked at her.

"Hello, Nastia Sobieski. You had quite a day, didn't you?"

"Yes, including almost getting eaten by a real shark," she said. "You should be proud of me, though. I used the verse you gave me."

"Yes, I noticed. That was good of you."

"What?" she said in mock surprise, placing her fingers over her gaping mouth. "Did I actually do something *right*? Wow, oh wow."

A red glass fish embraced the candleholder. Suddenly, it moved and blinked at Nastia. "Why are you upset, Tia?"

"Because of Erlend!" she sighed. "He was a nice guy, Aini. Even though I talked to him about how fallen the world is, some of what he said sank in. Why should I pray if God doesn't answer prayers?"

"God never lies," the hammerhead stated firmly. "He has instructed you to pray and said he will answer. Thus, you should pray."

"I don't know about that." She turned toward the window, her eyes sad and suffering. "I think God has lied many times."

"That is not true at all —" the red fish began, but Nastia interrupted, waving her hand.

"I don't want to argue about it. Please, let's not argue tonight. I'm not at all in the mood. Besides, I feel guilty about letting him kiss me. What will Anton say? He will probably be mad that I spent the whole day with another guy."

The fish and the hammerhead shark glanced at each other. "Apologize to him," said Aini. "A small step is good. But your guilt comes from somewhere else."

"What!" Defensive anger rose. "Where do you think it comes from?"

They were gone. Nastia examined her water glass and the candleholder, but there was no red fish or blue shark.

"Darn it! They left me again." She was ashamed of being disrespectful toward the angels, but she didn't feel like fighting her mood, so she remained silent.

"It *is* you," Anton Shepherd walked up and pulled out his chair, a wide playful grin on his face. "They need to put in more lights. I was thinking I would reach over and kiss someone I thought was you but find out it was some creepy old lady." He grimaced and then laughed.

At least he's in a good mood. "Hello, my boyfriend." She smiled for him as he sat, leaned forward on the table, and sipped from his glass. "How was work?"

"Good. I made contacts with several potential investors. My boss will be happy about that. How was your day? What did you do?"

Oh boy, here it goes. She shrugged. "It was interesting."

"Don't tell me you spent it alone? I didn't want you to."

"Actually, just the opposite. A guy named Erlend came over and talked to me while I was sunbathing on the beach. He invited me to lunch and then scuba diving."

"Did you go?" he asked without any opinion on his face.

"Yes. We spent the whole afternoon together."

"I'm glad. Did you have a good time?"

"Yes, it was fun." The image of the foiled shark flashed through her mind. "He was a cool friend and had an interesting story." She cleared her throat and looked down at the nibbled roll on her plate. "However, he didn't think of me as just a friend."

Anton's forehead crinkled as his eyebrows rose. "He didn't? How do you know?" His voice curled on the last word.

Nastia's red hair sparkled with a shake of concern. *How am I supposed to say this?* "Well, he kind of kissed me."

Anton's eyes became wide and the edges of his mouth dropped. "Really?"

"I'm sorry, Anton! I didn't want him to. He just reached over and kissed when I wasn't looking. I know you're mad at me."

"I'm not mad at you." His face relaxed and his dimples showed again.

"You're not?"

"No. I trust you, Nastia. I want to punch this Erlend guy in the face, but I don't blame you at all. You're a very attractive woman. I can't be surprised when other guys notice."

The waitress came, and they ordered their meals. Once she left, Nastia spoke, "Well, good grace, you are a *phenomenal* man. I don't deserve you."

He chuckled. "I think the same thing about you all the time. But I want to hear more about this guy who took liberties with you."

"Are you jealous?"

"Yeah, of course. You said he had an interesting story? What was it?"

"He just finished college and came up here for vacation. He used to live in Hawaii but moved in his early teens because his best friend lost his wits from a shark attack while they were surfing. He visited that same friend yesterday and found out he has brain cancer and will die in a few months."

"Wow!" Anton shook his head. "It's no excuse for kissing you, but that's tough."

"Yes, it is. I've been sad all evening because of it." She recalled how he had lost his belief in prayer.

"I might be able to cure that. Are you interested?"

"Yes. Please free me from this stupid sadness."

A mischievous smile crossed his face. "I'll show you after dinner. It's a place someone at work told me about today. You'll love it."

———————◆———————

NASTIA HAD NO idea where they were going, but she trusted Anton as he drove them through the night. Instead of worrying, she mused about the new roach on her waist. All she had done was look at Erlend and admire his six-pack. Was that really the sin of lust? Yes, there had been a tiny little thought in her vibrant imagination, but that was all.

"We're here." Anton parked the car on the half-moon section of dirt beside the road. Nastia saw the ocean in the distance about thirty feet down. Anton opened her door, his backpack slung over his shoulder. He led her to the edge of what she thought was a cliff. "Down this way. Careful — it's steep."

Nastia gingerly placed her feet down the path, slipping on a few occasions. Finally, they reached the bottom. A surge of pleasure rushed through her. The moonlight illuminated the isolated beach, the moist sand shimmering while the waves crashed. Weatherworn cliffs enclosed around them with a few coarse rocks scattered about. Everything else was smooth.

"Oh, my grace!" Nastia jumped up to Anton's face and kissed him. "This is so gorgeous!" She walked up to the water and dipped her feet, the froth retreating. She looked back at Anton. Even in the dim moonlight she could see his big smile.

"That's not all." He pointed up.

Nastia leaned her head back and gasped and then giggled. "Anton, this is what I've always dreamed of doing — coming to the perfect beach and stargazing with my perfect man! I just want to lie down and look at them."

"I planned for that too." He removed a blanket from his backpack.

"Did you get this from the hotel? Did they let you?"

"Yeah, they let me, they just don't know it." Anton reached deeper into the backpack and pulled out two mangoes and a pocketknife. "These were sitting in a bowl at the conference today. No one was using them, and they were perfectly ripe so you know…" He flashed his eyebrows hoping she would laugh, which she did.

Nastia shook her head playfully. "You're such a guy."

They lay down on the blanket and gazed up at the stars while eating fresh slices of mango. After a while, Anton spoke, "Remember the day we met on the plane, when you said being a Christian is like the life of a star?"

"Yeah?" She hadn't thought about it since the incident. "Why?"

"If stars are Christians then what are shooting stars?"

Nastia thought for a moment. She had faced doubt about her faith today and didn't possess the enthusiasm she had when she compared her life to a star three weeks before. So much had changed since she first met Anton. She had changed significantly. She wasn't sure about God anymore. She half wanted to stop being a Christian so she could be released from the guilt of living with Anton. In the back of her mind, Nastia kept telling herself she would repent and leave Anton once they got back to D.C. But she felt so happy and secure, resting there in his arms — much more secure than she had felt with Erlend. She felt safe with Anton.

"I think shooting stars are a celebration when someone becomes a Christian." The response popped out before Nastia really thought about it.

"Huh," he muttered. "Do you like being a Christian?"

Oh no! Anton can't challenge me on my faith now, not when I've been so unsure and confused. "Yes, I do. It's the only way I can live." She said the words because they sounded good, not because she meant them.

"Why?"

She looked at him. "Why are you asking all of a sudden? You didn't seem this interested before."

He shrugged defensively. "I'm just curious about the faith of my girlfriend. We do sleep in the same bed every night. I'm interested in what goes on in your sexy head."

"Oh, sure that was convincing." She poked his shoulder. "Why do I like being a Christian? Hmm…" The black outline of a bird suddenly flapped in her face. "Aini! I'm busy. What is it?"

"Don't let this ministry opportunity pass, Tia," said the sweet voice. "This is your chance to tell Anton about Jesus — the one who paid the price for his sins. Tell him about the complete spiritual satisfaction that is found in Christ and only in Christ. Even while you live in sin, God can use your imperfect words to tell Anton about the only relationship that brings deliverance from condemnation — the relationship with Jesus Christ."

"But I don't know what I believe anymore," she replied desperately. "I don't know who I am. I don't know where I'm going. There are too many decisions before me. I can't handle them now."

"You have to handle them," Aini continued. "God has placed these choices before you now. You made the wrong choice before, but it's never too late to make the right choice! Ask God for strength and wisdom. He won't keep it from you. Remember 1st Corinthians 10:13, 'God is faithful; he will not let you be tempted beyond what

206

you can bear. But when you are tempted, he will also provide a way out so that you can stand up under it.' You are facing the temptation to be weak right now, Tia, but you can endure it. You can get past this and do what you know is right. Just depend on Jesus."

"Oh, please not now. I'm tired —" Nastia began but the bird's silhouette flew away.

Nastia sighed and decided to answer her boyfriend. "I like being a Christian because it's the cure for loneliness. Even though I can't see Jesus in person, I know he is there. I have a relationship with him. He is more than a limited physical person; he is a strong spiritual being. Jesus knows every thought of every person. He knows just how broken and lost we are. He knows every sin we have committed." She paused. "I can trust Jesus. I know he accepts me and wants me even though I am a huge mess."

"What do you mean by sin?"

Nastia was surprised by the question. It sounded elementary to her. "Come on, Anton. You know what sin is. You told me you went to church when you were a kid."

He chuckled. "They never defined sin, which is funny, considering how much they talked about it."

"Okay, um…sin is an offense against God." She felt satisfied with the response as if she was checking off an answer on a test.

"But what does that mean?"

"I'm sorry, Anton. It's been a long day. My brain seems to have shut down."

"We can talk about something else if you want," he said in a tone that didn't care.

"No, no. I've got this. I just have to think for a moment." She shut her eyes, trying to find the right words in her jumbled thoughts. "Well, Christianity is based on the Holy Bible. If you want to know everything about my faith, just read that book. The New Testament especially is where we find the definition of right and wrong that undoubtedly applies today, but also in the Ten Commandments, which is a timeless law. We can't put anything before God; He has to be the most important part of our lives. When we put anything before God, we sin."

"Give me an example."

"Okay. Stealing is a sin, and lying, and sexual immorality." She stopped and shut her mouth, wishing she hadn't said the last one.

"You mean like us, how we are living together without being married?"

"Yes. And adultery and homosexuality." She felt strangely humbled. "But those sins are worse than what we are doing."

"Are they?" He kissed her on the forehead and silently watched the stars.

"Seriously now, Anton. What made you ask? Why are you curious? I'm allowed to ask questions too, you know."

"Fair enough." He exhaled and scratched his shoulder. "Sometimes, I don't see much that matters in the world and our culture. It makes me wonder if there's something more, something better."

Wait? Is he actually considering becoming a Christian? Nastia prayed in her head, Oh God, please save him! May he know you and pursue you! Please make him!

"But," Anton continued. "I'm a solid atheist. It would take a pretty big crisis to change my mind. I'm 96 percent sure the world evolved and there is no God."

Darn it. Maybe he was just curious. Nastia didn't want to talk about it anymore and jumped to her feet. "Do you want to walk by the water?"

"Sure, or better yet, would you like to go swimming?"

"But I didn't bring my bathing suit!"

"Do you need one?" He grinned slyly.

"Yes, I don't feel comfortable."

He rolled his eyes. "Oh brother, you never feel uncomfortable."

"Yes, I do."

"No, you don't."

"Anton, if you've noticed something about me by now, it must be my stubbornness. No one can get past my stubbornness."

"Oh yeah? You are living with me."

She shook her head. "That's different. I wanted to live with you. I don't want to go skinny dipping tonight. Besides, it's cold."

"Okay, princess, go in fully clothed." With a sudden burst of abrupt masculinity, he raced toward her, picked her up in his arms and threw her into the water. She screamed, landing with a splash.

"It's freezing! *Anton.*"

He sauntered toward her with a grin of success. Nastia climbed onto him, in a piggyback position. She was surprised by how easily he carried her. Had his muscles really been this huge? She pressed her fingers on his ribs.

"What are you doing?" he said, chuckling.

"Trying to find your bones!"

"Why? Do you think I'm all muscle?"

"You wish."

She held on tightly as he walked further into the ocean. She grew a little nervous but could only see thrill written in his moonlit face. She decided not to protest. As they got deeper, the waves grew stronger. One wave splashed and a dark voice spoke faintly, "There is no God. You are a fool and an idiot." And with the next one, "There is no God. Your faith is an illusion." She wailed inaudibly.

"Don't you think this is far enough?" she said, but he didn't seem to hear her.

A colder wave hit them, and the dark voice spoke again, "You are nothing but a random speck. Nothing matters. No one matters. You are nothing but a random speck."

No! No! She thought. *I can't stand it! I can't stand it!* She wanted to order Anton to turn back for the shore, but she restrained herself, screaming inside. She looked back and saw the outline of a person touching their belongings in the blackness. "Anton! Someone is back there messing with our stuff!" she panicked.

"What?" He turned around and hurried for the shore, plowing through the inhibiting water. Nastia slid off him, and they ran over to the blanket and his backpack. Anton slowed and looked around, a wary shadow over his face. "I don't see anyone." His eyes narrowed at her. "Did you say that just to make me turn around?"

"No, I didn't. I saw someone. Look," she pointed to the blanket, which was freshly folded and had a seashell on it. "See, it wasn't folded before."

"Yeah, it was. I folded it."

"You did?" Fear continued to pound in and out of her heart. "Did you put a seashell on it?"

"No." His face was more serious as he looked up at the steep path and the rental car. "All right, this is strange. We can go now." He put a towel over her shoulders and pressed her toward the car as he swung his backpack on.

Nastia was glad to feel Anton's hand on her shoulder as they climbed up to the car. Every bit of darkness around them frightened her. Was the person hiding in that shadow or behind that bush? She wanted to drive far away from this beach!

Breathing heavily, she felt calmer as they loaded up the car, and Anton got into the driver's seat. Standing alone for a moment, Nastia looked around. Had she seen anyone? Or was it just an illusion? The dark voice echoed in her ears and she closed her eyes, trying to shake it out.

"So, you sleep with him every night?"

"Ah!" Nastia jumped and opened her eyes. A small girl with red hair stood in front of her, smiling casually. She had large innocent eyes and a curious expression. "Who are you?" Nastia inquired. "Why are you out here by yourself? Where are your parents?"

The girl ignored her questions and held out her hand. "You forgot to take my shell. I gave it to you." The girl placed the small shell in Nastia's hand, but once it touched her palm it disappeared like smoke.

"Who are you?" She demanded again.

"My name is Mythia." Suddenly, the girl turned around and skipped away while humming the hymn, "It Is Well with My Soul."

"Are you coming?" Anton called.

"Yeah, I'm coming." Nastia hesitated, squinting around for the mysterious girl.

The outline of a tiger approached her. She would have screamed if she hadn't noticed the blue tinge in the car's light.

"Is that Jianyu? Who was the little girl? Should I run after her?"

"You could chase her, but you would never catch her alone," said the tiger.

"Who was she? Or *what* was she?"

"She is the spirit of your faith. She is not a real person but the embodiment of your faith. If you want to know the state of your beliefs then watch her." He turned and loped away.

Nastia hopped into the passenger seat and slammed the door.

"What's wrong?" Anton asked. "You took a little while. Did you see anyone?"

"Oh no. I was just admiring the view one last time."

After five minutes of driving, Anton broke the silence, his face kind but still serious. "You know how you have been talking about your faith being a barrier in our relationship?"

"Yes?"

"Well I think I have come to a conclusion about it."

"Okay."

Anton paused and continued. "Every couple has barriers and differences between them. The successful couples overcome those barriers and consider the differences as an addition to the team. I think your Christianity is a beneficial addition to our relationship. There is a lot of good and respect for others in Christianity, and I'm glad you possess that side of us. I possess the side of science and reason. Your faith is just another part of you. Please don't treat it as a problem between us."

"I'll think about it," Nastia replied.

"Thank you." Anton leaned over and kissed her. "I do love you — more than anyone else alive."

Nastia smiled.

As she sat quietly, her mind raced, and she wanted Anton to be a Christian more than ever. Nastia thought about the Bible verse that Erlend had stopped believing, John 15:7, "If you remain in me and my words remain in you, ask whatever you wish and it will be given you." Nastia decided to try it. She would pray and believe with all her heart that God would convert Anton into a Christian and then it would happen. She prayed in her head, *Father God, please make Anton Shepherd a Christian by sunset on Monday before we leave. With every bit of my desires, I pray this! In Jesus name, amen!*

24

PEARL TRUTH

NASTIA KNEW THAT Anton wouldn't allow himself to visit Oahu without touring Pearl Harbor. She didn't care too much about the battleship or the aircraft hangar except for her boyfriend's sake. Anton looked around the naval base with somber admiration and respect. Nastia copied his mood, even though it wasn't her own. However, once they watched the graphic documentary and took the boat to the Arizona Memorial, Nastia's saddened mood became sincere. The azure sky was bright and clear as they quietly wandered around the floating memorial with the other tourists.

"I'm going to go pray for a little while, Anton. Is that all right?"

"Sure. I'll be over here."

Nastia moved away from him and leaned against the large aperture, gazing at the water below. Over one thousand men had died somewhere down there. The thought gave her a chill; Nastia was very glad to be above water.

The same small red-haired girl from last night walked up beside her, hopped onto the aperture, and dangled her feet over the edge.

"What are you doing up there?" Nastia asked, still questioning the legitimacy of the pretty little toddler.

The girl laughed carelessly. "I told you, my name is Mythia. You must have a bad memory."

"Okay then, Mythia. You should come down and act more serious. We are here to remember those who gave their lives for the

213

United States during World War II. Pearl Harbor was a horrible tragedy. You need to act more reverent."

Mythia giggled obnoxiously. "I don't care about some stupid soldiers who drowned ages ago. I care about me. It's actually pretty funny when you think how they were trapped in the boat and couldn't get out."

Nastia was indignant. "How can you be so completely disrespectful? That was a terrible thing to say! Take it back!"

Nastia tried to put her hands on Mythia's shoulders, but the girl simply giggled once more and dove into the water, disappearing.

Nastia shook her head furiously. "What a little brat!"

The red bird flew in from behind and landed on the sill, exactly where Mythia had been. "I agree, she is a brat."

"Hello, Aini. I don't get how she is supposed to reflect my faith. What was the point of all that?"

"Mythia is very similar to you, Tia. The way she disrespects the lost soldiers of Pearl Harbor is like the way you disrespect God."

"Oh brother. Every single human being disrespects God. How am I especially bad?"

"Because you are proclaiming the name of Christ while living in sin, even though you know exactly what you're doing is active rebellion against God. And don't compare yourself to other people. Don't try to justify your actions by saying that everyone disrespects God. Galatians 6:4–5 says, 'Each one should test his own actions. Then he can take pride in himself, without comparing himself to somebody else, for each one should carry his own load.' "

"Why can't they say 'herself' every now and then? The Bible can be rather sexist."

Aini sighed. "Oh, Tia. How long will you shirk your responsibility and ignore the one who loves you more than anyone else? I can't help you when you're like this."

The red bird flew away, leaving Nastia to herself.

She tried to ignore the nipping conviction inside her. All Nastia had to do was hold out for a little and then it would go away.

"Feeling sorry for angels doesn't help anything," she said, even though her conviction wasn't remorse for being rude toward Aini; it was shame because of her irreverence toward God. She knew it all too clearly.

———————————◆———————————

AS ANTON DROVE them back to Waikiki beach, he said, "I have one last session this afternoon. What do you think you'll do?"

Nastia wondered if her boyfriend was worried. "Anton, I am so sorry for spending the day with another guy yesterday. I should have stayed alone in my room. I know I hurt you, even though you don't admit it."

Anton rolled his eyes. "No, I am honestly not mad at you; I'm just mad at him for kissing you. I say what I mean. Please trust me. I trust you. I know you won't cheat on me."

"Oh no, of course I won't cheat on you! But thank you, Anton. It's good to hear that you trust me. You are the best boyfriend a girl could ever have. You need to tell me more about the other girls who have liked you in the past. I mean, they would have to be idiots not to have at least a small crush on you, even though you are all mine now."

He laughed, and his wide grin took over his face. "But I don't care about those girls anymore. I care about you. Hey, sometime you need to tell me about all the guys who have liked you in the past."

Nastia's eyebrows rose. "But there are so many. I can't remember all of them."

"Then why did you ask me?" He chuckled.

"Yeah, I guess you're right. Too many people have liked us."

"Let's not get prideful, though," he said. "We are no better than the ugliest people."

"Do you really believe that?"

215

"Yes, I do."

Nastia wanted to believe that she was beautiful, regardless of the repellent sight the car mirror showed her. She looked like an old lady who was starving to death with a bruised and swollen face. Why not remember the many men who had crushes on her? She wanted to feel desirable again. Yes, Anton's love made her feel appreciated and valued, but he was so good — so genuine. He would value anyone. However, she suspected that Anton would leave her in a second if he saw the ugliness of her soul. Or would he?

◆

AFTER THEY ATE lunch and Anton left for his session, Nastia stepped out of the hotel and headed for the beach in short jean shorts and a pink striped blouse that revealed one of her shoulders. Her large brown sunglasses shielded her eyes. People strolled in and out of shops, toting bags filled with expensive products while others headed for the beach in their bathing suits. Nastia didn't want to talk to anyone. She wanted to be alone. Was it possible to find someplace alone at the over-populated Waikiki beach on a Sunday?

She passed the surfboard booth with the tall man who had an extra-long torso. He looked up at her and stared for a while. *Gosh, he comes here too much*, she thought, annoyed.

The only place that wasn't swarming with people was the rock-lined jetty with a paved path running down the middle. *I think I'll go there.*

At the very end of the jetty, Nastia gingerly stepped off the walkway, found a smooth rock, and sat on it while the waves splashed. She didn't care if she got wet. She was here to be alone and remember herself.

The wind blew as she watched people playing in the water. The sunlight tingled her skin along with the refreshing ocean spray, launching and falling in a hypnotic pattern. It was steadfast, like the love of God. Nastia wanted to talk to him again.

"Okay, God. This is how it is," she prayed aloud. "I love Anton, and he loves me, and I can't give him up. He's wonderful, God. He's so good! No one has ever cared for me like he does. Why would you ask me to leave him? Wouldn't it be right to stay as his loving, supportive, and loyal girlfriend? Maybe you do actually want me to live with him. How could something so thoroughly good be wrong?"

She exhaled deeply. Hawaii was magnificent, and so was Anton's love. Combine the two and you get paradise. It was that simple in Nastia's mind. This was like a honeymoon beginning their future together.

"At least I'm not judgmental," she continued praying. "At least I don't depend on works to get me into heaven. I depend on you, Jesus — you and your grace. That's good, right? Isn't it better to live in sin and depend on your grace instead of depending on good works? Yes. I think I am much better off than the Christians who believe they're saved because of the good things they've done. I have it right. I depend on grace."

The biggest wave yet hit against the rocks and splashed Nastia more than the others. She removed her sunglasses, wincing, and dabbed the droplets away with the end of her blouse. Gliding her hair behind her ears again, she placed the glasses back on.

The red bird peered at her from the next rock, her tiny black-bead eyes glistening.

"You always like to surprise me, don't you?" said Nastia, recovering herself.

"I suppose so. Really, I just come when you need me the most."

"Okay then. What do you have for me?"

Aini began quoting immediately, " 'What shall we say, then? Shall we go on sinning so that grace may increase? By no means! We died to sin; how can we live in it any longer?' Romans 6 verses 1 and 2. No matter how you look at it, Tia, living with Anton is sinful. How can you continue with a lifestyle of death when that is the very thing from which God has saved you? Is Anton really more wonderful than God?"

"I never said that!"

"Maybe not, but you are living as if he were. Just remember that Jesus is the source of all goodness, truth, and love — not Anton or anybody else. You have a choice: Jesus or Anton."

Aini flew away before the next wave splashed.

Nastia groaned in exasperation. "Can't I have both Jesus and Anton? Isn't there a middle ground?" She sighed and tried to ignore everything the red bird had just said while praying, "God, please make Anton a Christian! You are all powerful. You can do all things. I believe it, Lord! Please, *please* save Anton's soul so that he can join the kingdom of God. He has to be one of yours!"

"Excuse me?"

Nastia twisted around and saw the surfboard salesman with the extra-long torso, standing behind her. "What do you want?"

"You looked lonely over here by yourself. Is everything okay? Would you like some company?"

Nastia laughed sarcastically. "Wish I was grateful, dude, but I am not lonely at all, and I don't appreciate you hitting on me. No, I will not go out with you, and I don't want to talk to you. Now go back to your pretty surfboards and make sure they don't get stolen. I'm sure some delusional bikini girl will fall for your ploys eventually. Bye!"

He frowned at her for a long moment, and then left.

Nastia turned back to the ocean. "Good grace! Can't I have one afternoon on the beach without some guy trying to get me?" She shook her head and decided to go for a walk.

ONCE NIGHTTIME FINALLY rolled around and Anton was done with all his sessions, he asked if she wanted to tour the shops and find a more casual dinner. She was pleased by his offer, and they left the hotel. Anton bought her a box of unbelievably delicious chocolates at an extravagant shop while laughing at Nastia's objections to the high price. She was determined to "get him back" and purchased a colorful tank top she thought would look marvelous on him. He gazed at her in the most adoring way as she tried to put it on him outside the store, forcing her to grin and giggle as she said, "Anton, you are a little distracting."

"No, Nastia, *you* are distracting. I don't feel worthy."

"Oh psh! That's a lie."

"Is it?"

They ended the conversation with laughter and kissing.

As they passed another shop, Anton said he had to find something for her to wear. He selected a pair of purplish-silver sunglasses for her. "Do you like these?"

"Yeah. They're cool. I like them if you like them."

For dinner, they ordered cheap Korean food and watched a group of native musicians play a quintessential Hawaiian song while a girl in orange danced in flowing movements. After the music and light applause ended, Anton said, "I'm going to get some ice cream for us. What flavor would you like?"

"Something very Hawaiian," she replied playfully.

"All right," he grinned and left.

Nastia absentmindedly listened to a plump family argue about who would get the glazed chicken while she waited.

"Nastia?"

She felt a light touch on her shoulder and looked up. "Erlend! I was hoping I would see you one last time. How are you?"

He appeared distressed by the words *last time* and said, "I wish you didn't have to go. Where is your boyfriend?"

"He's over there, getting ice cream. He's the tall one in the colorful tank top."

Erlend's face became somber. "Did you tell him about the kiss?"

"Yes. He knows that you kissed me."

"Was he very upset?"

"Not really." She laughed. "He just said he wanted to punch you in the face."

"Haha. Well, maybe I should go then. Goodbye Nastia. Please find me on Facebook."

"Will do. Bye."

She narrowed her eyes a little as he left in a nervous manner. God, please take care of Erlend. Help him to be confident in your ways.

Even though she felt hypocritical, she was glad to pray for him.

25

WILL HE DIE?

IN THE MIDDLE of the night, Nastia squirmed uncomfortably beside Anton on their resort bed, her mind plunging into a dream.

———————◆———————

THE AIR WHISTLED loudly, speeding through the red clouds, over the black ocean, and inside the red sun. The rocky hills collapsed like falling waves building up quickly and slamming down again and again as if the wind were everywhere and everything.

A surfer — with a sail on his board — splashed into view, launching over the violent curves and dips in the black water. An especially vicious wave grew higher and higher. Nastia's heart sped in the madness. "No, don't! You won't make it!" she cried. The surfer didn't listen. He flew toward the colossal mass of water, crashed into the wave, and launched backwards, falling upside down.

———————◆———————

NASTIA'S EYES SHOT open. The room was still. Anton slept peacefully. But Nastia was far from peace. She took deep breaths, trying to calm her high-paced heart, but whenever she closed her eyes the scene repeated. She saw the silhouettes of the wave and windsurfer. What did it mean? Why did the dream affect her so deeply?

After an hour of tossing and turning, Nastia found sleep again, but the images remained, and the powerful wind continued to whistle in her mind.

———————◆———————

AFTER CHURCH, LAUREN Henson walked into her apartment. She sighed, weary concern on her dark brown face. She had been thinking of Nastia all day. She and her boyfriend were still on their Hawaii trip. People had approached Lauren after the service, asking, "Where is your friend? Isn't she living with you?"

Lauren avoided the last question and replied with a different truth, "She is out of town this weekend. That's why she couldn't make it."

"Really? Where did she go?" someone had pressed.

"Hawaii," Lauren was forced to say, "With a friend of hers." She had to say *friend* for Nastia's own protection. This Anton guy must be a friend as well as a lover. It wasn't Lauren's secret to tell.

"Hawaii!" the listeners had said with excited smiles. "Wow. That's wonderful."

Lauren would have described it differently. In her mind, as she set her keys and purse down with a long exhale, she thought of another word — painful. Her spirit had been burdened ever since Nastia went to live with Anton, but today, Lauren felt especially strained. Why? Hawaii was just another place for them to sin together. What made today different?

A knock sounded on the door, startling Lauren. She took a deep breath and opened it. Stephanie Rivers, Nastia's work supervisor at the church, stood in the hallway with a small plate of sugar cookies.

"Stephanie!" Lauren greeted her politely. "What are you doing in this part of town?"

"I came to see Nastia," she said sweetly. "She emailed me and told me that she was sick and couldn't make it to work tomorrow. Is she asleep? If so, I can just leave these cookies with you. I don't want to disturb her."

Lauren's smile vanished. She almost lied and said, "Yes, she is sleeping." But she knew that was wrong. There was a time to shield Nastia and keep her secret, but that time had passed. It had gone too far. Sometimes, true Christian love has to make hard choices. Lauren decided to reject what was easy and do what was right.

"Come on in, Stephanie. I have to tell you something that Nastia should have told you weeks ago."

"What is it?" the woman said as she entered and the door closed. "Isn't she here?"

Lauren steeled herself. "No, she is in Hawaii with a guy named Anton."

———◆———

THE STUNNING AZURE sky and the breathtaking green and blue Pacific Ocean seemed even more magnificent that Sunday afternoon as Nastia and Anton lay on Waikiki beach, soaking in the vibrant sun. The wind blew steadily from the west, strong and powerful. Anton lay on his back with his blue shirt over his eyes while Nastia watched the windsurfers glide onto the thousands of white-capped waves.

"I had a dream about windsurfers last night," she told him.

"Cool. Were they out yesterday?" he said, very relaxed.

"No. There wasn't much wind yesterday, and the waves were pretty small. Actually, I've never seen them before in my life. I barely knew they existed."

"Maybe your dream has a deep meaning to it, something that will apply to the rest of your life." He smiled jokingly, but she had already been thinking of the meaning. The image of the surfer's silhouette in front of the red sky and black ocean refused to leave her mind. It was as if her whole feeling of insecurity and desperate need for something was captured in the dream.

"Why don't you tell me what it means, oh great dream interpreter?" she asked. He looked so marvelous with his shirt off.

"Let's see," he adjusted his legs as his white teeth shone. "The dream is telling you that when you lie on a beach, watching windsurfers with your boyfriend, you need to kiss him."

She smiled. "Is that what it means, oh great one?"

"Mhmm, that's what it means. And you have to do it for at least thirty seconds." He removed the shirt from his eyes, squinting at her.

She moved closer to him. "How did you get that?"

"I just know these things." He chuckled, and she kissed him for more than thirty seconds. "That's what I'm talking about, beautiful."

Nastia stared at his handsome grin for a moment. This was hers. He was all hers. She remembered her prayer two nights before. She had asked God to make Anton a Christian by sunset on Monday. Today was Monday. "Do you know what I want more than anything?"

"What?"

"I want you to put all your faith and hope in Jesus Christ and believe in him more than anyone or anything else."

His smile faded, and his eyes turned to mystery. "Why do you want that?"

"Because, if you don't, you will go to hell and suffer more horrifically than you could ever imagine." She pressed up against him and kissed his shoulder. "I don't want you to experience that! Please, *please*, don't go to hell!"

Her tear fell onto the side of his face and slid into his ear. He wrapped his arms around her and whispered, "I won't, Nastia. I'll always be here for you. You're safe with me. You don't have to be afraid anymore because we're together now, and that's all that matters."

"But it won't last! Both of us will die one day. What if you die tomorrow by some accident without believing in Jesus? You would go to hell, and I would go insane — literally insane, knowing that you were there because of me."

"No, Nastia." He pulled her head up and looked straight into her tear-clouded eyes. "If I go to hell, it's not because of you. You are saving me with your love. Every night, every time you lie on top of me like you are now, you save me from hell."

She sniffled, her eyes still sad. She couldn't enjoy the compliments. "Are you worshiping me, Anton?"

"Nastia," he said with a comforting grin. "I have worshiped you since the day we met."

"Belief in me will never save you. I'm just a girl — another flawed and sinful human being. You were made for much more than me."

"I don't need anyone else."

"Yes, you *do*, Anton."

He sighed. "Nastia, you know I don't believe in heaven and hell. They are fairy tales that have no application to the life I know."

"They are not fairy tales! God is everything, and heaven and hell are far more real than any of us could ever imagine, even if we spent our entire lives thinking about it. This world is the closest to heaven you will ever get if you don't come to believe in Jesus Christ. All you have to do is believe that he is the Son of God and conquered all sin when he died on the cross — including your sin — and believe that you need him."

They listened to the wind for a moment.

"That's just it," he replied. "I don't believe that a dude who walked around in Jewish sandals and said a lot of good things could clean up the mess of mankind. I don't believe I need someone I can't see, someone who died thousands of years ago. Nastia, I don't want to attack your faith, but can't you see how ridiculous that is?"

"Oh brother, Anton. Aren't you the one who asked me about Christianity just two nights ago? Aren't you the one who said you wanted something more?"

"I was just curious about what my girlfriend believes," he replied simply.

Nastia shook her head. "You know you need more. You know that nothing in your life has been good enough to make you whole."

"No, I *don't* know that. Besides, you don't really believe it either."

"What? That's stupid! Of course I do!"

"No, you don't. If you did, you wouldn't live with me. You've said yourself that Christianity forbids this."

Nastia was stunned. She moved away from him, speechless.

"See, I got you on that one," he said triumphantly.

Nastia didn't reply. She stared at the horizon to distract herself. Anton's resistance was a heavy weight.

She looked around at the beach, at the glimmering white tower-resorts, the deep blue shades in the wind-teased ocean, and the hundreds of people walking about. People covered the beach on the other side of the rock-lined jetty while a few middle-aged adults lounged in the green park behind Nastia and Anton. Only a few young men and women occupied the sandy volleyball court, and none of the guys had blond hair or blank aviator sunglasses.

Nastia wondered if Erlend was on the beach. The waves were much bigger today. Maybe he would try to surf them. What if he had walked by when she wasn't looking? What if he had seen her lying on top of Anton and decided that he could never talk to her again because of his frustrated desire for her?

Nastia glimpsed a pair of red swim trunks. Was it Erlend? She didn't know why she spontaneously wanted to talk to Erlend rather than Anton. Maybe it was because Erlend was a Christian.

A small girl with bright red hair was making a sand castle at the edge of the waves. Nastia recognized her as Mythia.

"Hey, I'm going to go over there," she told Anton while she climbed to her feet. "I want to step into the water."

"Are you okay?"

"Yeah, I'm fine. I just want to play in the Pacific a bit more before we fly home tonight."

"Have fun." He turned on his side to watch her.

Nastia tried to appear as if she was only picking up sand when she leaned down to talk to Mythia. "What are you doing out here? Are you trying to disrespect people again?"

The girl giggled pleasantly. "I'm building a water castle."

To her great surprise, Nastia realized that Mythia was not making a sand castle but a castle of water. The towers swirled up and down as the girl packed on handfuls of seawater that behaved like sand granules. "That's impossible!" Nastia exclaimed. "How do you do that?"

Mythia's red hair flapped in the strong wind. "It's easy! I just reach down my hand," she grabbed a handful of water, "and put it on top. Once it's on, I press it into the shapes."

"It doesn't look easy to me." Perplexed by the water castle, Nastia reached out to touch it, but once her fingers landed, the castle collapsed with a splash and retreated into the ocean with a flattened wave.

"What did you do?" Mythia screamed.

"I'm sorry, I didn't mean to." Nastia was bewildered.

With a childish scowl, Mythia ran onto the ocean, not sinking but running on it as if it was firm ground. She halted and made a clear pouty face toward Nastia. A wave built up behind her.

"Watch out!" Nastia cried, but Mythia didn't listen, and the roaring wave enveloped her. She was gone.

"What the heck? What the heck!" said Nastia in distress. Anton was still watching her, as calm as ever. Nastia concluded that only she could see the red-haired girl, who was supposed to symbolize Nastia's faith.

She sighed.

THREE HOURS LATER, after driving to the Honolulu airport and passing through security, Nastia and Anton sat beside their gate, waiting for the plane. They hadn't talked anymore about the state of her faith. Anton didn't push her for an answer.

Nastia looked down and noticed the light-brown fishhook sewn into the leather strap of Anton's size thirteen flip-flops. She looked up again, blinking. A large photograph of a plane flying over a snowy arctic hill advertised an airline. She thought it ironic to see in Hawaii — America's tropical paradise. The other photograph seemed more appropriate — a Polynesian woman in a white skirt and white lei necklace dancing in front of a rosy sunset.

The sunset!

She gazed out the window and saw the golden disk sinking toward the horizon. Oh no! Anton had to become a Christian before the sun passed the horizon or everything was ruined! On Saturday night, Nastia had prayed with all her might when she asked for Anton to become a Christian. If he didn't, then Erlend's doubts would be confirmed — God doesn't really answer prayers.

The hope that Anton would become a Christian in less than five minutes became even more important to Nastia. Everything was on the line now. Anton's salvation, Nastia's belief in prayer, and maybe even Nastia's own salvation as well as her entire worldview. Everything would change in the time it took the bright sun to cross the few inches of sky, unless Anton came to believe in God. She decided to try harder.

"What if I died tomorrow? What would you do?" she asked carefully.

Anton faced her and didn't speak until he saw the sincerity in her eyes. "I hope more than anything that you won't."

"But what if I did? It's possible. It has happened to couples before. You would lose me forever."

"Then I would be miserable for the rest of my life."

"Say you died two weeks later without changing your beliefs. I would be in one place, and you would be in another. We would be separated for time that never ends."

Even though he was as calm and controlled as ever, Anton's face became sad just like it had done three nights before when they sat in the Jacuzzi and Nastia expressed her anger about his previous girlfriend. "Nastia, I know you want me to become a Christian, but —"

"Don't say it!" she interrupted. "You have to believe in Jesus! You have to! I can't live if you don't!"

He looked even sadder. "Of course you can live —"

"No, no, I can't!" she ignored the stare of a lonely man nearby. "You don't understand! You thought I didn't believe in the power of Jesus because I'm living with you. But I do believe it! It's just — when you entered my life and we talked for the first time on the plane from Dallas to D.C. — my whole world was thrown upside down. You entered my mind, and I couldn't forget you. Now the only way I can live is to live with you. Maybe life isn't the way it's supposed to be; I've made mistakes; I've done things I regret. But you are different from everyone. What is supposed to be isn't as clear as the words printed on the thin pages of the Bible. Most other Christians would call living with you the biggest sin I have ever committed, but I don't agree. You are right, and living with you is right, but Jesus is right also. Our living together is not about life and death. Jesus is the savior from true death. And the only way we can be fully and truly together is if you believe in him."

It took all the energy she felt she possessed to say the answer. Now was the moment that would make or break everything. The edge of the sun was barely above the horizon.

Anton looked at the photograph of the plane above cold white hills, his eyes serious. "When you say 'believe' it means to think and feel that you know in your heart and your mind that something is true. Even though I love you more than anyone else, my love doesn't transcend belief. I'm still here for you, and it's not the end of the world, but I can't put my faith in Jesus. I'm sorry."

Nastia's heart sank with the sun.

The woman announced the time to board over the speakers that sounded like a hollow, empty echo to Nastia. They gathered their things and walked down the jet bridge. She fought the tears that refused to retreat, but when she blinked, they came. The flight attendant welcoming them looked at her sympathetically, but Nastia turned away. She didn't want to see or talk to anyone. The passengers in business class stared at her — one man lowering his glasses and narrowing his small eyes. Why did they have to do that? All Nastia wanted was to be back home in D.C., lying quietly beside Anton. But somehow, even that wasn't good enough. Her sense of comfort, security, and peace had changed. She felt like she didn't know how to live anymore.

Nastia was thankful that she and Anton had the three-seat row to themselves. She leaned against the window and gazed out unceasingly, tears streaming down her cheeks. Anton wasn't going to heaven. But that could change! Couldn't it? Doubt and hopelessness refused to let go of her. Anton didn't believe. To him Jesus was nothing but a dead man who once walked the earth in Jewish sandals.

As the plane quickly raced and lifted off the ground, rising higher and higher, Nastia felt more and more pain. Anton moved the armrest from between them and placed his arm around Nastia. She rested her head on his shoulder, sobbing.

Two wings fluttered, and something landed on her knee. Nastia opened her eyes and distinguished a small red bird in the darkness of the plane.

"Aini?" she whispered as if Anton would hear this time.

The red bird's tiny black eyes were sweet and compassionate. "Hello, Tia. It's been a crazy trip for you, hasn't it?"

"Yes, it has. I don't know what I believe anymore."

"Oh, Tia. Have you allowed Lunosh to deceive you? Do you really believe his lies?"

"No. I don't think so. He hasn't spoken to me at all today."

"He has in a way. He has allowed his lies to sink in. You cannot let them, Tia. All Lunosh wants is your complete destruction."

"Then maybe he is accomplishing that because I feel like I'm dying."

"Then you need to hear from true life again." Aini flew over to the small window, stuck her beak in the crevice on the side, and pulled out a page with words written in the color of the ocean. "Can you read this to me?"

Nastia looked down at the page, noticing the faint image of the Hawaiian shore at sunset behind the words. She read, "Proverbs 3:5-8: 'Trust in the LORD with all your heart and lean not on your own understanding; in all your ways acknowledge him, and he will make your paths straight. Do not be wise in your own eyes; fear the LORD and shun evil. This will bring health to your body and nourishment to your bones.' " She tried to smile. "So, if I do this, I'll have healthy bones?"

Aini made a soft chirp like a laugh. "Much more than that, Tia."

"So, what do you want me to get from this?"

"I want you to say this over and over to yourself tonight. God will give you physical strength to do what is right as well as spiritual strength. During this trip, you began to doubt that God answers prayers at all; you even called him a liar. God is not a liar. He does answer prayers. There are three answers that He gives to a prayer: yes, no, or not now. If you listen, God will reveal his answer to you. One thing that God understands much better than people is the value of the process.

"Also, your specific prayer had to do with Anton's salvation. It is good to pray for him to come to belief. This is very good! But God will not force anyone to have faith. He pursues people, He seeks them out, but He does not make a person choose Him. In order to be saved, Anton would have to surrender his life to Jesus of his own free will. True love can only exist when there is true choice. That is why you, Tia, still have the option to push God away, even though you have given your life to Him.

Nastia sniffled. "I guess you're right."

"Tia, there is something else," said the red bird gravely.

"What's that?"

"In this prayer," Aini explained, "you attempted to test God. You gave Him a specific timeline to answer your prayer. This is not right! 'Do not put the Lord your God to the test' Jesus said in Luke chapter 4 verse 12, when he was being tempted by the devil. Do not ask God to prove his power to you by performing a grand feat. He is the Lord, the Creator. He gathers the storehouses of rain; he directs the paths of the wind; He sees every person on the face of the earth; He formed every living creature and he understands them all. Trust that the Lord knows the bigger picture. If you submit your life to his plan, with an obedient heart, then he can show you the way."

Nastia sighed heavily. "What must I do?"

Aini twittered. "A wonderful response, Tia! Wonderful! The first step is to tell the Lord that you are sorry for putting Him to the test. The next step, is to turn away from all your sin, allowing God to lead you to a life of blessings."

Nastia squirmed uncomfortably, readjusting her head on Anton's shoulder.

"I'll let you think about these passages," said Aini. "But never forget Proverbs 3 verse 5: 'Trust in the LORD with all your heart.' Just to give you a glimpse into the love of God, think about the waves of Hawaii. How many did you see?"

"Oh gosh, thousands."

"Consider each one a symbol of his endless love. One wave is his kindness, the next his patience, and the next his forgiveness. They go on forever. Thank God for each wave, each part of his love. This is a taste of worship."

The red bird flew off into the slow, rumbling plane, leaving Nastia with the page on her lap. She wondered how many waves were splashing in the dark ocean below the plane. She examined the faint image behind the words and counted twenty-five waves. She would start with that.

26

CONFRONTED

NASTIA WAS THE first to wake up from their late afternoon nap. She and Anton had arrived back in Washington D.C. at 12:30 p.m. and returned to the familiar hotel room in which they lived. The time was 3:00 p.m. now, and Nastia wanted to see her best friend, Lauren Henson.

She found her cell phone on the kitchen counter, located the contact, and dialed the number. She had missed Lauren on their trip. Wouldn't it be wonderful to have dinner with her? She couldn't wait!

"Hello?" the voice answered.

"Hey, Lauren! It's Nastia. I'm back from Hawaii and I'd love to tell you all about it. Are you free for dinner tonight?"

Lauren hesitated. "I would like to talk to you."

"It's settled then! I'll meet you at Shalom Shy at 6:30. Look it up online. It's right by the river. Are you fine with that?"

"I guess so. See you then."

"Great! Bye!" Nastia pressed *End* as she wondered if anything was troubling her friend.

She softly entered the bedroom and saw Anton sleeping. "Anton? I'm going to dinner with Lauren, okay?" He didn't seem to hear, but she didn't want to wake him. "Ah well. I'll just leave you a note."

———————◆———————

AS SHE SAT at a white-clothed table, waiting for Lauren, everything about the restaurant Shalom Shy reminded Nastia of her first date with Anton. The grayish paint on the walls reminded her of Anton's easy-going nature, the vivid blue centerpiece shone like his love for life, and the view of the sun setting over the Potomac River made Nastia think of the college stories they shared.

She recalled the overpowering emotions she had experienced far away in a land that many believe to be paradise — Oahu, Hawaii. Only yesterday Nastia had tried with all her strength to persuade Anton to become a Christian — tried and failed. She couldn't think of another time in which the world felt at its end.

But today was different. Nastia had slept and rested, and now she would receive the life-giving encouragement of her best friend. Lauren was the best Christian Nastia had ever met; she was a living example of someone who never stopped believing in Jesus. Nastia couldn't wait to receive her support.

Clad in slimming black pants and a velvety purple shirt, Lauren Henson entered the restaurant and looked around. She wore a few touches of makeup on her face, but nothing like Nastia, who exhibited sparkling blue eyeshadow and shimmering lip gloss.

"It's my best friend!" Nastia stood, and they hugged.

"Hi, Tia. It's good to see you again." Lauren wasn't smiling.

"I have so much to tell you about our trip. Honolulu is a fascinating city…" Nastia noticed her friend's grim countenance. "What's wrong?"

Lauren pressed her lips together. "I have to tell you something."

Nastia's heart panicked. "Oh no! What happened?"

"Stephanie Rivers came by my apartment after church on Sunday. She said that you told her you were sick and couldn't make it to work. Did you say that?"

"Yes, I did," Nastia admitted. "I couldn't tell her I was going to Hawaii with my atheist boyfriend. They would fire me! Since I don't work on Fridays, Saturdays, and Sundays, I only had to cover for Monday and Tuesday. It's not a big deal, Lauren. Please don't look like I've betrayed the whole church." She grinned but Lauren did not. "What did you say to her? You covered for me, right? Just like you always do."

Her silence was the answer.

"Oh, good grace, Lauren, you *didn't*. You couldn't have! How much did you tell her?"

"I invited her into the apartment and told her right away that you were in Hawaii with a guy named Anton."

"No. No, you didn't." Nastia gasped, sitting up in her chair.

"She wanted to know how it developed. 'When did she meet him?' she asked. I said 'On the plane when she first arrived.' Then I told her that you have been living with each other for almost two weeks."

Nastia tried to hold in her rage by not speaking.

"I had to tell her," Lauren explained with a pleading look in her eyes. "It was wrong of you to deceive her and everyone else on the church staff. They need to have employees who set examples for the believers — Christians who pursue God with their hearts and their actions. 'Faith without deeds is dead,' James 2:26 says. Also, Matthew 18 talks about dealing with the sinning members of the body of Christ."

"Don't tell me there is a scripture that justifies what you did." Nastia's anger was groping to come out.

Lauren's eyes grieved, but she continued. "Matthew 18 verses 15 and 16 say, 'If your brother sins against you, go and show him his fault, just between the two of you. If he listens to you, you have won your brother over. But if he will not listen, take one or two others along, so that "every matter may be established by the testimony of two or three witnesses." ' "

"I'm not one of your brothers, Lauren."

"Please, Nastia. You know it means both brothers and sisters in Christ."

"But I haven't sinned against you!" Nastia declared, red anger now flushing her cheeks. "What have I done to offend you?"

"You stopped being my roommate to go live outside of wedlock with an unbelieving man," Lauren answered, keeping her voice gentle. "I was the only one who knew about it. It's not that your sin is directly against me; it's against God. I have been pleading with you to stop living with Anton, but you haven't listened. And since you refused to listen, I had to take the next step." Lauren took a deep breath. "I love you very much as a dear sister in Christ. I want to help free you from Satan's hold on you. Please leave Anton and come back and live in my apartment, where you know you will always be welcome. It doesn't even have to be my apartment, but that is the most available solution right now. Turn away from your sin and beg for God's forgiveness. He has paid the price for you, Tia. *Please.* Stephanie will give you a second chance. You can keep your job, but only if you repent from living with Anton and begin a life of purity again."

"You don't understand!" Nastia hurled out the words. "I can't just up and leave Anton. We are basically husband and wife now."

"Have you committed to each other until death, with at least one witness?" Lauren asked.

Nastia scowled. "No."

"Then you aren't married, even by the broadest worldly definition of the word" Lauren took another deep breath. "But the Christian definition of marriage is different. It's a covenant between God and the church, a commitment. You see," Lauren blushed a little, "love making is when the two become one flesh, and one flesh should not be separated. That's why God's blessing is so important, because it gives a marriage the greatest chance of survival. You two have just come together without taking the proper steps. Besides, he
— "

"Isn't a Christian?" Nastia finished Lauren's sentence for her. "Is that what you were going to say? Well, you're right! He isn't a Christian. But that doesn't mean we don't love each other. We do — very much. I could never leave him now. He is the best man I have ever met. We've been over this before. You of all people know how much I need a good man in my life. You know what my Dad did. Anton isn't like that at all. He's so good to me."

"Nastia, I know your father's mistake has scarred you deeply," Lauren said, with a sincere look glistening in her brown eyes. "I know that's true and it's hard. But you can't blame him. His choice to sin is separate from your choice to sin. You inherited the sinful nature from Adam and Eve just like the rest of us. Just like me. But even so, we can't blame Adam and Eve. We all have to take responsibility for our own actions."

"I am..." Her voice trailed off. Nastia had to think of more reasonable things to say. But what good would it do? Lauren firmly believed that Nastia was living in sin, and neither of them were going to change their minds. "What's the use of our arguing? It's just going to put more strain on our friendship. Can't we agree to disagree? Don't you want to hear about Hawaii?"

"Yes, I would, but this is far more important," said Lauren. "We can talk about Hawaii and whatever else you would like for hours, but why don't we do it after you move back in with me? Can we do that?"

Nastia's eyes were getting moist. "I really, *really* hate it when we clash so much. I know I can be stubborn and selfish sometimes, but my relationship with Anton is more important to me than anything else right now."

Lauren leaned forward with a serious expression, as if the words she was about to say were the most important words she would ever say. "Is that even more important to you than God?"

Nastia shook her head, not wanting to face the question. "God is very important to me. He is. Don't worry. But I don't believe that living with Anton is wrong anymore. It's far too right, far too superior to any other human relationship I have ever known for it to be wrong."

Lauren didn't reply. She looked exhausted and shook her head back and forth, tears filling her lamp-like eyes. "I'm not rejecting you," she whispered as she scooted her chair back and stood.

"What? What the heck are you talking about?" Nastia didn't want to deal with something difficult.

Lauren spoke her words clearly and carefully. "I have agreed to disagree with a lot of people, but you and I once agreed that living unmarried with a guy is living in sin. I know you believe it's wrong; you're just trying to run from the responsibility. But I can't help you run. I can't take my faith where you are taking yours. So, I have to go now."

"Good grace, no! Don't do this to me! I will be destroyed, and it will be your fault."

"No, Tia, no. Sin is a painkiller that brings more pain. That's what's happening now." Lauren lowered her head for a few seconds, blinking. "You are still the polka to my dotta. You will always be a very special friend to me."

When Lauren's eyelids lifted, Nastia felt a sinking feeling in her stomach. Her best friend was crying.

"My door is still open to you," Lauren squeaked out the words, her voice fading. "Okay? It will always be open to you. But I cannot be close friends with someone who is actively rejecting God."

Nastia watched as her best friend opened the glass door and left.

She wanted to hit the table. She wanted to hit it with all her strength! But she knew it wouldn't do any good.

"Can I take your order?" the waiter asked.

"No. I'm going home. I'm not going to eat here."

The waiter seemed worried. "Are you unsatisfied with our service?"

Nastia was annoyed by the question. "No! It's a completely different matter. Please, leave me alone."

The waiter did so.

Nastia lingered at the table for a moment. What was she supposed to do now? How was she supposed to handle this? She had to return to Anton. He would support her. He would love her!

The two wires of pride clenched tightly around Nastia's left calf and right forearm, reminding her of their existence. "Ouch!" She grimaced. They felt like they were cutting off her circulation.

Something fell from the ceiling and collided loudly on the plate in front of Nastia. A small metal ball rolled toward her. "Oh no!"

She jumped out of her chair, grabbed her purse, and raced for the door as fast as she could, disregarding the shocked hostess. Once outside, she hurried down the steps toward her car. She heard the metal ball smash into the concrete and onto the hood of the car as she fumbled with her key. It leapt onto her neck and unraveled into a string of six metal ants that immediately began to pinch their way into her skin. She held her breath as she finally unlocked the car, climbed into the driver's seat, and slammed the door shut.

She cried and bit her lip so hard that it bled.

◆

ANTON WAS SITTING in front of the TV in the colorful Hawaiian tank-top Nastia had purchased for him when she opened the door to their hotel room. He turned around to look at her and clicked off the set.

"Hey," he said. "I didn't expect you back for a while."

"So, you got my note?" she said dimly.

"Yeah, I did." His eyes sensed a problem. "Is everything all right between you and Lauren? What happened to your lip?" He reached to touch the tiny spot of dried blood.

"It's just a scratch. And no, nothing is all right between me and Lauren."

"Oh no." He hugged her. "What went wrong?"

"Everything! She told Stephanie, my supervisor at the church, that I'm living with you. Both of them agree that it's *very* wrong. She basically said if I don't stop living with you, they will fire me."

Anton released a heavy exhale as he hung his head over her shoulder. "What are you going to do?"

"I think I'll quit."

"Okay."

Her cell phone started to ring.

"Oh grace, speak of the devil." The screen read *Stephanie Rivers*. She answered it. "Hello?"

"Hi, is this Nastia?" said the timid voice.

"Yes, it is."

"Are you free to talk right now?"

"Yeah, sure. What's up?" Nastia rolled her eyes so Anton could see how irritated she was.

"This is difficult for me to say, but something has come up. Two of the elders and I need to talk to you."

"That sounds very serious. What's wrong?"

"We will address that when you come in," Stephanie said. "Does eleven o'clock tomorrow work for you?"

"Why can't you just tell me now?" Nastia heard the semblance of anger in her own voice.

"It's not something I can disclose over the phone — only in person."

"Is this about me living with my boyfriend?" Nastia blurted out.

There was a long pause. "It might be."

Nastia looked at Anton. He was simply and lovingly standing there for her. She made her decision. "If you and those elders are planning to judge me, then I don't want any part of it! You can start looking for another schedule girl. As of this moment, I quit! It was nice knowing you." She pressed the *End* button as if she was crushing an ant.

Anton wrapped his arms around her. "You really do love me."

"Yes, I do." Nastia pressed her chin into his neck.

"You've had a hard couple of days," Anton said. "Me saying no to what you wanted, and now losing your job and this trouble with your best friend. You know, you don't have to worry about money. I make more than enough for the two of us. But, hey, you need to relax. Would you like to go down to our comfy old hot tub again? There's no sense in trying to sleep now. I'm still on Hawaii time."

"That would be nice."

They kissed.

———————◆———————

AT 2:00 A.M., Anton clicked off the TV and said, "I have to get up for work in the morning."

Nastia wormed around in the covers for two more hours. The new ants of idolatry pulsed painfully on her neck. Frustrated by her insomnia, Nastia got out of bed.

She opened the refrigerator and poured herself a glass of organic milk. Maybe milk would not have the inky hypocrite's brew like everything else she drank. She didn't taste the bitterness in the first sip, or the second.

Curling up on the couch, she noticed the silhouette of a tiger and a small bird on the deck, but she didn't go out. She was cold. Wouldn't it be colder outside?

The faintest hint of a splash sounded from her glass of milk resting on the coffee table. What was it? She wrapped her arms around herself and rubbed her skin, uncomfortable and depressed. All she wanted to do was rest! Couldn't God give her that?

Something crawled on her lower back. She reached to scratch it, but nothing was there. She felt the crawling again, up her spine, then at her upper back. She strained to touch the spot, and when she did, she felt a small metal spider.

Nastia gasped and frantically tried to brush it off, but the spider refused to move. It had connected with her skin, but it wasn't beneath the skin like the other sin-bugs and it didn't hurt either. Still, she was greatly disturbed and headed out for the balcony.

"Aini? Jianyu?" she wailed. "Are you out here?"

Lying on the couch, the tiger raised its head. The bird stopped preening.

"Hello, Nastia," said the tiger's deep voice. "What is troubling you?"

"A spider just crawled onto my back! What is it? What does it mean?"

"That is the spider of resentment," Jianyu explained. "It will pinch you when you actively resent someone. Each leg represents a person in your life. Right now, the spider probably has four legs. They will grow longer and longer the more you resent those four people."

Nastia gingerly touched the immobile spider again. "Who do they represent?"

"Who do you think has offended you or harmed you today?"

"Well," she thought for a moment, "I'm upset with Lauren and probably will be for a long time, and also Stephanie. I don't know how I can forgive her for being such a judgmental Pharisee!"

One of the spider's legs twitched, causing Nastia to tense up. "Is my father the third one?"

"Yes, if you have not forgiven him."

"I guess I haven't. But who does the fourth leg represent?"

"Who do you think?" the tiger replied.

"I don't know!" Nastia glared at the sky as a wave of chills rushed up and down her body. "Is it God?"

"Yes. You resent God for letting all of this happen, even though God is without sin. That leg represents your immoral anger toward God."

Nastia slumped into the plastic chair as a siren mourned in the distance.

27

DRUNK ON SALT WATER

A WEEK AFTER returning from Hawaii, Nastia closed the door of her car and began crossing the large supermarket parking lot, the sunless sky rapidly growing darker. Two days earlier Nastia had visited a new church by herself. She had sung the songs, listened to the sermon, and left feeling just as lonely as before. She missed her best friend, even though she simply could not forgive Lauren for ratting on her.

Nastia had been looking for a job all week but still hadn't found one. Hopefully, at least one of the many applications she had sent would be accepted. She felt like she would go crazy if she didn't find a good job soon! She was growing horribly restless and had been thinking of the new hurts over and over. But more than that, she wanted a distraction from the spider on her upper back that twitched uncomfortably every time she thought of someone who had wounded her, which was several times a day.

The supermarket felt like a refrigerator. Nastia rubbed her upper arm, trying to warm herself. The memory of Lauren's words at Shalom Shy made her want to cry every time she thought of them, and now, in the frigid supermarket, Nastia strained to fight the tears. *My door is still open to you. Okay? It will always be open to you. But I cannot be close friends with someone who is actively rejecting God.*

Why did Nastia constantly remember those words? She wasn't rejecting God! Was she? No, she was living with the man whom God had provided. It was Lauren who was rejecting *her*. She was the one who refused to be her only supportive friend. Nastia was attaching to Anton even more because he was the only person — besides acquaintances — with whom she talked.

Nastia turned a corner toward the refrigerated sauces and saw a middle-aged woman rushing away with her cart and young child. *What just happened?* An overpowering smell filled her nostrils as she tripped on the slippery floor and hit her head. Instantly, a memory flooded Nastia's mind as strong and forceful as the smell, but much more painful.

———————◆———————

A GLASS JAR shattered on the floor, and the stressed Mrs. Sobieski bent down, hurting and wincing, her red bangs ruffled and moist.

"Don't do that, Mom. You'll hurt your knees. I'll get it," said fifteen-year-old Nastia, grabbing her mother's arm and trying to pull her up to a standing position again.

"No, thank you, Nastia Jane. I'm already down here. But could you please take the sandwich to your father? He's in the band house counseling someone."

Nastia grabbed the plate and headed out the back door, still concerned about her mother. The band house was what they called the old guesthouse in the backyard where Mr. Sobieski spent most of his time, preparing sermons, counseling, and occasionally working on music recordings for the church's worship group.

The late afternoon sky was clustered with dark clouds that usually only brought excessive wind rather than rain to the Sedona desert. That day was especially windy. Nastia heard thunder as she walked up the steps and opened the screen door.

She usually knocked, and her dad would say, "Who is it?" and then "Come in." But, for some reason, Nastia simply opened the door and walked in that time. Maybe she didn't think he could hear with the loud wind in the sparse trees around the house. It didn't matter. Why had she thought of that irrelevant detail so many times? What she saw next was the pain of years.

In the dim brown glow of the band house, Mr. Sobieski had his shirt off while he embraced a woman, his hand on her leg. They both looked at Nastia with wide eyes.

Nastia froze for a moment, realizing what she saw. Once she did, she dropped the plate, raced over the back yard, climbed the fence, and ran as fast as she could for her secret spot on the other side of the dirt hill. The wind blew even louder and a deep crack of thunder resounded with a flash, but Nastia didn't care about the lightning. She didn't care about anything!

She sat down in the soft dirt behind a large bush and opened her waterproof box where she kept her CD player and a few albums. She put in her favorite, turned up the volume, and listened to the music through her headphones. It began to rain, and she tossed her clear poncho over herself, clutching the CD player to her neck. All she wanted was to keep it dry! All she wanted was to be left alone and not talk to anyone! She hated the thought of her father! Oh, her horrible father! Nastia knew the woman he was committing adultery with. She was a wife and a mother in their small church.

———————— ♦ ————————

"ARE YOU ALL right?"

Nastia opened her eyes and realized she was back in the Washington D.C. supermarket. Cheap yellow mustard pooled all over the floor, giving off a potent odor. A grocer leaned over her.

"Yes, I'm fine. Thank you. Just a little dizzy."

He helped her to her feet.

A blue tiger watched Nastia from behind a stand. She gave him an agonized look and turned to leave.

———————————◆———————————

AFTER PURCHASING HER items and driving home, Nastia opened the door, entered the silent hotel room, and set the crinkling plastic bags on the counter. She rubbed her forehead. Had she just experienced a concussion? She shook her head and tried to think of something else. She was glad their room possessed a full kitchen with a refrigerator, stove, dishwasher, sink, and appliances. They had rarely used it, but today, Nastia wanted to cook dinner for Anton.

The sky was black outside the sliding glass door. It was nighttime already. Anton had texted her earlier to say that he wouldn't be home until ten. That gave Nastia time to prepare a late dinner.

She began chopping the carrots, onions, and mushrooms as the butter melted in the stainless-steel pot. The image of Erlend's rare smile flashed in her mind. Nastia had been thinking of him all week. She remembered what he said in the motorboat above the reef after they saw the shark: "Are you an idiot? Why didn't you come up immediately with me? You could have been killed!" He had saved her life. Erlend was probably the only person who had saved Nastia's life. He was such a nice guy, and a Christian too. Nastia wished she could have helped him more with his troubles. "I wonder," she whispered. "What if I had dated Erlend instead of Anton? We could have been a Christian couple instead of a clashing one." Somehow, she knew that it would not have worked out.

Suddenly, the suppressed memory of her father committing adultery rushed in as clear as ever, overpowering the comforting thought of Erlend. "No! Darn it! I thought I had just forgotten that again!" It was her worst memory. If she could have removed it from her mind and thrown it into a filthy dumpster to be gone forever, she would have. But memories didn't work that way, unfortunately.

Rage and hate for her father surged into her heart. She resented him more than anyone else. After that day, she never let him hug her again. Whenever he would reach over to put his hand on her,

Nastia would pull away. She did not want to be touched by her father at all; she was very glad to be out of the house and away from the entire state of Arizona, just to be away from her father.

Two legs of the spider on her back twitched and she could feel them grow half an inch. "What? Ahh!" She reached behind her neck and touched it. The body felt slightly bigger.

"What's happening? I didn't do anything! I didn't do anything but fall, hurt my head, and remember. Why are you doing this to me?" She was angry with God.

A red bird stood on the granite countertop right beside the wooden cutting board and the two large tomatoes. Nastia gasped. "Aini! I could have mistaken you for a tomato."

"I would have let you know." The bird made a sound like a laugh. "So, you're making dinner?"

"Yes. I feel like a Christian housewife. All I need now is a sermon playing on the radio." She chuckled.

Aini flew over to the pot and peered in. "Mmm. Smells good."

"It's just butter and vegetables, silly." Even so, Nastia was pleased by the compliment.

"What are you making?"

"Smoked salmon bisque; my mother's recipe."

"Sounds perfectly delicious."

Nastia began slicing the tomatoes. "What are you doing here, Aini? Is there anything you wanted to say?"

"Jianyu told me what happened at the grocery store," the bird replied, flying back to the counter. "He senses that you resent him."

"Resent him?" Nastia was shocked at first by the statement. "Well, he does tell me what to do a lot."

"Part of the role of a good authority is to provide instruction," Aini responded.

Nastia shrugged. "Maybe I don't understand him."

"I didn't think so. If you did, you would not resent him. It's a bad idea to resent your protection, Nastia. He represents authority just as I represent kindness. Both are different parts of love."

"Wait, I thought you represented love, and he represented some vague concept of authority?"

"No, I represent kindness, though not adequately I might add. Both of us show a part of love. Mere kindness without the vital protection of authority isn't enough. You need both. God's authority is most important."

"Don't put yourself down, Aini. You are my favorite of the two angels." Nastia thought the bird would appreciate the compliment, but she was wrong.

"I shouldn't be. You must appreciate us both equally. But more importantly, you must stop resenting God and his fatherly guidance and protection. We are only angels, but he is the creator of the universe and the source of all goodness."

"I don't want fatherly guidance. I hate my father."

The bird's small eyes became sad. "This is a very serious problem. If you resent God along with your earthly father, then you will fall into horrible darkness even worse than what you experience now."

The blue tiger rested quietly in the dark living room, bearing a commanding yet humble expression. He held a scroll between his fangs. The red bird flew over, clenched the scroll with her feet, and carried it to the counter.

"What's this?" Nastia observed the moving sketches of waves on the partially unrolled scroll.

"This is a short story called 'Drunk on Salt Water,'" Aini replied. "Please read it to Anton during dinner."

Nastia examined the paper and scanned over the story. "Why can't I read it to him in bed?"

"It would be better if you didn't associate the good themes of this story with your daily sin of sleeping with him."

The bird flew off the counter, met up with Jianyu, and headed out onto the balcony.

———————◆———————

TWO HOURS LATER, Nastia sat alone at the circular glass table beneath the dim light. The hot bisque waited on the table, along with bowls and spoons. Nastia had already eaten one full ladle because she was so hungry. Finally, the door opened, and Anton entered, wearing a light-blue shirt and a gray tie.

"Hey, sorry I'm so late. I didn't mean to keep you waiting. But I have some great news to tell you!" He set his briefcase down, kissed her, and took his place on the other side of the table.

"Really? What's the news?"

He lifted the lid and inhaled. "*Mhmm…*this smells delectable! What is it?"

"Smoked salmon bisque, my mother's recipe. Now, come on, tell me."

Anton flashed his wide, mischievous grin, and Nastia knew it was something special.

"Okay," he chuckled. "I know we just got back from Hawaii a week ago, but I have been working through the glitches of a sudden invitation we have received."

"What invitation?"

"You know that woman at our table the first night in Honolulu?"

Nastia thought for a moment. "Yes. You mean the one who asked all those questions about us?"

"Yes, her. She contacted my employer and invited both you and me to visit her mansion off the coast of Athens, Greece."

"Whoa! Really? When? And for how long?"

"My boss told me that we should leave a week from Friday, and we can stay there for three days. It would be a total of four days, including travel."

"Hmm," Nastia didn't know if she was excited or not. "Sounds interesting."

Anton sensed her hesitation. "I know you're tired of horribly long flights. I am too, but my boss wants us to do this. Ms. Barlas said it's about a major investment she wants to contribute to the company I work for."

"All right. I'm up for it."

"Great!"

Nastia filled his bowl with bisque, and he began eating.

"This is delicious!" he exclaimed. "Why didn't you tell me you could cook so well?"

She shrugged. "I really can't. I think I got lucky this time."

He rolled his eyes. "Oh brother, I don't believe a word of that, Miss Modest."

They smiled at each other.

"Anton?" She was ready to tell her story.

"Nastia?" He grinned widely again.

"I have a dinnertime story to tell you. Consider it the evening show."

"Are you going to belly dance for me? That'd be nice."

"Oh, be quiet, silly." They both laughed. "Are you ready for me to tell it?"

"Sure. The floor is yours, great narrator."

"Thank you." She paused for a moment to prepare herself and began, "Once upon a time, there was a lone island in the tropics with three stranded inhabitants — a female prostitute, a young man just out of seminary (that's college for aspiring pastors, in case you were wondering, Anton)."

"Thanks, Nastia, but I know what seminary is," he said with a grin.

"Okay, good. Anyway, there was a prostitute, a young male pastor, and a little preteen girl with red hair named Faith."

"Hmm, I think I have met that girl before."

"Congratulations on having a memory. Will you let me tell the story now?" Nastia said, impatiently.

"Yes. I will not interrupt anymore." Anton lowered his head and lifted another spoonful of bisque to his lips, attempting to hide his grin.

"Good boy. Okay. Every morning, they would go out to the beach and spend the day there. The prostitute, desperate to quench her thirst, would leap into the waves and swallow handfuls of seawater. The young pastor would shake his head with disgust, realizing that salt water only makes someone thirstier, before he returned to his studies. Meanwhile, Faith would scavenge around in the forest, looking for dew on the big leaves to put into her small cup. One day, she found a map lying in the sand beside a rock. She ran out to the beach and said to the prostitute and pastor, 'Look! I found a map that will lead us to the spring of fresh water on top of the hill!'

" 'You did? Wonderful! Let's go now!' said the prostitute, but the pastor hesitated.

" 'Wait,' he said, taking the map from the girl. 'We have to examine the map first and see if it's legitimate.' He scrutinized it with suspicious eyes, but soon his face brightened, and he said, 'Yes, this does look like a map to the spring. Follow me, I will lead you there.'

So, Faith and the prostitute followed the pastor. He read the signs and found the paths, saying, 'This way!' and 'Over here!'

"Finally, they climbed the last part of the hill and arrived at the spring. A beautiful cascade of water trickled into a clear pond. But an angel stood in front of it, preventing them from rushing toward the stream. He wore polished silver armor and an intimidating helmet, and he was armed with a sharp iron spear.

" 'Please move aside,' the prostitute begged. 'We are extremely thirsty!'

" 'Yes,' the pastor added. 'We have been traveling *all day*. Please let us drink.'

" 'I will let you,' said the angel. 'But only if you give up everything else and recognize that this is a gift you can never deserve.'

" 'What do you mean by give up everything else?' said the prostitute, in a concerned tone. 'I desperately need fresh water, but can't I drink salt water also, every now and then? I have acquired a taste for it.'

" 'No!' replied the angel, pounding the end of his spear on the ground. 'You must give up your entire life and only drink and live here at the pool of fresh water.'

" 'But I can't give up seawater,' the prostitute protested. 'I just can't! It's impossible for me."

" 'Then you cannot drink any fresh water,' the angel stated in an absolute tone.

"Meanwhile, the pastor waited for the angel and the prostitute to stop talking. Once they did, he spoke to the guard. 'Please, good sir, I can see that you value the laws of God.'

"The angel addressed him cautiously, 'Yes. I certainly do.'

" 'I do as well!' he said with a smile. 'I have studied the laws of God tirelessly with all my efforts. I have read many marvelous books written by the best biblical scholars and I have pursued understanding of the most complex theologies. I have never tasted any seawater, I deciphered the map, and I led these two women up here to the spring. Do you not agree that I, of all people, deserve a refreshing drink of fresh water as a reward for all my good works?'

" 'No, you do not deserve a taste,' the angel replied firmly. 'No stranded human being has ever deserved a drink of the divine fresh water, and you are no exception. You must simply accept God's gift with gratitude.'

"The pastor was shocked. 'But surely you have heard what I just said! I have contributed so much good to the world. I helped these two women, and I kept myself from giving into the vast temptations of the great ocean. God would definitely want me more than anyone else.'

" 'Your heart is full of pride and self-righteousness. If you do not humble yourself before God, you can never taste the perfect water.'

"The pastor stepped back, feeling that this was very unjust treatment.

"Faith had remained silent for a long time. Once the angel turned to her, she spoke, 'Sir, I have tasted salt water, but it only made me thirstier, and I have tried to understand the deep complexities of the pastor's studies, but it was very hard, and I gave up. I have been searching for fresh water to quench my thirst for weeks. If I don't have a drink now, I will die of dehydration. There is nothing else in the entire world that I need and want more than the life-giving water of God.' "

"The angel smiled with satisfaction at Faith. He motioned for her to approach the pond. 'You have a pure heart, young one. You will not only taste fresh water; you will live in the palace of God and see the savior's face.' "

"The end." Nastia finished her story.

Anton slurped his final spoonful of bisque.

"How did you like it?"

Anton shrugged. "Very interesting. You should write a book about the adventures of Faith."

Nastia giggled in amusement. "I think God already did."

28

BARLAS ISLAND

NASTIA FELT SOMETHING like a feather slide down her spine as she boarded the plane with Anton on a late Friday afternoon, embarking on a direct flight to Athens, Greece.

"I'm sorry I couldn't get our seats together, Nastia," Anton apologized as they walked down. He had told her before, and she was disappointed. Now he felt bad. "I'll sit in the one in the back, and you can have the better one."

"No. No. I refuse to let you. I will take the one in the back. You have the good seat because you deserve it more than me." She kissed him and hurried away.

"No, come on. It's ladies first!" he started to say but she was already placing her carry-on suitcase in the compartment above her row. She sent him a stubborn smile. He shook his head and couldn't help but grin widely.

Nastia took a deep, fortifying breath. This would be the first flight she hadn't spent with Anton since before they had met. She wasn't too disappointed, however. Maybe it would be a good experience to talk to someone else and not be so completely dependent on his company.

A teenage girl, with very straight brown hair, warily placed her pink suitcase beside Nastia's. She glanced at her boarding pass one more time and sat in the aisle seat. Her thin mother and father came over to check on her before they settled in the next row.

After the plane raced over the runway and rose into the sky, Nastia turned to the girl and introduced herself. "Looks like we will be spending nine hours next to each other," she smiled. "My name is Nastia."

The pretty girl looked at her with acutely well-meaning eyes and said, "Hi, I'm Taylor. It's nice to meet you."

They shook hands.

"What are you going to Greece for?" Nastia inquired.

"My parents, my younger brother, and I are visiting Athens for a short sightseeing trip," Taylor replied. "What about you?"

"My boyfriend and I are going on a random trip to some tiny island off the coast of Athens. A mysterious woman, whom we met only once at a crazy-late business dinner in Hawaii, invited us to her mansion there."

"Really?" Taylor's face lit up like a mocha candle. "Wow! That sounds extremely exciting! Our trip isn't nearly as interesting as that. We are only visiting the Acropolis and museums."

"Oh, I don't know. You might have more fun than me. I have no idea if this trip will be a huge failure or a success. I have a strange feeling about it. Besides, I only found out that we were going a week before Tuesday." Nastia laughed.

"You mean this past week? Just *ten days ago*?" The girl was shocked. "Gosh, my family has been planning this trip for months. Did you say you were going with your boyfriend?"

"Yes. He's amazing."

After a while, the air conditioning in the plane became noticeably colder. "Good grace," Nastia lamented. "This is what I hate about flights. They get so cold."

"Yeah, I know what you mean," Taylor commiserated. "But better too cold than too hot."

Nastia opened a paper-thin airplane blanket and started spreading it over her shoulders. "But they don't have to make it *so* cold. I don't feel comfortable in my own sin."

Taylor seemed confused. "Sorry? Don't you mean skin?"

Nastia laughed at herself, realizing her mistake. "Yes, thank you. I did mean skin not sin." She thought of the irony of her accidental wording. "I feel far more comfortable in my sin than my skin."

"What do you mean by that?"

"Oh, nothing. Never mind."

Taylor waited for a few moments and pressed again. "Can I ask you something?"

"Definitely. Go ahead."

"How is it, living every day with your boyfriend? Are you living with him? I didn't mean to assume."

"Don't apologize. I am living with him — and it's great. My relationship with him is the best human relationship I have ever experienced in my life. I love him so much, more than anyone else in the world." She paused. "How old are you?"

"Fifteen."

"Oh, my grace, that is young! You probably shouldn't be thinking about a serious dating relationship until you're much older."

"But why? You just said it's the best human relationship you've ever experienced. That makes me want a boyfriend even more than I do already."

"Oh no! What have I done?" Nastia decided that she wasn't being a good influence on Taylor. "Please don't listen to me. You know, a lot of my good friends don't like that I'm living with a guy, and we aren't married."

"They shouldn't say that," said Taylor sympathetically. "I think marriage is getting a little outdated. Most of my friends at school have parents who have either divorced or separated at least once. I think simply living together is a good way to find the closeness of marriage without the difficulty of legal issues."

Nastia was surprised that such an innocent-looking girl would say what Nastia had been secretly thinking for months. "You are very mature for your age."

Taylor smiled. "Besides my parents, you are the first person to ever say that."

Nastia felt a kinship with the girl. "You remind me of my younger sister, Megan."

"Thank you. You have sisters? How many?"

"Three."

"Wow. I only have a younger brother, but I've always wanted a sister."

The flight was long, but Nastia adequately passed the time with Taylor. They talked about many different things — clothes, movies, books, art, experiences in high school, how this was Taylor's third time to Europe but Nastia's second, what college is like and what Taylor should expect, and picking a career — but mostly they discussed dating and boys. Taylor was very interested in everything Nastia had learned during her five weeks of living with Anton, and Nastia was more than happy to share. She even opened up about her thoughts on Erlend. "I met the most adorable blond surfer in Hawaii. He was a wonderful guy. One thing you have to realize about dating, even living together, is that you will still encounter other guys who you are strongly attracted to." Taylor soaked up everything Nastia said.

After dinner, Anton came over on his way to the bathroom and checked on Nastia. An hour later, she walked up to the bathroom in the middle of the plane just so she could visit Anton as well. Taylor slept for a bit, and Nastia tried for a few dark hours, but soon she was wide awake again, and they were playing a word game she had invented.

Once they landed and started getting off the plane, Nastia wished Taylor a good vacation, promising to connect on Facebook. Taylor thanked Nastia for her company, saying, "I'm very glad we met."

ANTON WAITED FOR Nastia right outside their gate. "Looks like you made a friend."

"Yes, I did," Nastia said as they made their way through the busy and bright Athens international airport. "She was great company. How about you? Did you meet anyone?"

Anton shrugged. "I sat between two businessmen who were either completely silent or talking about boring work. But it was okay. I watched a couple movies."

"Where to now?" she asked.

"I thought we could go see the Parthenon before we leave for Barlas Island."

"Sounds great."

They took the public metro system through the busy city and to the Acropolis. The sun shone strongly upon them as they stood before the ancient pillars of the Parthenon. "Almost 2,500 years old, the Parthenon is one of the most iconic buildings in the history of the world. It was built as a temple for the virgin goddess, Athena," a tour guide said as they passed. Nastia and Anton quietly strolled around the building, holding hands. Despite how tired and overwhelmed she was by the travel, Nastia felt happier than she had in weeks. If only she could seal this moment in time and forever walk through life hand-in-hand with Anton. He appeared so magnificently himself in his blue jeans and T-shirt as they surveyed the impressive vista of Athens.

After finding a bite to eat, they took another bus to the pier at the edge of the Aegean Sea. Enyo Barlas patiently waited for them, her raspberry-colored hair just as short and glossy as the day they had met. She pinched her hands behind her back, bearing a proud satisfaction in her thin eyes.

"Welcome to Greece!" Enyo greeted with a sly grin. "I hope your trip was not uncomfortable."

"It was fine, thank you," Anton replied, putting on his black sunglasses to shield his eyes from the powerful sun.

"Did you get to visit the Acropolis like your supervisor told me in an e-mail? The Parthenon is my favorite building in the entire world! And I don't mean that lightly."

"Yes, we did," he said.

She turned to Nastia, hugging her abruptly. "How wonderful to see you again! Those flights over the Atlantic are absolutely *dreadful*. We must get you to the island as soon as possible so you can rest."

"We are a bit tired, but the flight wasn't too bad." Nastia wondered why Enyo seemed to disregard Anton's answers.

An elderly Greek man stood at the wheel of a weather-worn boat. Enyo, Nastia, and Anton climbed into three of the seven passenger seats. The driver turned up the engine and pulled out of the pier.

The warm, salty wind rushed over them as Anton and Nastia sat together, his arm around her. The clear sky displayed a spectacular azure above the blue Aegean Sea. Nastia looked through her purplish sunglasses and thought that the Pacific Ocean around Hawaii was greener than the Aegean. The scenery did remind her of Hawaii, but it was very different. Greece seemed drier and busier and didn't possess the aura of paradise like Oahu did. There were no romantic palm trees or tropical flowers. Nastia could only think one thing: *This is so European!*

Soon, after about ten minutes of racing through the watery spray, the island became visible. It was one piece of flattened rock sticking out of the immense sea like an enormous stone eye. That was Nastia's first impression. She felt a piercing gaze transferring its searing desires into her own heart, as if the island were the top of a drowning statue — brutally beaten and mistreated. She felt a strange suspicion rise within her. *What is this island? Who is Enyo Barlas, really?*

As they drew closer, Nastia could make out the design of the house on top of the island. It was a white two-story building with a blue glass dome on top, mixing classic Greek with contemporary style. She craned her neck to keep looking at the beautiful structure as the boat slowed and suddenly stopped with a jolt. She looked down, and the wrinkled boatman was already hunching over to unload their bags. Once the three passengers had wobbled onto the dock, Enyo whispered something into the old man's ear, and he hopped back into his boat and drove away. She turned to them, her eyes now shockingly circular.

"Come this way," Enyo directed, heading toward some steep steps. "You'll have to carry your luggage yourselves up this part. I'm so sorry. The old boatman thinks these stairs will cause his death if he climbs them. Isn't that silly?"

Nastia and Anton exchanged uncertain glances and followed Enyo up the rocky steps. Once they navigated the challenge, they arrived at a beige tile platform in front of the white house. They climbed up five tile steps framed by two spindly trees, across another tile platform, then up five more steps framed by two male statues, across another platform, and finally, up five steps that reached the polished beige pillars of the front deck. Nastia and Anton dropped their suitcases and pulled out the handles, panting and sweating.

Enyo fiddled with the doorknob until it surrendered, and she walked in. "Come on, come on!" She hastily waved her hand. They followed her inside as cooler air rushed over them. The room was completely beige, with the exception of thin white curtains, light-blue sofas, and marble statuettes.

"Wow! You have a gorgeous place," Anton commented.

"Thank you, thank you!" Enyo replied.

"How did you get all the building materials up here to make this?" Nastia asked, greatly awed by everything.

"Money, darling. Lots of money." Enyo strode further in and shifted her head back and forth. "Damon! Damon! Where are you?" she called. "Damon is my son, my dears. He and I are a family of two."

"Is it just you two up here?" Nastia asked.

"Not just," Enyo said from behind the blue-glass dining table. "The cook and her daughter — who works as our maid — live in the little house at the end of the island, but they keep to themselves. I am so glad that Damon and I have real guests for a change. We love each other very much, but sometimes, we just want to kill each other like gladiators in the arena." Her eyes became lines again as she grinned.

"Yes, splendid Mum?" came the response of a sleek voice. From the stairwell beside the kitchen, a skinny, extremely-tanned young man about six-feet tall entered, wearing white shorts and a see-through white shirt. He looked at Anton first as a faint smile grew on his face. "Hello. Good to meet you. My name is," he chuckled. "Well, you already know my name. My mother was screaming it so loudly!" He leaned over and kissed Enyo on the cheek and smiled fully now, exposing his small but white teeth. "It's Damon Barlas."

"Good to meet you. My name is Anton Shepherd, and this," he motioned to Nastia, "is my girlfriend, Nastia Sobieski."

"Oh gods!" He jerked his head back, as if he had just tasted the most delicious chocolate truffle and was praying for more. "That is the most beautiful last name I have ever heard in my life!"

"Sounds like you have never seen a man with a herd of sheep before," Nastia grinned, and Damon looked straight at her.

For the first time, Nastia caught a good look at his eyes; she was instantly taken aback. Damon's irises were so black that they mixed with his pupils. They were sly, foxy eyes. And his face was an adolescent kind of handsome, but loveable and very streetwise.

"No, no. I was talking about *your* name," Damon clarified. "Sobieski — what does it mean? Do you know?"

"I don't know. I'm sorry," said Nastia. "But my great grandfather was known to say that the first Sobieski was a priest who saved a town from slaughter."

"Mmm!" Damon murmured. "I sense a fascinating story hidden in your family heritage —"

"And you'll have to tell us over dinner," Enyo interrupted, her eyes quickly changing from wide circles to thin lines. "You two must be exhausted. I'll show you to your room. You did want one for the two of you, right?" She eagerly tilted her head for the answer.

"Yes," Anton confirmed while Nastia said "Definitely!" at the same time.

"I thought so." Enyo led them up the stairwell, to the second floor. She opened a door on the left of the hall. The bedroom had a long wall-to-wall window about three feet above the floor and a low white bed with blue pillows. It smelled of jasmine. "The bathroom is right in there," she pointed to a blue-glass door. "I should think you both want to take a nap before dinner. We always eat late. I hope you don't mind eight o'clock?"

"Whatever you planned is good with us," said Anton.

"I had my cook fetch some fruit and cheese for you," she pointed to a blue plate on the nightstand, "if you'd like a snack. I wish you happy napping!"

She smiled thinly and shut the door.

"Oh gosh!" Anton stretched his arms above his head. "I'm beat. Man, I only got two hours of sleep on the plane."

"I didn't sleep at all. Yes, please — let's take a nap together."

"But I have to admit, I am hungry." He sauntered over to the cheese and fruit plate and dropped a couple bites into his mouth. "How about you? Those pita pockets we had for lunch were not enough for me."

"Don't mind if I do."

They ate together, showered, and crawled into the bed to sleep. Nastia didn't have trouble finding rest immediately.

———————◆———————

THE NEXT THING she knew, Anton was caressing her cheek with his finger, his eyes sleepy and content.

"Hi, my Galaxy Girl," he whispered. "Have I told you how beautiful you are lately?"

"Not very lately," she smiled.

"Well shame on me. You are the *most* attractive woman in the entire world. I'm so lucky to have you."

"Oh, Anton," she searched her mind for the words. How could she give him an adequate picture of her love when she loved him more than all the world and everything? "You are life, as far as I am concerned. You have infected my mind, and there is no getting you out."

They kissed.

"I wish I could take you with me tomorrow. Maybe I'll ask," he said, his eyes closed.

"What?" She opened hers. "Why wouldn't you take me with you?"

"Because it's business — just standing around and talking. You're not work to me, baby, you're pleasure."

"What if I want to wait for you while you work?"

"You wouldn't enjoy it."

"I don't know…" she let her voice trail off.

After a while, Anton looked at the time. "We should probably get up," he said, pulling off the covers. "It's almost seven thirty."

"All right." Her voice was faint.

"How about we let the Barlases decide whether you come to work with me tomorrow or not? After all, we're here on their generosity."

Nastia hesitated. "Okay." She didn't want to spend time in the mansion without Anton, but she reasoned that a good girl would support her boyfriend in his job. She didn't want to be a distraction. He was right. They were there on the generosity of two people. She would have to respect that, even though those two confused her.

———————◆———————

THE SUN HAD set by the time they arrived at the blue-glass dinner table. The hanging wave-like chandelier cast a soft light over the table, where Enyo and Damon were discussing something in dim tones. They looked up at Nastia and Anton.

"Ah! My guests!" Enyo said pleasantly, motioning toward two chairs. "Please sit. We are having swordfish tonight, lamb and red-wine soup, and of course, Greek salad. Dessert will follow."

Nastia found her goblet already filled with red wine beside a small glass of water. Waiting until Enyo and Damon began, Nastia and Anton started to eat.

"Did my wish come true?" Enyo asked. "Was your napping happy?"

"Yes, it was," Anton replied while Nastia nodded. "The bed was very comfortable."

Nastia wondered about Damon's inaudible snigger. His dark eyes again were shadowed in mystery.

"Very good!" Enyo smiled while she lifted her second forkful of salad. She nodded to Damon.

"Uh," he stammered and looked at the couple. "My mum and I were talking, and we thought you both should know a little more about us. For one, we are not complete foreigners." He smiled at Nastia. "I was born in Athens, but we live in New York now. We just come here to our Greek paradise for the summer and a few holidays."

"That's the intro," Enyo jumped in. "But if you want to get down to the interesting stuff, I will." Damon smirked as his mother continued. "I was married three times but divorced seven. How can that be? Divorce is what I call any breakup of a relationship that lasted longer than two years. I've had my experiences with men but now I am content to be single." Enyo looked at her son endearingly as a waft of the swordfish filled Nastia's nose.

"I have had my experiences with men too," Damon said, raising his wine goblet, "because I am gay."

So, he is gay, Nastia thought casually. But once she noticed how Damon gazed into Anton's eyes, her emotions switched, and she felt protective.

"That's really cool," Anton said encouragingly. "My brother is gay."

"Really good for him."

"Mind if I ask you a few questions about it?" Nastia asked in a sweet voice.

"Please do. I love questions about my sexuality." Damon turned to her, but Nastia didn't trust his face. "Ask away."

"When did you first decide it?"

Damon tittered. "Oh, that old question. It really wasn't something I *decided*. I plopped out of my mother's belly gay, just as you came out of your mom's straight. It was an inseparable part of me from my first second. I've wanted a boyfriend since I was seven."

"So, there has never been any doubt in your mind that you're gay?"

"No. There has not." He looked straight at her. "Do you mind if I ask *you* a few questions?"

"Not at all." Nastia wanted to hear them.

"Are you a *ho-mo-phobe*?" Damon pronounced each syllable too slowly, as if talking to a child.

"No. I'm not afraid of gay people at all."

"Do you believe it's wrong?"

Nastia thought carefully but decided to be honest. "Yes, I do. I am a Christian, and I believe the Bible clearly says that practicing homosexuality is wrong."

"Gracious me." Damon glanced at Anton. "Sounds like you wouldn't approve of my boyfriends."

"Do you have one right now?" Nastia inquired.

"Unfortunately, no. It's terrible."

"Well, it sounds like you two have a lot to talk about over the next couple of days," Enyo interrupted, her eyes fierce with pleasure. "Anton and I will be leaving for the mainland at around 2 p.m. That will give you and Damon plenty of time to discuss whatever you want for as long as you like. We have a beach — believe it or not — on the side of the island that you didn't see coming in. It's small, but we hold it dear to our hearts, our toes, and our backs." She grinned, narrowing her eyes to thin lines as if punctuating her sentence.

"Nastia and I would like some good beach time tomorrow," Anton quickly replied. "We didn't get as much time together as we wanted in Hawaii."

"Certainly! Certainly!" Enyo said. "Consider yourselves pharaoh and empress of Egypt while you're here. I have to say, if any couple looked like Anthony and Cleopatra, it's you."

"Thank you." Nastia grinned comically.

During dessert, Enyo went wide-eyed again and said, "At ten thirty or eleven, Damon and I *always* go out to the hot tub and look at the lights of Athens. It's perfectly remarkable from here. Please, join us."

"I'd love to," Anton said. "That's something of a special tradition for Nastia and me. How about you, baby, would you like to go out with them?"

———————◆———————

A COLD GUST swirled around Nastia and Anton as they walked out to the back of the house, after quickly changing into their swimwear. The steamy hot tub radiated aquamarine light between two enflamed fire pits.

"I guess we were faster," Anton remarked concerning the absence of Enyo and Damon. He peered at Nastia romantically, his eyes low, and his lips very kissable. She leaned in, but before their mouths touched, Enyo came out.

"Don't let me stop you, my dears," she said, scuttling to the hot tub and stepping in immediately. "Well, come on in! I don't want you freezing on my icy tiles."

Without kissing, Nastia and Anton walked over to the tub and slowly made their way in.

"Great father Julius!" Enyo exclaimed. "You have the figure of Cleopatra too, my darling."

"Thanks," Nastia grinned.

"What did you do to get so sexy?" Enyo said, but before Nastia could answer, Damon shuffled out from behind the silhouetted pillars, his arms folded tightly in front of him.

"I think she was born as sexy as a goddess, Mommy," he said, racing over to join them. "It comes naturally to her."

"You have a nicely cut body yourself," Anton commented casually, and Nastia felt a shiver rush through her.

"Thank you, Anthony." Damon's black eyes smiled. "That's going to be my new nickname for you now. I always love a body compliment from a straight hunk like yourself."

What! Nastia thought enviously. Is Anton seriously complimenting a gay guy's body?

"I know how hard it is for skinny guys like you to show some muscle," Anton continued, "but you've done it."

"Very perceptive," Damon sat down gingerly, his mouth wide open in a motion that said, "It's hot!" He breathed again. "But you're body. Dude! What did you do? Kill Hercules and put your spirit inside his body?"

Enyo, Anton, and Damon laughed together.

"I wish I could do that to a goddess," Enyo complained.

"Oh pshhh, Mother. You are plenty sexy. Thousands of women your age would kill for your body."

Enyo grinned, and her eyes looked less conniving than they had all night.

"I mean, think of all the men going bug-eyed for you *as we speak*," Damon said.

"What about all the men going bug-eyed for *you*?" Enyo retorted.

The three roared with laughter again.

"I have a juicy parent-embarrasses-the-son story to tell." Enyo's look of plotting didn't stay away for long.

"Oh no," Damon groaned. "Well, go ahead. Tell it fast."

"One time, when Damon was sixteen," Enyo began, looking excitedly at Nastia and Anton, "he had a boyfriend over here, and I had mine. We were all sitting like this in the hot tub, and no one was really talking. My boyfriend and I were simply relaxing like mature adults, but Damon," she rolled her eyes, "Damon and his boyfriend were tenderly poking each other's nipples. I tried not to laugh, but it didn't work, and soon my boyfriend and I were crying with laughter."

Damon chuckled. "Yeah, I bet that was pretty funny." He turned to Nastia and Anton to explain. "The guy was only my third boyfriend."

"Only?" Nastia blurted out, but no one seemed to notice. Anton and Enyo were busy laughing.

"That reminds me of a story about my brother," Anton said. "It was after my freshmen year of college. I was at my mom's house for the summer. One day, when my mom was out, I walked into the living room and saw my brother making out on the couch with some guy I had never seen before. I had to go outside so he couldn't hear me laughing. I thought it was hysterical. They were in," he shook his head while smiling, "an awkward position that just made me crack up."

Anton, Damon, and Enyo laughed together again. Nastia smiled but only because Anton had told the story.

As the three continued talking, Nastia gazed out at the distant lights of Athens. She thought she saw a blue tiger leap into the bushes, but it was too dark to be sure.

29

RED WIND

DURING THE LONG night, in the darkness of the guest bedroom, Nastia slept beside Anton, while her mind filled with a dream:

---◆---

SHE STOOD ON a rock, the wind blowing louder than ever in front of the red sky and black ocean. Other large rocks crashed down and rose up again and again, as if they were water. The black silhouette of a windsurfer rushed into view. A large wave grew higher and higher, and the windsurfer sped toward it. "Don't! You'll get smashed into the rocks!" Nastia shouted, but the wind was too loud. The surfer hit the wave and launched into a flip. While he was still in the air, the sky and ocean switched colors. Suddenly, the ocean was molten lava, and the sky was black as death. The surfer plunged into the lava.

---◆---

THE FOLLOWING MORNING, Nastia lounged in a cushioned chair beneath a large umbrella while Anton tanned on the island's small beach; his broad, muscular body changed position every now and then.

"Are you relaxed, baby?" she asked.

"Yes. Very. How about you?"

"I guess so."

"Why don't you come out here on the sand and tan with me?"

"I can't. My skin is too white. I got badly burned in Hawaii."

The two lovers spent the remainder of the morning on the beach. Eventually, they walked back up the slippery steps to the mansion, where Enyo and Damon were eating lunch.

"Please join us," Enyo insisted.

After lunch, Anton dressed into beige shorts and a white button-up. Nastia walked with him down the other set of stairs to the dock, where a boat and Enyo waited for him.

"Have a good time here," the woman said, her smile as thin as her eyes. "We will be back tomorrow."

"What time tomorrow?" Nastia whimpered dimly.

"Hopefully the middle of the morning, but definitely before 2:00 p.m.," Enyo replied.

Anton turned to Nastia and looked down at her tenderly. "I have this work stuff to get over with, but please try to enjoy yourself here. Damon might make a good friend."

"I'll try."

They kissed, and he jumped into the boat, which turned around and headed in the opposite direction. Anton craned his neck and waved.

"Bye," she said, weakly moving her hand in return.

A sense of panic stabbed her heart like a dart. Suddenly, the sky felt like it was closing in on her, and the Aegean Sea was a great mass of water, waiting to drown her. "Bye?" Her voice was weighted with pain. "It can't be bye. No. I'm alone? Is he gone? No, no, no, it can't be! Anton, turn that stupid boat around and come back right now!"

The boat maintained its course, traveling farther and farther away. Nastia felt horribly alone. Gnawing fears rose in her mind.

She looked down at the waves splashing beside the warped dock. Inky gray swelled in one spot. The spot leapt out of the water and landed on a board beside Nastia. It quickly formed into a silver creature.

"Well, if it isn't *the silver dragon*," Nastia said in a dramatic tone. "I haven't seen you in a while."

"It *has* been a while," the deep, cunning voice replied. "When was the last time we spoke? Was it that day on the beach when you first met Erlend?"

"Yeah, I think that was it. Exactly three weeks ago."

"Erlend was *very* handsome and *very* nice, wasn't he? Yet God stole him away from you. Why would a 'loving God' do such a thing? It has hurt you, hasn't it? It has hurt you so much in the past three weeks."

"I guess it has." Nastia heaved a weary breath. "But I'm missing someone else right now."

The dragon's thick mane curled and grew as the scales rippled on his snake-like body. He darted his head oddly toward the distant boat that was now only a speck. "Oh, Anton," his voice whispered as if Lunosh dearly missed Nastia's boyfriend. "The perfect man. He has so much, gorgeous toned muscle on his six-foot-three body, doesn't he? And every single strand of it loves you. You are everything to him, and he is so good. It's terribly sad what God is planning to do to him."

"Do to him?" Nastia's heart skipped two beats and then started pumping faster and faster. "What is God planning to do? Tell me!"

"I'm not supposed to tell you the secrets I have learned."

"Since when have you done what you're supposed to do, Lunosh? Tell me! Tell me now!"

"All right." The silver dragon paused for a moment. "God is going to kill him."

"What! When?"

"Tonight."

272

"So, I'll never see him again?" Tears built up in Nastia's hazel eyes.

"No. Never again," Lunosh answered. "God is sending him to hell where he will suffer forever. Can you believe how unjust God is? It's absolutely horrendous."

The tears dripped onto Nastia's cheeks, and she wiped them away. The silver dragon disappeared as Nastia climbed the tiring set of stairs, up to the house. Crying and groaning softly, she opened the front door and walked in. Hearing the closing door, Damon came into the living room.

"So, they left?" He noticed her puffy eyes. "Aw…what's wrong?"

Nastia tried to get a hold of herself. "Oh, it's just hard to part with Anton these days." She didn't know whether to believe Lunosh or not, but she was terrified of the possibility that Anton might die.

"Can I give you a hug?" Damon offered.

"No, thanks." Nastia didn't want to make any physical contact with him.

"Well, okay. If it means anything, I'm really, really glad that you're here. I can't stand being on this island by myself."

"How old are you?" Nastia changed the subject.

"I just turned twenty a month ago."

"You look younger, like seventeen."

"The perks of baby face syndrome. How old are you?"

"I turned twenty-one in the spring."

"You're only a year older than me," Damon said.

"Maybe I've experienced more than you."

Damon chuckled. "I seriously doubt it. Few people our age have experienced as much as me. But hey, would you like to go down to the beach? It's better than sitting in here."

Nastia thought for a moment. She was a little afraid of Damon. But what else would she do? She didn't want to be alone, and she felt like she had enough discernment to sense if Damon was trying to manipulate her or not. Besides, she wanted to ask him more questions.

"All right. I'll dress into my bathing suit."

NASTIA AND DAMON carefully made their way down the steep stairs that led to the beach. She wished she had brought a one-piece swimsuit instead of a bikini.

A small red bird was perched on a bush beside the path. Nastia stopped. "Aini! I'm so glad you're here."

"It's great to see you too." The red bird smiled but only for a second. "Be careful today. Don't listen to the lies of Lunosh. He is out to destroy you. Don't forget the passage in Proverbs that I recited to you on the plane back from Hawaii, Proverbs 3:5-8: 'Trust in the LORD with all your heart and lean not on your own understanding; in all your ways acknowledge him, and he will make your paths straight. Do not be wise in your own eyes; fear the LORD and shun evil. This will bring health to your body and nourishment to your bones.' "

"But how can I trust God?" Nastia retorted. "I've been ignoring him. He might punish me by killing Anton! What if he does? I will be completely ruined, and life will be horribly empty!"

"Nastia, you know you have sinned, and you feel the unavoidable guilt. If you want to be truly happy, then do as the passage says. Trust in God! Trust that he knows and wants what is best for you. Repent and turn back to God! He wants to love, protect, and care for you, but how can he when you actively reject him?"

"Why do you have to use the same words as Lauren did?"

"Because it's true. Do what is right! Leave your sinful lifestyle and ask for God's forgiveness, and he will heal you!"

"I can't think about that now."

The red bird flew away, and Nastia continued down the path.

———————◆———————

THE SUN SHONE brightly onto Damon and Nastia as they lay on separate towels, the waves rolling methodically only a few feet away.

"So where are you from?" Damon asked.

"I was born and raised in Arizona, but Anton and I live in Washington D.C. now." Nastia observed his extremely tan and slim body, clad only in a black Speedo streaked with neon blue. His abdominal muscles were acutely defined, but his chest was quite flat. "How about you? Are you Greek?"

"I am three-fourths Greek. I was born in Athens, but Mum and I moved to New York soon after she divorced my dad. Do you want to know why we have the same last name?"

"Sure."

"Barlas is her maiden name. She changed mine when she changed hers back to Barlas when I was two. I never knew my dad, and from what my mother tells me, he wasn't a good man at all. I'm glad she changed my last name. I don't want the shadow of some creepy old guy hanging over me for the rest of my life."

"I can understand that."

"Do you like your dad?"

Nastia hesitated. "Yeah. He's a good father," she lied. She didn't want to expose that wound to Damon. One of the spider's legs quivered on her back. "Do you wish you had known him just to see what he was like?"

"I've thought about it." Damon put his arm over his closed eyes. "But I decided no."

"Can I ask you a potentially hard question about your homosexuality?"

He chuckled. "Yes, you may. Shoot me your straight-woman arrows."

"Do you think your decision to be gay has anything to do with the absence of your father?"

275

"You really don't know anything about gays, do you? I told you last night: I have been gay since the day I was born. I have always been naturally attracted to men, not women. It's as simple as that."

"Have you ever been attracted to girls?"

"Not really. I mean, I've noticed how some women are pretty, and I can see why someone might find them sexually attractive, but I don't. I actually tried to feel something for a girl at one point in my life, but when it didn't work, I gave it up and decided that it's stupid to try to be someone I'm not. You see, something you have to know about gay people is that our sexuality is entwined with every part of our person. So, when someone asks for us to change, they are asking for us to deny every part of our being — our sexuality, our emotional structure, our view of the world, even our spirituality. I know you said you're a Christian, but do you see any truth in the yin and yang symbol?"

"Yes. Some," Nastia answered. "There is both good and evil in all of us."

"Exactly. But the yin and yang can apply to sexuality too. Every straight person has a little bit of homosexuality in them just as every gay person has a little bit of heterosexuality in them."

"I had never thought of it that way before."

"Do you agree?" He turned onto his stomach and looked at her with his piercing black eyes. Nastia noticed for the first time the small yin and yang tattoo in the center of his lower back. "Do you like my tattoo?" He smiled.

"Yeah. It's cool."

"Are you against tattoos also?" he asked as if he were addressing a toddler.

"No. Not at all," she said firmly. "Anton has a nice tattoo on his arm."

"Yeah. I saw it last night in the hot tub." His voice became respectful again. "You didn't say much while we were talking last night. What was wrong? Do you hate me because you think I have feelings for him?"

276

Nastia was surprised by the question. "Do you?"

"No, I don't. He is freak'n hot, but he's straight. I've learned that it just doesn't work out when I have feelings for a straight guy. I can't like him because he's straight just as much as you can't like me because I'm gay." He grinned.

"Yeah. That's quite a lot."

"But we can be friends, right? Most of my best friends are girls."

"Yes, we can be friends. Certainly."

"Good." Damon rested his face down on the towel and closed his eyes again.

They listened to the soft washing of the Aegean waves for a few moments. Nastia decided to try something.

"You are a solid person, Damon," she said. "You don't fit into that unfair stereotype of gay guys who go off and cry when people challenge them on their homosexuality."

"Glad to hear it."

"But I still hold true to my convictions. Do you mind if I tell you a short allegorical story?"

"What about?" Damon asked.

"Straight versus gay."

"Ooo fun! Yes, please. Tell me the story."

30

THE MOUNTAIN AND THE COLD TOWN

NASTIA READJUSTED HER purplish sunglasses as she gathered her thoughts and prepared to tell her allegorical story to the skinny and tan Damon Barlas, whose jet-black hair shimmered with a blue tinge. The sun-blessed wind swam through Nastia's red hair and she began:

ONCE UPON A TIME, there was a tiny settlement up in a mountain far from any town or city. Only four married couples lived there — two straight couples, a lesbian couple, and a gay couple. The first straight couple had a daughter and the second had a son. The gay couple had a son and the lesbian couple had a daughter. One day, the eight adults held a meeting together in one of the cabins.

"I am concerned about my daughter," one of the lesbian women said. "She has been playing with the gays' son, and they are great friends, but she needs another girl to play with."

The mother in the first straight couple looked to her husband. "We sympathize with your desire to find a female companion for your daughter," the husband said. "But we wish to raise our daughter differently than you are raising yours."

"What do you mean by 'differently'?" the second lesbian woman asked suspiciously. "You're not judging us for our lifestyle are you?"

"No, no. Not at all," the wife in the first straight couple clarified. "We just have varying definitions of what is best for our children. You want what's best for your daughter just as we want what is best for ours."

The gay couple asked the same thing to the second straight couple. They wanted their son to have a male companion, but the second straight couple resisted. The meeting ended on cold terms of disagreement, and the two straight couples went to have dinner together in one of their cabins while the gay and lesbian couples ate separately in one of their cabins.

Two years passed, and soon, the daughter of the first straight couple turned eleven years old. "I saw the other girl," she told her mother one spring day when the father was out hunting. "She was in the field, picking flowers and invited me to join her."

"Did you?" the mother asked in a concerned tone.

"Yes. We played all day," the daughter replied. "I asked her to come over today. Is that all right?"

"I wish you had talked to me first," the mother started to say, but before she could finish, they heard a knock on the door. The daughter of the lesbian women stood there, eager to play again. The mother put her hand to her mouth, looking down at the two girls, who both seemed quite innocent.

"All right. You can play together," she said. "Just please stay close to the house." The girls ran off to play imaginary games, and the mother carefully watched from the kitchen window while she washed dishes and cooked dinner.

She heard another knock on the door, and the mother in the second straight couple entered. "Elizabeth?" she said (that was the name of the mother in the first straight couple). "I brought the green beans." The two families had planned to have dinner together that night.

"Thank you, Ruth," Elizabeth said, greeting her friend with a hug. "I was just about to start making the corn bread."

"Good. I'll help you." Ruth set down her bowl and approached the window, her eyebrows knitted. She noticed the two girls playing. "Is that the lesbians' daughter?" Ruth asked, receiving a nod for a reply.

"So, you conceded to let them play together?"

"I didn't see how I could do anything else," Elizabeth answered, measuring corn flour into a bowl. "Actually, I feel sorry for the girl. And it's true — I want a female companion for my daughter, just as you have been for me."

"It's different, Elizabeth," Ruth said, her eyes narrowed and serious. "You and I both believe in the traditional roles for men and women. A woman should only give in to her romantic interests if it applies to the man she wants to marry. Same with men. Same gender relationships should only be pure friendship. That is the way God intended things to be."

"Yes. You're right," Elizabeth agreed.

"My husband and I had a discussion about this the other day," Ruth said while she chopped pieces of corn. "He let our son start playing with the gays' son at the beginning of the week. He thinks that we should help and reach out to the boy. I support him in that — it's just I'm not so sure if our son is ready for that kind of challenge. The good book says that bad company corrupts good morals."

"Maybe you can help the gays' son," Elizabeth encouraged, "just like we can help the lesbians' daughter."

"We definitely should!" Ruth said, still worried. "I just don't think letting our children play with them is the best way to do it."

Five years passed, and soon, all the four children were sixteen years old. The gays' son became very close friends with Ruth's son, and the lesbians' daughter became very close friends with Elizabeth's daughter.

One night, the two boys were talking in the woods and Ruth's son, David, said, "I think I like Hannah (Elizabeth's daughter)."

"Are you sure?" Troy asked in a disappointed voice. "What makes you say that?"

David shrugged. "I don't know. She is really pretty, and I just want to be alone with her. I want to protect and care for her."

"Yeah, you might feel that way sometimes," Troy said. "My oldest dad told me that he once had feelings for a girl when he was young. But then, he realized that she could never fully understand him no matter how much they tried and tried and tried to make it work. Eventually, his companionship with the girl became worse than it was when they were just friends. Then he met my other dad and realized that only another guy could fully and completely understand him."

"But it works out for my parents and Hannah's parents," David argued. "They are really close and love each other. My dad says that men and women were created to complement one another in marriage."

Troy didn't say anything more on the subject that night.

Soon, David decided to go on a summer date with Hannah. They talked a little, and David noticed her sadness. He asked her what was wrong, but she didn't want to tell him. After the date, Hannah and David went their separate ways.

The following night — despite the contradiction from David's dad — David and Troy snuck out into the woods to go camping.

"I had trouble connecting with Hannah on our date," David said while he poked the fire. "She had something on her mind but refused to tell me."

"Do you still like her, or do you see past her pretty face now?" Troy asked, hopefully. In case you haven't guessed yet, he had a crush on David.

"I'm not as into her as I was before," David replied with a disappointed shake of his head.

"I'm sorry you had to find it out the hard way," Troy empathized. "This is what I was talking about before. Straight relationships just don't work. I have watched yours and Hannah's parents over the years and noticed that they are wasting their entire lives trying to understand each other when they could be experiencing the superior same-sex oneness of a homosexual marriage. Traditional marriage doesn't work because men will never fully understand women, nor can women ever fully understand men."

That night, David yielded to Troy's reasoning, and they committed evil together.

Word quickly spread about David and Troy's sin. Hannah — who secretly had a strong crush on David — was heartbroken. Both the straight couples were furious with David, and soon, he went back to Troy and said, "Okay. I'll become your gay husband because you're the only one who loves me now."

Troy and David went off to build their own cabin where they could live together. Hannah was even more heartbroken than before. Her parents didn't want her to spend any more time with the lesbians' daughter, because they feared that she might do the same as David. Hannah felt very alone. For two years, Elizabeth and Ruth were her good female companions, but Hannah could never stop thinking of David and would weep every single day.

Suddenly, a terrible plague struck the village, and both of Hannah's parents died. Ruth and her husband took Hannah into their house, feeling extremely sorry for her. They treated her with great kindness and generosity, but Hannah couldn't get over the fact that they were David's parents.

One day, she went out alone into the flower field, thoroughly overcome with sorrow and grief. The lesbians' daughter, Lois, saw Hannah and went out to talk with her for the first time in three years. Lois hugged her, sang a soft song to her, and said, 'You need romantic love, Hannah. I can provide this for you. I am the only one who can heal your broken heart.'

Seeing no other light in her darkness of grief, Hannah gave in, and she and Lois went to live in the cabin that once belonged to Hannah's parents.

As the years went by, the older lesbian and gay couples died, and then David's parents also. Only the young people remained.

The following winter was colder than ever, and Lois became sick. Hannah struggled to cut more firewood and make more healing soup, but it wasn't enough. David had compassion on Hannah and tried to help her with her chores. They got to know each other again and had some happy moments together. Meanwhile, Lois grew sicker and sicker and then died. David comforted Hannah in her grief.

"I'm so sorry," he told her while she cried on his shoulder. "You have lost more than any of us on the mountain. If only you knew how I felt about you when we were teenagers."

"You had feelings for me?" Hannah asked in surprise.

"Yes. I did," David said, hugging her more.

"Did you know that I have loved you ever since we were toddlers?"

"You *have*?" David was overcome with happiness, and they kissed.

At that moment, Troy burst into the cabin and saw them together. He was furious and raced back to his cabin, through the snow. David decided not to run after Troy or ever go back to him again. Instead, David and Hannah committed their lives to each other.

A few weeks passed, and Christmas came. Troy was extremely distraught and lonely. He cried and cried and scrapped himself. Eventually, he decided he couldn't live without David.

Troy snuck through the early morning and hid behind a tree to watch David and Hannah's cabin. Soon, David stepped out to go hunting, leaving Hannah alone in the cabin. Troy rushed in, strangled Hannah, and then returned to his cabin, covering his footprints with the branch of a spruce tree.

Troy waited for a week and then walked back over to the other cabin. He found David weeping beside a grave he had made for Hannah.

"What happened?" Troy asked.

David looked up at him. "Last week, I came to the house, and Hannah was lying on the floor — dead."

"Oh no, that's horrible!" Troy sat beside David and embraced him.

"You were angry with me, weren't you? When I left you to live with Hannah?"

"Yes," Troy responded carefully. "I was very angry. I missed you like crazy and hurt more than I ever have before. But I never ever wanted something like this to happen. Hannah was a sweet and wonderful girl."

David and Troy went back to their own cabin to live together again. Eventually, David died of disease and Troy killed himself.

The end.

———————◆———————

NASTIA STOPPED TALKING. She took a deep breath and stretched out on her towel, the sun shining as brightly as before. "So?" she turned to look at Damon, who was lying on his back again with his other arm over his closed eyes. "What did you think?"

"Very depressing." He turned onto his stomach and looked at her. "I bet Lois was distraught when she saw how David and Hannah enjoyed each other's company."

"Yeah. I decided to leave that out. But did you hear my message hidden within the lines of the story?"

"Oh, I definitely heard your message. It wasn't hidden very well." He grinned. "Don't worry, I'm not diss'n your story-telling skills. I just disagree with your whole point."

"What do you think my message was?"

"That homosexual relationships destroy happiness."

"Very good." Nastia watched a wave crash onto a rock. "That's why I believe that same-sex marriage should be illegal. The two definitions of marriage naturally strive to overpower each other. One has to triumph over the other, and if gay marriage is added into the legal definition of marriage, then heterosexuality will be greatly suppressed — and people will stop having children. I don't mean to offend you, Damon, but I am a straight woman all the way, and I believe that heterosexuality is the way human marriage should be."

"Yeah, I can tell." He chuckled. "You believe that homosexuality is wrong."

They sunbathed for a while longer until Damon sat up and smiled.

"What is it?" Nastia wondered what was going on in his head.

"I have an allegorical story of my own to tell about homosexuality." Damon wrapped his arms around himself, one down behind his stomach and the other up behind his neck. "Do you mind? I promise to make it shorter than yours."

Nastia allowed her curiosity to appear in the pale skin around her lightly freckled nose. "I don't mind at all. Please. Go right ahead."

Damon put his arms behind his head and wiggled his torso, as if dancing. "Let's see." He pulled up his slightly hairy legs and hugged them. "Okay. Here we go:

———————◆———————

SOMEWHERE, IN THE grand world of storytelling, there was an isolated town in a place that was always very cold and cloudy. All

285

the houses were made of stone, and no one really knew what material the rooftops were made of because they were always covered in icy white snow. The only warmth and plant life in the village came from those who were in love with each other. They grew gardens in the backyards of the houses and lit their fires with the flame of love — only created when the in-love couples kissed.

Long ago, the first priest of the town had outlawed homosexuality, and thus, the only couples that existed were heterosexual husbands and wives.

Now there was an enormous and awe-inspiring stone cathedral in the center of the cold stone town. It was the most respected part of the whole area, and all the people were required to go there every Wednesday, Friday, and Sunday night to listen to the priest, who lived in the cathedral. Inside, there was a great, roaring fire pit that always burned.

"Ever since the beginning of our fair town," the priest would say, "we have relied upon the love, affection, and devotion of the husband-and-wife couples who were united in these walls. Without them — the center of our community — the bond that protects us from the evil wolves and the slaughtering cold could never burn." The priest would point to the great fire, and everyone would look to it as if it were a god. "For the safety of all of us — for the very welfare of our souls — I beg you to keep this fire burning. None of us can survive without it. The only thing that can destroy it is homosexuality."

After the priest was done talking, each townsperson would walk up to the great fire and throw in a bit of wood. The husbands and wives would kiss and then flick their newly created flames into the huge fire.

The cathedral was also the school, run by the priest. All the children in the town were required to go to the cathedral until 4 p.m. every weekday.

There was one couple that had trouble keeping their garden strong. People said it was because the husband and wife didn't love each other enough; thus, the couple was treated poorly throughout the town. Since their garden was weak, the couple had few trees to light their fire with, and soon, they were all out of wood.

One day, while their twelve-year-old son was at school, the husband and wife wandered away from the town and out to the great forest on the hill a mile away. Everywhere else was snow-covered plains.

The husband hurried to cut down a moderately sized tree. While he and his wife were dragging it home, a large pack of wolves emerged from the forest and raced after them. The couple dropped the tree and ran as fast as they could. Some of the townsfolk saw this, and everyone raced to the walls to watch. The husband and wife almost made it to the gate, but just before they did, a wolf leapt onto the wife and mauled her face. The husband tried to pull the wolf off his wife, but the other wolves caught up and killed him too.

The town held a funeral for the couple, burning their bodies in the great fire. The priest said that he would take care of the orphaned son, Philon, so he gave him a small room in the back of the cathedral.

A year passed, and Philon became best friends with another guy named Icelos. One day, when the children were playing in the snowy courtyard, the priest thought he saw homosexuality in Philon's manner. During dinner, he noticed that Philon seemed a little bit feminine.

"Are there any girls in whom you are interested?" the priest asked while the two ate in a cold room.

Philon shrugged. "Not right now."

"Do you see any appeal in the bodies of girls?"

Philon sensed that something was out of place. "Um, maybe."

The priest jumped to his feet and shouted his next question. "Are you attracted to boys? Are you?" Philon looked up fearfully, but he didn't answer.

The priest seized his arm and forced Philon down the hall and to the basement of the cathedral. "I am going to lock you up. You are not allowed to go to school or see another child until you stop being attracted to boys and start being attracted to girls." He locked Philon into a freezing dungeon lined only with hay and rough blankets.

"How will I keep warm?" Philon pleaded as he raced to the barred door and called out to the priest, who was almost at the top of the stairs. "Won't you give me any flames of love?"

"No!" the priest answered roughly. "You do not deserve warmth. The cold and pain will purge your homosexuality from you. Tomorrow I will return, and if you haven't stopped being queer, then I will whip you. Every day that goes by I will whip you for as many days as you have remained homosexual." He shut the door loudly and locked it.

Imprisoned by stone walls, harsh frost, and two locked doors, Philon crawled into the corner, wrapped a rough blanket around himself, and wept into his hands.

The next day — which was a Friday — Icelos looked around the school for Philon, but he couldn't find him. After all the other children had gone, Icelos walked up to the priest and asked, "Where is Philon?"

The priest glared down at the boy suspiciously. "You will find out tonight during the town meeting."

Everyone gathered closely together in the cathedral, for it was especially cold, and the meeting began. The priest climbed up to his podium, in front of the great fire, and said, "A horrible evil has been discovered in our town. One of the boys is a homosexual!"

Murmurs rippled among the people and someone asked, "Who is it?"

"The orphan, Philon, is the queer!" the priest answered.

The people of the town gasped.

"I have locked him away, so he cannot harm any of us. Please, I ask that none of you try to visit him. He can hurt you with a single touch. If he comes in contact with another boy his age, our great fire will certainly be destroyed." The townsfolk left the cathedral in utter silence.

A week passed, and Icelos missed Philon tremendously. He snuck around the cathedral and found a small barred window with dim coughing sounds rising from it. "Philon? Is that you?"

"Yes," the prisoner answered. "Is that Icelos?"

"Yes, It's me! I'm here for you. I'm going to get you out!" Icelos pulled on the bars but they were too strong. "Do you know where the keys are?"

"Beneath the papers in the second drawer of the priest's desk," Philon replied.

"Okay. I'll be down there soon!" Icelos raced into the priest's office — while the priest was teaching a class — and found the keys in the second drawer. He rushed to the dungeon door, unlocked it, ran down the stairs, and unlocked the prison cell. The two boys hugged, and Icelos noticed that Philon had red cuts across his back.

"Philon! What happened to you?" Icelos saw the sadness in Philon's eyes and knew that the priest had whipped him. They hugged more tenderly than before while Icelos stroked the back of Philon's neck. "Don't worry. I'm with you now, and I will never leave you again."

At that moment, the priest entered the dungeon and saw the two boys. He bound them with chains and dragged them out into the center of the town. He ordered the warning bell to be rung, and everyone gathered in front of the cathedral.

"These two boys were found engaging in homosexual wickedness!" he shouted, and all the townsfolk groaned with despair. "For such an offense — and for the very survival of our community — we must banish these two criminals and never allow them inside the walls of our town again!"

The people agreed and helped to drag the two boys outside the gate. The priest removed their chains, pushed the boys to the snowy ground, went back inside the gate, and locked it securely. Everyone rushed to the top of the walls to see what the banished boys would do.

A haunting wolf howl sounded from the forest, and Icelos and Philon looked to each other in terror. Icelos's mother screamed and embraced her husband. Many more howls sounded and the wolf pack emerged from the forest. The wolves started running toward the two boys.

Icelos looked at Philon with deep affection and said, "I love you."

"I love you too," Philon replied, and they kissed.

Suddenly, a red flame appeared, and they removed their lips. Icelos and Philon took hold of the red flame together and pointed it toward the wolves.

"We will avenge your parents!" Icelos shouted, and they locked their hands together and then opened them toward the incoming wolves. A huge ring of red flame pushed out, making a deep sound, and destroyed the entire pack of wolves. The townsfolk couldn't help but cheer because they hated the wolves so much.

"We need these boys!" one man called. The people opened the gates and let the boys inside.

The crowd moved back to the cathedral and placed Icelos and Philon in front of the great fire. The boys kissed again, and the great fire exploded into a huge burst of smoke. Everyone raced back outside, coughing and then looked up. The clouds pulled back, the sun shone through, and the town filled with light and warmth and joy. Colorful flowers popped up all over the town and the people began dancing while singing, "The cold has pulled away! / The great fire was our enemy / not homosexuality!"

The priest panicked and shouted, "No, no! The gay boys are our enemies! Please help me to lock them up or they will destroy us!" The people booed at the priest and locked him up instead.

The townsfolk made Icelos and Philon their kings, and everyone lived happily ever after.

The end.

———————◆———————

DAMON GRINNED AND closed his eyes with satisfaction. The sun was getting low in the sky. "Now, what did *you* think of *my* story?"

Nastia pondered for a moment. "It was interesting. You are very creative."

"Thank you," he said, moving around on his towel as if dancing again. "You hated it then?"

"No, I honestly believe that it was interesting and very creative." She brushed her red hair lightly.

"Very good, miss straight woman." Damon laughed and jumped to his feet. "It's about time for dinner. You want to go back up to the house and get food?"

"Sure. I am kind of hungry."

As Nastia and Damon left the beach and walked up the earthy steps, Nastia remembered what Anton had told Damon the night before, *"You have a nicely cut body yourself...I know how hard it is for skinny guys like you to show some muscle, but you've done it."*

Nastia felt jealousy erupt in her heart, and she looked at the back of Damon again. *He is pretty sexy*, she thought, but her mind went past the doorpost of "sexy" and into the windowless room of lust. She lusted after him in her heart.

Nastia grabbed the steep hill as she tripped on a step. A metal roach rolled down her arm, entered her skin, and scuttled down to her waist. "What!" Nastia exclaimed in pain, knowing that Damon might be able to hear her. "There's no way I could have lusted after him. He's gay! This isn't fair!" She pounded her foot against the step, her body tightening hurtfully.

Damon turned around. "Having trouble?"

"No. I just dropped my towel," she lied.

After Nastia showered and dressed into a green summer skirt, a sleeveless magenta shirt, and a glittering set of jewelry, Nastia left the room and met the blue tiger in the hallway. "Gosh, you startled me!" Jianyu looked intimidating with his long indigo body, swaying tail, and thin black stripes. "What is it?"

"Watch yourself tonight, Nastia Sobieski. Do not let down your guard. Remember Proverbs chapter 6 verses 27 and 28: 'Can a man scoop fire into his lap without his clothes being burned? Can a man walk on hot coals without his feet being scorched?' You will be burned if you give into temptation tonight. It will seem harmless at first, but it will lead you to the flame of sin that wishes to scorch your soul."

The tiger leapt over Nastia, scaring her half to death, and disappeared into the shadows.

31

THE WAY OUT

THE PLUMP GREEK cook set the food-filled plates wordlessly before Nastia and Damon as they ate dinner on the pool deck behind the polished marble pillars. The sun glowed a soft orange as it crept toward the distant hills, causing the sparkles in Nastia's hair to glisten.

"What's her name?" Nastia asked Damon in a whisper after the cook had left. Damon wore khaki shorts and a see-through red button-up. Nastia couldn't help but look over his torso.

"Akeldama," he replied. "She doesn't talk much."

"She seemed sad. I wonder if something was troubling her." Nastia thought the ancient Greek athlete design on the rim of her plate looked strangely sinister.

Damon shrugged. "Maybe she hates it here. Her daughter is quiet too. She cleans most of the house but always runs away when we enter a room while she's working."

"Where do they stay?" Nastia felt sorry for the girl she had never seen.

"Over there." Damon pointed to a small building at the end of the island. "It's not much, but they never complain."

Nastia felt a surge in her heart, telling her to get off the island now. But she knew she couldn't, and the desire dimmed.

"I thought of a different ending to your story," Nastia said, dipping her pita bread in a bowl of tzatziki sauce.

"But it's *muy* story," Damon defended in a pitiful voice.

"I don't have to share if you don't want me to, but I couldn't help but think of how things might have developed."

Damon turned his head in a circle. "So, it's more of a continuation? Okay, okay. You've got me curious now. Go ahead and relate your version of the ending."

"Don't worry. I'm not telling an entire new story," she clarified like an older sister would. "I was just going to say that if Philon and Icelos lived for a few years as co-kings, they would eventually destroy each other because of the struggle for power. One of them would try to be the *only* king, and the other would get killed."

Damon imitated the frown of a child. "So, you killed off Philon and made Icelos a tyrant? Oh alas, alas!"

Nastia didn't expect the last words. "Do you think that was a possible course your story could have taken?"

"Maybe, if you're a defeatist." Damon looked a bit sad, but his smile bounced back. "Did you notice that my story was the one with the happy ending while both of your endings were sad? Everyone died in your mountain story. That's really depressing."

"Well, yeah," Nastia replied. "They ended that way because the theme was homosexuality. I think it's wrong, thus my endings exposed the consequences."

"That's a wee bit extreme, wouldn't you say?" He chuckled.

After dinner, they watched a long movie about Greek gods. Once the credits began, Nastia sprang to her feet. "I think I'll head to my room now. Good night, Damon. See you tomorrow morning."

A shadow of disappointment swept over his face. "Okay. Good night, Nastia."

She hurried up the stairs, down the hall, and into her room, locking the door immediately. She sighed, feeling relieved and safer.

The room was dark despite the efforts of the weak bathroom lamp. She turned the dimming lights all the way up. The long, horizontal window above the bed flashed a glimpse of her reflection.

She looked away and closed the bathroom door, so she couldn't see the large, all-too-clear mirror.

Tap...tap...tap...

Nastia jerked her head at the hollow ceramic sound. *What the heck is that?*

Tap...tap...

She heard it again and shot her gaze toward a blue vase that wobbled back and forth on its stand.

Something's inside the vase. Is it another roach? No, no — please. I can't stand another roach. I can't stand another painful metal insect!

The vase wobbled once more, and Nastia became too curious to ignore it. She walked over and lifted the tiny lid.

A red bird shot out of the vase and in front of her eyes faster than a second, giving Nastia a nerve-racking jolt. She dropped the vase, but the small bird swooped down and grabbed the rim with her feet before it crashed to the ground. She set it back on its stand.

"Good grace — Aini! Why did you have to scare me like that?" Nastia released her shaking tension with a deep exhale.

"So, you were startled? Good," the bird replied with a satisfied look in her miniscule black eyes.

"What? You mean you were trying to terrorize me out of my skin?" Nastia glared down at the red bird. "What's wrong with you?"

"You weren't that scared of me," the bird responded. "But you have been afraid and unsettled all day. Tell me, what has been bothering you?"

"Oh, Aini — you have no idea. I have a horrible feeling about this trip. Something really bad is going to happen, I just know it!" She grimaced painfully. "I'm afraid that Anton will die tonight."

"Are you still worried about that?" Aini sighed, calmly perched on the rim of the vase. "I don't pretend to know what God is planning for the future, but I do know there is a threat of a completely different kind lurking in this house."

"Really?" Nastia put her hand over her lower lip, her hazel eyes fierce with concern. "So, Damon is a bad man? I knew it."

"There is a force of darkness in this house, Tia," said the red bird gravely. "You're not safe here. This isn't going to be good for you. But there is a way out."

Aini flew over to the bathroom, pressed down on the handle, and opened the door. The blue tiger sauntered out with a golden scroll held between his sharp teeth. He and Aini carefully unrolled it onto the floor. The scroll contained five colorful illustrated instructions.

Aini landed on the scroll and pointed a wing toward the first illustration, which depicted a small weatherworn motorboat. "Akeldama the cook and her daughter will be leaving the island tonight."

"What? Tonight?" Nastia interjected.

"Yes," purred Jianyu in a deep tone. "For your protection, you must flee this island tonight."

Nastia took a deep breath. "Okay. Interesting. I'm listening."

Aini pecked at the boat illustration. "Step one: go down to the dock and ask the cook if you can leave with her. She will say yes."

"Oh, but I don't speak any Greek," said Nastia. "How can I ask her?"

"Akeldama's daughter speaks English. She can translate for you." Aini fluttered down the scroll, where she pointed at the second illustration. This one depicted a yellow car with a faded white sign atop the roof. "Step two: take a taxi to the airport."

Nastia gasped. "The airport? So you're asking me to fly out of Greece in the next few hours?"

The red bird nodded her tiny head. "Yes, Tia. That is step three." Aini hopped over to the illustration of a plane encircled by clouds. "There is a direct flight from Athens to Washington D.C., departing at 1:40 a.m. You have enough money in your account to purchase the ticket home."

Nastia couldn't help but consider the idea. "It is appealing. I've had this horrible feeling about this island ever since we got here. It might be good to leave. Are you sure there are seats available?"

"There are," answered Jianyu with a growl.

Nastia fiddled with a lock of her hair, twirling it around her fingers. "But wait. What is step four?" She pointed to the black and grey illustration of a smart phone.

Aini peered up at Nastia with her black bead eyes. "Step four: call Anton and break up with him."

Nastia jumped backwards. "I knew it! You two are just scheming to get me to break up with Anton. But that's not my intention at all. No, I don't like being stuck on this island with a stranger and Anton staying the night off in Athens for some reason. No, I don't like that at all. I wish he was here instead. But to break up with him? You know I don't want to!"

Aini let out a soft exhale from her cone-shaped beak and waddled a little further down the scroll. There was an illustration of a red-haired woman bowing with her face in her hands. Kneeling beside her was a bearded man garbed in white with a crown of thorns on his head. "Step five: repent before Jesus and he will clothe you in his pure love."

"Of course I love Jesus, of course," Nastia reacted quickly. "But he understands how much I love Anton too. Come on, you can't ask me to give up what I cherish with all my heart."

Aini and Jianyu simply stared at Nastia.

"So you're asking me to run away from Anton and choose Jesus instead?"

The red bird and the blue tiger both nodded.

Nastia turned away, closing her eyes and shaking her head. "No. No! This isn't fair. You're making me choose. Can't I have both Anton and Jesus?"

Aini flapped over to the dresser beside Naista. " 'Suppose a woman has ten silver coins and loses one,' " said the bird, quoting Luke 15:8-9. " ' Does she not light a lamp, sweep the house and search carefully until she finds it? And when she finds it, she calls her friends and neighbors together and says, "Rejoice with me; I have found my lost coin." ' Tia, you are like a lost coin to our Lord Jesus. He wants to find you again. He is calling you back to himself. He loves you."

Nastia opened her mouth to argue, but the words never reached her lips. She didn't know what to say.

The blue tiger spoke this time. "The Lord is gracious and compassionate, slow to anger and rich in love."

"Oh, I recognize that one," said Nastia, "It's, oh it's on the tip of my tongue. It's Psalms 145, right?"

Jianyu nodded his large blue head. "Verse 8. Well done."

Aini sprang onto Nastia's shoulder, brushing her ever-so-soft feathers against Nastia's neck. "You are God's precious daughter. Tonight, he calls you back to himself. Tonight, a way out has been provided for you. What do you say?"

Sitting like a noble dog, Jianyu flicked his tail back and forth in S-shaped curves as the angels waited for Nastia's answer.

Nastia suddenly remembered a time in college, when she was taking a morning walk around campus. The sun illuminated a thin mist like a crown of glory around the forest. The tall eucalyptus trees seemed to reach out their branches, as if they were lifting their arms in praise. Nastia was overcome with a sense of inexplicable joy during that walk. The presence of God was clear as the light of the sun. A deep, satisfying peace filled her whole body. Her life had not been easy that week. There had been drama with a guy. But during her prayer walk with God, there was peace and joy, and the contentment that resulted was all Nastia needed. God was gracious.

Maybe I could go back to Him, Nastia thought. God will take care of me. He really loves me, doesn't he? Oh, but Anton...

Nastia blinked at the red bird and the blue tiger, who both stared at her expectantly. "I'm only going to agree to steps one, two and three. I'll go back to D.C., but I'm not yet agreeing to break up with Anton. I need to think about it. Okay?"

"We'll take it," chirped Aini, soaring around the room exuberantly.

"Now pack your bags," said Jianyu. "We don't have much time."

32

TO FLEE

CLAD IN A matching dusk blue pants and blouse set, her beige sandals firmly fastened, Nastia emerged from a side door adjacent to the pool deck. She carefully rested her suitcase on the stone path, striving to be soundless. A gust of wind plucked out a thin white curtain from the window above, like a veil being removed from a corpse. Nastia held her breath.

"It is nothing, Nastia," said the blue tiger. "Follow me." Jianyu stalked ahead, glancing left and right cautiously.

"Oh Tia, I am so proud of you!" said the red bird, unable to contain her elation as she did a figure eight in the air. "You are taking the right path! You are beginning to make such good choices! Believe me, you will be rewarded."

"Yes, she will," said Jianyu. "But we must focus on the task at hand. There is evil nearby."

"Yes, yes we must." Aini landed on Nastia's shoulder. "Mind if I rest here during the walk?"

"Not at all," said Nastia with a smile.

They followed the path beside the pool deck in the back of the mansion. The sound of the wind grew louder, as if a storm was brewing. Nastia wondered where Damon could be. Maybe inside? In his room? But she had a funny feeling that the angels weren't worried about him.

The path was quite rocky. Nastia struggled to step down a narrow ledge whilst lifting her suitcase. "It feels like it got heavier," she whispered.

"Don't worry. We are almost there," the blue tiger prompted. He led them to the small building at the end of the island, which was painted in the same white and blue of the mansion. As they got closer, a staircase came into view that led from the building to a second dock with a run-down motorboat tied to a wooden post.

A young girl rushed down the stairs, carrying two boxes. She dropped them into the motorboat and ran back up. She didn't notice Nastia.

"All right," said Jianyu, "go down to the boat and speak with the girl. Ask her for a ride to Athens."

"Okay," Nastia answered compliantly. She took a deep breath and made her way down the final few steps.

Right then, a wisp of silvery smoke glided off the roof of the house, swirling into a condensed cloud until it became the shape of a dragon. Jianyu crouched and bared his fangs.

"Don't listen to the dragon," said Aini into Nastia's right ear. "He is trying to take you off your path."

Nastia walked on, refusing to acknowledge Lunosh.

"Escaping into the night with your suitcase, are we?" said the silver dragon in a mocking tone. "Oh, what will Anton think of this? After all the trust you were slowly rebuilding with him again. But now... what a shame."

Nastia didn't respond. She hurried ahead until she got to the stairs.

Akeldama the cook charged out the door and noticed Nastia. She stopped in her tracks as if shocked by electricity.

"Oh, hello," greeted Nastia. "Can I, I mean, may I ride with you to Athens tonight?"

Akeldama only returned a blank stare, her hair in a loose bun. "*Then kah-tah-lah-veh-noh,*" she replied.

"Oh, right of course, you don't speak English. If only your daughter was here. Is she inside?" Nastia gestured to the door.

Akeldama glared at her, frowning furiously for a moment, and then went inside and shut the door.

"What's happening?" Nastia asked Aini. "Why did she just disappear like that?"

"She'll come back," the red bird answered in a whisper. "Now this moment is key, Tia. Do not listen to Lunosh."

"Did I hear my name?" Lunosh slithered through the air, back into Nastia's view. He analyzed her with his fish-meat colored eyes, the silver mane around his face curling and twisting. "You will miss him. Oh, you will miss so much. Won't you miss the way he holds you at night? What a shame that this will completely shatter his trust. He won't take you back after this. You're abandoning him. He's out there in the big city of Athens counting on you being here. But, poor man... Are you really going to give up Anton and run away in that rickety motorboat?"

Nastia glanced down at her suitcase. She did feel funny, escaping like this.

"Tia, don't listen to him. Ignore him," said Aini. "Just wait a few more minutes. Akeldama's about to come back out with her daughter."

But Nastia had already started retreating up the path. "He's right. I'll really miss Anton."

In a swift motion, the silver dragon dove down and clutched Nastia's hand with his tail, forcefully tugging her up the path.

"You may not touch her!" Jianyu roared. He crouched on a rock and then launched at the dragon, his many mighty fangs exposed in his wide-open mouth. Jianyu bit down on the middle of the silver dragon's body, landed, and pinned the slithering creature to the ground. But Lunosh would not be dismissed so easily. He whipped up, pulling Jianyu into the air. And then it was all silvery scales and blue fur as the tiger fought the dragon.

"Go back and ask them now!" said Aini urgently. "Now is your chance."

Nastia slowly headed back to the building. Akeldama and her short daughter waited for them on the dock, more bags in hand. "*Viasini!*"

"She says to please hurry," the girl translated in a kind voice. "I'm sorry, but we need to leave now."

Nastia breathed rapidly. And then she called out. "Tell your mother you can go on without me. I'm going to stay here. I'm sorry for distracting you." Nastia whirled around and stomped back up the path.

Aini sprang off her shoulder and flapped in front of Nastia's eyes. "What are you doing, Tia?"

"I'm changing my mind," said Nastia angrily, crossing her arms so tightly it was as if she was hugging herself. "I'm staying here tonight. I'm going to wait for Anton to get back tomorrow. I'm not going!"

Suddenly, Lunosh broke away from Jianyu's claws. He seemed to grow as he rose and swirled, swimming through the air like one huge silver ribbon. "Excellent choice, Nastia."

———————————◆———————————

AFTER RETURNING HER suitcase to her bedroom, Nastia heard a cold, scraping whisper emerged from the darkness. "Anton is dead," said the voice. "Anton is gone forever. God has killed him. He is in hell now, and there is nothing you can do. You are going to hell, too. Salvation is a lie."

"I can't stay in here anymore!" Nastia told herself. "I have to get out of this room!" She lunged for the door and left the room.

The hallway was unbelievably dark. Nastia thought she saw a vile grin at the end of the hall, atop a huge mass of coiled silver flesh.

She raced in the other direction, down the stairs, and into the living room.

She heard the scream of a young girl.

"What is that?" Nastia ran out the side door and onto the long, hall-like balcony on the side of the mansion. A wailing gust swept through the transparent white curtains — billowing in, out, and around six pillars.

Nastia saw the outline of a girl at the end of the hall, staring at her. "Mythia? Is that you?" Nastia ran toward the shape, but before she arrived, the red-haired girl dove over the railing with another scream. "Mythia!" Nastia leaned over the railing. The girl held on to a protruding rock, barely preventing herself from plunging into the waves thirty feet below.

Nastia strained to reach the girl. "Come on. Take my hand. I can save you."

The girl scowled back as if Nastia had told her to die. "No! I don't want *your* help," Mythia released her grasp.

Nastia was the one who screamed now. "Why does she have to do that? Why does she have to destroy herself?" She covered her face with her hands and raced inside.

———————◆———————

CONTRASTING WITH THE loud chaos Nastia had been feeling, the living room was completely dark yet serene. She switched on a lamp that glowed just as kindly as she wanted. Nastia knew she couldn't sleep if she tried to go back to bed, so she curled up on one of the couches and rested her head on a blue pillow. A beige blanket lay on the coffee table. Nastia spread it over herself, finally relaxing. "Are you asleep?" a voice whispered from across the room.

Nastia saw Damon standing at the bottom of the stairs, wearing only small shorts. "No. Not yet. Sorry, did I wake you?"

"No," he smiled. "That should have been my question." He walked over and sat on the couch across from Nastia. "What's keeping you up?"

"It's hard to explain," she replied. "I always have trouble sleeping, even when I'm really tired. Like now."

"Did you enjoy the movie?"

Nastia shrugged. "Yeah. It was exciting."

An idea grew in Damon's black eyes. "Do you mind if I tell you what Greek goddess you would be?"

She laughed. "Not at all."

"Athena."

She smiled. "Would I make my home in the Parthenon?"

"You could if you wanted. Now you try for me. What Greek mythological person would I be?"

"Hmm…" Nastia pulled the blanket up to her lips. "Hermes, maybe."

"Hermes?" Damon retorted. "You think I would make a good messenger for the gods?"

"Sure. Would you rather be someone else? Who would you choose to be?"

"Hyacinth. He wasn't a god, but he was gay and a hero."

"I'm not sure I remember whether he was gay." Nastia frowned. The room was quiet for a moment.

"I can't sleep either," Damon said. "Would you mind if I pull this couch beside the one you're on and sleep on it?"

"Of course you may," Nastia said. "It's your house. You don't have to ask me."

"I didn't know if it would make you uncomfortable." He dragged the coffee table away and then struggled to pull the other couch. After much effort, he managed to position it directly against Nastia's couch. "Sometimes I hate this place." He climbed in and put a different beige blanket over himself. His face was only two feet away, much closer than Nastia first thought it would be.

"Why do you hate it here?" she asked.

"Because it's so isolated." Damon huddled against the back of his couch and faced her. "Have you ever thought up your own Greek god before?"

"No. Never. Have you?"

"Yes. I thought up the goddess of loneliness."

Nastia's face lit up. "Wow. She really gets around, doesn't she? What do you call her?"

"Tempesta," he said with a grin. "Because she creates terrible storms inside of people, even when there is absolutely nothing going on around them."

"That's wonderful! Have you thought up a legend for her as well?"

"Yes, I have."

"Can you tell me?"

Damon yawned. "Not today. How about tomorrow? I think we have had enough storytelling for one day."

"All right." Nastia reached up to the lamp above her head, but hesitated. "Do you mind if I turn off the light?"

"Not in the least. Please do."

The room went dark and sleep came quickly.

33

THE BURN

THE ROOM WAS filled with calm sunlight when Nastia woke on the couch. Damon's face was pressed against her shoulder while he continued sleeping. She laughed when she noticed how he lay on his stomach, half on her couch and half on his own with his left arm awkwardly caught in the gap between the two. She didn't want to disturb him and carefully lifted her beige blanket, crawled over the armrest, and walked toward the dining room and kitchen. While sipping some water, she saw the time, 10:38.

"Wow," she muttered, surprised. "I haven't slept that well in months."

———◆———

OUT BY THE pool deck table, Nastia felt splendidly comfortable and quite free in the strong sunlight for she had just applied plenty of sunblock to her soft white skin. *No red and rashy scorches today*, she thought.

The red bird flew in from the bright sky and landed on the table.

"Hello, Aini," Nastia greeted casually.

The tiny, shimmering black eyes blinked up at her. "Good morning, Tia."

"Last night was crazy! I'm very glad Damon found me and kept me company. I was finally able to sleep."

"Yes, the company of another human being created in the image of God was intended to be soothing. But are you sure it was wise to sleep so close together, especially when only you two were in the house?"

Nastia shook away the suggestion. "Please don't talk to me about wisdom now, Aini. I was enjoying the freedom from loneliness. I could not have asked for anything better at that moment than his company. I was so horribly tired. Anton was right, Damon is a good friend."

"I'm not talking about his friendship abilities," the bird clarified peacefully. "I'm talking about your susceptibility to temptation. Don't forget the passage Jianyu quoted to you, Proverbs 6:27-28: 'Can a man scoop fire into his lap without his clothes being burned? Can a man walk on hot coals without his feet being scorched?' You got dangerously near the fire of sin by sleeping so close to Damon last night. Just a slight step farther, and you will fall into the burning coals."

Nastia didn't want to lose her cheerful mood and said jokingly, "Don't worry — I've put on plenty of sunblock." She could almost imagine a smile on the red bird's face, but it wasn't there.

"Have you tasted your lunch yet, Tia?" Aini asked, pointing her small wing at a glass refrigerator.

"No, why?" Nastia was slightly disconcerted by the question.

"Nothing, it just smells like mustard." With that, the bird took off and flew away.

"What? Mustard!" Now Nastia felt uncomfortable. The scene of her mother painfully bending down to clean up a puddle of mustard flashed in her mind. She looked down at the sauce, which resembled the same puddle from that day of adultery.

Nastia opened the refrigerator and removed one of the two plates of saucy chicken. She sniffed it. "Darn it Aini!" Nastia said to the air. "If you hadn't told me, I might have enjoyed this."

Now the mustard smell was so clear she left the table and sat in a lounge chair ten feet away, taking her glass of water with her. She noticed the inky swirls in the liquid and tasted the bitterness more than usual. Nastia realized for the first time that she was growing accustomed to the taste of hypocrite's brew, as if it were black coffee.

Damon walked out of the mansion in the same black Speedo with neon blue streaks he had worn for the past two days. "Hi, Nastia! What a gorgeous day, although *you* are *much*-better looking."

She smiled, simply.

He walked over to the refrigerator. "Great! Akeldama left us food. I am famished." He laughed. "You didn't have to wait for me, you know." He stepped up to the very edge of the pool, looking at her as if the water wasn't there.

"I don't mind. Are you going to swim first?"

"I'd like to just for a bit. It is a warm day."

As Damon wiggled his body and leapt into the pool, Nastia looked at him in a different way, as if she just had to have his body up against hers again. The third roach she had received yesterday suddenly popped out of her waist, painlessly, and crawled on the edge of the chair. It scurried up the backrest and onto Nastia's sunglasses. She didn't care and let it stay there, dying her purplish glasses silver while she watched Damon swim around. He swam as if he had forgotten every problem and woe that the world possessed, and there was only him and the water. *I wish I could feel that way*, she thought.

Just as quickly as before, the metal roach leapt off Nastia's sunglasses and disappeared in the bushes.

Damon swam over to the edge of the pool nearest Nastia and leaned on it, pointing his elbows up while pulling his body down. "Are you ready for lunch?" he asked from behind his tan arms.

"Sure." She got up.

After heating up their plates, Nastia and Damon made their way back to the table on the pool deck. The mustard didn't bother Nastia as much as she thought it would. She forced down the first few bites, but her stomach tightened after her third, and she decided not to eat anymore. She pushed her plate away and curled up in her chair.

"Do you not like it?" he asked with a childishly sad face.

"No, it's fine," she lied. "I guess I'm not as hungry as I thought."

"Would you like me to tell you the tale of the goddess of loneliness now?" he asked excitedly.

"Please do."

Nastia sipped some water as Damon tilted his head in thought and began:

TEMPESTA — THE GODDESS of loneliness — is the eldest daughter of Poseidon, the god of the sea and the brother of Zeus and Hades. Only a few months after Poseidon claimed his watery domain, Tempesta was born to him, not from a woman, but directly from the sea. She came into existence while Poseidon evaluated the bounds of his new water-controlling powers. In the middle of the night, when the sky was completely overcast with the most horrible storm the world had ever seen, Poseidon created the highest wave that had ever been and crashed it into an island, destroying it in the process. While the storm continued to whirl around him in horrible strength, Poseidon noticed a form floating in the water where the island and wave had been. He picked it up, and seeing that it was a baby mermaid, he said, "I name you Tempesta because you came out of the most powerful storm I have ever created."

And so Tempesta came into being. Poseidon raised her by himself in his deep, cold, underwater castle in the middle of the ocean. She never knew what it was like to have a mother, and Poseidon rarely ever said anything to her. For the vast majority of her childhood days, Tempesta was completely alone in the underwater castle with only imaginary characters as her companions.

Once she turned twenty years old, Tempesta asked her father for a merman who would be her companion. Poseidon agreed, turned a human man named Rachialga into a merman, and united him with his daughter in marriage.

Tempesta and her husband Rachialga deeply loved each other for one year. Then one day, while she was filled with great bliss and overflowing delight about Rachialga, Tempesta swam into the small underwater castle that Poseidon had given them and found that Rachialga was not there. She called after him playfully, thinking he was teasing her. An idea came to her mind, and she decided to swim to the enchanting beach where she and her husband had spent their happiest moments together. But when Tempesta poked her head out of the water, she saw Rachialga making love to a mortal woman in the very spot where Tempesta had first made love to him on their wedding night.

Instantly a hellish rage tore through every vein in her body. "He's mine! He's mine! Get away!" she shouted while using her powers to raise the ocean waves and darken the sky. Rachialga and the mortal woman turned toward her in terrified surprise. Once Tempesta noticed how beautiful the woman was, she froze a launching wave in her hand, turned it into a spear, and threw it at the woman, but Rachialga was embracing her, and the spear pierced them both.

Immediately, Tempesta's rage dropped, and she was tormented by overwhelming guilt. She rushed to Rachialga, but Charon (the ferryman of the dead) was too quick; Tempesta's husband was already gone.

The combination of guilt and longing for Rachialga was more than Tempesta could bear. She wept for days and days, scarring her face so she would no longer be beautiful and cutting her body so she wouldn't be desirable anymore. Tempesta tried to make a deal with Hades, offering him her ability to bare children in exchange for her deceased husband, but Hades refused no matter how much she pressed him.

After Tempesta left the netherworld and was swimming inside the vast ocean, the guilt pounded inside her more than she could stand. She felt so alone she thought her immortality would leave her in the next second. In that moment, Tempesta refused to believe that she had killed her husband. She created a story in her head in which the mortal woman was the murderer, but Tempesta was the only one to be pitied. She vowed to haunt all humans with the loneliness she felt, saying to herself over and over, "They deserve it. They killed him!"

Two dolphins were swimming past, and Tempesta cursed them, turning them into wrinkled forms with no eyes. They became her enchanted slaves and pulled her chariot throughout the world while she tirelessly searched for any mortals whom she could curse with her newfound power of loneliness. For the rest of time, she traveled the world, cursing and cursing, never sleeping, and always denying the reality that she had killed her husband."

———————◆———————

"THE END," DAMON said after a long pause. "What did you think?"

"That was so beautiful!" Nastia said, her face creased with sincere pity. "I don't know why, but I loved it. Wow. You thought up your own Greek goddess of loneliness and the legend too? I'm very impressed."

He smiled dimly as eagerness grew in his black eyes. "I have a small statuette of her in my room," he said. "Would you like to see it?"

"Yes, please!" Nastia stood quickly. Damon laughed and led her into the house, up the stairs, and into his bedroom.

"Here it is." He reached into one of the square block shelves and removed a ceramic statuette of a sullen-faced mermaid tightly holding the reins of two wrinkled and eyeless dolphins. "Mum had it made for me." Damon handed it to Nastia.

"Very interesting." She turned the statuette around in her hands. "How nice of her to make it for you."

Nastia looked up, and something very strange happened. Damon was wordlessly motioning for her to sin with him. She was shocked at first, but then a sudden thrill of excitement tugged strongly inside her, and she thought that it would be very nice to have sex with Damon.

Just before she got into the bed, Aini flew in front of her face, flashing small red wings. "Don't do this, Nastia! You are about to plunge into the fire that will burn you severely!"

"But I do it with Anton all the time," Nastia said far too casually. "Lately, I've wanted to try someone else's body. This isn't serious, silly bird!"

Aini flew away.

◆

"NASTIA! I'M BACK!" the voice of Anton called in the distance. Nastia was very distracted and wondered if the sound was only her imagination. She heard a few muffled thumps in the hall. They grew louder and stopped. She and Damon turned around at the same time to find Anton standing in the doorway.

◆

NASTIA SAT MOTIONLESS in the dim bedroom where she and Anton had slept together two nights before. She felt completely naked even though she was fully clothed.

The air was stiff with a horrible wrenching silence as Anton vigorously stuffed his suitcase. Nastia desperately wanted to say something to him, but she dared not. His masculine dimples and handsome face did not show the least resemblance of the wonderful smiles Nastia had once known. There was only pain.

Anton avoided her eyes as he turned to walk out of the room. He stopped in the doorway and said with his back to her, "I'm going to the dock now. Be down there in ten minutes."

"Okay," she whispered, scared of saying anything more. Anton left.

Nastia remained on the bed. Her bag was packed, and she was ready to travel into Athens, stay the night at a hotel, and then fly back to D.C. the following morning as Anton had said they would. But she was exhausted and stunned.

Nastia knew she should feel extremely ashamed, but she didn't. She knew her actions had deeply wounded Anton's heart — Anton, her favorite person in the entire world — but her remorse was only a tiny ripple. She didn't hate herself. In fact, she was almost glad she had given in. *Why would I think such a horrible thing?* She asked herself, and she was immediately hit by the reality of her actions: she had actually done it with Damon; she had *actually* cheated on Anton, not only emotionally, but all the way. It was real.

The softest knock sounded on the wall, and Nastia looked up. Damon stood in the doorway, looking quite normal; he even smiled. The only difference was the word *woops* in his dark eyes.

Nastia rolled her hazel eyes in utter distaste. "So, you're gay, huh? Oh yeah, *sure*, Mr. seducing prostitute!"

He shrugged, came closer into the room, and leaned on the wall. "I am still gay."

She dropped her chin and glared at him. "What the heck! Then why did you want to have sex with me? Why did you do it?"

He looked at her as if she were a toddler, surprising Nastia. She thought the expression was horribly out of place.

"Did you forget what I said to you on the beach yesterday? How I think that the yin and yang applies to sexuality too? I am definitely mostly gay, and that is right for me, but I do have a little bit of heterosexuality in me also."

"Do you think I give a crap about your stupid yin and yang?" She wanted to hit him but she closed her eyes instead. "I just cheated on my boyfriend!"

"You asked the question," he retorted. Nastia couldn't believe that even Damon was making her feel like it was all her fault.

"You are the most beautiful woman I have ever met," Damon said. "Honestly. You are more beautiful than all of the Greek goddesses — more beautiful than Aphrodite, Hera, Psyche, and even Athena. Ever since I first saw you in the living room two days ago, I have been looking for a flaw in your physical appearance. But I haven't found any!" He paused. "Having sex with you was like having sex with a goddess. Who wouldn't want that?"

Nastia released a sarcastic laugh. She didn't know if Damon was mocking her or being serious. He sounded truthful, but she didn't care. "Thank you so much!" She rolled her eyes again as a question entered her mind. "Have you ever had sex with a girl before me?"

He shook his head. "No. Actually I haven't. They have all been guys before you."

Nastia stood up, shivered, and backed away from him, throwing her hands into the air. "I can't stand it! I can't stand it! You are such a wicked person!"

"Maybe," Damon replied. "But if I am, you are too."

He strolled out, and Nastia was alone once more. "Tempesta," she said. "Oh, that stupid Tempesta!"

She reached down and lifted her suitcase, revealing a roach beneath it, glowing like a hot coal. She gasped. Somehow she knew it was the very same roach that had left her waist only a few hours before. "Oh no!" She bolted toward the hallway, carrying her suitcase, but before she reached it, something started to burn in her waist — a burning she had never felt before. She screamed, dropped her suitcase, and lifted her shirt. The hot-coal roach was imbedded in the same spot it had been before, next to the other two roaches —

but instead of bruises, grey ashes surrounded it. "Is that my skin? It's burning my skin!"

The angels were nowhere to be seen.

EXHAUSTED FROM THE silent tension with Anton during the return flight, Nastia went to the airplane bathroom for a break. When her eyes hit the mirror, a heavy weight plunged inside her heart as she observed her reflection. Her face was uglier than it ever had been before. The whites of her eyes were blood red, her nose was bruised and disfigured, and her cheeks were only thin, blotchy skin, like an old woman's.

Nastia reached up and fingered her greasy red locks. Two chunks of hair dropped to the floor, revealing a swollen bald patch. "AHHH!" she gasped, horrified.

The wire on her leg had spiraled all the way to her upper thigh, surrounded by vomit-green splotches. The wire on her arm had almost reached her shoulder. Coloring her waist a rusty orange, the three roaches pulled the skin of Nastia's torso, making her look anorexic. Around her neck, the many ants of idolatry suddenly unified, forming a multi-link chain. But what affected Nastia the most was the new sight of a spider's leg that had just appeared beneath her chin, creeping from its swollen source on her back.

Hot tears stung her eyes. Nastia slumped to the floor, her knees pressed up against the plastic wall of the tiny airplane bathroom. She tried to forget everything she had just seen, everything that had just happened — but a pulsating numbness swept over her in aching waves, preventing her from dismissing the images. Nastia had lost so much — her best friend, her boyfriend's affection, even her sense of the presence of God. The weight of it all crashed down on her with an overwhelming force. Nastia cried and cried and cried.

34

WHEN IT'S ALL ON YOUR SHOULDERS

NASTIA SLAMMED THE passenger door of Anton's SUV and settled into the seat with a deep, shaking breath — weighted but relieved. Holding the steering wheel as naturally as anything, Anton ignored her, put the car into drive, and raced away toward the fading dusk and his hotel.

Good grace! Nastia thought in utter distress. The past two days had to be the worst in her whole life. Anton had silently carried his pained expression throughout their half day in Athens, right after he discovered her and Damon, and then the entire following day as they flew back from Greece to Washington D.C. Had it really only been two days? Nastia thought it had been three at least! The inner aching was more than she had suffered in years. It was horrible! Just horrible! Everything was thrown off. She felt like she would die if this continued.

Nastia had tried to make conversation with Anton. During the flight, she couldn't hold it in any longer and blurted out, "For the love of life, Anton! Just yell at me already! Say *something*. I can't stand this silence; it's driving me mad. Tell me how much you hate me, and what I've done. Tell me how you are annoyed with me and can't stand me. Just please talk!"

He had merely turned to her, his eyes pink with hurt, and said, "No. Not on the plane."

"Okay fine!" she had replied. "You just shut up, and I will watch movies." She was lucky to have the choice of many different movies, but none of them were enough to distract her. Nastia found herself thinking about her day with Damon again and again, striving to remember when exactly she had gone wrong. Was it because he told the story of Tempesta right before? Or maybe when she had entered his room? Or was it before that? The flight lasted for over nine hours, and Nastia didn't figure out anything.

The drive through D.C. was peaceful in comparison. Nastia was simply happy to be away from Greece and back in the United States. Everything would be put right here. She would apologize to Anton with all her heart, he would forgive her, and they would be passionate lovers again. They could get through this, couldn't they? She didn't want to admit it to herself, but maybe Anton was considering breaking up. *No, no, that can't be true. He loves me more than anyone else, doesn't he? Of course, he won't want to live without me. This is only a phase of anger that will soon pass.*

They pulled into the parking garage, unloaded their suitcases, and quietly made their way through the hotel system. Maybe he was cooling down. Walking side by side was like being good lovers.

They entered the room and Nastia spoke, "Finally we're home!" She dropped onto the couch and exhaled. "Gosh, it's good to be back!"

"It shouldn't be," Anton whispered.

"Shouldn't be what?"

"You shouldn't feel good being back in my hotel room." He calmly walked away, into the bedroom. Nastia followed and found him removing her clothes from the dresser and throwing them onto the bed.

"What are you doing?" she demanded.

"I'm taking your clothes out of my hotel room." He moved to the closet and began tugging her clothes off the hangers.

"I can see that, but *why?*"

Anton looked at her with complete disappointment. He seemed taller than usual. "Nastia, I can't put into words how absolutely upset I am with you right now. You cheated on me. People who love each other don't cheat. I left you on the island with Damon for not even two days, and you couldn't stay faithful to me? What am I supposed to make of that?"

"What?" Nastia scoffed. "How can you say that? You have no idea what I was going through while you were gone for your stupid business investment. *You* left me alone with Damon. I wanted to be with you the whole time. I was craving for you with every part of me. Yes, I made a mistake, a huge mistake — but I was going through such a hard, inner struggle. Just try — *try* to understand!"

"So, you're saying your emotions and inner struggle were too strong for you to resist temptation? That sounds like zero self-control to me." He gave a chuckle but swallowed it rapidly. "You completely shattered my trust, and there is no way it will ever heal. I thought you loved me — and I was really taken in by your beauty. But now I see the truth. You are ugly, uglier than any girl I have ever dated. I am done with you, and I mean it."

Nastia was speechless for a second, but it didn't last long. "Anton! You can't do this to me! No, I'm not leaving! I *do* love you. Don't put my gold dress in the bag. Give me back my dress! *Anton…*"

———————◆———————

NASTIA STOOD BEFORE the apartment door that she had hated once for its simplicity, but now she didn't care. She couldn't stand to be alone a moment longer. She had to see the only person in the world who truly knew her — Lauren Henson.

The door swung open, and Lauren saw her, not surprised only sad because she could read Nastia's face and the way she carried her suitcase.

"Can I come in, please?" Nastia pleaded.

"Yes, of course," Lauren replied, passively stepping to the side.

"Thank you." Nastia let her case thump to the floor. "Uh!" She turned around to see Lauren, silent and motionless. "Oh, don't be a statue! I cheated on Anton okay! We flew to Greece for some possible investment thingy of his, and I slept with a mostly-gay bisexual guy in an island mansion. Is there any better way for me to explain it? Stop skulking around and looking dumb." She hated how she was venting to Lauren, but Lauren was tough. She had handled much worse from Nastia.

"I'm not dumb," Lauren said calmly.

"Oh. Good. Grace. I know you're not dumb! Can't you tell that I will be saying crazy things right now? I just lost the most important person in my life! Are you going to kick me out? Are you going to say I haven't truly repented because *he* broke up with *me*, and I didn't leave him first?"

"No, Tia. I will not kick you out. You are very welcome here. I've missed you."

Nastia smirked. She couldn't appreciate an, "I've missed you" now. Ugh — but she knew she should. "Thank you, Lauren. That means a lot."

Lauren saw past the forced words, her prominent cheeks swelling. "Please don't say 'that means a lot' when you're not sincere."

"Oh, Lauren. You are making this hard! Why? Where is your compassion? I'm really hurting right now, and this is how you're treating me?"

"I'm sorry, Tia. I just see how you're struggling to care for anyone but yourself. You haven't come back to God yet, but I know it takes time." Compassion returned. "But I love you, and I don't want you to suffer. Come here." Lauren opened her arms, and Nastia obliged. They embraced tightly for half a minute.

"Come on. Let's go into the kitchen and have some tea," Lauren suggested, stepping toward the entryway.

"No, Lauren. I'm not ready to sit down. I've got to go off by myself. Please tell me something, though. Some comfort."

"It might be difficult comfort."

"I don't mind. I just need something. Anything."

"Okay." Lauren pondered momentarily and began. "You made Anton into an idol. It's as if you were trying to live inside a dollhouse when there was a royal palace right beside you. You chose fake love instead of the true love of God.

"But God is waiting for you, Tia! He still cares for you and wants you with all his heart. Never take for granted the love of God. That's one of the biggest mistakes any believer can make because — in the process — we let ourselves see God's love like a joke, like his name used in vain. But God's love is not a joke. It's steadfast and dominant and breathtaking and colorful and — satisfying.

"This is what it means to fear God: we fear his love because it's the real deal. It's something so completely greater than anything else. God's love is so mysterious and huge that it's terrifying."

Lauren paused, allowing Nastia to absorb the concepts.

"Thank you for saying that, Lauren. I need to go out by myself for a while. I need to think — in the right way."

Lauren smiled her sweet and encouraging smile. "I understand. Be safe!"

———————◆———————

THE NIGHT WIND chilled Nastia as she stepped outside the door and folded her arms, brushing her oh-so-pretty red hair to the side. But no, her hair wasn't pretty today. Not to her. She felt like a dirty burden. Yet her heart fought anything that resembled worthlessness, like it had always done. Nastia rarely struggled with low self-esteem or insecurity. Too many people had confirmed her beauty, attractive confidence, likeable personality, and intriguing countenance for her to believe otherwise. But, really, only her agreement with the compliments mattered.

She started walking beside a low-traffic street, heading for the bridge nearby. A pair of blinding headlights raced toward her. "Turn off your brights, you jerk!" she shouted, unafraid of the crimes that happen in the big city. Nastia didn't care about dangers right now. She had a fresh can of pepper spray in her purse.

The car zoomed on.

Voices from people she knew before Anton flashed in her head.

Nastia, I love you! You are so beautiful!

We love you! You are so awesome! Oh my gosh!

Ever since I met you I haven't been able to get you off my mind. Please, I just want a kiss. Just one kiss!

Hey, Nastia! Wow, I wish I had your number...

She saw faces too — wide-eyed girls who wanted to be just like her, handsome jocks with nothing but lust on their brains, and insecure guys who obsessed over stupid things like her ears or her favorite green shoes. Many people had noticed her in some way. Many people had a thought about Nastia Sobieski.

She climbed onto a grassy hill between the road and the river. Embracing her knees, she gazed at the dark water reflecting the milky glow of orange streetlights.

Those people didn't really matter to Nastia. They loved her one minute and hated her the next. But she didn't care. In the end, she was just as happy whether those people adored her, hated her, or ignored her.

The opinions that did matter came from very different sources — her mother, her sisters, Lauren, and the men she actually loved. First there was the football player in high school, named Cody, who she hunted down almost every school day.

Sadly, he grew annoyed with her and said, "Just leave me alone. You are the most legitimate stalker I have ever met." Nastia was deeply hurt by his rejection, and she vowed to never hunt down a guy again. They would have to come to her!

And they did. College proved to be a favorable place for male admirers. Each day was a new social adventure. Yet, she only gained one boyfriend in the three years, and he only lasted for a month. Jaden pursued Nastia constantly, and she enjoyed his interest. He would send her cards, flowers, and chocolates with invitations to dinner. After a while, she gave in, and they started dating. But when she decided to be his girlfriend, she really wanted the best relationship possible and texted him a lot, expecting to see him almost every day. When they didn't talk much and Jaden was casually absent-minded, Nastia wanted to discuss it with him in order to improve their relationship. He was turned off by the responsibility and broke up with her.

And then — so unexpectedly it seemed to be a miracle — Nastia Sobieski met Anton Shepherd on a plane from Dallas to Washington D.C. Anton was different from all the other guys. He was both confident and kind; he was muscular and handsome but not lustful. He cared about her. He valued her as a wonderful person, not an object. How could Nastia not fall head over heels in love with him? Anton was the shining knight Nastia had dreamed about since she was a little girl.

But what went wrong? What happened? How did she lose her shining knight?

"It was Aini and Jianyu!" she blamed, looking around and not seeing them. "They were constantly nagging me to leave Anton and repent. They tripped me up and made me depressed."

Nastia knew this was wrong the moment it left her lips. The bird and the tiger were envoys of God.

"Then it was the silver dragon!" she said aloud. "It was Lunosh! He tempted me. He whispered in my ear and played on my deepest desires like a piano."

But this didn't work either. Everyone is tempted, and being tempted isn't a good-enough excuse.

As Anton said, just an hour ago, "So, you're saying your emotions and inner struggle were too strong for you to resist temptation?"

A fresh idea came to her, one that was much stronger than blaming angels or even Lunosh — her father. No one had hurt Nastia more than Mr. Sobieski. Her high school years were the most painful of her life. He cheated on her mom, her wonderful and amazing mom! Mr. Sobieski was a hypocritical, lying, and selfish man. Once she found out that he had committed adultery, Nastia passionately resented him. She hated her father. He was the last person in the world she ever wanted to hug or touch in any way, even a simple handshake. Oh no, that would be like dipping your hand in slime. Nastia was repulsed by the mere idea of her father.

"But that is why I needed Anton so much!" she wailed into the night wind, tears blurring her vision. "He was truly good in a world of wicked, lustful, and all-out disgusting men."

She looked up at the sky and addressed God, the tears rolling down her cheeks like spilled beads. "God, I need Anton! I need, need, need him! Why did you put him in my life if it was wrong to love him, and you knew I would want him so much? Why did you let him sit next to me on that stupid flight? And now I don't have him at all — and I never will again. How could you do this to me, God? How could you tease me with the one thing I needed the most?"

Nastia knew the answer. She knew the truth as if God had spoken it before her question. God had tested her. It was a challenge to see whom she loved more — Jesus or a shining knight. Nastia had chosen the shining knight. She had broken the first commandment with such a determined lustful passion it was frightening.

Had she really *loved* Anton? She had wanted him for sure. She adored him but in a very selfish way. She had turned her back on God in order to have Anton, and in doing so, she had turned her back on God's true love — the kind that is patient, loyal, humble, forgiving, and self-sacrificial. Nastia had only thought of her own desires when she went to live with Anton. She saw it now.

"I never loved him," she announced as if the realization would save her. "I loved what he would do for me and what he would provide for me. I never loved him at all. The only person I've cared for is myself. All my physical gifts, sweet words, stories and teasing were nothing but a form of currency to purchase his affections, just like any old prostitute. It wasn't love at all.

"But I was so wrapped up in my emotions and my past pain. I blamed my father — I blamed circumstances, I've even blamed the person who created both Anton and me. I blamed God!

"What does all my past pain amount to, then? The hours each day, for almost ten years, when I would dream of the man who would be the antithesis of my father? What does all my agony and frustration about his sin amount to?"

Nastia stilled her thoughts for a moment, disregarding a frosty gust caused by another racing car. These conclusions were more important than anything right now because they led to the truth. She yearned for the truth!

Nastia spoke aloud but calmly, "I guess hurtful memories and the desires that result are just excuses in the end. They are only means to justify sinning and seeking my own selfish way. Yes, I've been hurt — it was definitely wrong of my father — but I allowed my hurts to rule my life. I allowed the scars from my past to make me into a horrible selfish mess, complete with roaches, ants, wires, and a spider on my body.

"Anton was right. I am ugly, just as ugly as my father. We are the same — selfish and lustful. Ugh! I have become the monster I despised."

The craving returned. "I want Anton! Oh, if only I hadn't cheated on him, then he would still be here, and I would be with him and…"

An idea suddenly entered her mind, like the first sight of light in a midnight storm. "Wait! I don't have to want Anton at all. Just now, I wanted him out of guilt as if I were supposed to suffer in hopeless longing. But I'm not! I don't have to! Yes, I was wrong to cheat on him. Yes, I've been a bad girlfriend, but the whole thing with Anton was wrong. I don't have to miss any of it!"

A glimpse of freedom lit up in her eyes. "I don't love Anton. I don't want him. Yes, he was nice, fun, and considerate, but we did nasty stuff together — and I hate that. I don't want to be his girlfriend. I wouldn't mind if I never saw him again. Oh, my grace, this is the most freeing thing I have ever decided!"

She looked up at the stars and instantly felt ashamed, more than any person could make her feel.

"Lord Jesus," she breathed softly, "I'm sorry. I still want my ideal guy — a good man to love me. Not Anton anymore. No. I want a Christian guy like Erlend, the blond man in Hawaii. I liked him very much, God. He was sweet, handsome, personable, deep, and he liked me too. He is just the kind of guy I've always wanted. Erlend is the guy of my dreams not Anton!"

The new dream faded too, like an especially pretty wave quickly forgotten. It wasn't strong enough. Nastia remembered Erlend for who he was — a simple guy with flaws, not the ideal shining knight. He wouldn't satisfy her either. She could imagine frustration with him, just like the snorkeling conflict with the shark. He wasn't perfect, and life with him would have been rough, too.

Who exactly was this shining knight she had always wanted? It was more than just a good man. The perfect man she had imagined was impossible to find among fallen humanity. She wasn't searching only for a husband; she was searching for an everlasting companion who could satisfy all of her deepest and most fundamental needs. Nastia wanted divine love.

"How stupid can I be? I was trying to make Anton into Jesus! I was looking for Christ among attractive guys. I am such an idiot! Jesus is so much better than they could ever be — he is God!"

She realized the truth. She wanted and needed God. He was the only one who could satisfy her to the extent she desired, but at the same time she still wanted a husband — a good man who would love her, and she could love in physical and personal ways.

"Oh, God," she prayed, disappointed with herself. "I have turned my desire for a good husband into an idol that has taken me from you. I know romance is a very good thing you have created, but I turned it into a wreck!

"I miss you, God," she groaned. "I feel selfish even in this, even as I pray and come back to you. But it's not about me, it's about you, Father God! I'm a mess, but you're not! And that's the whole point of the world! I desperately need you, Lord Jesus Christ. You are the resurrected Son of God. You were born in the flesh, but you conquered sin and death."

Nastia gazed up at the twinkling stars above the Washington D.C. skyline. "One day, you will reign in the heavens in all your mighty glory. And all people will see that you are the true Lord.

"Please forgive me, God! I turned away from you. How stupid I was! Even as a Christian who had met you, I looked the other way at some flashy distraction. Please forgive my idolatry...

"Lord, Jesus. I don't want sin anymore. I don't want the idols. I want you. Please forgive me. God! Please forgive me!" Tears rolled down her cheeks. "I've done wrong. I see it now. I finally see it. I've lived the wrong way, even before Anton. I've been such a proud woman. The way I scowled down at people. It was as if I searched for a confirmation of my own worth by criticizing others. I can't treat people like that anymore, Lord. I can't do that anymore. I don't want to be a finger-pointer or a stone-thrower. Lord, help me! Help me to lift people up, to encourage, to cherish people the way that you cherish me. I've lashed out at people enough for one lifetime. From now on, Lord, help me to change! I can't be the same anymore. I must be kind. I must be compassionate. I must be more like you.

"And Lord please remove this lust from my soul. It is poison to relationships! Lust is such a thief of human quality. I don't want this in my eyes anymore! Please Lord, I will wait for the wholesome physical love that you have for a husband and wife. In the meantime, help me God! Remove this lust from my eyes! Please! I can't be like this anymore. I can't view the world through these lenses anymore…"

Nastia clenched a fistful of dirt and rubbed it between her fingers. "Oh God! My attempts to get what I want have brought me to ruin." Her arms slackened and her head fell forward. "Please forgive me, God! Have mercy on me. I have sinned. Have mercy on me, mighty Lord. Please!"

Suddenly, it was as though a hand was resting on her shoulder. And then she heard in her soul, "Nastia Sobieski, I love you. Your sins are forgiven."

A chill swept over Nastia. She opened her eyes and looked down at her arm. She gasped, and pleasure raced through her veins. Her arm was clean with no wire or ugly bruises. It was the way it had been before Anton!

She quickly lifted up the bottom of her shirt and touched her stomach. The roaches were gone too! Even the burning red one! They were gone, and her stomach was clean skin again!

She jumped to her feet and started running for the apartment, a thrill of joy rushing all through her. Tears grew in her eyes as she shouted, "I'm set free! I'm set free! Jesus, I'm forgiven!"

Beneath the white light in the otherwise dark parking lot, she found her car and looked in the side-view mirror. The spider of resentment was gone too, with its hideous, clenching legs. They were no more, and she had a lovely neck once again. She felt it with her hand. "Oh, it's soft and painless!" She touched her collarbone. "The ants are taken too!" She ran her fingers through her silky red hair. "My hair is clean! No more grease! Oh, God, thank you! Thank you!"

And then she looked at her face, disbelieving the mirror's image at first.

"I am beautiful," she whispered in a breaking voice, tears rolling faster from her eyes. "Only by the power of God, I am beautiful!"

Overwhelmed, Nastia sobbed with joy and sank to the ground. "Oh, God, Lord Jesus, I don't deserve your love. I don't deserve this gift. You are the true beautiful one. We your followers are only recipients of the salvation we could never earn. But I thank you from the bottom of my heart." Nastia inhaled a deep, life-giving breath. "I love you, Jesus! Thank you! Thank you, thank you, thank you!"

35

HOPE

A WEEK LATER, after a day of job hunting, Nastia climbed the stairs up to Lauren's apartment. Once she turned down the hallway, she stopped in her tracks. A blue tiger sat nobly just outside the apartment door — flinging his tale to and fro — while a red bird preened on the door handle. Nastia took a deep breath and walked forward.

Without breaking his perfect posture, the tiger stared at her. The bird fluffed her scarlet feathers one more time and said, "Hello Tia. How wonderful to see you again!"

"You too!" she replied, glancing at the tiger's unwavering gaze. "Where have you guys been? I haven't seen you since — that day."

"We needed to step aside so you could consider the paths before you," Jianyu growled.

"And it appears you made the right decision," Aini chirped. "Congratulations Tia! You repented and turned back to God. We are so proud of you."

Nastia couldn't help from smiling. "Aw…thank you, Aini."

Jianyu lowered his head, as if bowing. "We honor you today, Nastia Sobieski. Well done. You have already begun to experience the rewards of choosing Jesus above all else. Your soul was made beautiful when you submitted to the healing power of God's love."

"I-I really don't deserve God's love," Nastia replied, exhaling. "How am I allowed to feel this happy after everything I've done?"

" 'The Lord is gracious and compassionate, slow to anger and rich in love,' " answered Jianyu, quoting Psalm 145:8. He raised his blue head, strong and formidable. "Your body will no longer represent your soul. You no longer have to worry about wires or roaches or ants or spiders on your body, or hypocrites brew in everything you drink."

"Praise God! I'm so glad to be free from hypocrite's brew. Uck! It was nasty stuff."

"Hypocrite's brew prompted you to drink much less water," Aini chimed. "Sin has taken a toll on your physical body. In this upcoming season, we suggest that you devote yourself to spiritual and physical healing. Rest, offer prayers of thanksgiving to the Lord, go on walks, eat well, and please rehydrate your parched body."

"I can do that," said Nastia. "Resting is so much easier now. I am grateful for the chance to recover."

Aini fluttered her scarlet wings. "You have reconciled with the Messiah. There is no safer place than that."

Nastia smiled "I suppose you're right."

"Nastia Sobieski," Jianyu purred. "We have come to you today to let you know that we must leave you now. We must return to heaven. You no longer need us."

"What?" Nastia gasped. "But who will I talk to about my heart? Who will help me to deal with temptation?"

"You have the Lord Jesus," said Aini. "And the fellowship of believers. That's what you need now."

Nastia took a deep breath.

"Can I hop onto your shoulder one more time?" the red bird asked.

Nastia nodded. Suddenly, Aini was on her right shoulder and Nastia felt the softest feathers in the world brushing against her neck. "I am overcome with joy over you, Tia. You did what was right! You repented. Your life will be much better from here forward."

When Aini sprang back to the floor, Nastia turned to the blue tiger. "Jianyu, may I give you a hug?"

Sitting up in a noble position, Jianyu bowed his striped head. "You may."

Resting on her knees, Nastia hesitantly wrapped her arms around Jianyu, his long prickly whiskers tickling her. She petted the fur on his back briefly; it was thick but smooth. "Thank you for fighting Lunosh that one time. Your protection helped me in my dark hours."

"You're welcome, young one."

When Nastia let go, she noticed a large tear gliding down Jianyu's big blue face. But at the same time, he was smiling.

"All right," Aini interjected. "Farewell Tia! We will see you again one day!"

Just as Nastia was thinking, *Wait, I'll see them again?* Aini fluttered down the hall, toward a sunlit archway, with Jianyu loping beneath her.

Sighing, Nastia glanced to the opposite end of the hall. The silver dragon sneered in obvious fury, but once he caught Nastia's eye, he dissipated into the shadows.

＊

INSIDE THE FRENCH-THEMED kitchen, Nastia gathered a couple of tea bags while Lauren carefully poured boiling water into two fleur-de-lis mugs.

"Here you are, Tia," Lauren handed over a steaming mug.

"Thank you, Lauren. You're the best."

They both sat around the pale wooden table beneath the Eiffel tower lamp. With a curious brow, Lauren glanced at the new painting of a surfer silhouette upon a bright red sunset.

"So, Tia," she asked. "What's been going on with you this week? You've been pretty quiet. I can't help but be concerned. Have you been hurting? Please fill me in. How are you doing?"

Nastia took a slow sip of her Paris blend tea. "Yes, I have been hurting. This week was hard. As I told you, I turned back to God the night after I got back from Greece. I repented and asked for forgiveness. That was seriously the most freeing experience of my life, but it didn't make life easy. God is definitely bringing healing, but it's taking time." Nastia sighed. "You were right, Lauren. Sin is a painkiller that brings more pain."

Lauren's lamp-like eyes were filled with compassion. "Have you missed Anton very much? I'm sure it's hard to go from living with him and being that close to not at all."

"Oh, my grace, yes. It's been very difficult. I think it would be easier to get over a mean guy, but Anton was so nice. Yes, he was an unbeliever, but he was quite good-natured. It hurts so much more because he was good, and *I* betrayed *him*. Uh…" She closed her eyes for a moment and took a deep, steadying breath.

"I'm just starting to get over the denial part of it," Nastia continued. "I would think, 'I'll talk about this with Anton tonight, and we'll laugh and love each other,' but then I realize that it's over, and I don't have him anymore. Every time that happens, I feel this horrible sinking pain, and I turn to Jesus in prayer because I don't know how I'll make it otherwise. God has been faithful; he's helped me through this week, but it has been very hard. I haven't been so desperate for Jesus in years. I've been reading my Bible and praying about the verses, striving with all my heart to understand them."

"And what have you found?"

"A lot, Lauren." She took another sip. "I've gone back to the Lord's prayer. Jesus told us to pray this way and address our Father in heaven. I've been thinking about what that really means. I don't think we have to pray the precise words all the time, but more the concepts."

"Yes, exactly," Lauren chimed in, leaning over to touch Nastia on the arm. "It's very good to start a prayer by recognizing God's sovereignty and the glory of his name and kingdom, then asking for his will to be done in our lives, giving our requests to him. It's so important to express to God whatever we want and feel. My Dad used to say that any desire will become an infection in our spirit if we don't express it to God in prayer. Whether it be a sinful desire that we need to confess, or a request for good things, we need to talk with God about all of it."

"I remember him saying something like that," Nastia confirmed, recalling the good days with the Henson family. "I was over for dinner one time, and he said it in his deep, rumbling voice. Your dad had such a powerful voice, Lauren."

Lauren laughed her contagious, pure-comfort laugh that naturally caused people to forget their hardships. "It's true. He has a solid voice."

Nastia grinned happily. "I loved it when he talked. When I was going through all my inner confusion in high school, my fears would seem much less powerful after your dad said something profound."

Lauren's face was covered in a bright smile. "Well, I am glad he was a blessing to you."

"He was. Your whole family was, but mostly you of course, Lauren."

"Thank you, Tia. I care for you very much."

"That leads me to the point I was saying about the Lord's Prayer!" Nastia leaned in, emphasizing the importance. "It says, 'forgive us of our sins as we forgive those who trespass against us.' In order for me to truly accept God's forgiveness, I have to forgive everyone else in my life. This is hard for me to say but," she took a deep breath, "I want to forgive my dad. I am going to forgive him."

Lauren's eyebrows rose so high they almost reached her hairline. "Wow. That is huge. I am proud of you, Tia."

"It will take a while," said Nastia. "I try praying about it, but whenever I think of what he did, this restraining rage builds up inside me, and I can't. Someday, I will get past that barrier and fully forgive, but it will take time."

Nastia shook her head, disappointed in herself. "I have a love-hate relationship with time. Sometimes, I wish I could just have it now and get over it now, but it doesn't work that way. I wish I could fully forgive my dad and stop resenting him now. I read somewhere in the Bible recently that we should not be resentful. I wish I could just get over Anton and move on completely. But on the other hand, I see that God uses time to create a lasting conviction within us. Without time, our faith would be worthless — just whims of emotion. But with time, God actually builds strong relationships with us."

"Yes!" Lauren rejoiced. "I love to hear you say these things, Tia. I can see a real change in you. Our relationship with God is the most important part of life made through acceptance and dependence on Jesus. One of my favorite verses is 1st Corinthians 13:13, 'And now these three remain: faith, hope, and love. But the greatest of these is love.' "

"Oh, Lauren," Nastia smiled jubilantly. "I have to tell you about a lesson that is changing my life. Besides my first conversation and acceptance of Jesus, this is the most important choice I have ever made."

"Okay. I'm listening," Lauren waited eagerly.

"Hope," Nastia said simply.

"Hope?" Lauren was expecting more. "What do you mean?"

"Hope is absolutely key to worshiping and loving God! It's the whole reason I created this painting," Nastia pointed to the artwork, depicting a surfer stilled in the height of his jump. "How do I explain this? It's everything! It's saving my life!" Nastia pressed her palms against her face.

"Just try," Lauren nudged. "Start anywhere."

"Okay." Convicted passion emanated from Nastia's face. "I didn't genuinely place my hope in Jesus in the past, not even in college when I stood up for my faith and defended Christianity without a care for what other people thought. My motivation wasn't pure then. I thought my hope was in Christ, but I didn't know what that meant. I believed in Jesus and recognized his love for me, but the worldly things attracted my eyes. The core of my desires was somewhere else. That's what hope is — the core of the heart.

"I placed my hope in dating, in finding the ideal man and living intimately with him. I pushed that desire beneath the surface in college, but it was still there. When I came here on the flight from Dallas, that desire was suddenly awakened. I craved a good boyfriend more than anything. I felt lonely and empty, and even while I prayed and told myself that God was all I needed, I didn't really believe it because my hope was in a dream of the ideal boyfriend. I sincerely recognized that Jesus is the only way, but my dream of a tender loving relationship was more — attractive. I longed for it more than I longed for God.

"And then Anton came along. I was ripe for the picking. Anton represented everything I had always wanted in a guy — except faith. But I went after him anyway. I hardly even considered denying the chance to become his lover. He became the center of my life. My hope was in that specific affection — not in God. Hope resides in what we view as the most beautiful and desirable thing in all existence. All-the-way romantic affection, found in a close relationship with the ideal man, was what I viewed as the most desirable thing. I worshiped that idea instead of God."

Lauren nodded. "You made him an idol. He became the focus of your heart."

"Actually, no," Nastia corrected. "I was the focus of my heart. Anton was the object of my desires — but in the end, it was all about me. I did it for me, not him."

"How does the painting fit in?" Lauren gestured to the red, blue, and black artwork. "It really is gorgeous, Tia. You did a beautiful job."

"Thank you." She smiled. "It represents me and how I sinned. Ever since Hawaii, I had this image in my mind of a falling surfer — falling like Christians when we stumble. Following Christ doesn't mean being flawless — it means accepting that we are awful and then turning to God because we need him. I have been horrible. I am not better than anyone else. I turn to Jesus because he is the only one who can be righteous. I can share in his righteousness only when I humble myself before him and recognize that I deserve to go to hell. I do deserve hell, but Jesus has given me life instead."

Nastia sighed. "I'm heartbroken, Lauren. My idolatrous dream devastated me. Living with Anton there at the end was so painful, especially with the breakup. But I'm done with it now. I'm done with misplaced hope! I'm done expecting anything besides Jesus Christ to complete me because it ruins me when I do. Everything — whether it's good or bad in nature — turns into ravaging death if we place our hope in it instead of in Jesus."

"I hadn't thought of hope quite that way before," Lauren replied. "It makes me so happy to hear you talk again — as a person who loves Jesus. You honestly seem to have repented, and that is tremendous!"

Nastia's face was sad. "I don't deserve your encouragement, Lauren. Can you believe what I did? I cheated on Anton! I feel bad for him; I really do. You know what he told me? He said, 'You are ugly, uglier than any girl I have ever dated.' Gosh — talk about a blow. But he was right; I was terrible. I just wish there was some way I could make it up to him." She sighed.

Lauren pressed her lips together. "You can try to apologize to him. That would be godly."

"But I can't! He cut me off completely. He blocked my number and my social media accounts. There's no way I can contact him anymore."

"One day maybe. You can pray for the chance to apologize and explain how it was wrong for you to live with him."

"Yes. I would like that opportunity." Nastia's face grieved. "Oh, Lauren, I'm sorry. I've wronged you too. I never thought how you would feel when I moved out. I only thought of myself."

"I forgive you, Tia." Lauren grasped Nastia's hand. "We're friends, and that's not going to change. But more importantly, God has forgiven you. He loves you so, so much."

The kitchen timer rang. "Ah!" Lauren dashed to the oven. "That'll be dinner."

"Love?" Nastia whispered, as if she had never heard the word correctly before. "Love of God?"

Lauren carried the glass dish to the table, her hand in a fleur-de-lis oven mitt. "It smells delicious, doesn't it? My mom would make this a lot, mac and cheese with ham."

"It looks fantastic," Nastia commented. "Hey, how about a toast?"

"Great idea."

They lifted their mugs, and Nastia said, "To Christ and his genuine forgiveness. He is the only one who satisfies us."

"Amen!"

They sipped and began dinner together, chatting about childhood stories and laughing, as best friends do.

ONE NIGHT, NASTIA had the apartment to herself. Lauren was working a late shift. Wearing a matching set of white pajamas with thin blue stripes, Nastia rested peacefully under the window in the living room, the Bible in her hands. She was thinking about the father in the story of the prodigal son, when suddenly she felt a stirring in her heart. She felt God's presence wrap around her like a warm blanket. And then she felt a strong desire to look out the window.

It happened so fast. For just a second.

Among the stars in the sky were two gigantic golden doors, sleek and bright. They were wide open. Between the doors was a river of light, pouring out into the world with a soft murmur of distant singing.

There, standing in front of the river of light, was a figure of a man in a white robe. Nastia wondered if he was the angel of the

Lord. She didn't know. On his head was a shimmering golden crown. The man was extending his hand, leaning down toward Nastia.

And then she blinked. The image was gone from her eyes, but it was imprinted on her memory as clear as day.

Nastia heard a voice speak to her spirit with calm authority, "I love you, Nastia."

She clutched her Bible to her collarbone and pressed her chin onto it, making an indentation into the well-worn leather. Nastia was filled with a tremendous elation. She couldn't remember feeling happier than she did at that moment. Her eyes grew moist as she responded, "I love you too, God."

The End

ACKNOWLEDGMENTS

I WOULD LIKE to thank a few friends back in my college days —
John, Claire, and Esther. Your encouragement made a huge
difference to me while I wrote the first draft. I also want to recognize
Rosetta Ann Photography for doing such amazing work on the
cover art. I am very happy with the cover photo. I can't thank you
enough for helping me out.

More recently, I want to thank Temple Russell Christiansen for
editing this book and providing much-needed feedback. Rita was a
key part as well. In addition to the proofreading assistance, Rita
prompted me to think about a theological point that I needed to
work through. Thank you so much for bringing up that topic! My
mentor Rob also helped to improve this story, through a pivotal
discussion about the character of God.

Lastly, I want to thank my dearest mother, who supported me
from start to finish.

ABOUT THE AUTHOR

C. R. Kelchner grew up in a home that cultivated imagination. He played story-inspired games with his brother and sister, his parents often read books aloud, and he frequently explored the Bosque forest in Albuquerque, New Mexico. The Kelchners were great fans of fantastical fiction, like the *Narnia* books by C. S. Lewis and *The Lord of The Rings* by J. R. R. Tolkien.

After receiving a bachelor's in psychology with a minor in biblical studies from a Christian college in Tennessee, Kelchner began his first children's fantasy book, *Lady Glimmer and the Children of Doubt.* He moved to Alaska in his mid-twenties, where he got a job as a foster care worker. Surrounded by the majestic snow-capped mountains and countless birch trees, Kelchner completed a psychological drama called *The Blue of Torches: Ignited.* In his free time, Kelchner enjoys reading, hiking, movie nights with friends, coffee shops, Bible studies, and traveling.